Thomas Hardy, Metaphysics and Music

Thomas Hardy, Metaphysics and Music

Mark Asquith

First published 2005 by
PALGRAVE MACMILLAN
Houndmills, Basingstoke, Hampshire RG21 6XS and
175 Fifth Avenue, New York, N.Y. 10010
Companies and representatives throughout the world

PALGRAVE MACMILLAN is the global academic imprint of the Palgrave Macmillan division of St. Martin's Press, LLC and of Palgrave Macmillan Ltd. Macmillan® is a registered trademark in the United States, United Kingdom and other countries. Palgrave is a registered trademark in the European Union and other countries.

ISBN-13: 978–1–4039–4138–1 hardback
ISBN-10: 1–4039–4138–6 hardback

This book is printed on paper suitable for recycling and made from fully managed and sustained forest sources.

A catalogue record for this book is available from the British Library.

Library of Congress Cataloging-in-Publication Data
Asquith, Mark.
    Thomas Hardy, metaphysics and music / Mark Asquith.
        p. cm.
    Includes bibliographical references and index.
    ISBN 1–4039–4138–6 (cloth)
    1. Hardy, Thomas, 1840–1928—Knowledge—Music.   2. Music—England—19th century—History and criticism.   3. Music and literature—History—19th century.   4. Hardy, Thomas, 1840–1928—Fictional works.   5. Hardy, Thomas, 1840–1928—Philosophy.   6. Hardy, Thomas, 1840–1928—Aesthetics.   7. Aesthetics, British—19th century.   8. Metaphysics in literature.   9. Music in literature.
    I. Title.
    PR4757.M74A87 2005
    823'.8—dc22   2005041537

10   9   8   7   6   5   4   3   2   1
14   13   12   11   10   09   08   07   06   05

For Anne-Marie, Thomas and Emma

Contents

Acknowledgements

This project would not have come to fruition without the help and support of many individuals whom I would like to thank silently here. In addition I would like to extend my special thanks to the following:

I would like to thank Max Saunders and Leonee Ormonde for their perceptive reading of the manuscript, advice and support during the whole writing process. I would also like to thank Tim Armstrong for his excellent suggestions as to how the manuscript could be improved. I would also like to acknowledge a special debt of gratitude to Ross King whose constant support, discerning reading and willingness to discuss the main ideas in the book were invaluable. My thanks are also extended to Jörg Rademacher and John Woolford for their advice during the early stages of the project.

I would also like to thank my editors at Palgrave Macmillan, Paula Kennedy and Helen Craine; the production team at Integra Software Services, especially Satishna Gokuldas, for all their hard work on the manuscript; the staff of the Senate House Library, London for their efficient assistance, kindness and moral support; and Lilian Swindall, the curator of the Hardy archive in Dorset, for her helpful advice. Thanks are also due to the staff of Harberdashers' Aske's Hatcham College and Trinity School, Croydon for their encouragement over the years.

I would also like to acknowledge a debt to a number of habitués of the British library, particularly Sophie Oxenham, Nicky Santilli, Simone Murray, Ruth Meads, Sarah Wood, Brian Chadwick, Edward Neil and Susie Jordan for their friendship during life-saving coffee breaks.

I would also like to thank my parents for their moral support over the years. My main debt, however, is to my wife, Anne-Marie, without whose patience, affection and common sense this book would not have been completed.

Introduction

In Chapter 6 of *The Return of the Native* Thomas Hardy provides the following description of the isolated figure of Eustacia Vye as she stands motionless upon Egdon Heath:

> It might reasonably have been supposed that she was listening to the wind, which rose somewhat as the night advanced, and laid hold of the attention.... Gusts in innumerable series followed each other from the north-west, and when each one of them raced past the sound of its progress resolved into three. Treble, tenor, and bass notes were to be found therein. The general ricochet of the whole over pits and prominences had the gravest pitch of the chime. Next there could be heard the baritone buzz of a holly tree. Below these in force, above them in pitch, a dwindled voice strove hard at a husky tune, which was the peculiar local sound alluded to ...
>
> 'The spirit moved them.' A meaning of the phrase forced itself upon the attention; and an emotional listener's fetichistic mood might have ended in one of more advanced quality. It was not, after all, that the left-hand expanse of old blooms spoke, or the right-hand, or those of the slope in front; but it was the single person of something else speaking through each at once.
>
> Suddenly, on the barrow, there mingled with all this wild rhetoric of the night a sound which modulated so naturally into the rest that its beginning and ending were hardly to be distinguished. The bluffs, and the bushes, and the heather-bells had broken silence; at last, so did the woman; and her articulation was but as another phrase of the same discourse of theirs. Thrown out on the winds it became twined in with them, and with them it flew away.[1]

1

I quote this passage at some length because it presents clearly the type of musical allusion with which this book will be concerned. To begin with, Hardy's detailed description of the Aeolian modulations surrounding Eustacia is significant because it indicates the prominence that the art of music had achieved in his writing at this stage of his development. Furthermore, this description typifies Hardy's use of musical allusion in that it centres upon a mysterious 'music of nature' rather than the conscious expression of an executant. A more detailed appraisal of the passage reveals a number of more idiosyncratic features: namely the authorial speculation as to whether Eustacia might be listening to the music, the attribution of distinct tones to individual natural phenomena and the addition of Eustacia's sighs to the surrounding music. Perhaps most importantly, this music is not simply decorative, for as the listening consciousness drifts between Eustacia and that of an 'emotional listener' the various heterogeneous tones are galvanised into the expressive agency of a 'single spirit'.

Quite what Hardy means by the term 'spirit' is a question considered in the following pages, but what is unquestionable is the dominance of the musical metaphor as a means of objectifying its agency both in this scene, in the novel as a whole and in various other Hardy texts. It forms a soundscape that underpins the domestic drama played out amongst competing characters, laying bare a deeper metaphysical resonance. An appreciation of such musical allusion is central to our understanding of Hardy's philosophical and aesthetic ambitions in the novels – indeed, it is essential if the behaviour of some of his characters is to be understood at all. And appreciation implies contextualising such music within an age when terms such as 'spirit' were being subjected to careful dissection through the newly fashionable tools of biological, physiological and psychological analysis. Central to this book, therefore, is an attempt to place Hardy's use of musical tropes within his contemporary scientific and philosophical community, a process that leads to very different interpretations of the key texts.

To some extent Hardy's use of musical allusion reflects changing attitudes towards the art during the nineteenth century, a period which saw it elevated to a position in which the aesthete Walter Pater was able to write in 1877 that '*all art constantly aspires towards the condition of music*'.[2] Its lowly position in Enlightenment thinking is typified by the aesthetic judgement of Immanuel Kant, who argued that if 'we estimate the worth of the fine arts by the culture they supply to the mind ... music then, since it plays merely with sensations, has the lowest place among the fine arts'.[3] The field of musical aesthetics barely existed:

writing about music tended to encompass technical points and was done by musicians for musicians. In the second half of the eighteenth century, however, the social philosopher Jean-Jacques Rousseau and the contributors to the French *Encyclopédie* began writing about music in abstract philosophical terms, which in turn was highly influential upon the first writers of the German Romantic movement. One such writer was Wilhelm Wackenroder, who has his fictional musician, Joseph Berlinger, question the soundness of the Kantian position by comparing the arts and concluding that though music is the youngest, no other is capable of fusing the qualities of profundity and sensuality and raising the listener to a transcendent level above the strife of the world.[4] In effect, the listener leaves the world of mundane worries and is introduced to a semi-religious realm of pure feeling in which he experiences the essence of all emotions, in particular the typically Romantic feeling of inexpressible longing. Music therefore becomes, in the words of the short-story writer E. T. A. Hoffmann, not simply an art worthy of regard, but 'the most romantic of all the arts – one might say, the only purely romantic art – for its sole subject is the infinite'.[5] As such, popular Romantic writers like Johann Herder, Johann Goethe and Friedrich Schiller all turned to musical execution and musical allusion for literary effect.

The revolution surrounding the status of music was essentially generated by literary means: the first truly Romantic composers, such as Schubert and Weber, followed the lead of the 'Sturm und Drang' movement rather than vice versa. Indeed the musicologist R. M. Longyear states quite bluntly in his study of the period that 'the influence of Romantic writers on composers was greater than the influence of composers, even in Germany, on the writers'.[6] One result of the marginalising of musical composition and performance was the growth in the number of sounds that might be considered musical. Whereas in the poetry of the eighteenth century music was treated as a decorative metaphor lacking any real substance, to the Romantics its capacity to move the listener without being seen made it the ideal artistic medium with which to characterise the Kantian 'thing in itself'. Hence, music became a means of expressing the divine spirit that existed in nature, Hoffmann noting that

> There is about the imperceptible beginning, the swelling and the dying of the tones of nature, something which has a most powerful and indescribable effect on us; and any instrument which could be capable of reproducing this would undoubtedly affect us in a similar way.[7]

One such instrument was the Aeolian harp, which became, in the words of M. H. Abrams, the 'toy' of the movement.[8] Such popularity is easily explicable: the combination of the precise tuning and the variability of nature made it the perfect representation of the Apollonian and Dionysian elements of artistic creation explored later in John Ruskin's *Queen of the Air* (1869).[9] One of its earliest appearances was in James Thomson's *The Castle of Indolence* (1748), in which the presence of a discarded harp suspended in the midst of a wood 'sooth[es] the pensive melancholy Mind' of the listener, 'with certain Music, never known'.[10] Samuel Taylor Coleridge uses the same music to prompt the poetic voice in 'To Dejection', and to animate the feelings of the lovers in 'The Eolian Harp'. Significantly, in this latter poem the effects of the natural melody cause the poet to speculate whether 'all of animated nature' may be 'but organic Harps diversely fram'd' which tremble 'as o'er them sweeps / Plastic and vast, one intellectual breeze, / At once the soul of each, and God of all'.[11] Henceforward, Nature itself is transformed into a giant harp which announces the presence of God. With the development of the 'inward ear' and the cult of the sublime, which gave poetic significance to previously dissonant noises, sounds in nature evolved into a 'music' which could be heard in the tossing of waves, murmuring of brooks and moaning of wind in trees.[12]

The identification of music in natural phenomena, its capacity to express emotions and its potential to lever the individual to a transcendent level are typical features of the Romantic attitude towards music that remained central to musical discourse throughout the nineteenth century. Since Hardy's early reading focussed on those English poets whose work embodied the above principles, it is unsurprising to find him employing musical allusion in what might be considered a typically Romantic fashion in early novels, *Desperate Remedies*, *A Pair of Blue Eyes* and *Under the Greenwood Tree*. However, even here it is possible to detect uneasiness in Hardy's cosmic vision, for despite the lavish and carefully composed descriptions of nature, the one absent element is the benevolent God. It seems that even at this stage Hardy balked at the idea of 'Nature's Holy Plan', allowing the reader instead to snatch glimpses of a world governed by an uncaring universal process.[13] Between the publication of *Far from the Madding Crowd* and *The Return of the Native* his darkening vision appears to coalesce into a set of metaphysically coherent principles, allowing the 'giants' embodied within 'the Cliff without a Name' and Norcombe Hill to transform themselves into the central 'character' of Egdon Heath.[14] As the Heath replaces God, it brings its own music, not the Aeolian melodies that convinced Coleridge and Wordsworth of deistic benevolence, but rather the dirge-like groan of the blasted pine which announces the misery of existence in an ambivalent universe.

The change in Hardy's use of musical allusion therefore is dependent upon the evolution of a gloomy understanding of man's relationship with the universe. In this he was not alone, but rather his sense of doubt and despair is symptomatic of the late Victorian malaise caused by the recession of faith and the inability to find a suitable substitute. A number of factors help to explain this uneasiness: the perceived threat of democracy brought about by the 1867 Reform Bill; suspicions concerning mass urbanisation and industrialisation; the crumbling of faith before the onslaught from German Biblical scholarship and scientific inquiry; and the possibility, highlighted by determinist philosophers and Charles Darwin's *Origin of the Species* (1859), that man was simply part of a meaningless universe. During the first half of the century, doubts concerning man's ascendancy had been countered by varying mechanisms. Tennyson, for example, found himself faltering in his attempts to reconcile a benevolent God with his perception of a 'Nature, red in tooth and claw', but used such doubt to bolster his faith.[15] In *In Memoriam* the discoveries of modern science gnaw at his belief, whispering that 'the stars...blindly run' and that God is nothing more than a First Cause in a mechanistic universe.[16] Tennyson responds by embracing doubt and regarding it as a strengthening process: 'He faced the spectres of the mind / And laid them: thus he came at length / To find a stronger faith his own'.[17] For Tennyson, then, religious dislocation is a necessary prelude to the emergence of a 'crowning race' that will be able to mix scientific inquiry and religious reverence, and therefore create 'one music as before'.[18]

Tennyson's belief in man's perfectibility was shared by Thomas Carlyle and J. S. Mill, both of whom adopted the philosophy of Auguste Comte and the St Simonians to give a humanist answer to man's predicament. According to his *Autobiography* (1873), Mill found a clear conception of the nature of the age in the Positivist idea that between two 'organic periods' in which man recognises a positive creed, there lie critical periods of 'transition'.[19] His consternation in *The Spirit of the Age* is therefore tempered by optimism, which suggests that 'so long as this intellectual anarchy shall endure, we may be warranted in believing that we are in a fair way to become wiser than our forefathers'.[20] Mill's optimism was shared by Carlyle who surrounds his Teufelsdröckh with a Godless world in *Sartor Resartus* (1834), so that he can pose the question 'If our era is the Era of Unbelief, why murmur under it; is there not a better coming, nay come?'[21] The new age manifests itself in the image of a Phoenix which rises from the ashes and fills the 'Earth with her music',[22] so that 'amid the rushing and the waving of the Whirlwind-Element come tones of a melodious Deathsong, which end not but in tones of a more melodious Birthsong'.[23]

Throughout the mid-century man continued to search for signs of this rebirth, Matthew Arnold noting in 1877 that 'amid that break-up of traditional and conventional notions respecting our life' he was still hankering after 'some clear light and some sure stay'.[24] His Empedocles is unable to find a satisfactory reconciliation between human inquiry and religious reverence, and discovering the reality of Tennyson's fear that 'God and Nature [are] at strife' he turns to suicide as the only means to 'cut his oscillations short, and so / Bring him to poise. There is no other way'.[25] In 1874 John Ruskin visited Mount Etna himself, and found that the 'dreadfully painful... discordant and violent ringing' of nearby church bells, as he gazed upon the mountain, 'was in a strange sympathy with the horror of the morning light – rose red – on the dreadful cone'.[26] Perhaps, during the exuberance of the first two volumes of *Modern Painters*, he might have perceived in such a sublime scene an indication of the majesty of God. The scene before him now, however, is simply one of sinister discord: a mind weighed down by the encroaching gloom, which finds itself out of tune with the harshness of nature.

By the late 1860s man's failure to capture the new melodic strains that had kept the optimism of Carlyle and Tennyson alive left Hardy, like Arnold, stranded on the shore of Dover Beach whilst the comforting 'Sea of Faith' receded. Alone and in the darkness Arnold exhorts us to listen to the 'grating roar':

> Of pebbles which the waves draw back and fling,
> ... With tremulous cadence slow, and bring
> The eternal note of sadness in.
> Sophocles long ago
> Heard it on the Aegaean, and it brought
> Into his mind the turbid ebb and flow
> Of human misery.[27]

Arnold's mixture of sea and musical metaphor are just two of many used by the mid-Victorians to describe and explore the perplexing state of melancholia that beset their mind. J. H. Newman saw his conversion to Catholicism as something akin to setting out to sail Arnold's choppy 'Sea of Faith'. For Ruskin the clear blue skies of Medieval England were transformed into 'The Storm-Cloud of the Nineteenth Century',[28] and in Thomson's *The City of Dreadful Night* (1874) modern England is transformed into a nightmare urban landscape in which a labyrinth of streets is built upon 'waste marshes' and held together by 'crumbling bridges'.[29]

The most pervasive metaphor of all, however, is that of the descent from harmony to discord, something which can be observed as we move from the poetry of Wordsworth to Arnold. Wordsworth's music of babbling brooks and singing trees reveals a benevolent God, whose harmony enables the individual to cope with the groans making up the 'sad music of humanity'. In Arnold's darker vision, the benevolent God has disappeared leaving man with the 'eternal note of sadness' ringing in his ears. This is the tradition into which Hardy moves: and yet it would be incorrect to think of his use of musical allusion in the novels in terms of a series of isolated metaphors, for its role is far more fundamental to the construction of his narratives. Instead, music forms a web which weaves together the events unfolding in the narratives into a unified expression of his gloomily coherent metaphysical vision. Central to both the aesthetic and philosophical function of such music, I believe, is Hardy's exposure to a number of contemporary philosophical and musical theories during his research for *The Return of the Native*.

Research is the important term here, for whereas prior to this period it is easy to believe in the persona created in *The Life of Thomas Hardy* of the journeyman novelist fluctuating between the genres of social satire, detective sensation and the pastoral, sacrificing any 'proper artistic balance' for the desire to be 'merely...considered a good hand at a serial',[30] both the increasing number of artistic pronouncements to be found in *The Life*, and the commencement of the *Literary Notebooks* suggest that during the writing of *The Return of the Native* his attitude towards his writing changed dramatically. There are various reasons for this: the success of *Far from the Madding Crowd* gave him a little more financial security and artistic licence; his decision to support his new wife, Emma Gifford, by means of his art caused him to take it more seriously; and finally he was terrified at being branded as a purely rustic writer, and wanted to add substance to his work.[31]

The overriding sense that emerges from these *Notebooks* is of Hardy's general dissatisfaction with the constraints of the contemporary novelistic form, a frustration articulated in a letter to H. W. Massingham which states, 'ever since I began to write...I have felt that the doll of English fiction must be demolished'.[32] It is a theme explored further in Hardy's assertion in the late essay 'A Profitable Reading of Fiction' that the art of writing [novels] is as yet in its youth, if not in its infancy. Narrative art is neither mature in its artistic aspect, nor in its ethical or philosophical aspect; neither in *form* nor in *substance*.[33]

Essentially, the *Notebooks* were Hardy's response to this fear: a shorthand record of the ideas of the most influential scientific, philosophical and artistic authorities of the day, which was to provide the form and substance and act, as Robert Gittings has noted, as the 'ammunition in Hardy's new campaign to capture the heights of a really great novel'.[34] Interestingly, whilst Emma's brother was visiting their Sturminster Newton home during the summer of 1876, he appears to have made a comment to the effect that Hardy was not getting on with his next novel, which resulted in an alteration in the latter's research techniques, leading him away from large texts towards short journal articles published in the mainstream journals of the day.[35] It is, therefore, by careful analysis of these periodicals that it is possible to both understand and account for the alteration in Hardy's artistic outlook between the writing of *Far from and Madding Crowd* and *The Return of the Native*. Central to this change is a darkening of Hardy's cosmic vision combined with the more consistent use of musical allusion to express it.

It has already been noted that to some degree Hardy was the product of his age, and nowhere is this clearer than in his voracious appetite for periodical literature. The mid-century journal press was one of the wonders of the age: it fulfilled the needs of the educated and would-be-educated for information; and such were the eclectic interests exhibited by the mid-Victorian gentleman, and the desire for improvement amongst those intelligent but not university-educated members of the middle class (into which category can be placed all women), that such information covered a wide variety of different topics. Articles were needed to inform on the latest political controversies, the more fashionable artistic movements and introduce a host of new areas of interest, such as Biblical scholarship, geology, evolution, Benthanism, Puseyism and the new sciences. Music simply provided another area about which the upper classes and aspirant middle classes felt they should be informed. It contains qualities which make it ideal for discussion in journals of this type: most middle-class readers would have been used to music making in the home and therefore it did not suffer from quite the same degree of educational and social exclusivity that still hung over the fine arts. Mozart might be reproduced on a piano in any drawing room in the country. What the mainstream periodicals offered, therefore, were challenging articles on musical genres, pieces and composers, as well as in-depth analyses of musical theory, as a supplement to this most democratic of art forms.

Perhaps surprisingly, not simply music, but the science of musicology proved to be an extremely popular subject for debate in the mid-century. The affective power of music on listeners combined with its mysterious origins made it the perfect art with which to speculate using the newly fashionable sciences of anthropology, psychology and physiology. By the mid-sixties the aural arts in general had become the focus of laboratory experiments and biological speculation. Hearing, for so long considered the least problematic of the senses, became the perfect means by which the individual could be dissected and problematised. Accordingly, both music and voice tone – the latter maintaining its pre-eminent epistemo-logical significance in defining the individual 'self' and the former moving this 'self' in mysterious ways – became the focus of recording and measurement in terms of vibrations. By the middle of the 1870s, this was supplemented by a wider interest in metaphysics, as is attested by the founding of the philosophical journal, *Mind* (1876ff.), and the journal of the metaphysical society, *Nineteenth Century* (1877ff.). Significantly, the mystery of music's affective power was amenable to both scientific and metaphysical methods of analysis and accordingly attracted some of the most popular exponents of these disciplines to write articles on its origins, influence and function. Judging by their number, such articles proved popular, possibly because they offered the perfect link between fashionable means of inquiry and the personal experience of the reader. As a consequence of their editorial appeal, some of the most ground-breaking work in the field of the aural arts of the day found their first expression not in specialist journals but in the mid-century mainstream periodical.

Such articles tended to be published in nine important periodicals: The *Edinburgh Review* (1802ff.) and the *Westminster Review* (1824ff.) were expensive quarterlies which consisted of long, carefully written articles for a well-educated readership. The work of Walter Houghton has established that throughout the 1860s their circulations stood at around 7000 and 4000 respectively, though, as Houghton has pointed out, there is a 'great difference between circulation and readership': most of the influential quarterlies and monthlies could be perused in club rooms, reading rooms, common rooms and were also available from Mudie's Circulating Library.[36] *Blackwood's Edinburgh Magazine* (1824ff.) and *Fraser's Town and Country Magazine* (1830ff.) were comparatively inexpensive monthlies made up of a mixture of serious articles, fiction and poetry, which were designed for the educated middle classes. In 1860 they had circulations of 10,000 and 8000 respectively. *Macmillan's Magazine* (1859ff.) and *Cornhill Magazine* (1860ff.) were shilling monthlies offering entertainment and instruction for middle-class readers. Initially they were extremely successful with circulation figures of 20,000 and 80,000 respectively, though these figures soon dropped. The *Fortnightly Review* (1865ff.) *Contemporary Review* (1866ff.) and the *Nineteenth Century* (1877ff.) were monthlies intended for liberal intellectuals, with circulations of between 2500 and 4000 in the later 1860s. Finally, *The Athenaeum* (1828ff.) was the largest-selling serious weekly journal, with an estimated circulation of 20,000 in 1860. It sought to both entertain and instruct its middle-class readership with short articles on contemporary political and artistic subjects.[37]

Interestingly, it was the more liberal journals that tended to publish musical articles. Liberalism seems to have been a necessary prerequisite because, as Lynn Ruth, Binstock has argued in her unpublished doctoral thesis, 'A Study of Music in Victorian Prose', the scandalous private lives of a number of prominent musicians outraged many conservative critics.[38] Furthermore, the mid-century movements headed by John Hullah and John Curwen, which engaged music as a tool for mass education, were associated with progressive political movements. Thus, the liberal and progressive *Westminster* devoted far more space to music than its Whig rival the *Edinburgh*, whilst their quarterly competitor, the Tory *Quarterly Review* (1809ff.), published hardly any musical articles at all. Similarly, the liberal *Fraser's* ran far more musical articles than the Tory *Blackwoods*. The Positivist sympathies of the *Fortnightly Review* ensured that the journal carried a number of articles exploring the scientific basis of music, a feature mirrored by the composition of the *Nineteenth Century*, which was the organ of the Metaphysical Society. Finally, the connection between the *Contemporary Review* and the church ensured that the journal always carried a large number of articles on music, particularly those which sought to invest the art with a moral function.

Generally speaking then, it is these liberal monthlies, catering for middle-class intellectuals seeking to read articles at the forefront of aesthetic and scientific theory, which were responsible for introducing the vast majority of the English public to the groundbreaking ideas of contemporary musical theorists such as Richard Wagner, Arthur Schopenhauer, Herbert Spencer, James Sully, H. R. Haweis and Edmund Gurney. Such articles, whether produced by apologists or the theorists themselves, tended to be lengthy, intellectually challenging and rigorous in a way that it is difficult for the modern reader to grasp.

It is the aim of this book to place Hardy's novels within the context of these contemporary scientific, philosophical, aural and more specifically musical debates and explore how knowledge of such cultural background enriches our reading of them. I have sought to identify how the work of particular thinkers may have shaped Hardy's thought and also, to avoid the reductionism implicit in this method, how his ideas reflect a more general cultural framework. In doing this I have sought to reposition Hardy amongst his peers, as both a more theoretically consistent and artistically innovative artist, and not the 'good little Thomas Hardy' dismissed so patronisingly by Henry James.[39]

The book opens in Chapter 1 with an assessment of Hardy's own well-documented sensitivity to instrumental music before analysing his employment of musical tropes and metaphor in his earliest fiction: *The Poor Man and the Lady* (1866), *Desperate Remedies* (1871), *Under the Greenwood Tree* (1872) and *A Pair of Blue Eyes* (1873). In these novels music is employed in a way common to other mid-century writers as a means of exploring sexual attraction without exciting the bowdlerising pens of editors constrained by the prurience of Victorian sexual mores. Even within such early work, however, it is possible to trace the roots of Hardy's more mature use of music as an expression of his conception of man's place in the universe. Accordingly, the second half of the chapter is concerned with tracing the Classical and Romantic influences that shaped this embryonic musical metaphysics, particularly the conception of the 'music of the spheres' and also musical allusion in the work of Milton, Shelley and Wordsworth. The chapter closes with an assessment of the transitional novels *Under the Greenwood Tree* (1872) and *Far from the Madding Crowd* (1874).

Chapter 2 moves on to an appraisal of Hardy the philosopher combined with an analysis of how his gloomy metaphysical outlook was shaped by the influence of contemporaries such as Charles Darwin, Herbert Spencer, W. L. Clifford, Walter Pater and the German metaphysician Arthur Schopenhauer. An appreciation of Hardy's metaphysical evolution is essential to our understanding of the handling of musical allusion in his mature work. Of particular interest is the collapse of a belief in materialist certainties in favour of a universe conceived of in terms of 'process': a world governed by determining laws – such as those of Newtonian physics, the Immanent Will, the Darwinian principle of sexual selection, materialist laws of determinism and the principle of heredity – unified under a partially anthropomorphised process indifferent to the suffering of man. The chapter also teases out and contextualises Hardy's ideas concerning consciousness and free will within his contemporary scientific and philosophical community, ideas which will have ramifications for his depiction of the effects of musical performance in the novels.

Chapter 3 focuses on the way in which Hardy's metaphysics was transformed into a form of narrative musical allusion influenced by the musical theory of Arthur Schopenhauer – who was enjoying a great deal of critical interest in the periodical press of 1876, the year of Hardy's reading campaign. It is only through an understanding of Schopenhauer, I argue, that we can fully appreciate the music of Egdon Heath or that of the trees around Little Hintock. Hardy's narrative deployment of such music was influenced by another figure who was coincidentally gaining a great deal of journalistic attention in 1876: the composer Richard Wagner. Though a number of critics have drawn compelling parallels between the work of Hardy and Wagner, there has remained within their work both a vagueness and an elasticity of historical perspective that has rendered their observations interesting rather than significant. Joan Grundy is typical of this in her intuitive assertion that:

> my own feeling is that Hardy's novels are . . . a literary counterpart to Wagner's music dramas, in which the voices and actions of the personages are both set against and blended with a continuous tissue of melody from the orchestra.[40]

Despite the perceptiveness of this observation, it remains, as the opening phrase suggests, an impression in need of justification. Accordingly, a significant part of this chapter is spent surveying a large number of periodical and newspaper articles on Wagnerian aesthetics published in 1876 to coincide with the first Bayreuth Festival. Put simply, Wagner's revitalisation of the Classical theatre demonstrated how Schopenhauer's musical metaphysics might be translated into an art form: the orchestra becoming the equivalent of a Greek Chorus weaving together the disparate emotional events unfolding on stage and exploring the forces motivating the behaviour of his central characters. Exposure to Wagner allowed Hardy to conceive of a literary counterpart to the music drama, the Aeolian music of Egdon and Little Hintock providing a Wagnerian chorus that explores the wider process underpinning the behaviour of his characters. This understanding of Hardy's music offers a new interpretation of Hardy's depiction of dancing in the novels, which is transformed from a simple portrayal of a quaint rural custom to a metaphor demonstrating the powerlessness of individual action. The chapter closes with a discussion of how Hardy explores consciousness and free will in relation to this metaphysical music (with particular emphasis on Mrs Yeobright's apprehension of the music of the Devil's Bellows and Sue Bridehead's perception of the First Cause as a dreamy composer), and an analysis of how Schopenhauerian theory enriches our appreciation of Tess' sensitivity to music.

Chapter 4 focuses on how contemporary scientific and anthropological discussions concerning the aural arts in general and the origin, meaning, physiological affectiveness and function of music in particular illuminate our understanding of Hardy's portrayal of the activity of falling in love in the novels. Desire is reduced to the conditioning influence of hereditary, physiological and biological determinants which find expression in the narratives through the response of susceptible female characters (since they are nearly all females) to the performance of music. In accordance with the popular contemporary analogy of the female nervous system as an Aeolian harp responsive to male touch, Hardy's 'highly strung' heroines are made to vibrate in consonance with the musical strings 'plucked' by the musical performance of their male suitors. Such is their powerlessness that Hardy evokes metaphors taken from the sinister force of mesmerism (which, in the Victorian mind, was directly analogous to the power of music), contemporary interest in physiological experimentation, materialist philosophy and biology – particularly Darwinian 'courtship ritual'. I also argue that, in accordance with contemporary theories concerning the relationship between the evolution of music and speech, the emotional power of music in Hardy's novels is shared by his depiction of musically delineated voice tone. (Indeed, it is difficult to account for Hardy's insistence on this unusual aspect in the portrayal of his characters without an understanding of Victorian attitudes to the development of speech.) In brief, voice tone becomes a privileged means of 'musical' communication between Hardy's lovers, undermining the stilted dialogue that characterises so many of their exchanges. I think particularly here of the way in which Angel is drawn to the 'fluty' voice of Tess, Eustacia is drawn to Clym through a single 'goodnight' and the attraction of Jocclyn Pierston to the musical voice of Avice Caro.

Chapters 5, 6 and 7 consist of separate readings of those novels that demonstrate a sustained use of musical allusion: namely *The Return of the Native* (1878), *The Mayor of Casterbridge* (1886) and *Jude the Obscure* (1895). All share the broad characteristics explored in Chapters 3 and 4, but each presents variations that preclude a more thematic type of study. One particular advantage of this approach is that it enables us to appreciate how musical allusion adds to the unity of the separate novels. Another advantage of this chronological method of analysis is that the evolution of Hardy's art towards a more experimental novelistic genre can be seen clearly. Critics are fond of describing *Jude the Obscure* as the first modern novel – which in many respects it is, but it is also a novel in which Hardy reaches the limits of music's capacity to represent the metaphysical characteristics of his cosmic vision. His rejection of the novelistic form following the clamour arising from its publication, therefore, says as much about the difficulties arising from attempting to graft the avant-garde onto an established genre, as it does about the limits imposed by Victorian sexual mores.

Chapter 5 demonstrates how in *The Return of the Native* Hardy creates a reinvigorated Classical tragedy in which the music of Egdon functions as a form of Wagnerian chorus constantly reminding the reader of the ambivalent process underpinning the domestic plot concerning the Yeobrights and the Vyes. My reading gives rise to several new inter-pretations in the novel: it connects together the dances as an expres-sion of complicity with the ambivalent universal process; it presents a Schopenhauerian interpretation of Clym's singing; and it analyses the musicality of the dialogue in the novel, in so doing repositioning the mummers scene as a clear expression of Hardy's ideas concerning free will and determinism.

Chapter 6 focuses on Hardy's 'man of character', Michael Henchard, whose grandiose vision of his own suffering is continually undermined by a Wagnerian chorus of natural music designed to remind the reader that in Hardy's world there are no vindictive gods, just a cosmic process indifferent to the plight of man. It can be heard in the musically buzzing fly that seems to taunt him following the wife-sale, in the Aeolian modulations that blow over the Roman Ruins undermining his grand gesture of the reconciliation with his wife and in the mockery of the Aeolian tones made by the wind that blows through the tent-ropes following his disastrous entertainment. In the second half of the novel this set of ambivalent laws is transformed into the 'lampless orchestra' that creates the purling water of the Blackwater, a river into which Henchard continually finds himself staring in an effort to understand himself. Unfortunately, he remains deaf to this music, rejecting the vagaries of personal analysis in favour of a fetishistic belief in external agents. The chapter also includes an analysis of the musically adept Farfrae, whose musicality allows him to play upon both Elizabeth-Jane and Henchard himself.

Chapter 7 demonstrates how, like Henchard, Jude is unable to under-stand the forces motivating his behaviour: 'events did not rhyme quite as he had thought' becomes a constant refrain. He is transformed into a 'little cell' upon whom the external world 'rattl[es]' and 'glar[es]', an epistemological representation that can be interpreted in the light of modern theories concerning aurality and human development.[41] I focus particularly on the way in which the Christminster dream and his ambitions of becoming a church licentiate are represented by means of an idealised Aeolian music. The chapter also explores the ways in which Jude's dreams are sacrificed to his sexual desire, in particular the part played by music in his relationship with Sue. Both characters are emotionally mute, the only time they seem to connect is under the influence of music, or through the musical element of voice tone, which offers a subtext to the empty dialogue that passes between them.

In seeking to place Hardy within the context of Victorian debates concerning the nature, status and origins of both music and voice, the book enters a relatively new and expanding field focussed on the cultural interpretation of different kinds of sound and music. This ranges from art historical works such as Richard Leppert's *The Sight of Sound: Music, Representation and the Human Body*[42] – which centres on how Victorian painters used musical subjects to subvert the parameters of female sexuality conditioned by the constraints of a patriarchal market – to more theoretical works such as Jonathan Crary's *Suspensions of Perception: Attention, Spectacle; And Modern Culture*, which offers a more general picture of how the work of painters such as Manet and Seurat can be reinterpreted in the light of nineteenth-century advances in psychophysical research.[43] Crary's work is of particular significance in placing Schopenhauer's ideas within the context of contemporary physiological research, and positioning the work of Wagner within the context of competing visual entertainments.

Also of great interest are theoretical works focussing more specifically on aural arts. Foremost amongst them is Douglas Kahn's *Noise, Water, Meat: Sound, Voice and Aurality in the Arts*,[44] which explores the cultural implication of changing attitudes towards noise, music and voice tone and hearing in the arts. Two recent works which have concentrated more specifically on the cultural history of attitudes towards hearing and voice are Steven Connor's *Dumbstruck – A Cultural History of Ventriloquism*[45] and Jonathan Reé's *I See a Voice*,[46] both of which assess how the epistemological importance of the voice as a means of individuation has been altered by a variety of historical inventions. Such work, as will be seen, helps to contextualise Hardy's own responses to sound and voice tone within a framework which is both historical and theoretical. It helps to decode Hardy's insistence on the aural element in his creation of so many of his novels, which at times appear as a complex soundscape made up of natural music mixed with musically delineated voice tone.

As yet there has been little work on literary responses to changing attitudes in the aural arts. One of the most interesting is Delia da Sousa Correa's *George Eliot, Music and Victorian Culture*,[47] which weaves together an analysis of how music became part of the 'role of woman' question of the mid-century with a study of how science was being used to study the affective power of music. Her work is particularly interesting in the way that she explores how Eliot's presentation of music and seduction is enlightened by our understanding of contemporary musical theory, particularly the work of Herbert Spencer and G. H. Lewes, both intimates of the novelist. Her work builds on earlier, though less specialised contributions to the field such as Gillian Beer's *Darwin's Plots: Narrative in Darwin, George Eliot and Nineteenth-Century Fiction*, and Sally Shuttleworth's *George Eliot and Nineteenth Century Science: The Make Believe of a Beginning*. It is a work which makes a number of points relevant to Hardy's portrayal of desire in the novels, and will be reintroduced in Chapter 4 accordingly.

Another recent study which is relevant to the present work and adds a different critical dimension to that of the cultural/historical texts mentioned above is John Hughes' *'Ecstatic Sound': Music and Individuality in the Work of Thomas Hardy*,[48] which uses the work of modern critical theorists such as Deleuze to explore the way in which Hardy employs musical motifs as a way of developing his characters. Deleuze is of particular interest because of the way that he conceives of thought in physical terms as materially conducted through the senses, an idea peculiarly in tune with the nineteenth-century focus on the physiology of the mind. He argues that Hardy's characters are not to be conceived of in terms of the pre-given form of personality, but are 'variable sensations' that exist in a state of perpetual 'becoming'. It is the function of the writer, he argues, not simply to represent such a process but also reproduce it in the reader through his syntactical skills. Thus, in certain passages of the novels, there is a blurring of subjective experience as character, narrator, artist and reader meet in a process of 'becoming'.

For Hughes, it is the art of music, whether manifested in the Aeolian tones of the wind or in the notes produced by a musical instrument, which becomes the clearly observable means by which Hardy seeks to illustrate the process by which an individual momentarily coalesces into a new set of relationships concerning those around them: a process typified by Hardy's use of instrumental music as a means of bringing to the surface previously buried desire. Hughes' employment of Deleuze adds a modern theoretical framework to Hardy's delineation of characters in terms of process, a tendency which, I argue in Chapter 2, developed out of his engagement with the work of Darwin, Pater and Schopenhauer.

Hughes' work, therefore, as with the other studies discussed above, will be used throughout the present book to add another dimension to my own cultural/historical research.

The overriding sense emerging from this brief survey of critical opinion is that there is a need for a study that places Hardy's thought in the philosophical, scientific and musical context of his time. It is only through an understanding of such contexts that we are able to grasp how music moved from the periphery of his art, where it remains in *Far from the Madding Crowd*, to the dominant source of allusion in the tragedies. In these novels Hardy reveals a subtle and complex use of musical allusion which offers new interpretations of both narrative structure and characterisation, and enriches our reading experience.

1
The Road to Norcombe Hill: Hardy's Musical Evolution

Through the pages of *The Life* Hardy recounts that as an infant he was 'extraordinarily sensitive to music', with a 'sensitiveness to melody... [which] remained with him through life'.[1] Memories of his youth are dominated by evocative descriptions of his 'adventures with the fiddle' in the villages neighbouring Bockhampton.[2] This early musicality is a characteristic upon which most modern critics agree:[3] Michael Millgate notes that 'the sounds of his father's violin of an evening could move him to dance and weep simultaneously'; Martin Seymour-Smith that 'as a boy he sought relief in the joy to be found in music';[4] and Elna Sherman that Hardy 'possessed a sensitive ear...was quickly and profoundly moved by the music he heard; [and] as he matured his musical taste became discriminating'.[5] And maturation did not see a discernible diminishing in his passion, leading Sherman to ask whether 'music is the greatest unifying factor in his poetry and prose alike?'[6] A question answered in the affirmative by Carl C. Weber, whose exhaustive bibliography of Hardy's 'musical poems' concludes that 'throughout his long life music remained one of Hardy's chief interests'.[7] This conclusion is echoed by Robert Gittings who notes that 'the chief draw, as always in his life, was music'.[8]

As well as with his own performances, *The Life* also abounds with records of the many concerts Hardy attended. One in particular, per-formed at Prince's Hall in June 1887, moved Hardy to write that he 'saw Souls outside Bodies', a description that he employs repeatedly in the fiction to characterise the effects of listening to music.[9] It also records his love of opera, an interest corroborated by Millgate's observation that during his first visit to London he was an 'enthusiastic opera-goer', and Grundy's assertion that throughout the 'impressionable period of his life...he attended performances at Covent Garden and His Majesty's several times a week'.[10] Modern criticism, then, which is divided over so many of Hardy's biographical details, is unanimous in the identification of sensitivity to music which remained with him throughout his life: a passion echoed in the author's own admission, 'to be honest I am never tired of music'.[11]

This love of music is evident in all of Hardy's early writings, *Under the Greenwood Tree* being the most autobiographical evocation of his youthful musical experiences. In such works, however, musical allusion does not provide the means of expressing Hardy's complex metaphysical vision, as it will in the more mature novels, but rather, in common with many mid-century writers, it is employed as a means of exploring disruptive social and sexual relations. For it is during this period that the public performance of parlour music becomes symbolic of the tension underlying contemporary constructions of femininity. da Sousa Correa has demonstrated that musical articles in the social-conduct pages of the plethora of women's journals and advice books on the training of girls published for the middle classes elicited very different and sometimes paradoxical responses.[12] Women were actively encouraged to play music in the home to foster domestic harmony and religious sentiment amongst their brothers and father.[13] The highly successful *Cornhill* sought to educate and inform its readers, a policy which, like the journal itself, was implicitly gendered. Hence, Charles Aidé's comprehensive review of the state of the contemporary music scene, 'Amateur Music', is an exhortation to indulge in private music making, encouraging its female readership to fill their homes with music since it 'elevates and enlarges the imagination, while it induces clearness of thought'.[14] Such a role is captured in countless saccharine canvases, the research of Richard Leppert into this field guiding us to pictures such as Charles West Cope's *The Music Lesson* (1863), in which the female pianist becomes a figure responsible for the domestic harmony of the hearth and home.[15]

However, at the same time women were being warned through the pages of the same journals that excessive music making detracted from the performance of their domestic duties and transformed them into idle dreamers. Worse, the learning of accomplishments for social display was roundly condemned. It was seen as training women for the marketplace and incompatible with domestic and charitable work. Yet how, as da Sousa Correa has noted, women were to succeed in the 'marketplace' without using their musical accomplishments to 'sell' themselves and thereby enter the realm of domestic contentment is a paradox which is continually avoided.[16] It is this inconsistency which is explored in the mid-century novels of Anne and Charlotte Brontë, William Makepeace

Thackeray, Elizabeth Gaskell, and George Eliot, and also in the paintings of Holman Hunt and William Breakspeare.

In the nineteenth-century novel music is both a symbol of spiritual and domestic harmony and dangerous sexuality. Whilst private enjoyment of music can reveal depth of character, public display is often used to determine shallow and morally corrupt characters. The piano becomes the favoured site of nineteenth-century fictional seduction, with women either portrayed as victims to male charms through their emotional susceptibility, or predators, artfully using their accomplishments to play upon male sexual sensitivity like latter day sirens. In *Vanity Fair* (1848), for example, music is instrumental in Becky Sharp's manipulative seduction of Rawdon Crawley: 'When she sang, every note thrilled in his dull soul and tingled through his huge frame.'[17] In *The Tenant of Wildfell Hall* (1848), as da Sousa Correa has noted, Anabella Wilmott is presented as a corrupt figure who coldly uses her casual musical facility and the close proximity afforded by musical performance to seduce the heroine's husband.[18] Similarly, da Sousa Correa notes that in *Wives and Daughters* (1864–1866), Elizabeth Gaskell contrasts the careless brilliance of Cynthia with her heroine's genuine love of music, but distaste for performance. Thus, Molly is presented as the guardian of domestic harmony, whilst Cynthia is transformed into a siren figure threatening Molly's possibilities of success in love.[19] In *Middlemarch* (1871–1872), Eliot contrasts Dorothea's distain for 'practising silly rhythms on the hated piano' (which asserts her moral superiority) with the siren Rosamand Vincy, who uses her exceptional musical mastery to entrap the unworldly Lydgate.[20] Finally, in Margaret Oliphant's *Phoebe Junior* (1876), the heroine's choice of music functions as an indicator of her internal struggle between two competing suitors. Eventually she marries Clarence Copperhead, who even couches his proposal in musical terms, 'you suit me down to the ground, music and everything', since she is able to provide an accomplished accompaniment to his violin playing.[21]

For Victorian painters the representation of musical performance in social settings becomes a means of subverting accepted patriarchal norms and exploring female sexuality. William Breakspeare's *The Reluctant Pianist*, for example, shows an erotically posed young woman at the piano (with coquettish smile), who refuses to play for her forlorn husband. As Richard Leppert has argued, her refusal to play signifies her pleasure in withholding her sexual favour from her powerless husband.[22] In a later canvas, *The Tiff*, however, the resignation of the male has been replaced by the sinister and phallic violence suggested by his brandishing of a riding crop.[23] The ambiguity of music and female sexuality is perhaps made clearest in Holman Hunt's *The Awakening Conscience* (1853), in which a girl is depicted starting to her feet from the lap of her lover as his hand idly plays a few chords on the piano at which they are both sitting. Music fulfils an ambiguous role as both the means of seduction and also the medium by which the female sitter's moral censure is awakened.[24]

In Hardy's earliest work *The Poor Man and the Lady* (1866), it appears from William Rutland's attempts to piece together the lost manuscript that music was central to the lovemaking of the central characters. According to Edmund Gosse's conversations with Hardy with regard to the novel, one particular scene involves both the hero and heroine being reconciled as lovers under the emotional influence of the music of a public concert.[25] This, William Rutland takes to have been recast, 'with the alteration of two or three sentences', in *An Indiscretion in the Life of an Heiress*, in a scene in which the estranged lovers, Geraldine Allenville and Egbert Mayne, are reunited during a performance of Handel's *Messiah*.[26] Hardy describes the effects of the music on Egbert as follows:

> The varying strains shook and bent him to themselves as a rippling brook shakes and bends a shadow. The music did not show its power by attracting his attention to its subject; it rather dropped its own libretto and took up in place of that the poem of his life and love.[27]

What is interesting here is that Hardy is using music as a means of exploring the sexual attraction of his protagonists whilst subverting class distinctions. Unusually it is the male character, Egbert, who is presented as the more susceptible. He is transformed into a shadow of his rational self, sustaining violent physiological contortions inflicted by a source that is as irresistible as a constantly flowing brook. The nature of the music remains unrecorded, indeed its value resides in its relation to the effects on Egbert, which is to lead him through a new series of emotions concerning the love of his life. To invoke the Deleuzean model employed by Hughes, music becomes a means by which the 'packet of sensations' that is Egbert momentarily coalesces into a new set of relationships concerning Geraldine. For her part, as Geraldine also finds herself moved by the music, Hardy makes the point that it is their social differences that are annihilated as their hands stretch across the rope dividing the cheap from the expensive seats. Music here becomes the great social leveller, privileging their love above the restrictions imposed by class considerations and lending to it nobleness. Class censure, however, continues to threaten, as is implied by Hardy's transformation of them into 'frail and sorry wrecks upon that sea of symphony'.[28]

Interestingly, Hardy uses almost the same words and imagery for different purposes in one particular scene in his first published novel, *Desperate Remedies* (1871).[29] Here it is Hardy's heroine, Cytherea Craye, who proves susceptible to music as she is drawn to the organ playing of the sinister Charles Manston:

> The varying strains…shook and bent her to themselves, as a gushing brook shakes and bends a shadow cast across its surface. The power of the music did not show itself so much by attracting her attention to the subject of the piece, as by taking up and developing as its libretto the poem of her own life and soul, shifting her deeds and intentions from the hands of her judgement and holding them in its own.
>
> She was swayed into emotional opinions concerning the strange man before her; new impulses of thought came with new harmonies, and entered into her with a gnawing thrill.[30]

Here Hardy's use of music does not signal the happy reunion of lovers mutually attracted, but rather it explores Cytherea's overmastering attraction to a man whom she regards in normal circumstances as unpleasant. He himself anticipates the sinister Mop Ollamoor of Hardy's story 'The Fiddler of the Reels', both his physical description and the potency of his mystical power being grounded in the mid-century interest in mesmerism (a subject that will be dealt with in detail in Chapter 4). The brook 'gushes' rather than ripples, suggesting an uncomfortable emotional intensity, which though thrilling, 'gnaws' like an animal into her very being. The choice of instrument itself, with its 'reverberating', 'weird' tones, adds a sinister note to the seduction, which is echoed in the Gothic addition of the 'unearthly weirdness' of the thunder and lightning outside. Under the power of music, and by implication her newly awakened sexual desire, Cytherea is alternately shaken and thrilled, becoming a supplicant 'involuntarily shrinking up beside him, and looking with parted lips at his face'. John Hughes notes how Manston's virtuosity as he adapts his music according to his musical sense is reflected in Hardy's writing, the continuous present conveying 'the power of the music to hold and move Cytherea, and to channel all the natural power of the storm into its own intense effects'. As Hardy attempts to capture the effects of the music there is a lapse in his narrative responsibility as he becomes immersed in the scene: his sentences and paragraphs dilate as he struggles with the representation of both 'perception and desire'.[31]

Significantly, when reason is restored, Hardy once again gives into the restraint required of the narrative, and has his heroine swiftly dispatch a letter blaming the music for the release of their feelings: it is a note that excuses the behaviour of both character and writer.

Despite betraying a poetic disregard for Hardy's handling of the narrative form, such scenes in the early fiction are conventional in that they allow the author to explore the sexuality of his heroine, whilst maintaining her virtue. Here, however, she remains an auditor and is therefore saved from the more morally dubious role of performer. It is a pattern that is anticipated by other nineteenth-century novels such as Eliot's *The Mill on the Floss* (1860), in which music is used to demonstrate the struggle between Maggie Tulliver's duty to her friends and desire for Stephen Guest. In a series of carefully crafted musical scenes the weak singing tenor of Philip Wakem, urging caution, is contrasted with the deep bass of Stephen, until finally during one particular concert she finds that 'in spite of her resistance to the spirit of the song and to the singer, [she] was taken hold of and shaken by the invisible influence – was borne along by a wave too strong for her'.[32] As with Hardy, the musical metaphor is transformed as the dam of female sexuality finally finds release.

In Hardy's second published novel, *A Pair of Blue Eyes* (1873), it is the heroine, Elfride Swancourt, who is the musical executant and the young architect, Stephen Smith, the susceptible listener. The music fires his heart like 'a small Troy'[33] and he is depicted squeezing into a small nook between the piano and the corner of the room from which he 'gaze[s] wistfully up into Elfride's face' in a state of supplication.[34] Hardy, however, does not create a Rosamand Vincy (*Middlemarch* had been appearing whilst Hardy was writing his novel) for he does not use his heroine's musical facility to demonstrate her delight in her own sexual attractiveness, but rather he uses her choice of music to explore her own complex sexual identity and the harsh nature of love in general. Both themes, as will be seen in Chapter 4, are far more typical of Hardy.

She begins with 'Should he Upbraid' from Henry Rowley Bishop's arrangement of songs from *The Two Gentlemen of Verona*, the main theme of which is that man's censure 'will prevail' and make the performer 'sing as sweetly as a nightingale'.[35] It is Hardy's, possibly Elfride's, covert warning to Stephen that in love his youthful good looks will not succeed in seduction as effectively as the harsh treatment of his mentor, Henry Knight. It is his damning review of her novel and merciless treatment on the chessboard that will act as the most potent aphrodisiac. Through the next song, from which two lines are quoted in French, Hardy makes clear that Elfride has planted the seeds of love in Stephen's heart. This leads to the warning implied by the last song, her mother's setting of Shelley's poem 'When the Lamp is Shattered'.[36] Hardy quotes the second half of the third verse, which cautions: love is transient, and since it chooses the 'frailest for [its] cradle' it will become a thing to be endured rather than enjoyed.

In *Under the Greenwood Tree*, Hardy's use of musical allusion becomes the central metaphor through which he explores the underlying themes of community and sexuality. The opening carolling of the Mellstock Quire not only presents the reader with a humorous depiction of Hardy's childhood music making, but also introduces the idea of a community in which each man has his allotted role, fulfilling a traditional ritual. Reverential talk of past members, and the comfortable way they slip from hymn accompaniment to secular dance music, indicates that their sense of tradition outweighs other considerations. Yet it is a tradition under threat, for their painfully discordant performance during the Christmas morning service, in which they are forced to duel with the women led by Fancy Day, brings a reproving glare from Parson Maybold and indicates that they are not in tune with the prevailing feeling. Diana Unwin's unpublished doctoral thesis 'Narratives of Gender and Music in the English Novel 1850–1900' traces within Hardy's apparently simple tale how music making as a patriarchal communal activity (typified by Anthony Trollope's use of church music in *The Warden*) became fragmented by the emergence of the individual female performer. She notes that such female incursions into a male preserve reflect the more general need, illustrated clearly by George Eliot in *Daniel Deronda*, for the mid-century female to find a voice.[37]

Hardy's meaning here, however, is sexual as well as sociological. Fancy's earlier dislocation of the young Dick Dewey from the rest of the Christmas carollers anticipates not only her dismantling of the quire but his sexual awakening. It is a theme which is explored through the rhythms of various dances at the Tranter's Christmas party, in which both he and the wealthy Mr Shiner compete for Fancy's hand through their competent execution of appropriately named figures such as 'Follow my Lover'. Of course, this use of dance as a metaphor for sexual manoeuvring would not look out of place in the pages of Jane Austen, and yet in Hardy's hands it takes on significance beyond the immediate domestic dispute. As the dancing becomes more frenetic the reader's perspective is transformed into the observing consciousness of Dick, to whom the room seems 'like a picture in a dream' in which 'fiddlers going to sleep as humming-tops sleep' animate the 'incandescent' and 'cadaverous' dancers.[38] Momentarily Dick appears to see beyond the living room to a wider 'dance of life', so that when he complains that Shiner's monopolisation of Fancy has transgressed 'what was *ordained by the regular dance-maker'* he seems to be looking past tradition to a single unifying power governing the 'steps' of all mankind.[39]

We catch another glimpse of the capacity of music to evoke the presence of a transcendental power in Hardy's description of the sobbing, hissing and moaning of the trees of Mellstock Lane at the beginning of the novel.[40] Here Hardy does not use the trees to explore the inner turmoil of his characters, as he does in the chapter 'Fancy in the Rain';[41] rather the voice of each tree is first and foremost an individual voice revealing an essence independent of perception. Indeed, collectively they create a sinister keynote which is deliberately at odds with the jolly singing of Dick Dewey as he enters the scene. It is this use of a keynote and the way that Hardy stages the gradual emergence of man on the scene that has caused Frances Pietch to draw parallels with Wagner's 'prelude technique'. In this she is mistaken, for the music here is not Wagnerian in either form or function, but derives, as will be seen in due course, from Hardy's reading of the Romantic poets. At present, however, it is enough to recognise that in this scene Hardy's use of music is not merely decorative, or simply an extension of the pathetic fallacy, but suggestive of a metaphysical power acting independently of man.

Hardy lifts the veil still further on a transcendental power in *Far from the Madding Crowd* when he invites the reader to 'stand on Norcombe Hill during a clear midnight' and observe the stars which 'seemed to be but *throbs of one body, timed by a common pulse'* and listen to the thin grasses 'touched by the wind in breezes of differing powers' so that they 'wailed or chaunted to each other in the regular antiphonies of a cathedral choir'.[42] In this example, Hardy combines his chanting grasses with the Classical conception of 'the music of the spheres' to evoke the presence of a wider transcendental process analogous to the shape of music. Once glimpsed, however, the curtain drops and Hardy returns to a variety of different methods for describing man's position in the universe. In this combination of Aeolian and cosmic tones, however, it is possible to recognise Hardy's later metaphysical music in embryo. Therefore, in the remainder of this chapter I would like to turn to a consideration of the Classical and Romantic influences which paved the road to Norcombe Hill.

Hardy's allusion to music as a 'sphere-descended Maid' in *Desperate Remedies* suggests that his interest in the idea of a cosmic melody extends to the beginning of his writing career.[43] It is not inconceivable that he read Plato's account of the theory: *The Literary Notebooks* are full of quotations from the *Ion, Charmides, The Republic* and *Cratylus*,[44] and the Platonic influence on all his work is apparent in a letter to Edmund Gosse which excuses the ultra-romantic nature of the story on the grounds that it was sketched 'when I was virtually a young man, and interested in the Platonic Idea'.[45]

It is more probable, however, that Hardy's interest in a form of cosmic music derives from the reinvention of the music of the spheres at the hands of the English poets who made up his early reading. A Christianised version appears in Lorenzo's reference in *The Merchant of Venice* to the 'smallest orb which thou beholdest / ... in his motion like an angel sings'.[46] It appears again in Dryden's 'A Song for St. Cecilia's Day', in which on the day of 'Creation' a sleeping Nature is awakened by a 'tuneful voice ... from high' which animates all phenomena 'the diapason closing full in man'.[47] It is a musical creation myth which is later explored in George Eliot's 'The Legend of Jubal', and which triggered a number of notes in Hardy's *Studies and Specimens Notebook*.[48]

Another version of the creation myth that appears to have interested Hardy is Milton's 'On the Morning of Christ's Nativity'.[49] Here God is depicted as a craftsman who sets his 'constellations' and hangs 'the well-ballanc't world on hinges', and then, on the morning of Christ's birth, sets in motion a sweet music 'as never was by mortall finger strook'.[50] Man is in harmony with the stars and his destiny and therefore he is able to hear the angelic orchestra playing a commemorative fanfare.[51] However, such cosmic harmony is short-lived, because the wisest Fate decrees that it is misplaced and must follow the redemption of Christ's crucifixion.[52] What follows is a descent into a jarring harmony of weeping voices and dissonant clangs, to which Pagan gods perform a 'dismall dance' before each 'slips to his severall grave'.[53] It is the descent into dissonance which appears to have appealed to Hardy, the notes in his *Studies and Specimens Notebook* nearly all being taken from the latter half of the poem and focussing on the images of discord and the dance macabre of 'fettered Ghost[s]'.[54]

This picture of an earth animated by the music of misery is also central to Milton's 'On the Late Massacher in Piedmont' from which Hardy noted the poet's exhortation to God not to forget the 'moans' of the massacred Saints.[55] Shelley's *Prometheus Unbound* depicts a similarly inharmonious world, which, judging by the wealth of pencil marks and annotations in his 1865 edition of the poem, was also the focus of close study by Hardy.[56] For Shelley, the suffering Prometheus is not simply a thief who severed man from the gods, but he symbolises the belief that though tyranny will always yield, man must suffer, defy his tormentors and yet still renounce revenge. Shelley depicts two worlds in the poem: the first is that which the Furies show to Prometheus in an effort to break his resistance, the second is that which dawns following his release. The second vision is one in which Earth and Moon dance in harmony according to the laws of gravity, and man is placed in an Arcadian idyll in which he communicates through a type of 'orphic song'.[57] The first revelation, and perhaps the one most interesting to Hardy, presents the reader with Milton's savage land, in which the despairing self-obsession of a spiritually bankrupt mankind is echoed by the groans of the Titan, which merge into the moans of the sea.[58]

John Keats appears to be alluding to the same anguished moans when describing the way the sighs of his heroine mingle with the music of celebration on 'The Eve of St. Agnes' to create a sound of 'yearning like a God in pain'. Although largely unread in Keats, Hardy appears to have been attracted to this Promethean expression of agony for he notes it in its entirety in his *Literary Notebook*.[59] These are the cries which are to echo through Hardy's own work – most notably in the 'Strange orchestras of victim-shriek and song' heard in the 1901 poem 'The Sleep-Worker', and Shade of the Earth's cry that *'My echoes are men's groans, my dews are red'*.[60]

The other aspect of the music of Norcombe that deserves our attention is that of the thin grasses 'touched by the wind in breezes of differing powers' so that they 'wailed or chaunted to each other in the regular antiphonies of a cathedral choir'.[61] This form of Aeolian musical allusion has its roots in the Romantic conception of the earth as a giant 'Aeolian Harp', the tones of which reveal the essence of phenomenal nature. Once again it is an image that clearly interested Hardy: when reading Shelley's *The Revolt of Islam*, for example, he made numerous entries in his *Studies and Specimens Notebook* detailing the episode when the lovers Laon and Cythna, like the reader upon Norcombe Hill, are placed 'beneath the golden stars of the clear azure air' whilst the breezes blowing upon the winter blooms create 'music wild and soft that filled the listening air' unifying the vision under the 'sweet melodies / Of love'.[62]

Perhaps the most significant influence on Hardy, however, is Wordsworth, whose employment of natural sounds as a springboard for metaphysical fancy was grounded in the close analysis of natural phenomena. This process can be seen clearly in the early poem 'An Evening Walk' in which the reader is presented with an almost forensic accretion of natural detail. What saves such writing from the accusation of formlessness that Hardy levels at the realists, however, is Wordsworth's awareness, suggested in the later poem 'Yarrow Revisited', that 'Nature's Self' is not

to be discovered without the 'poetic voice'.[63] It is this means of perception that enables the sounds that accompany the poet during his walk
to be transformed into 'the song of mountain-streams' and 'the spiritual
music of the hill'.[64] This 'music of nature' is not to be confused with the
'harmony of the spheres' because Wordsworth does not conceive of
these tones in rhythmic terms, and also each flower and mountain
possesses an individual voice which is not simply a means to a higher
metaphysical truth, nor a reflection of human emotions, but is first and
foremost the voice of the individual natural object.

Despite their heterogeneous nature, these tones are not conceived of
as dissonant with each other, but form a concord which can only be
captured by the poetic imagination. In poems such as 'To The Cuckoo'
and the 'Solitary Reaper' various natural sounds are unified by the
poetic imagination under a single keynote.[65] In the first, the echoing
voice of the bird is disengaged from its corporeal substance to lend a
'mystical' keynote to that part of nature in which it is heard; in the
latter, the voice of the reaper provides the harmonising keynote for
the whole valley in which she works, thus unifying 'man' with the
valley.

In 'The Power of Sound', Wordsworth asks whether earth has any
'scheme' for all this music.[66] In his reply, the cave of Aeolus is transformed
into the labyrinthine auricular cavity, through which the 'poetic-ear' can
perceive the 'one pervading spirit'.[67] Since, he argues, the same forces
which make the 'heavens' make our minds, man will echo the harmony
or dissonance of the outer world. When man perceives the 'mighty
harmonist' of the ocean, he is brought into a state of tranquillity, and
when the winds howl during 'Stern Winter' they create a 'dirge-like
sound' which has a chastening effect upon him.[68] Here, Wordsworth
creates a benevolent connection between mind and nature through sound,
a relationship which becomes far more caring in *The Prelude*, where the
River Derwent becomes something of an earth mother to the poet,
blending 'his murmurs with my nurse's song' and 'mak[ing] ceaseless
music that composed my thoughts', giving a foretaste of the calm which
'Nature breathes among hills and groves'.[69] In 'Tintern Abbey' Wordsworth
continues this theme, noting that as man grows older it is the memory
of such 'sweet sounds and harmonies' experienced in youth that will be
of comfort in times of 'pain and grief':

> For I have learned
> To look on nature, not as in the hour
> Of thoughtless youth; but hearing oftentimes

The still, sad music of humanity,
Nor harsh nor grating, though of ample power
To chasten and subdue. And I have felt
A presence that disturbs me with the joy
Of elevated thoughts.[70]

It is this statement of the relationship between man and nature which appears to have held such fascination for Hardy – he not only marked it in his 1864 and 1896 editions of 'Tintern Abbey',[71] but he also copied it into his *Literary Notebooks*[72] and then employed it himself in a later essay on the realist school of fiction[73] – and it is easy to understand why. For here, music does not function in the traditional Romantic fashion as an invisible lever to a transcendent haven from the world's ills, but educates man through the poetic imagination. Close contemplation of nature will lend to the 'sad music of humanity' a 'chastening' quality, which will not simply offer man respite, but enable him to come to terms with his existence, in the process making him into a better human being. It is this idea of calm acceptance rather than escape that is central to Hardy's own philosophy.

This music of nature, I believe, informs Hardy's description of the music heard in Mellstock Lane and on Norcombe Hill, and forms the foundation of the musical allusion employed in the tragedies. Hardy certainly considered himself a 'faithful Wordsworthian', his 'much-marked' 1864 edition of the poet's collected works bearing testimony to his careful study, and an entry in *The Life* for January 1881 suggesting his full grasp of the Wordsworthian poetic method:

Consider the Wordsworthian dictum (the more perfectly the natural object is reproduced, the more truly poetic the picture). This reproduction is achieved by seeing into *the heart of a thing* (as rain, wind, for instance), and is realism, in fact, though through being pursued by means of the imagination it is confounded with invention, which is pursued by the same means.[74]

The lists found on a loose leaf from an unidentified notebook of the different sounds made by the wind and rain testify to Hardy's close attention to the sounds of nature. These find artistic expression in the careful description of the rain falling upon various types of vegetation in *Desperate Remedies*, and the detailing of the sounds of various animals heard by Stephen Smith as he waits for Elfride in the porch of Endelstow church in *A Pair of Blue Eyes*.[75] When the trees of Mellstock Lane are considered, it is important to recognise that the 'tones' of the trees are those idiosyncratic features that enable the 'dwellers in the wood' to distinguish one type of tree from another. Hardy's deliberate vagueness concerning both the time and appearance of the 'man' who enters the scene allows the reader to assume the role of the observing consciousness to whose 'intelligence' the trees 'whispered thus distinctively'.[76] These whispered tones create a sinister 'keynote' thereby undermining the happy song of Dick Dewey (into whom the lightly drawn figure of 'a man' eventually metamorphoses). It is this keynote which is later taken up in the equally sinister 'liquid tones' of the nightingale accompanying Dick's apparently happy marriage to Fancy Day.[77]

The essence of Hardy's construction of the scene on Norcombe Hill is careful attention to detail, exemplified by the depiction of the way winds of differing power blow upon the grasses: 'one rubbing the blades heavily, another raking them piercingly, another brushing them like a soft broom'.[78] Once again, it is the reader who becomes the observing consciousness as Hardy makes the bold authorial observation that 'the instinctive act of human-kind was to stand and listen'. And when we do listen, we hear the 'sobbing' of hedgerows, the 'moaning' of trees and the insistent throb of the stars as they orbit each other. This is the world envisaged by Milton and Shelley: a godless universe in which an Aeolian music announces the agony felt by all living things. Crucially, because man possesses the gift of consciousness he both participates in this mournful music and transcends it: a philosophical principle that Hardy signals through the barely discernible notes of Gabriel Oak's flute, which are part of this chorus and yet a 'sequence which was to be found nowhere in nature'.[79]

We catch other glimpses of Hardy moving towards the conception of an ambivalent universal process in his depiction of Norcombe Hill as a giant, and also in his description of the 'silent workings of an invisible hand' seen by Joseph Poorgrass as he enters Yalbury Great Wood. These remain, however, captured moments, which hint at the presence of a cosmic power rather than embody a coherent metaphysical vision.[80] Indeed, when the curtain falls upon Norcombe Hill, Hardy returns to the more traditional means of representing man's relationship with his environment, such as the weather, time and coincidence. And yet, it is undoubtedly true that in its representation of a unified discordant universe with which man is out of tune, the music of Norcombe antici-pates that of Egdon.

Two things need to happen to Hardy's art for this music to become the pervasive metaphor observed in *The Return of the Native*: first, the various cosmic agencies Hardy manipulates to explore the relationship between his characters and their environment have to be reduced to a more coherent set of metaphysical principles; and secondly Hardy has to find a means of translating these principles into a musical analogy capable of sustaining itself throughout the complexities of his narrative. What made this transformation possible is Hardy's periodical research of 1876–1877, which introduced him to a number of contemporary thinkers, such as Spencer, Darwin and Schopenhauer, whose modern science and philosophy not only vindicated his own darkening vision, but also explained it in terms of easily digestible biological and meta-physical theories. Furthermore, this period of research also introduced him to the work of Wagner, who indicated how such views of life might be translated into musical tropes. Such is the importance of this period of research in Hardy's artistic evolution that it is the aim of the following chapter to set out some of the more pertinent ideas to which he was exposed in the mainstream journals.

2
'Silent Workings of the Invisible Hand': Hardy's Metaphysical Evolution

In a rather playful passage in a letter to an unidentified correspondent Hardy claimed 'I have no philosophy – merely what I have often explained to be only a confused heap of impressions, like those of a bewildered child at a conjuring show.'[1] It is a sentiment repeated in a letter to John Galsworthy in which he claims 'I am not a philosopher' and 'a miserable reasoner'.[2] Such admissions mean that it has become fashionable to dismiss Hardy as a systematic thinker, Millgate, for one, arguing that Hardy's mind was 'not naturally equipped to move easily in realms of philosophical discourse'.[3] It is a sentiment seemingly vindicated by the lapses in his treatment of determinism and idealism (pinpointed by Simon Gatrell and Robert Schweik) in both *The Mayor of Casterbridge* and *Tess of the D'Urbervilles*.[4]

A number of critics, however, have dismissed Hardy's protestations (which simply reflect his lack of intellectual confidence) and have argued that this 'confused heap' is amenable to philosophical analysis. Pierre D'Exideuil, for example, argues that although Hardy 'always sets his face against presenting a system in the sense congenial to a theorist ... [the] rough apanage of ideas and concepts, which form the substance of the *Wessex Novels* and *Poems*, and, above all, of *The Dynasts*, makes it possible *to reconstruct a real metaphysical system*'.[5] More recently, Miller J. Hillis, Brian Green and Deborah Collins have sought to identify general themes in Hardy's work, whilst openly acknowledging his deficiencies as a systematic thinker.[6] Green is perhaps the most candid here, for although he rejects the notion that the novels and poems represent a systematic philosophy, he claims that it is possible to distil from Hardy's 'tentatively' expressed ideas a 'master theme' around which the various strands of his thought are woven.[7] Put simply, the world envisaged in *The Return of the Native* and subsequent novels is constructed upon principles which can be summarised as follows: Hardy conceives of a world governed by determining laws – such as those of Newtonian physics, the Immanent Will, the Darwinian principle of sexual selection, materialist laws of determinism and the principle of heredity – which are unified under a partially anthropomorphised unified process indifferent to the suffering of man. Man is part of this determined universe, but possesses the double-edged 'gift' of consciousness, which not only enables him to perceive the misery of existence in such a harshly determined world, but also allows him to rebel against the dictates of his environment, therefore creating a tragic tension.

Green's reluctance to proceed beyond the identification of 'themes' is surely right here, for whilst it is possible to identify the broad principles underlying much of Hardy's work, his 'tentativeness' continually undermines attempts at systematisation. Millgate explains this trend in Hardy's writing in terms of a 'Laodiceanism' that enabled him 'to see virtue in all sides of a question' and present his thoughts as a series of impressions.[8] It is a pertinent point, and yet as an explanation it emphasises Hardy's undisciplined vacillation at the expense of what might be construed as his virtuous acknowledgement of complexity. Essentially, the task facing Hardy, like all artists, was one of how to represent the perplexing nature of the world around him without falsifying it through simplification and systematisation. Hardy's answer appears to have been to offer the main threads of a coherent view, whilst never losing the bemusement of the child before the conjuror. Collins goes further, explaining Hardy's philosophical inconsistencies as a product of the confusing age in which he lived, and also a deliberate aesthetic ploy designed to undermine the readers' demand for certainty in its authorial discourse.[9] She invokes Mikhail Bakhtin's concept of 'polyphony' to argue that Hardy's constant disavowal of a single authorial voice freed him from the 'danger of philosophical tunnel vision' and allowed him to explore the world around him through competing and sometimes contradictory voices.[10]

The idea that Hardy's philosophical uncertainty may have been worked out in his narratives is also significant in the light of Pater's ultra-Romantic manifesto *The Renaissance* (1873), which transformed the spirit of 'tentativeness' into something approaching a philosophical methodology. In his conclusion to the 1877 edition he states that although science is reducing the world to a series of 'elementary forces', their complexity is such that the very concept of knowledge is reduced to a series of 'unstable' and 'inconsistent' impressions experienced by the 'individual in his isolation'.[11] Thus, although deterministic laws may govern man's activities, Pater resists Enlightenment attempts to discover their nature in favour of exhorting the artist to focus on the momentary manifestation of these forces. In this context a letter written by Hardy to Alfred Noyes is of interest, since in it he chastises the poet for picking passages from his poems that give contradictory interpretations of what should be considered a clearly defined general view. Hardy notes that although he has 'called this Power [the Cause of Things] all sorts of names' they are mere 'expression[s] of fancy', and are not to be confused with the 'expression of belief' in which this Power has 'been defined in scores of places...[as] neither moral nor immoral, but *un*moral: – "loveless and hateless" '.[12] The reasoning seems entirely Paterian; his attempts to capture the isolated moment do not preclude his 'belief' in a coherent metaphysical universe, while his 'belief' in the latter does not annihilate his impression of the moment.

Pater's conclusion has significant ramifications with regard to Hardy's aesthetic thought and particularly his use of music in the novels, and this will form the focus of Chapter 3. In this chapter, however, I would like to establish the philosophical and scientific context underpinning the cosmic vision explored in Hardy's later fiction and summarised by the three principles outlined above.

The idea that an ambivalent process rather than a benevolent God governed the universe was part of the malaise that plagued the mid-Victorian world. Tennyson's anxiety that man may be left stranded in a cold, Godless universe 'Born of the brainless Nature who knew not that which she bore!' led him to build doubt into his faith, and therefore perceive the advances of modern science as part of a strengthening process.[13] For Hardy, however, such theistic contortions were an early casualty of his loss of faith in 1865, as is recorded with a tone of regret in late poems such as 'The Impercipient' and 'God's Funeral'.[14] The speakers in both poems echo the sentiments expressed by Markham Sutherland in Froude's *The Nemesis of Faith* (1849), who pledges to 'give away all I am, and all I ever may become...for one week of my old child's faith'.[15] It is a theme to which he returns in an authorial comment in *Tess of the D'Urbervilles*, which refers to 'the chronic melancholy which is taking hold of the civilised races with the decline of belief in a beneficent Power'.[16] In 'A Plaint to Man' Hardy explores the same theme from the perspective of a Feuerbachian God who was created by man as a 'phasm on a lantern-slide' to confront the 'gloomy aisles / Of this wailful world'.[17] As the creation of need, he acknowledges that his power to comfort man is dwindling, and he therefore encourages him to come to terms with his isolation.

Unable to sustain his belief in a 'man-projected Figure', and even less in a careless God,[18] Hardy is to be found in the mid-seventies drifting towards the conception of a metaphysical process indifferent to the plight of man: the 'brainless Nature' feared by Tennyson.[19] In this, Hardy fell very much under the long shadow of evolutionary theory, in which ideas of a benevolent God were replaced by the idea of a semi-anthropomorphised 'process'. The Darwinian process of natural selection, according to which a species constantly adapts in order to gain an advantage over its competitors in the struggle for existence, offered scope for anthropomorphism, even within the *Origin of the Species* itself, where Darwin refers to an 'ever-watchful Nature, with an infallible eye and "unerring skill" [which] scrutinises, picks out, and favours each successful competitor, but rejects failures'.[20] For Herbert Spencer, evolutionary process was a mixture of natural selection and Lamarckian inheritance of acquired characteristics partially anthropomorphised into 'The Absolute', which is neither conscious nor unconscious, nor part of the universe or distinguishable from it.[21] This is the kind of Nature about which Hardy is to be found complaining in a letter printed in *The Academy and Literature* concerning Maurice Maeterlinck's *Apology for Nature*, which states that the only way to save Nature's good name is by assuming ' "that she is blind and not a judge of her actions" or that she is an automaton, and unable to control them'.[22]

However, evolutionary theory did not simply mechanise God, it brought into question not only the dominance of man in the universe, but also his very autonomy. Roger Ebbatson makes this point succinctly in his observation that

> Darwin, in his brilliant demolition of the ideas of fixed species unveiled a world in which essence is replaced by becoming, a world where there operates what Huxley designated 'a transitory adjustment of contending forces'. The notion of transition, of a world which was to be comprehended, as Engels wrote, not 'as a complex of ready-made things, but as a complex of processes.'[23]

For Pater, arguing in *Plato and Platonism*, the evolutionary theory of Darwin had simply vindicated the fear of the Ancients of a world in 'flux' – the idea that any particular phenomenon, whether it be a plant or person, exists as a result of forces which are in constant motion in the universe.[24] It is quite clear from the *Literary Notebooks* that in 1876–1877 Hardy was taking an interest in those theorists who focussed on man's participation in a world of flux. In the summer of 1877 he read John

Morley's analysis of 'Holbach's System of Nature' in the *Fortnightly Review*, which presents the reader with the image of a raging sandstorm, in which, despite the apparent chaos, every grain of sand obeys the laws of molecular necessity. Hardy was evidently drawn to this conception, marking this passage in his own copy of Morley's works and copying into his *Notebook* the assertion that *'All phenomena are necessary.* No creature in the universe, in its circumstances and according to its given property, can act otherwise than as it does act.'[25] This view is echoed in John Tulloch's 'Morality without Metaphysics', which denies the existence of free will on the grounds that man's supposedly independent conscience falls 'under the empire of force which rules all nature' and is simply the 'last transformation of the great natural forces of light and heat and electricity, passing through the mysterious involvements of the human nervous system',[26] and also the 1876 essay of physicist John Tyndall, where the world of flux is likewise conceived of in terms of a vortex of continuously combining molecules, in which even man's thoughts and feelings have 'a definite mechanical correlative in the nervous system – that ... is accompanied by a certain separation and remarshalling of the atoms of the brain'.[27]

What this meant for thinkers like Spencer is that there was no transcendent 'self', simply a series of 'psychical states' which conform to laws just as easily as simple reflex action in muscles. In *The Principles of Psychology* he argues that it is the 'extreme complication' of the causal forces determining these states which gives man the 'illusion' of free will. It is an 'illusion' to suggest that 'at each moment the *ego* is something more than the composite state of consciousness which then exists'.[28] Hardy, of course, remained a fervent supporter of Spencer throughout his life, and furthermore was reading very similar conclusions in Frederic W. H. Myers' 'Human Personality', published in the *Fortnightly Review* of 1885. The article argues, as Hardy's notes in the *Literary Notebooks* make clear, that human beings have a multiplex nature, human as other; that what we suppose to be choice is reflex action only. Quoting from the article he asks, 'does my consciousness testify that I am a single entity?'[29] A question that he seems to answer in a revealing entry in *The Life*: 'I am more than ever convinced that persons are successively various persons, according as each special strand of their characters is brought uppermost by circumstances.'[30]

It is, however, in the work of Arthur Schopenhauer that such epistemological speculations and evolutionary theory were to be most comfortably unified in the Victorian mind. Indeed, to a large extent he was treated by an intellectual community fashioned in the empirical tradition and dominated by the biological methodology of Darwin as a philosopher who had 'taught deductively what Darwin has proved inductively'.[31] For Schopenhauer, that element which prevented the self from being conceived simply as a Paterian jumble of fragments of representations and ideas was our perception of the human body, an object in the phenomenal world over which we have a special knowledge. Through observation of the body's extension into the world, Schopenhauer identifies the Kantian 'thing in itself' (that element independent of the perceiving mind which prevents the phenomenal world from becoming merely the product of individual perception) as the 'will'. For Schopenhauer then, as for Pater, the individual is conceived as a product of sensation, but this chaotic succession of perception is determined by the blind movement of the will and experienced by the individual through his own body, often primarily sexual. Since, Schopenhauer reasons, there is no difference between our body and any other object of perception in the phenomenal world, the will must constitute the inner state of all things, both animate and inanimate. The phenomenal world, therefore, from the smallest crystal to the most complex animal is an objectification of the will.

It is a theory that rivalled the Darwinian principle of sexual selection in terms of its simplicity, but, despite its publication in *The World as Will and Idea* as early as 1819 it had remained largely ignored in both this country and his native Germany. By the mid-seventies, however, he found himself peculiarly in tune with the greater emphasis on physiological understanding of the human subject. Indeed such was the interest in 1876 that the contemporary philosopher R. Adamson could claim that 'the spirit of the age seems to be impregnated with the pessimist view of things' so that 'one can scarcely open any philosophical work without finding reference to [Schopenhauer's] name and thoughts'.[32] Helen Zimmern also identified the onset of a stage of 'pessimism' in an article in *Academy*,[33] and responded with her biography of the philosopher, which, according to a review by the philosopher C. A Simcox was well timed to satisfy 'the growing public that is curious about his philosophy'.[34] A month later the *Cornhill*, then under the editorship of Leslie Stephen (ed. 1871–1882), published James Sully's 'The Pessimist's View of Life', which was later expanded into *Pessimism: A History and Criticism* (1877).[35] At the end of the year, *The Fortnightly* published a comprehensive piece by the German émigré Francis Hueffer, who had been a student of the philosopher at Gottingen.[36] There were also a number of short articles and reviews published in journals such as *The Athenaeum, Academy* and the new philosophical journal *Mind*, the first volume of which appeared in 1876 and resembled a tribute to Schopenhauer's life and works.

Schopenhauer's popularity rested on both his emphasis on physiology – allowing Hueffer to assert with great clarity that 'our body itself, with its nerves and fibres, its blood and its brain, is indeed nothing but this Will become conscious' – and also the belief that he offered a philosophical vindication of Darwin.[37] Indeed, Zimmern argued that Schopenhauer 'had to a certain extent anticipated the generalisation of the universal "struggle for existence", with its corollary of "the survival of the fittest" '.[38] As a consequence there is a great deal of elasticity in the terminology applied to both thinkers. Zimmern, for example, employs 'will', 'impulse' and 'striving' interchangeably in her attempts to suggest a lack of planning and inevitability which are central to her interpretation of the essentially irrational, blind and purposeless nature of the Schopenhauerian universe.[39] This feature is also made clear in Hueffer's juggling of the terminology of both men:

> Will and interminable desire are the essence of our being, and the same desire is at the bottom of the phenomena of the world. These phenomena themselves, although we recognise their essence by analogy, surround us with bewildering horror. Everywhere we see struggle for existence, species devouring species, race contending with race;... Surely this is not a bright picture, and Schopenhauer has painted it with the sombrest hues of despair. He lays bare the revolting cruelty of nature, which at the cost of inconceivable individual suffering creates new types only to abandon them again to the universal doom of destruction.[40]

To the Victorian intellectual community, Schopenhauer bridged the scientific/philosophical divide, a sentiment that was extended to his compatriot, Edward von Hartmann, whose *Philosophy of the Unconscious* was the subject of a lengthy article by James Sully in the *Fortnightly Review* of August 1876.[41] Hartmann talks not of the will, but rather of unconscious wills lying behind such automatic human processes as the growth of the body, reflex reactions and the healing of a wound.[42] These separate wills unite in a single unconscious will, which, though it can be traced in the material processes, has a metaphysical existence presiding over the others.[43] It is this 'organizing Unconscious' which is more than simply a collection of bodily functions or material forces; 'it is a will enlightened by an intelligence' which unites all phenomena.[44] This conception of the unconscious will, Sully argues, is of particular significance when considering Darwinism. Hartmann's discussion of natural selection focuses on his belief that though it can explain how the modification of existing organs comes about, it is unable to account adequately for serious morphological change within a species. This can only be understood, he argues, if we consider the existence of an unconscious will which exploits the mechanical changes which take place within a species. In effect, the unconscious flows into the mould prepared for it by the mechanism of individual variation.

We do not have to look far in Hardy's work to find evidence of an 'unconscious will', or the 'sombrest hues of despair', indeed the reviewer R. H. Hutton noted as early as 1879 that 'Hardy speaks with the calm confidence of one who has found Schopenhauer far superior to all the prophets and all the seers.'[45] It is a sentiment echoed by Joan Grundy, who argues that Hardy 'may, I think, have been partly influenced by Schopenhauer, from whom, it is generally agreed, he in part derived his notion of the Immanent Will'.[46] There is, however, in her tentative modifying expressions a diffidence more articulate than the assertion, deriving, one suspects, from the practical difficulty of reconciling Hardy's inability to read German with the fact that Haldane's translation of *The World as Will and Idea* did not appear until 1883 – an argument articulated most recently by the critic Tim Hands who dismisses the notion of Schopenhauerian influence.[47] But, as has been suggested above, Schopenhauer was very much in the public domain in 1876 in precisely those journals that Hardy was studying as part of his campaign. That is not to say that he appropriated his entire metaphysical model from Schopenhauer, but rather, as John Hughes argues, he found in Schopenhauer points of contact which both confirmed and stimulated his own thinking.[48] For with Schopenhauer, as for Darwin, it is not necessary to know the philosopher's work in detail to be fully aware of Schopenhauerianism. These points of contact are evident in such general features as, as R. H. Hutton noted, the gloomy vision of *The Return of the Native*, but more particularly in the way that the monotheistic Egdon Heath mirrors the concept of the 'Immanent Will', and, more pertinently, in Hardy's use of music.

Schopenhauer's musical theory will be considered in detail in the next chapter, but for the present I would like to consider Hardy's depiction of Egdon in relation to the scene quoted at some length at the beginning of this book. In Spencer's terms, Eustacia's emergence from Rainbarrow offers an evolutionary metaphor, the ascent through increasing organisational complexity climaxing in the moment of 'individuation' when she demonstrates herself to be distinct from her environment. But there is a precision in Hardy's description (not to mention a musical dimension) which is closer to Schopenhauer. Schopenhauer classifies the degrees of objectification of the will into five levels, which are made explicit by the philosopher Edith Simcox (writing under the pseudonym of H. Lawrenny) in her essay 'Arthur Schopenhauer' (1873): the 'most powerful and varied [is] in man, diminishingly so in lower animals, less still in the vegetable kingdom, but present even in inorganic matter (attraction, electricity, & c.) as a faint, inarticulate consciousness diffused through the inert mass'.[49] As the observing consciousness of Diggory Venn takes the reader from the level of the road through a gradual series of ascents, which embrace hillocks, ridges and acclivities to the top of Rainbarrow, where the solitary figure of Eustacia is 'so much like an organic part of the entire motionless structure', that she becomes 'like a spike from a helmet',[50] it appears that we have travelled through the varying objectifications of the Immanent Will.

In simple terms, then, Egdon presents the reader with a partially anthropomorphised First Cause or Will whose haggard features indicate its subjection to the laws governing all phenomena. It re-emerges in a series of transparencies in *The Dynasts*, in which Hardy adopts specifically Schopenhauerian terminology to show 'the controlling Immanent Will,... as a brain-like network of currents and ejections, twitching, interpenetrating, entangling and thrusting hither and thither the human forms'.[51] In the novels his characters become little more than nerve endings of this wider process, following, as Ebbatson has noted, a Spencerian evolutionary pattern which sees them emerging from the homogenous darkness of the 'Unknowable', distinguishing themselves from their environment, before sinking back into the gloom.[52] They are reduced to the level of insects, the favoured image of both Darwin and Schopenhauer to exemplify a world governed by the principle of instinct, Zimmern noting, 'in the blind yet efficacious instinct of animals, more especially of insects, Schopenhauer discerns the clearest proof and illustration of the unconscious action of that impulse to which he ascribes the origination of the universe'.[53]

For Hardy they provided an admirable metaphor. Even in the early work *A Pair of Blue Eyes* he draws out the parallel between the 'Humanity Show' observed through the window of Henry Knight's Bede's Inn study and the 'many-coloured zoophytes' inhabiting the small aquarium standing in the corner of the room.[54] When in *Desperate Remedies* a contemplative Aeneus Manston finds himself staring into the depths of a water butt he sees 'hundreds of thousands of minute living creatures' dancing over his green-tinged reflection, 'perfectly happy, though consisting only of a head, or tail,... and all doomed to die within the twenty-four hours'.[55] Hardy returns to this image again in *The Return of the Native* through his reduction of the heathmen to ants and 'the maggoty shapes of innumerable obscure creatures' crawling over the face of haggard Egdon.[56] Here it is left to the unphilosophical Johnny Nunsuch to glimpse, like Manston, the uncomfortable truth of this analogy as he stares into Throope Great Pond looking for effects and instead sees 'myself looking up at myself'.[57] Hardy revisits this imagery in *The Dynasts*, reducing vast European armies into ants, cheese-mites and caterpillars crawling over the body of a supine Europe.[58]

However, man does not simply suffer in common with the insects; for characters such as Clym Yeobright a life given over to the simple satisfaction of instinct amongst the Egdon eremites is infinitely preferable to the possession of consciousness. It is this double-edged sword which raises Hardy's characters above the heath and lends to them a tragic stature. Quite what Hardy understood by consciousness remains difficult to tease out, as is made apparent by his assertion in a letter to Edward Wright concerning the philosophy of *The Dynasts* which states that the will of man is 'neither wholly free nor wholly unfree'.[59] Once again, however, apparent vacillation should not be condemned as intellectual uncertainty, but rather an admission of the complexity of the debate concerning how consciousness emerged in a materialist world – a debate that was engaging some of the foremost minds of the mid-seventies.

For Schopenhauer, for example, man can never escape the dominance of the will, even his intellectual activity is subordinate to its power. As Zimmern observes, the will is pre-eminent while the 'Intelligence is only a *tertiary* phenomenon', the 'Will is the substance of the man, Intelligence the accident.'[60] The way in which the will manifests itself in man is through the shaping of 'character', so that, as Zimmern claims, 'no man can change his character, for the character is the Will itself exhibited in a phenomenal form'.[61] This conception of free will is, as will be seen in due course, fundamental to our understanding of the behaviour of Michael Henchard, Hardy's 'man of character'.

Schopenhauer's subordination of the intellect to the will does more, however, than simply delineate the individual in a new way: it explains why man's life is a misery. Fundamental to this unhappiness is Schopenhauer's idea that the principle of necessity, which makes the contact of man with the outside world so traumatic, is repeated in the very dynamic of consciousness. Adamson notes, 'man is an accumulation of a thousand wants; his life is a struggle for existence, a constant succession of cravings, temporary gratifications, and renewed desires. Pleasure is impossible without pain; it presupposes pain, and is therefore secondary and negative in nature.'[62] Once again it is a conception that Hardy will have found clearly expressed in his copy of *Pessimism*:

> The deepest reason of this suffering lies in the nature of will itself. Will, as we have seen, is, in its nature, striving; but striving is necessarily suffering. 'All striving springs out of defect, and discontent with its condition, is therefore suffering, so long as it is not pacified.' Again, since the nature of will is to strive, and since will is the real and persistent element of our nature, permanent satisfaction is out of the question.[63]

According to Schopenhauer's more colourful metaphors, 'the subject of willing is thus constantly stretched on the revolving wheel of Ixion, pours water into the sieve of the Daniads, is the ever-longing Tantalus'.[64] In terms of his general theory, the misery of human existence is determined a priori by the dominance of the will, and is vindicated a posteriori by observation of human experience. Again, as will be seen in later chapters, this conception of conscious striving is pertinent to our understanding of the lives of such characters as Jude, whose life fluctuates between idealistic hope and despair, and Tess, whose 'low screams of entreaty and agony' following the death of Alec actually find her, according to Hardy's authorial intervention, 'bound to some Ixionian will'.[65]

It is quite clear from his presentation of consciousness in the novels, however, that for Hardy's characters it entailed a degree of freedom, an idea which reflects the views of contemporary thinkers such as von Hartmann and W. L. Clifford. Both J. O. Bailey and Walter Wright have drawn out significant parallels between the ideas of Hardy and Hartmann's view that the will is not blind, but consists of an unconscious energy existing in all phenomena becoming conscious.[66] Hardy certainly focuses upon this aspect of Hartmann's work in his notes taken from *The Philosophy of the Unconscious*: a work which Hardy praised in an interview with William Archer before launching into his own speculations as to whether there may be some 'consciousness, infinitely far off, at the other end of the chain of phenomena, always striving to express itself'.[67]

Sully's appraisal of Hartmann's ideas concerning the birth of consciousness is dramatically presented as the result of 'a collision of two wills, namely, the will of the unconscious individual mind and the reacting wills of the atoms of the brain'.[68] In essence, consciousness emerges from a rupture in the mind like the mushroom cloud arising from the collision of atoms following a nuclear explosion. So shocking is the impact of organised matter breaking in upon the unconscious that Hartmann concludes that pain 'is an inseparable ingredient of all conscious life'.[69] It is a conclusion that echoes that of Schopenhauer, but the methodology by which he attains this position is inductive rather than a priori. Beginning with his observation of the human condition, Hartmann argues that

> human existence is a miserable one, and so far from being made less so by the progress of human development, is in a sense growing more and more miserable as intelligence increases and the true value of human ends becomes calmly recognised.[70]

He distinguishes three stages in man's disillusion, which are reflected in the historical evolution of mankind. The youth has a naïve belief that happiness is attainable, but experience extinguishes this hope, and expectations of future joy are elevated to the concept of paradise. Man today, however, has left the partial comfort ensured by primitivism and medieval religiosity and has entered a new stage where he foregoes individual happiness in the hope that it may be attainable for future generations. But this is an illusion as fallacious as the others, the product of misguided hope rather than any real evidence. The only satisfactory solution is to escape the tyranny of the will through a 'common act of will-annihilation'.[71]

Similar ideas are also to be found in the work of the contemporary theorist W. L. Clifford, who in *Lectures and Essays* (1879) set out to answer the problem posed by Tyndall in his 'Belfast Address', as to how consciousness could arise in a materialist world.[72] In 'On The Nature of Things-in-Themselves' Clifford proposed the existence of a single universal consciousness made up of 'mind-stuff' permeating all inorganic and organic phenomena. He argues that 'a moving molecule of inorganic matter does not possess mind or consciousness; but it possesses a small piece of mind-stuff'.[73] When these molecules are combined in such a way to 'form the film on the under side of a jelly-fish' we have the 'faint beginnings of Sentience'.[74] Finally, when they combine to form 'the complex form of a living human brain, the corresponding mind-stuff takes the form of a human consciousness, having intelligence and volition'.[75] Whether Hardy came across these ideas through the original essay, or when making notes on W. H. Mallock's review of Clifford's work in the *Edinburgh Review*,[76] it is clear from a letter to Roden Noel that he found the concept of mind-stuff 'very attractive'.[77]

Perhaps there is little wonder, since it not only explains how consciousness may have emerged from unconscious material, therefore saving man from the determinist nightmare, but it also provides support for

Hardy's belief that consciousness is slowly penetrating into the universe and may eventually permeate the universal process itself – the basis of his meliorism. Hardy made a note to this effect from an article in the *Spectator* by G. H. Lewes which reads, 'unless you assume the ultimate atom or molecule to have some inner qualities analogous to those which we call mental – qualities such as the late Prof. Clifford used to speak of as those of mind-stuff – there is no explaining how the mental universe is developed out of the physical'.[78] Since this process is in its embryonic stage, however, man is left in the predicament of possessing consciousness in a world governed by harsh determinism. Thus, unlike the rest of the natural world the individual is able to perceive the hopelessness of his situation because of 'Nature's indifference to the advance of her species along... civilised lines'.[79] This quandary is explored in a number of Hardy's works: In *The Dynasts* the Pities rails against the 'intolerable antilogy / Of making figments feel' in a world in which 'Necessitation sways',[80] whilst in 'The Mother Mourns' an anthropomorphised nature concedes that she had 'not proposed me a Creature' exhibiting such 'brightness of brain' who could therefore find 'blemish / Throughout [her] domain'.[81] In the poem 'Before Life and After' Hardy depicts a mythical time 'Before the birth of consciousness, / When all went well', prior to describing the pain and anguish suffered by man after 'the disease of feeling germed'. In the last stanza the poet asks when the First Cause shall become conscious,[82] a question answered by the Prime Mover in the poem 'New Year's Eve':

> My labours – logicless –
> You may explain; not I:
> Sense-sealed have I wrought, without a guess
> That I evolved a Consciousness
> To ask for reasons why.[83]

Yet Hardy added another ingredient to this concept of consciousness to make the pain endured by a Promethean figure such as Clym Yeobright that much more exquisite. In *The Life* Hardy states, 'If the world stood still at a felicitous moment there would be no sadness in it'[84], which in the terms of the present discussion would suggest that a static state of consciousness would enable man to come to terms with his environment.[84] But Hardy extrapolated from *The Origin of the Species* that man is continually evolving 'a degree of intelligence which Nature never contemplated when framing her laws, and for which she consequently has provided no adequate satisfactions'.[85]

This position echoes the evolutionary pessimism of Schopenhauer, made clear in Sully's statement that 'all progress as intellectual development necessarily increases the amount of suffering, so that the world is tending to become worse instead of better'.[86] As has already been noted Schopenhauer's a priori conclusions were also reached through Hartmann's inductive methodology, according to which pain is 'an inseparable ingredient of all conscious life' because consciousness emerges from collision between two wills. As a consequence, not only is human existence miserable, but it is becoming worse as mankind begins to understand the meanness of its situation.[87] It is the development of this unique conspiracy of determinism and evolution that brought to Hardy's novels a concept of tragedy which not only highlighted the perpetuation of human misery, but asserted with scientific justification that things could only decline further. In *The Life*, therefore, it is a semi-anthropomorphised Nature who stands condemned for her 'indifference to the advance of her species along what we are accustomed to call civilised lines'.[88] The only logical conclusion reached by both Schopenhauer and Hartmann is the 'common act of will annihilation', which is reached in *Jude the Obscure* with the birth of a generation whose sensibilities have evolved to such a degree that they embody the 'universal wish not to live'.[89]

The possession of consciousness, however, does have a positive aspect, since it gives the individual a degree of free will. To understand Hardy's position on this subject it is necessary to return to the idea of a form of 'protoplasm', 'Immanent Will' or 'mind-stuff' unevenly distributed throughout nature. According to Hardy's view, each man possess a tiny part of the Immanent Will, which means that if all the other forces surrounding him are in a state of equilibrium he is able to act with freedom. It is a theme to which Hardy alludes in a letter to Edward Wright concerning the philosophy of *The Dynasts*:

> When swayed by the Universal Will (which he mostly must be as a subservient part of it) he is not individually free; but whenever it happens that all the rest of the Great Will is in equilibrium the minute portion called one person's will is free, just as a performer's fingers will go on playing the pianoforte of themselves when he talks or thinks of something else and the head does not rule them.[90]

In effect, man is transformed into the digit of a universal melodist, an image reflected in *The Dynasts* by Years' observation that 'the Will heaves through Space, and moulds the times, / With mortals for Its fingers!'.[91] The sentiment is entirely Schopenhauerian, though, as Tim Armstrong has noted, 'perhaps the specific image of the playing hands comes from Hardy's reading of a piece by the popular science writer C. W. Saleeby a few years earlier'.[92] Hardy's note on the article focuses on Saleeby's argument that reflex action is 'entirely independent of consciousness', and that 'Will, is the expression of imperfection [in this mechanism]... Whilst will emerges from reflex action, to reflex action will can return... eg. Piano playing & c....'[93] Suffice it to say the freedom granted is very little, for acting freely still entails acting in accordance with the will. Paradoxically, as Hillis Miller has observed, 'the more powerfully a man wills or desires, the more surely he becomes the puppet of an all-shaping energy, and the quicker he encompasses his own destruction'.[94]

Such a conclusion begs the question why Hardy should allow it to exist at all, a point to which he turns in the poem 'He Wonders About Himself'. Here the poet, like the Napoleon of *The Dynasts*, describes himself as 'tugged' by an invisible force of 'the general Will', wondering 'What I shall find me doing next!'[95] In the last stanza the poet asks whether his free will might 'Bend a digit the poise of forces, / And a fair desire fulfil?'.[96] The answer is given in the 'Apology' at the beginning of *Late Lyrics and Earlier*, in which Hardy asserts that when the forces of the universe are in equilibrium man is able to exercise his 'modicum of free will' to decide for himself what a morally correct course of action is and therefore keep pain and suffering 'down to a minimum'.[97] This ability to adapt becomes one of the key themes running through Hardy's fiction. Tess, for example, remains pure in Hardy's eyes because her free will constantly struggles against her sexual instinct and the hereditary disposition of her barbarous ancestors. Conversely, as will be seen in due course, the tragedy of Michael Henchard stems from his attempts to impose his own small portion of the will upon the universe through a series of acts which are both impulsive and massive in scale. In essence, in a world which rewards flexibility and adaptability he and characters like Eustacia, Clym and Jude are too forceful. It is those passive characters such as Thomasin and Elizabeth-Jane who survive because they use their small amount of the will to minimise the excesses caused by the vicissitudes of the determined world.

The aim of this chapter has been to establish a number of metaphysical themes underpinning the cosmic vision Hardy explores in the major novels. Although these themes are glimpsed in Hardy's early work, it is only following his campaign of periodical research conducted in 1876–1877 that his vision becomes more coherent. Understanding the emergence of Hardy's metaphysics is a crucial first step to appreciating his use of musical allusion in the later novels, and it is the transformation of metaphysics into music that will form the focus of the next chapter.

3
The Spider's Web: Metaphysics into Music Drama

A good novel, argues Hardy in 'A Profitable Reading of Fiction' (1888), must be 'well and artistically constructed' with a 'beauty of shape' which gives the reader a pleasure similar to that gained from the pictorial or plastic arts.[1] In *The Life* Hardy airs his more immediate fears concerning the modern novel, that it is 'gradually losing artistic form, with a beginning, middle, and end, and becoming a spasmodic inventory of items, which has nothing to do with art'.[2] In 'The Science of Fiction' (1891) he makes clear those he feels are responsible for this decline: the 'social realists'. Their search for emotional realism in the accretion of infinitesimal detail has, he argues, missed the point of the art, which relies on the captured essence of isolated moments crafted into a satisfying whole.[3] 'Good form' is central to artistic success, and in 'A Profitable Reading of Fiction' he quotes J. A. Symonds to indicate those forms that fulfil this criteria: 'good fiction may be defined here as that kind of imaginative writing which lies nearest to the epic, dramatic, or narrative masterpieces of the past'.[4] Thus, in common with a number of contemporary Hellenes, Hardy is to be found rejecting Romantic introspection as a means of exploring the mid-century religious, moral and social malaise, in favour of the detachment offered by structured Greek forms. As Arnold observes, 'the literature of ancient Greece is, even for modern times, a mighty agent of intellectual deliverance'.[5]

Why this should be so is suggested by Pater's essay 'Winckelmann', which reveals how Greek tragedy explores life's 'conflicts' with serenity and dignity, and shows how joy may be arrested from 'discouragement'.[6] He goes on to argue in 'Demeter and Persephone' that 'because [myths] arose naturally out of the spirit of man, and embodied, in adequate symbols, his deepest thoughts concerning the conditions of his physical and spiritual life', in a time of spiritual unrest, like the present, they are 'not without a solemnising power even for the modern mind'.[7] In essence, Greek literature was important to the Victorian mind because it revealed similar struggles: a point put succinctly by another Hellene whose work *Social Life in Greece from Homer to Meander* (1874) appears frequently in Hardy's *Literary Notebooks*, P. Mahaffy. He observes that 'every thinking man who becomes acquainted with the masterpieces of Greek writing, must see plainly that they stand to us in a far closer relation than the other remains of antiquity'.[8]

This belief in the contemporary relevance and educative benefits of Greek humanism was also shared by J. A. Symonds, whose *Studies of the Greek Poets* (1876) also appears on numerous occasions in the *Literary Notebooks*.[9] He encourages his contemporaries to 'emulate [Greek] spirit by cheerily accepting the world as we find it, acknowledging the value of each human impulse and aiming after virtues that depend upon self-regulation rather than on total abstinence and mortification'.[10] These sentiments are echoed by Arnold's claims in *Culture and Anarchy* that during a period of religious and moral upheaval individuals should revel in the Hellenic '*spontaneity of consciousnesses*'.[11] Similar ideas are to be found copied into Hardy's *Literary Notebooks* from an essay printed in the *Saturday Review* under the unappealing title 'The Ethics of Suicide' (1876), which observes that the 'Hellenic character' was one of 'native joyousness and exultation in life': sentiments that find expression in Tess' 'appetite to enjoy' and Sue's belief that she and Jude had returned to an age of 'Greek joyousness' to which Christianity had blinded them.[12]

These Hellenic ideals spawned a number of mid-century imitations such as Arnold's Sophoclean verse drama *Merope* (1858), and Swinburne's *Atalanta in Calydon* (1865)[13] and *Erechtheus* (1875). Hardy's admiration for Swinburne is well recorded (the *Studies and Specimens Notebook* is full of jottings taken from *Atalanta*[14]) and when we also consider that in 1876 Hardy was jotting down ideas for a 'grand drama' or 'Iliad of Europe' it seems that he was considering his own modern verse drama based on the Napoleonic wars: a project that was eventually to take shape as *The Dynasts*.[15] The postponement of this design, however, probably has less to do with artistic considerations than the belief that it would have proved a financially uncertain project for a recently married man who was in the midst of establishing himself as a novelist. Instead, what emerges in 1877 is *The Return of the Native*, a novel that embodies a number of features from Greek tragedy, such as the five-act structure, the unity of time and place, and Classical motifs such as that Oedipus theme of Clym's partial blindness. However, it would be incorrect to denounce the novel as an uneasy compromise between Hardy's epic plans and financial expediency. For, as the 1912 preface to the Wessex Edition of the novels makes plain, such Classical features were not merely cosmetic additions, but fundamental to the form of the narrative in which ordinary people were elevated to the level of the heroic, and Wessex was transformed into Attica.[16]

If the novels were to be Classical tragedies, however, it is clear that they were to be tragedies appropriate for their time, in which the Fates were replaced by the unconscious forces motivating the behaviour of Hardy's characters. As the most recent research by Henri F. Ellenberger has shown, the second half of the nineteenth-century saw great interest in the philosophical concept of the unconscious, with most contemporary philosophers admitting the existence of an unconscious mental life. Interestingly, as the Romantic approach to the psyche, which remained purely speculative, gave way to more experimental and clinical approaches to the unconscious, one of the most pervasive metaphors employed to represent unconscious activity remained the stage. The German philosopher J. F. Herbart, for example, offered the highly influential speculative model of the unconscious as 'a kind of chorus that accompanies the drama being played on the conscious stage'.[17] This model survived the first experimental explorations, the psychophysics of G. T. Fechner presenting the waking and dreaming subject as similar mental activities 'displayed alternately on different theatre scenes or stages' (a remark that was to be the starting point of Freud's topographical concept of the mind).[18] As suggested in the last chapter, Schopenhauer's theory of the will offered a model of the unconscious mind which was both amenable to the new emphasis on physiological enquiry and also possessed a natural theatricality. For Schopenhauer the Romantic conception of the unconscious was transformed into the will, a blind dynamic driving force, which not only reigned over the universe, but also conducted man. Thus man is reduced to the level of a puppet, carrying out his activities in a semi-somnolent state dictated by internal forces which are unknown to him and of which he is scarcely aware.

It is quite clear from *The Life* and *Literary Notebooks* that Hardy maintained a lifelong interest in the concept of the unconscious; indeed, his notes on von Hartmann's *Philosophy of the Unconscious* are amongst the most detailed in the *Notebooks*. In one of the occasional examples of aesthetic musing that we find in *The Life* Hardy projects the idea of a sensation novel in which the 'sensationalism is not causality, but evolution', and not 'physical but psychical'.[19] What he has in mind is suggested by one of his more colourful metaphors in which he proposes a narrative structure in which 'the human race [is] to be shown as one great network or tissue which quivers in every part when one point is shaken, like a spider's web if touched'.[20] Hardy realised his ambition in *The Dynasts*, where his 'visible essences' are transformed from a spider's web into the twitching nerves and fibrils through which the great brain of the Immanent Will animates the activities of man.[21] This is Hardy's most dramatic piece, taking advantage of the natural theatricality that derives from Schopenhauer's conception of the unconscious will. In it the reader is placed at the same aesthetic distance as the Chorus of Spirits so that he is able to observe both the activities of the European armies and also the wider process underpinning them. It is this theatricality, I would argue, that Hardy is seeking to achieve in his mature novels. In them the reader is placed at a similar aesthetic distance from which he is able to observe the unfolding of two separate but connected plots: the domestic world in which Hardy's characters carry out their everyday activities, and the unconscious world dominated by the controlling influence of a semi-anthropomorphised universal process. Significantly, the Chorus of Spirits is replaced by *musical allusion*, which, to use an image from *The Wood-landers*, weaves together the 'great web of human doings' and connects them to the wider universal process.[22]

In the novels, then, Hardy is seeking to create a 'modern myth' in which the unconscious activity of the universal process guiding the behaviour of his characters is explored through musical allusion. What made this possible was Hardy's exposure to the musical aesthetics of both Schopenhauer and the composer Richard Wagner, who were both enjoying something of a vogue in 1876.

Schopenhauer's musical theory, rather like Darwin's principle of natural selection, is constructed on a simple axiom, which seems to have been so commonplace by 1876 that a journal as mainstream as *The Athenaeum* could refer to it without any preliminary explanation.[23] Hardy certainly knew of it, having read the account of the musicologist and experimental psychologist, Edmund Gurney, in his 'On Some Disputed Points in Music' (1876):

> Wagner adopts with slight modifications Schopenhauer's notions on the ideal basis of music...to wit music is 'as immediate and direct an objectification or copy of the will of the world as the world itself is, as the ideas are of which the universe of things is the phenomenon. Music is not the copy of the ideas like the other arts, but a representation of the cosmical will co-ordinate with the ideas themselves.'[24]

Of central importance is the analogy between natural phenomena and music which dictates that bass tones are equivalent to the lowest grade of objectification found in inorganic nature and those that are 'higher represent...the world of plants and beasts'. The higher the pitch, the more sophisticated the will's objectification, until we arrive at 'the high, singing, principal voice' in which is recognised 'the highest grade of the objectification of will, the intellectual life and effort of man'.[25]

Music not only traces the outward activity of the will, but is also reflected internally through its similarity to the 'morphology' of human consciousness. Schopenhauer's ideas are rooted in Friedrich Schelling's observation that the element of 'succession' in musical rhythm is analogous to the 'self-awareness' of the individual brought about by the recognition of the unity of various moments of consciousness.[26] Similarly, in the *Asthestik* Hegel argues that music reflects consciousness because just as man's awareness of himself at one time is part of a unified experience making up his personal identity, the individual notes making up a melody are both independent and part of a unified whole.[27] Schopenhauer asserts that in the same way that a tone only gains significance in relation to those that preceded it and those that are expected to follow it, so man is aware of his life not as a series of disconnected moments, but as a unified sequence extending backwards and forwards.[28]

This connection forms the basis of Schopenhauer's analogy between music and man's experience of the world. In his daily intercourse the will of man is either satisfied, which brings happiness; blocked, which brings suffering; or directed towards the empty longing for a new desire, which brings languor or boredom. A melody is analogous to this pattern of striving and satisfaction, since any melodic phrase is built upon a key-note from which the rest of the phrase deviates through intricate tonal patterns before eventual return. If the keynote can be considered parallel to the satisfaction of the will, then the digression and the attempts to return to it are analogous to the perpetually striving will. This conception is similar to Pater's idea made clear in 'The School of Giorgione' in which he states that 'life itself is conceived as a sort of listening – listening to music...at such times, the stresses of our servile, everyday attentiveness being relaxed, the happier powers in things without are permitted free passage, and have their way with us'.[29] Once again it is an analogy that has its roots in the Romantic tradition, particularly the condition of 'infinite yearning'. Such sentiments were popularised in this country through the short stories of E. T. A. Hoffmann,[30] Ludwig Tieck's novels *The Pictures* and *The Betrothing*,[31] Carlyle's *German Romance* II, and also the anthologies of R. P. Gillies and R. Holcraft.[32] In Schopenhauer's hands, however, Romantic appeals to music's mystical power were systemised into what he called a 'philosophy' of life which explained not only why life was miserable, but also how to escape its worst excesses.[33]

For Schopenhauer, then, the activity of listening to music performs a dual function: it enables the individual to submerge their will in the wider process and therefore find solace from the misery of life, and it also allows the listener to experience a 'picture' of the inner-life of man governed by the will 'but entirely without reality and far removed from their pain'. An understanding of both of these principles enriches our appreciation of Hardy's ambitions in the novels as a whole and also helps to explain certain puzzling musical scenes: I think particularly of the musical interludes in which Tess seeks to escape her misery in the church, that between Jude and Sue over Phillotson's piano, Jude's visit to the composer, and the effect of Farfrae's singing on Elizabeth-Jane in the Three Mariners. Before consideration of such specific scenes, however, I would like to consider more generally how Schopenhauerian musical metaphysics were employed by Hardy to reinvigorate his vision of Classical tragedy. Instrumental in this transformation is an understanding of the work of Richard Wagner, who, like Hardy, extolled the virtues of the Greek drama, hailing it in *Art and Revolution* (1849) as man's greatest artistic achievement because it combined the separate disciplines into a semi-religious artwork, which used the myth to explore the emotional life of man.

In making the connection between Hardy and Wagner I am building upon the observations of several recent critics who have identified a number of Wagnerian features in Hardy's work, but have been unable to account for them. Karen Elizabeth Davis, for example, argues in her unpublished doctoral thesis, 'Native to the Night: Form, the Tragic Sense of Life, and the Metaphysics of Music in Hardy's Novels', that Hardy's narratives reveal

> a dominant musical pattern which, though Hardy may not have deliberately intended it, forms a natural underlying structure to the narrative.... There is no saying for certain whether Hardy ever consciously adapted the structural features of a particular musical genre such as the concerto, the symphony, sonata form, the Gregorian chant, or the symphonic poem. Yet this study shows that in the novels chosen for discussion these genres implicitly appear.[34]

In practice, Davis reads the novels in terms of competing musical themes that conform to the shape of a specific musical genre, though quite how

Hardy could unconsciously follow the complex prescribed movements making up a concerto grosso or a Classical concerto which she considers novels such as *Under the Greenwood Tree* and *Far from the Madding Crowd* to follow, is never explained.[35] Significantly, she also identifies a number of Wagnerian characteristics, most notably the 'leitmotif,' which, she argues, is present in the 'mechanical laugh' of Troy and the 'pulsations' of Bathsheba Everdene as organising sounds in *Far from the Madding Crowd*.[36] Her most striking observation is the link between Schopenhauerian metaphysics and Wagnerian music drama in relation to the music of Egdon Heath, but she concludes with the rather vague assertion that 'Hardy's perception of music and the Will puts him in a special company of nineteenth and twentieth-century artists that includes Schopenhauer, Nietzsche, Wagner, Mahler, Mann and Schweitzer'.[37] This may well be true, but there is a blurring of historical context here which undermines the usefulness of her otherwise perceptive comments.

Likewise, Elna Sherman's attempts to capture the musicality of the opening of *The Dynasts* finds her juggling with vague comparative terms such as 'may be likened to' with specifically Wagnerian terms:

> the Fore Scene may be likened to a prelude of a vast music drama or the introduction to a gigantic tone-poem. Although Hardy disclaims a perfect organic unity for his great epic drama, the musical undercurrent that flows through it from beginning to end supplies a unity of a more subtle kind. Whether or not Hardy was himself conscious of this is a matter of little consequence, but that a musical background was plainly in his mind cannot be denied.[38]

Once again there is a vagueness surrounding these assertions which tends to confuse rather than convince. Sherman is reluctant to identify what she means by the term 'musical background' and how deeply within the foundations of the drama Hardy's musicality is set. Her subsequent analysis does little to illuminate further. As with Davis, her use of the specifically Wagnerian terms 'prelude' and 'music drama' raises the issue of possible influence, which is not considered beyond the identification of the above ill-defined similarities. How is the Fore Scene similar to a Wagner 'prelude'? – shape, intensity, function or simply because it opens the drama? Her use of the term 'music drama' suggests an organic unity, which she then withdraws with her vacillation over whether this is conscious or unconscious. Like Grundy she has, I would argue, grasped by intuition the musical thread which runs through *The Dynasts*, but she appears at a loss to identify both its form and function.

Francis Pietch provides us with the most comprehensive assessment of Hardy's Wagnerism in her unpublished doctoral thesis 'The Relationship Between Music and Literature in the Victorian Period: Studies in Browning, Hardy and Shaw'. She argues that Hardy uses music of natural tones in three ways which might be considered Wagnerian: to comment on what is left unspoken; to evoke the appropriate atmosphere at the beginning of the novels; and to round off the novels with quiet endings. The beginning of *Under the Greenwood Tree*, she argues, behaves like a Wagnerian 'prelude': the characters are heard before they are seen and a general tone is set. Whilst being in full agreement with the generalities of the first two statements (the third is perhaps the least convincing) they remain little more than the generalities here presented, mainly because the wide-ranging scope of the thesis means that she is unable to develop her ideas in sufficient depth. Furthermore, her work is hampered by a failure to establish both the chronology and precise nature of Wagnerian influence in this country.[39]

In general, then, the link between Hardy and Wagner in Hardy criticism has been perceptive, leading to very interesting readings of the novels, but tenuous and occasionally unconvincing. I would argue that the simplest way to develop a real appreciation of the link between the two artists is to understand mid-Victorian attitudes towards the composer's aesthetics. For, significantly for Hardy, Wagner's musical theories were enjoying a great deal of periodical interest in 1876 to coincide with the staging of the first Bayreuth Festival. Significantly, because Wagner's ideas were iconoclastic, they proved popular amongst those intelligent but not university-educated members of the aspirant middle-class, who still felt socially and educationally excluded by Italian opera and the other fine arts. Commissioning editors, as is their wont, simply responded to the market, calling for articles which presented Wagner's philosophical ideas in a clear, detailed, and sometimes provocative manner for intelligent non-expert readers. For most Victorians, such articles provided their only exposure to Wagner's ideas.[40] However, because of the limitations of space, the idiosyncrasies of a number of writers, and the vagaries of editorial whims, the Wagnerism which arrived on these shores differs from that in Wagner's own prose works. What follows, therefore, is an outline of those aspects of Wagnerian aesthetics that were finding their way into the mainstream periodicals of the period to be read and digested by authors such as Hardy.

In *The Artwork of the Future* (1849) Wagner presents an alternative to what he considered to be the bloated Italian opera: a modern myth combining the expressive powers of Shakespearean drama and the current orchestra with the object of expressing the inner-man. Man, he argues in *Opera and Drama* (1851), is split into an 'outer' and 'inner', the latter of which can only find expression through the primitive language by which his distant progenitors communicated their feelings.[41] In *The Music of the Future* (1861) he argues that this language has since evolved into music, by which he means Beethoven, whose melodic complexity is 'so absorbing in [its] plastic motion that the hearer cannot tear himself from their influence for a single instant'.[42] Because this melody is seamless, when employed in the music drama it 'pour[s] throughout the work...like a ceaseless river' uttering all that the poet is unable to say,[43] exerting upon the listener 'the effect produced by a noble forest, of a summer evening' when he perceives 'the infinite diversity of voices waking in the wood'.[44] Thus, such music, he continues, has 'much the same relation in the drama meant by me, as the Tragic Chorus of the Greeks to theirs'[45] (a relational analogy, since his orchestral chorus explores the motives underpinning behaviour rather than comments on the unfolding drama).

The artwork of the future, then, must grow organically, embracing the audience in the act of artistic creation: a process that begins with the 'prelude'. Here, the orchestra creates an atmosphere of foreboding 'which necessarily calls for a definite phenomenon to finally fulfil it', an expectation satisfied by the appearance of a man who, in order not to destroy the feeling created by the orchestra, reveals himself in the language of music. Tone, however, must give way to the more specific form of speech, so 'as to *determine* the emotions roused in us' and give 'our vaguely raised emotions' a definite character with which to sympathise.[46] From this point, which by nature of the combination of word and tone-speech raises the drama above everyday life, the music drama can develop organically as a series of 'moments' linked together by the plastic qualities of music. The orchestra, by means of the 'continuous melody', leads the listener through the 'labyrinthine building of the drama', maintaining the emotional atmosphere when characters are forced to use speech to clarify the situation unfolding on stage.[47] Its power of 'remembrance' (Leitmotif) and 'foreboding' lend to the dramatic action a 'Unity of artistic Form', all exterior considerations are annihilated and the listener becomes absorbed in the organic creation of the drama.[48]

Wagner is first heard of in England in the early 1850s, when, unfortunately for him, the two leading critics of the time – Henry Fothergill Chorley, who reviewed for *The Edinburgh* and *The Athenaeum* between 1830 and 1866,[49] and James Davison (1813–1885), editor of *The Musical World; a Weekly Record of Musical Science, Literature, and Intelligence*

(1843–1865) and the music critic of *The Times* from 1846 to 1879 – were unified in their condemnation of his works. Davison's limitations of personal taste are even more frightening when the power of *The Times* is considered, which was, until the abolition of the newspaper stamp in 1855 and the repeal of the paper duty in 1861 (which opened the field for cheap newspapers) 'read by everybody who was anybody, [and] was indeed a power in art as in politics'.[50] His son described his father's opposition to the 'new music' in terms of a crusade against metaphysical pomposity,[51] which when linked to an acerbic wit could be damming. He extended sympathy to 'the general ear of "the future"' and called for 'some extra hospitals for the deaf wherever Herr Wagner and his compositions are allowed to penetrate',[52] later dismissing him as an unmusical system-maker who knew better how to 'theorise fancifully than to reduce his theories to practice': a view which remained more or less uncontested up to the early seventies.[53]

By 1876–1877, however, Wagner's ideas were enjoying something of a vogue in this country, largely due to the first staging of the *Ring* at Bayreuth and the Albert Hall Concerts in which the London public first heard Wagner's music. Such was the interest that *The Athenaeum* had difficulty responding to the 'many inquiries... made, verbally and by letters, about the purpose of the operatic representations which are to take place next month at Bayreuth', and *The Graphic* could report the existence of a very real 'Wagner mania'.[54] Instrumental in this change was the work of apologists such as, perhaps surprisingly, George Eliot, M. S. Mosely and the German émigré, Francis Hueffer, whose 'Richard Wagner' (1872) was, according to his own modest assessment, the birth of Wagnerism in this country.[55] Eliot, no doubt stirred by the rough handling of the London press in 1855, was moved to add some reflections concerning the composer onto her recollections of a recent trip to Germany to an article that she was producing for the liberal *Fraser's* (then under the editorship of John William Parker, which lasted from 1847 to 1860). Whilst not wholeheartedly supportive of Wagner's music she notes that he has 'pointed out the direction in which the lyric drama must develop itself, if it is to be developed at all'.[56] Mosely's 'Lyric Feuds' appeared in the *Westminster* in 1867, and reflects the desire of the then editor George Chapman (editor from 1851 to 1894) to publish the type of articles that the *Edinburgh* and *Quarterly Reviews* would reject on account of their advanced thinking.[57] Accordingly, Mosely presented Wagner as an avant-garde artist whose struggle for acceptance can be contextualised within such musical quarrels as those between Handel and Bononcini, Gluck and Piccinni; Mosely argues that all geniuses are condemned at first. In general, his essay calls for an unprejudiced discussion of Wagner's aesthetic principles (principles which, ironically, he regards as '*incontestable*'[58]).

Hueffer's essay is dense, and theoretically demanding, and exhorted precisely the kind of avant-gardism and iconoclasm that the editor of the *Fortnightly*, John Morley, was actively encouraging.[59] He appears to have relished his role of public apologist, setting out a vision of Wagner as an innovator on the scale of Carlyle's 'hero', who finding the established laws and forms of artistic expression inadequate supersedes them.[60] Central to his plan for elevating Wagner's reputation is his explanation of the way the composer unravelled the Gordian Knot of how poetry and music should synthesise, simplified, according to Hueffer's questionable rendition of Wagner's creative history, by his exposure to the metaphysics of Schopenhauer, which formalised new expressive parameters for the art of music. Significantly, his advocacy of Schopenhauer during the same period meant that the philosopher's role in Wagner's aesthetics was overemphasised (much, as a letter from Madame Wagner made clear, to the composer's evident delight[61]), a questionable privileging of the philosopher which remained a feature common to English reactions to Wagner. Quoting the same extract as Gurney, Hueffer argues that Wagner recognised that the capacity of music to represent broad groups of emotions made it the ideal means of exploring the inner-life unfolding upon the stage, whilst poetry added specific detail.[62]

Once again the conclusions are questionable, since, as the music critic of *The Daily Telegraph*, Joseph Bennett, was at pains to point out, the addition of language compromises the pureness of the musical art advocated by Schopenhauer.[63] Hueffer, however, remained highly selective in his use of the philosopher: in an expanded monograph version of this essay, *Richard Wagner and the Music of the Future* (1874), he adds a revealing analysis of *Tristan und Isolde* in which he states 'we hear for the first time the unimpaired language of dramatic passion, intensified by an uninterrupted flow of expressive melody, the stream of which is no longer obstructed' by artificial operatic forms.[64] The function of the orchestra, he explains, is similar to that of the 'chorus of an antique tragedy', lyricising the dialogue on stage without weakening the passionate intensity.[65] It is a point to which he returns in 'Richard Wagner and his *Ring of the Niblung*' [*sic*] (1875), in which he describes how a few orchestral chords could suggest the emotions underpinning the action unfolding on the stage 'which it would take pages of writing to explain in words'.[66] Thus, by combining poetry and music into one harmonious organism, Hueffer argues, Wagner has created a work of art that is superior to what either could be in their separate spheres.[67]

Another significant figure in the dissemination of Wagner's ideas in this country is the musicologist Edward Dannreuther, who founded the London 'Wagner Society' in 1873 and also translated Wagner's essay *The Music of the Future* into a one-shilling pamphlet.[68] This work provides the clearest adumbration of Wagner's ideas, which suggests that it was through its pages that many Victorians first encountered Wagner's ideas directly. It certainly acted as a source for many of the journal articles that followed its publication, a characteristic shared by Dannreuther's own meditations upon Wagnerian theory, published in the *Monthly Musical Record* of 22 May 1872 and reprinted in the 1873 collection *Richard Wagner: His Tendencies and Theories*.[69] He also published two important articles in the comparatively cheap shilling monthly, *Macmillan's*, which indicates that by the second half of the century the desire for challenging and informative pieces on Wagnerism was as well established amongst the middle classes as the upper.[70] Curiosity, however, does not signal agreement, a sentiment shared by George Grove (who edited the journal from 1868–1883, and who was responsible for the *Dictionary of Music and Musicians* [1878–1884]), who was also publishing rather more negative essays on Wagner, such as Joseph Bennett's 'The Condition of Opera in England' (1869).[71]

Like Hueffer, Dannreuther presents Wagner as an innovator, whose early adherence to Feuerbach suggested that art should demonstrate man's 'own nature in all its dignity'.[72] Goethe and Schiller had attempted the same (the latter even introducing a Greek Chorus into his tragedies), but had foundered upon the limitations of their art. Wagner overcame their problems because he understood that an entirely new form was required.[73] According to Dannreuther's reading of Wagner's aesthetics, metaphysics quickly gives way to Classicism, and the 'Will' is transformed into 'the spirit of music'. This insistence on the Classical nature of Wagner's project can best be explained by Dannreuther's knowledge of contemporary German archival research into the foundations of Aeschylan tragedy combined with a coincidental growth of an English Hellenism. Classical tragedy, he argues, was built upon '*poetry conceived and executed in the orgiastic spirit of musical sound*';[74] a hypothesis that, Dannreuther argues in his 'Musical Drama' (1875), is echoed in Wagner's contention that if the artwork of the future is to succeed in its Feuerbachian quest for spiritual humanism then it must combine the arts into a revitalisation of the Greek tragedy 'under the guidance of the spirit of music'.[75]

Thus, for Dannreuther, Wagner was led by the 'spirit of music' *unconsciously* to a drama of Classical proportions, in which legendary figures play out those massive emotions expressed by the orchestra.[76] Indeed, in many ways Wagner's music dramas are simply 'the realization of [the] strange suggestiveness inherent in instrumental music' itself.[77] In practice this music stands in relation to the drama like a Greek Chorus: it transports the audience to the 'ideal sphere' through the 'prelude', before becoming a 'tissue that covers the whole drama', drawing together the disparate scenes and events into an emotionally organic whole, exerting upon the listener an effect similar to that experienced by the solitary visitor who hears 'the multitudinous forest voices'.[78]

Not all were convinced by Wagner's Classical project: H. H. Statham's 'Wagner, and the Modern Theory of Music', which appeared in the Whig *Edinburgh* in 1876, continued to reflect the reactionary character of its editor – Henry Reeve – whose desire for 'old standards of thought and style' led to the journal's attacks upon the obscurity of Browning and the exuberance of Swinburne.[79] Unlike his predecessor, Chorley, Statham sought to temper prejudice masquerading as informed judgement with reasoned argument: nevertheless, his conclusions were similar. Thus, whilst he acknowledged the power of the orchestra to create 'tone picture[s] of the actions and passions of the drama' so that it 'occupies the same position as the chorus in the Greek drama', he then, in language that compromises his desire for even-handedness, reflects upon the 'extraordinary cacophony presented to us as music in some recent instrumental compositions, and in many parts of Wagner's operas'.[80] He concludes by stating that the beauty of music will always be compromised by attempts to make it express real emotions, and a man 'with a tin helmet and shield' standing behind the footlights is merely going to 'bring down music from its real "poetic basis" to the prosaic level demanded by listeners who are destitute of feeling and imagination'.[81]

Wagner's apparent disregard for musical beauty prompts Gurney to ask in his 'On Some Disputed Points in Music', published in the *Fortnightly Review* of July 1876, whether either the composer or his English apologist Hueffer were 'totally unconscious of any lofty beauty or meaning in music except as expressing some emotion or idea definable in other ways'.[82] Gurney's rejection of Wagner is hardly surprising considering his emphasis on the importance of melody in music. It is this intra-musical component, he argues, that moves the listener, not some extra-musical quality conjured up by calling music 'a language *for the emotions*'.[83] The continuous melos he rejects as a tautology, since melody cannot be sustained without either repetition, changing into something else or falling to pieces.[84] For similar reasons, in his essay 'On Wagner and Wagnerism' published in the *Nineteenth Century* in 1883, Gurney rejects the leitmotif which, he claims, works by mechanical convention and is read 'by the lamp, not of beauty, but of reason'.[85]

The reflections of the musicologist James Sully in the *Contemporary Review* of June, 1875 are of a somewhat different nature, since his criticism of the music drama acts as a foundation for his own speculations regarding the evolution of 'The Opera'. To focus on just one example of this process at work – having accepted Wagner's idea that 'the modern orchestra has the significance of the Greek chorus', Sully argues that it is therefore wasted as a 'mere support to vocal melody'.[86] Instead, in his version of the modern opera he envisages periods where there is a lull in the dramatic action, when 'the mind of the actor is cast in on itself in solitary thought' and when the 'orchestra may seek, by means of its rich and varied colouring and its subtle imitations of vocal tone, to give a beautiful, if a vague, expression to the inaudible movements of the soul'.[87]

Joseph Bennett reviewing *Das Rheingold* in *The Daily Telegraph* questioned whether music should 'be degraded to the condition of a mere reflector', since it turns music into the equivalent of 'bald, disjointed chat' which eventually becomes 'wearisome'.[88] Furthermore, he questioned the very validity of Wagner's attempts to re-establish the Greek drama as the basis for a modern art form, simply stating that it is 'as dead as the dodo in so far as regards its power over the popular mind'.[89]

For the Reverend H. R. Haweis, however, Wagner's synthesis of the arts offered more than simply a revitalisation of the Greek drama; it reinvented it for the modern audience. Vital to this was the modern orchestra, for though the traditional Classical chorus may 'have been adequate to the simple types of Greek tragedy', the modern psyche, with its 'questions, its doubts, its hopes', required a more 'complex organ of expression'.[90] The orchestra provided just such a tool since it 'fitted so closely about the soul of man, as to become the very Aeolian harp upon which the breath of his life could freely play'. This emotionally comprehensive quality of music allows the music drama to present to the listener, 'a true picture of human feeling with the utmost fullness and intensity . . . leaving nothing to the imagination', thus elevating the art form above all others.[91] Indeed, such was the emotional comprehensiveness of the orchestra in its expression of the feelings of the characters on the stage that Wagner was described by the musicologist C. Halford Hawkins in *Macmillan's* as 'the George Eliot of Music'.[92]

One thing is clear from this brief survey of articles on Wagner – although his aesthetics remained far from universally accepted, by 1877 he had gained such notoriety that music critic Percy Scholes could declare 'that in views of the British musical public, Wagner had at last "arrived"'.[93] Both symbolic of and instrumental in this change is the attitude of Davison, who, with a circulation of around 62,000 was vital in shaping public opinion.[94] Significantly, his editor, John Thaddeus Delane, had by 1876 perceived a growing divergence between public interest and the views of his music editor and accordingly instructed Davison to 'write pleasant letters upon Wagner and Wagnerism'.[95] Accordingly his reviews of *The Ring* are full of conciliatory statements, accepting the concept of a synthesis of the arts and also the 'continuous melody'. Indeed, so effusive was Davison's new found avant-gardism following the Albert Hall Concerts (particularly the review of the prelude to *Das Rheingold*[96]) that the reader begins to feel that he is attempting to excuse his earlier condemnation by suggesting that Wagner had evolved into something unrecognisable from the early works.[97] He had changed little, of course, whereas the British public, particularly the grass roots, was experiencing what Haweis identified as a very real 'Wagner *furor*'.[98]

That Hardy was aware of this 'furor' and the underlying Wagnerian project is clear from a note taken from his edition of the *Daily News* for May 1877 claiming that 'Wagner has told us that the Art-work of the Future is to be a combination of music, the drama, poetry, and painting'.[99] Furthermore, it is clear from a comment made in *The Life* that he enjoyed the later more avant-garde Wagner whom he bracketed with the artist J. M. W. Turner, because they exposed the 'deeper reality underlying the scenic'.[100] Such a comparison is of significance when considering one of Hardy's few remarks on Wagner's music:

> It was *weather* and *ghost* music – whistling of wind and storm, the strumming of a gale on iron railings, the creaking of doors; low screams of entreaty and agony through key-holes, amid which trumpet-voices are heard. Such music, like any other, may be made to express emotion of various kinds; but it cannot express the subject or reason of that emotion.[101]

Clearly Hardy considered Wagner's music as an actualisation of Schopenhauer's metaphysics, the varying tones reflecting the objectification of the will. Hardy's comment is also of interest in the light of Douglas Kahn's recent research into historical attempts to distinguish between noise and music. He draws attention to the highly influential work of the German physiologist Hermann Helmholtz, particularly his seminal *On Sensation of Tone* (1877), in which he draws a distinction between musical sensation (characterised by fixed scales) and noise (which exhibits the quality of sliding tones – 'glissandi').[102] Kahn goes on to argue that recent Modernist composers, however, have questioned such stringent definitions, arguing that noise is in fact deeply imbedded in musical materiality. The American musicologist, Henry Cowell, is the most interesting, arguing that

> Natural sounds, such as the wind playing through the trees or grasses, or whistling in the chimney, or the sound of the sea, or thunder, all make use of sliding tones. It is not impossible that such tones may be made the foundation of an art of composition by some composer who would reverse the programmatic concept. . . . Instead of trying to imitate the sounds of nature by using musical scales, which are based on steady pitches hardly to be found in nature, such a composer would build perhaps abstract music out of sounds of the same category as natural sound – that is, sliding pitches – not with the idea of trying to imitate nature, but as a new tonal foundation.[103]

It is quite clear that for Hardy, that later 'avant-garde' Wagner offered an example of just such 'abstract music'. Furthermore, though it has all the appearances of an off-the-cuff comment, there is a precision in each of his examples that guides us to incidents in the novels when musically delineated natural phenomena reveal the power of the underlying universal process. 'Weather' and 'storm' music, for instance, bring *The Return of the Native* to a close by indicating the folly of Eustacia's attempts to escape her destiny in the shape of the heath. Ghostly 'Aeolian modulations' accompany Henchard's meeting with the 'ghost' of his wife in the Roman amphitheatre, suggesting that in a world governed by the mechanism of necessity it is impossible for the individual to escape the consequences of his actions.[104] 'The iron railings before the houses' on top of Knollsea Harbour hum in 'a song of derision' at the attempts of Sol Chickeral and Mountclere to defy necessity in *The Hand of Ethelberta*.[105] Finally, just prior to the murder of Alec the 'low screams of entreaty and agony' of Tess make up the 'dirge' heard by Mrs Brookes through the keyhole of her boarding house room.[106]

If Schopenhauer indicated to Hardy the way in which his conception of the wider process could be translated into musical analogy, Wagner, as Joan Grundy has argued, demonstrated how such music could be transformed into music drama. Hardy's Wagnerism is not simply cosmetic, to be reduced to the identification of the occasional use of certain techniques, it is an essential part of the narrative structure of the major novels. In them Hardy is seeking to explore the psyche of a single individual – 'the native', 'the man of character', 'the pure woman' and 'the obscure' – by raising their story to the level of modern myth. This process of mythologising ostensibly ordinary characters begins with a form of 'prelude' through which Hardy raises the events about to unfold above the limitations of a particular time and place. From this point Hardy develops his 'psychical' drama, exploring the behaviour of his central protagonists through a Wagnerian chorus of Aeolian music which reminds the reader of the wider process controlling their behaviour. Furthermore, Hardy's revitalised Greek Chorus also reminds the reader of the Schopenhauerian message that is central to his meliorism: it is better to endure with flexibility and make the best of limited opportunities for happiness. It is this music that can be heard in the Aeolian modulations of Egdon, in the orchestral purling of the Casterbridge Schwarzwasser and also in the 'complex rhythms' of the sea surrounding the peninsula of Portland in *The Well-Beloved*.[107]

In effect, the mechanical 'First Cause' is transformed into a composer, the pianist of *The Dynasts*, whose dissonant tones animate Hardy's universe. For Schopenhauer, since music offers an alternative to the world of willing, the power of the composer is analogous to that of the First Cause:

> the composer reveals the inner nature of the world, and expresses the deepest wisdom in a language which his reason does not understand; as a person under the influence of mesmerism tells things of which he has no conception when he awakes.[108]

This analogy accords with Hardy's own, the youthful Sue Bridehead noting when her 'intellect scintillated like a star' that 'the world resembled a stanza or melody composed in a dream' produced by a 'First Cause [that] worked automatically like a somnambulist, and not reflectively like a sage'.[109]

Hardy's characters are little more than puppets of this 'automatic somnambulist', their free will only emerging to the degree to which they submerge their part of the will in the wider process. We are reminded of Hardy's discussion of free will concerning *The Dynasts*, in which the free individual is described as analogous to 'a performer's fingers [which] will go on playing the pianoforte of themselves when he talks or thinks of something else and the head does not rule them'.[110] Tim Armstrong has noted that the image of fingers playing by habit may appear a paradoxical image of freedom, 'but Hardy's formula reproduces the late nineteenth-century fascination with the borderlines of conscious activity as representing a freedom in which the material produced is liberated from intention – intention which, for Hardy as for Schopenhauer, is always bound to the Will'.[111] Armstrong argues that the popularity of such a concept is apparent from Pater's description of the importance of play in 'The School of Giorgione', those times in which 'the stress of our servile, everyday attentiveness being relaxed, the happier powers in things without are permitted free passage, and have their way with us'.[112] Thus, it is in moments of inattentiveness or reverie, when we submerge our portion of the individual will in the wider process, that we are most free. Schopenhauer depicts this distractedness in terms of mesmerism, somnambulism and the waking dream – an analogy which is crucial to our understanding of Hardy's portrayal of the activity of his characters in the novels.

The art of mesmerism, as the recent research of both Ellenberger and Alison Winter has demonstrated, held a remarkably strong hold on the Victorian mind, offering most people their clearest understanding of the workings of the unconscious mind.[113] People who attended the numerous mesmeric demonstrations observed individuals reduced to a puppet-like state, their activities carried out in a sleep-like trance.[114] Significantly, to the Victorians, as for Schopenhauer, the power of the mesmerist and that of music were analogous: both gave access to the unconscious mind, the ancient analogy of the mind as a musical instrument being retooled by mesmeric practitioners who claimed to be able to play upon the unconscious like a keyboard.[115] Indeed, many mesmerists strengthened this appeal by copying the dress and gestures of baton conductors.

One of the most influential models was Wagner himself, who was even caricatured as a mesmerist producing a hypnotic spell over Berlioz in the *Revue Trimestrielle* (1864).[116] According to Hueffer, Wagner had the same power over his orchestra, each individual player being 'equally under the influence of a personal fascination, which seems to have much in common with the effects of animal magnetism', and his audience, who were soon lulled into a trance-like state through the hypnotic power of the continuous melody.[117] There is little doubt, as Jonathan Crary has argued, that in his reinvigoration of the Greek tragedy, Wagner sought to produce a ritualistic communal spectacle that was so absorbing that it raised the individual to a transcendent level. His special effects, including the use of steam, burial of the orchestra, dimming of lights, use of coloured lights and use of lantern projections for the first performance of *Das*

Rheingold in 1876, were all designed to absorb the observer in a way similar to the popular competing attractions of the diorama, panorama and Zoëtrope. Such was their effect that according to Nietzsche, Wagner furnished 'the first example, only too insidious, only too successful, of hypnotism by means of music... persuasion by the nerves'. It was, he continued, a specifically modern 'counterfeiting of transcendence'.[118]

I would argue that in the mature novels and the multimedia work *The Dynasts,* and *The Famous Tragedy of the Queen of Cornwall,* Hardy employs his Wagnerian music to achieve a similar degree of hypnotic transcendence. The latter's parallels with Caliban's magic island are made apparent in Merlin's epilogue in which he concludes the 'shadowy and phantasmal show' which had 're-shaped and drawn' events and characters is 'now dead as dreams.'[119] In *The Dynasts,* even those who appear to control their destiny are simply 'people in a dream' ensnared by the web of the will weaved by a drowsy knitter.[120] Even Napoleon is simply a man touched by fate, his happiness secured by the success that he has been allotted; as he gives his final orders to Berthier at Waterloo he questions 'Am I awake, / Or is this all a dream?'. Hardy's conclusion is obvious, his power of self-determination is illusory, he remains nothing more than a figure on a lantern slide that follows the steps determined for him by a somnolent fate through the ghostly Aeolian music that pervades the drama.[121] Hardy's clearest depiction of the connection between his puppets and the music of the wider process comes in his description of the English army perishing off Welcheren: a scene animated by an 'Immanent Will' anthropomorphised into a mighty organist whose 'unweeting wind' blows over the contours of the ships' rigging, the heath-grass and through the organ-stops of the soldiers to produce a 'mewling music'.[122]

The same 'unweeting wind' blows through all Hardy's novels, producing a hypnotic quality in the behaviour of Hardy's characters, which reminds us of the wider process underpinning many of their activities. It finds its clearest expression in the Aeolian music that pervades the woods around little Hintock and the wind that blows over Egdon; the latter providing the clearest example of a Classically inspired work conceived under the influence of Wagnerian music. Indeed, Hardy claimed that it was a distillation of his vision of 'the art of the future'.[123] Such is its importance that the work will be discussed in detail in Chapter 5. For now, however, I would like to turn to an analysis of Hardy's employment of the specifically Wagnerian technique of the 'prelude' as a means of raising his reader to the appropriate level of transcendence for the work to follow. This is best exemplified by the opening portrait of Eustacia, which reflects many of the Schopenhauerian and Wagnerian ideas that we have been discussing.

As noted in the last chapter, in Spencerian terms, Eustacia's emergence from Rainbarrow offers an evolutionary metaphor, the ascent through increasing organisational complexity climaxing in the moment of 'individuation' when she demonstrates herself to be a distinct from her environment. Hardy is similarly concerned with process, but his careful orchestration of the heath music – which does not emerge haphazardly from the heath, rather the tones of the heathbells ascend in accordance with the physical features under examination, beginning with the 'gravest pitch of the chime' and ending in the 'linguistic peculiarity of the heath' which is 'above them in pitch' – emphasises that Eustacia's 'individuation' is a matter of degree rather than type. It is a unified music, the sound of a 'single person or something else speaking through each at once', and Eustacia's 'lengthened sighing', which he describes as the 'spasmodic abandonment', as if 'the woman's brain had authorised what it could not regulate', is simply 'another phrase of the same discourse as theirs'.[124] As the music makes clear, in Schopenhauerian terms the individuation of Eustacia is a product of her 'sensation', rather than an overarching conception of herself as a conscious individual. It reminds the reader that the movements of her innermost being are shared with the wider environment.

A number of Hardy scholars have also noted the Wagnerian undertones of this passage, particularly the similarity to the prelude to *Das Rheingold*, in which the Rhine maidens emerge from the river to add their high-pitched melody to the slow rhythmical movement of the water, but none have been unable to account for it.[125] Significantly, this particular prelude was frequently used as an illustration of Wagner's aesthetics, Davison claiming of the music that it 'suggests the idea of an Aeolian harp, under the influence of shifting currents, now generating one, now another, wayward melody'.[126] Hueffer noted:

> It has been compared to the 'Prologue in Heaven' of Goethe's *Faust*, foreshadowing in the minds of the divine beings the human actions of the ensuing piece. But, unlike the 'Lord' in Goethe's drama, Wagner's gods are not impassive lookers-on, but themselves the actors and sufferers in the great drama which ends with their doom. The subject of the trilogy is the struggle of free love and human impulse against the fetters of conventional laws. ... The opening scene shows the bottom of the great stream with the three Rhine Daughters floating amongst the rocks in merry gambols. Wagner's music here is graceful and

light, like the murmuring waves; from an orchestral undercurrent the song of the water-maidens rises in melodious strains.[127]

The parallels with the opening of Hardy's novel are striking: for not only does Hueffer's description reflect the ascent of Eustacia as she emerges from the inky blackness to give a necessary finish to Rainbarrow, but, like Wagner's gods, Egdon is both the controlling influence of events and also subject to the same laws of necessity.

These similarities become even more marked when the structure of Hardy's opening sequence is considered in detail. There is, for instance, a sense of universality encoded in the ambiguous identification of both the time and location of the story: it is to be Egdon's tale, a story related at the twilight of each day concerning one year's crop of the heath. Indeed, twilight and darkness pervade the opening scene, creating the sense of anticipation and foreboding appropriate for a tale of 'tragical possibilities'. This tension is relieved in the second chapter, 'Man Appears upon the Scene', and yet the arrival of Venn and Captain Vye replaces the heroic with the almost comic. The real prelude arrives in the form of the 'Figure Against the Sky' in which, as we follow the eye of the observing consciousness of Diggory Venn, we travel from the deep bass of the recesses of the heath to the tenor notes of the heathbells; and Eustacia's sighs, in accordance with Wagnerian doctrine, do not destroy the musical theme but rather supplement it. Indeed, the only difficulty with asserting that Hardy begins the novel with a Wagnerian prelude is the fact that it is not heard until half way through the first book. Simon Gatrell's analysis of the manuscript, however, is helpful here, because a false start on the verso of folio 18 suggests that our first glimpse of Eustacia on top of Rainbarrow at the end of Chapter 2 was in fact to have been more detailed and included the descriptions of the music of the heath. Hardy seems to have been deterred from his original plan due to pressures from Blackwood, the publisher.[128] Thus, the Wagnerian prelude appears to have been sacrificed, as is often the case with Hardy's bowdlerising, to financial expediency.

There is in Hardy's careful orchestration of this scene a hypnotic quality that embraces the reader in the process of individuation. To follow Hughes in invoking Deleuze, there is a sense of 'becoming' that haunts this scene, as the packet of variable sensation that is Eustacia is momentarily actualised according to a process of individuation which takes effect through the power of the music, a process which embraces author, narrator and reader.[129] The scene is infused with uncertainty: the narrative voice appears to drift between that of the observing consciousness of

Diggory Venn and a third-person narrator, whose tentative viewpoint is summed up in the observation that she 'might reasonably have been supposed'. Eustacia herself remains anonymous, her position replaced halfway through the scene by 'an emotional listener', and as the viewpoint telescopes from cinematic long shot to the precise description of her as descending like 'the glide of a water-drop' we, the reader, are actively embraced in the scene. In essence, it provides one of Hardy's 'moments of vision', a Paterian instance when writer, narrator and characters collapse into the ' "perpetual flux" of minds and things' under the influence of music.[130]

Despite the lateness of its publication, Hardy first began working on *The Woodlanders* during the same period of creativity that saw the publication of *The Return of the Native*, and as a consequence its Aeolian music is so pervasive that it offers a literary counterpart to Wagner's 'multitudinous forest voices'.[131] Once again, Hardy makes his intention to create a Classical drama explicit, this time in the authorial intrusion that transforms Little Hintock from a geographical location to 'one of those sequestered spots outside the gates of the world . . . where, from time to time, dramas of a grandeur and unity truly Sophoclean are enacted in the real'.[132] Its opening appears to share many of the features of the Wagnerian prelude: when the curtain rises it reveals a 'deserted highway' on a 'louring evening', a sense of foreboding which is increased by the 'tomb-like stillness' and the transformation of the reader into a 'loiterer' with no right to be there. Like the road bisecting Egdon, this highway is a symbol of human consciousness, its vulnerability suggested by the fact that it is nearly buried in dead leaves.[133]

Animating the entire scene is a sombre 'music in the breeze' which is 'produced by the instrumentation of the various species of tree'.[134] It is, as Hardy reveals during the pine-planting scene with Marty South, the 'soft musical breathing' that announces the pain of all living things in an uncaring universe.[135] As barber Peacomb, who is both lost and an outsider, becomes our observing consciousness, Hardy introduces the 'moveable attachment of the roadway' which is Mrs Dollery's van. The awkward description signals Hardy's reduction of the road into a spatial representation of time, a feature common to both *Tess of the D'Urbervilles* and *The Mayor of Casterbridge*, movement along which is central to his attempts to persuade the reader of his determinist views of life.[136] Through the back window of the van can be seen 'a square piece of the same sky and landscape that he saw without' against which Hardy sets 'the profiles of the seated passengers . . . their lips moving and heads nodding in animated private converse'.[137] It is an image of silent discourse that aptly

symbolises the powerlessness of man to alter his destiny, and anticipates the reduction of Napoleon to 'a figure on a lantern-slide'.[138]

Like the heath-cutters of Egdon, the characters appear to emerge from
the homogenous darkness of the woods around Little Hintock, contribute
their actions to the unfolding drama, and then sink back into its obscure
depths. Their powerlessness in determining their futures is emphasised
by the somnambulistic state which presides over so many of their actions.
The auctioneer of trees and faggots, for example, carries out his job in an
'abstracted mood', bringing down his walking stick on bystanders, his voice
being simply another 'one of the natural sounds of the woodland'.[139]
Marty cuts off her hair 'with a preoccupied countenance', Giles presides
over his party 'in a half unconscious state' and nearly all of Melbury's
speeches are given in a state of reverie.[140] It is a representation of human
activity which accords entirely with Schopenhauer's description of mankind acting in accordance with the will, the chorus of trees merely
reminding us of the futility of human action.

It can be heard in the 'melancholy Gregorian melodies which the air
wrung out of' the elm outside the bedroom window of the dying John
South.[141] He has a neurotic reverence for it, 'as the tree waved South
waved his head, making it his fugleman with abject obedience'; whereas
Marty, who can also hear its music, has a pessimistic belief that all will
turn out for the worst: she is rarely proved wrong.[142] Significantly,
although there is 'a sort of sympathy between [Giles] and the fir, oak, or
beech', he is deaf to their music.[143] When Marty makes her observation
concerning the sighing trees, Giles notes simply 'I've never noticed
it.'[144] He is both strong and honourable, but possesses a lack of flexibility
that prevents him from making the best of things. His music is that of
the old-fashioned bells 'chiming harmoniously' which adorn the heavy-
horse team that takes Melbury's oak to market.[145] It is an apt image,
Giles plodding in the fog, absorbed in his own misery, refusing to give
way to Mrs Charmond's coach coming in the opposite direction, and
through his obstinacy forfeiting his house and therefore Grace.

It is this combination of timidity and obstinacy that also prevents
Giles from beating Fitzpiers to the hand of Grace, a struggle that Hardy
relates through music. This conflict reaches its apogee in the woods during
the Midsummer Night rite, during which all the village girls attempt to
glimpse their future lovers. Hardy begins this scene by describing how
in Melbury's garden 'the two trees that had creaked all the winter left
off creaking, the whirr of the night-hawk, however, forming a very
satisfactory continuation of uncanny music from that quarter'.[146] In effect,
the creaking relationship of Giles and Grace will be replaced by the

music of the nighthawk, which, like Fitzpiers, seeks its prey at night. For, ironically, it is Fitzpiers, the sexual opportunist, who is at home in the woods in this scene, not Giles. As Marty, Grammer Oliver and Mrs Melbury attempt to 'act the part o' Providence' by driving Grace into the arms of their favoured suitor, it is Giles' character that proves decisive.[147] He exhibits an 'off-hand manner of indifference' to events, 'disdaining to shift his position' for better advantage and turning on his heal in resignation when he fails to capture Grace.[148] Thus, in the struggle for sexual selection, the obstinate Giles is eclipsed by Fitzpiers, who, having secured the affections of Grace, immediately seduces Suke Damson against the background music of the coarse whirring of the nighthawk.[149]

Although *The Woodlanders* and *The Return of the Native* provide the clearest examples of Hardy's Wagnerism, as will be seen in due course, Wagnerian innovations are to be found in a number of the novels. For now, however, I would like to turn to the way in which Hardy incorporates his conception of consciousness and free will into this musical model. As the last chapter demonstrated, the free will allotted to man is very small: it amounts to a portion of the will or Clifford's mind-stuff which must be in harmony with the dictates of the wider universal process for the individual to be truly free. The free individual, to use Hardy's analogy, is like the finger of a great universal pianist: he is free only when he resists the temptation to impose his own will on the universe in favour of submersion in the music of the wider process. This very Schopenhauerian conclusion is represented in the novels through the analogy with dancing: a communal activity in which the individual loses himself to the music according to predestined steps. To join the dance, therefore, is to give oneself up to one's fate. Simon Gatrell notes that in Hardy's dances

> neither soul nor mind seeks any longer to tyrannise the body, for all are combined in communication through the movements of the lived body, in what might be considered an image of the unity of being, of the indivisibility of the elements of our nature, an indivisibility innate, but only made palpable in dance.[150]

It is just such a dance that we catch sight of through the bleary eyes of the drunken Jude as he stands at Fourways in Christminster observing the 'book of humanity' in the form of the revellers frolicking to the music of a brass band.[151] In his description of the Duchess of Richmond's ball on the eve of Waterloo, Hardy even introduces musical notation in an attempt to connect the domestic scene to the rhythm of the Immanent Will. As the drums are taken up by the wider world outside the hall, all present abandon themselves to the movement of 'The Prime of Life', which they dance in a state of reverie.[152] This is not, as most critics have observed, simply an ironic commentary, but is a direct reference to 'The Prime, that willed ere wareness was, / Whose Brain perchance is Space, Whose Thought its laws'.[153] Through their participation in the dance, therefore, the dancers surrender themselves to the music and their fate, the latter of which Hardy personifies through the figure of Death, who leads from the floor those who are to perish in the following day's battle.[154]

In *A Laodicean* Hardy's description of the ball at De Stancy castle takes on a similar metaphysical significance. Paula and Somerset are depicted standing outside the marquee in the rain observing the dance through 'a tissue of glass threads', which Paula later recollects as 'a gauze between us and the dancers'.[155] Such gauzes are to be found masking the dumb shows of *The Dynasts*, obscuring the identity of specific characters and emphasising that since the individual is simply part of a wider process they are largely interchangeable.[156] Here the gauze serves the same function, elevating Paula's dance to that of dumb show, and reminding the reader that those who are happiest are those that submerge their will in the wider music of the universal process. Paula, however, remains on the outside in the rain, a Laodicean whose guiding principle is not acceptance, but rather 'to do what my fancy inclines me to do'.[157]

In *Tess of the D'Urbervilles*, submersion of the individual will entails rejecting obedience to a social moral code and giving in to the rhythms of Darwinian sexual selection. This is exemplified by the Chaseborough dance, the Darwinian theme of which is anticipated by the dance of 'innumerable winged insects' in the 'low-lit mistiness' outside the venue of the barn.[158] Within, individuals are transformed into pagan fertility gods writhing in a mist of 'floating, fusty *débris* of peat and hay, [that] mixed with the perspirations and warmth of the dancers, and form[ed] together a sort of vegeto-human pollen'.[159] As they dance Hardy emphasises the element of Darwinian selection, describing how the exchange of partners simply 'meant that a satisfactory choice had not as yet been arrived at by one or other of the pair', and finishing their performance in an orgiastic twitching of limbs amidst the pollen.[160] Significantly, although we are informed that Tess enjoyed dancing for its own sake, she remains an observer rather than a participant.[161] Like Jude she is an outsider, finding herself out of harmony with her environment, and appalled by the brutality of the Malthusian nightmare of her mother's home.[162]

Tess' timidity and sensitivity to her environment are central to her tragedy; an ominous truth that Hardy makes clear through his description of the Marlott dance at the beginning of the novel. Here Tess remains

unselected by a young Angel Clare, who has been so successful in dis-
ciplining his emotions according to the ascetic religious tradition of his
family that his momentary indulgence is brought to an abrupt end
through his obedience to the mechanical chiming of the church clock.[163]
This cameo introduces one of the main themes running through the
affairs of Hardy's tragic protagonists, that in a world governed by the
primitive sexual impulse the individual may find himself paired with
the wrong mate: Tess is seduced by Alec, Jude by Arabella, and Bathsheba
by Troy. This dance, however, is complicated further by Hardy's introduction of a new musical motif in the form of Mr Durbeyfield's performance of a 'slow recitative' concerning the family ancestry.[164] The dance,
therefore, does not simply anticipate the struggle for sexual selection,
but it also demonstrates that Tess is little more than a puppet performing
predetermined moves in accordance with the hereditary disposition of
her brutal ancestors.[165]

In each of the above examples, Hardy uses dancing to dramatise the
act of the individual giving themselves up to the wider will and therefore
their destiny. Life for Hardy's characters, however, rarely produces harmonious relations, largely because any positive action, such as the choice
of a potential partner, as opposed to a passive reaction, is a gamble, since
it may not coincide with the dictates of destiny. This dilemma is central to
Hardy's fiction and is dramatised in an incident in *The Hand of Ethelberta*
in which the heroine is depicted fretting over whether she should marry
the much older Mountclere or not. It is a scene presented not as a struggle
of conscience, as George Eliot would have written it, but rather as the
struggle of possessing consciousness. As it will be in *The Return of the
Native*, this latter quality is symbolised by a weak light amidst darkness;
this time 'the calm eye of the light-house', which is the 'single speck
perceptible of the outside world from the door of Ethelberta's temporary
home'.[166] Consciousness causes misery because it allows the individual
to perceive that any positive action, as opposed to a passive reaction, is
a gamble, since it may not coincide with the dictates of destiny. How
much easier, she observes to Picotee, if we were freed from consciousness
and simply followed our destiny: 'In a world where the blind only are
cheerful we should all do well to put out our eyes.'[167] And yet, as Hardy's
careful orchestration of the storm outside suggests, her fretting is simply
wasted time.

For outside, the attempts of Chickeral and Mountclere's brother to
dock their boat beneath the cliff at Knollsea (depicted with 'a forehead
with low-grown hair') and alter the destiny of Ethelberta, by warning
her of the latter's sinister brother, are prevented by a powerful east wind

which causes their proposed landing pier to 'trembl[e] like a spider's web' whilst raking the 'iron railings before the houses [on top of the bay] till they hummed in a song of derision'.[168] As they turn back, Ethelberta begins to sing so that 'the music of songs mingled with the stroke of the wind across the iron railings, and was swept on in the general tide of the gale, and the noise of the rolling sea, till not the echo of a tone remained'.[169] Her song reminds us that she remains little more than an organ-stop, and the wider process laughs at men's attempts to alter their destiny.

There are times, however, when like the youthful Sue Bridehead, Hardy's more sympathetic characters glimpse the true nature of things: a moment of epiphany when they become aware of the message encoded in the music surrounding them. As the intuitive Mrs Yeobright sits beneath the pines poised above Clym's cottage, she momentarily becomes an observing consciousness with access, like the reader and the Spirits of *The Dynasts*, to the 'single thread' which runs through both the domestic and the wider plot.[170] She is like the depiction of the artist in Velasquez's 'Las Meninas' – both a participant in the composition and an observer of it. Above her the 'perpetual moan' of the trees of the 'Devil's Bellows' provides a Wagnerian chorus which causes her to dismiss 'thoughts of her own storm-broken and exhausted state to contemplate theirs'.[171] It is a shared suffering: for theirs is the pain of vegetation which has risen above the heath, hers that of the 'intolerable antilogy' of possessing consciousness in a determined world.[172]

The madness of existence in such a world leads the Pities in *The Dynasts* to speculate as to whether 'some mean, monstrous ironist / Had built this mistimed fabric of the Spheres / To watch the throbbings of its captive lives'.[173] To illustrate this point, Hardy follows a description of the bloodshed of the battle of Albuera with a scene in a padded apartment in which courtiers tell an almost blind and gibbering king George of his bloody victory. This whole scene is animated by a 'brass band...playing in a distant part of Windsor', signifying the participation of all in the Pities' mistimed dance.[174] In response to the news, King George retorts:

He says I have won a battle? But I thought
I was a poor afflicted captive here,
In darkness lingering out my lonely days...
When will the speech of the world accord with truth.[175]

It is, indeed, a brutal summary of the plight of mankind in Hardy's universe, a fact perceived by one attendant who murmurs, 'Faith, 'twould seem / As if the madman were the sanest here!'. To understand the absurdity of man's position the individual must be blind or mad, since normal rational faculties will, as Hardy himself complained throughout his writing, continue to attribute to the First Cause a higher moral standard than their own.

Most of Hardy's sympathetic characters, including Jude, endure tragedy and strife to arrive at this understanding of the universe; others, like Henchard, never achieve this accommodation and continue to impose themselves on their surroundings. Conversely, Donald Farfrae and Thomasin Yeobright seem entirely in harmony with the universe from the outset, since they avoid extremes of action and accept the vagaries of events that befall them. Significantly, Hardy illustrates this by means of musical metaphor, representing Farfrae's flexibility by means of a 'voice [that] musically undulated between two semitones', and inviting the reader to observe in his portrait of the sleeping Thomasin 'an ingenuous, transparent life . . . as if the flow of her existence could be seen passing within her', an existence which 'seemed to belong rightly to a madrigal – to require viewing through rhyme and harmony'.[176] Sue, however, possesses insight without the necessary flexibility and when the tragedy of the children's suicide strikes she is to be found groping towards the religious belief abandoned earlier by Jude. However, this is perhaps less a criticism of Sue than a deliberate exploration of the limitations of the humanistic philosophy of 'making the best of it' in a harshly determined world.

Thus far, this chapter has been concerned with the way in which Hardy employs his Aeolian chorus to explore the activity of the wider process, and how the individual can signal his complicity with this process through the analogous activity of dancing. Listening to music in Hardy's novels, however, does not simply allow characters to escape from the misery of the will-governed universe, it also, in accordance with Schopenhauerian theory, offers a comprehensive and pain-free exploration of the inner-man. To trace the reception of this principle by English aestheticians is to observe a head-on collision between German metaphysics and late Victorian pragmatism. Typical of this tradition is the Rev. H. R. Haweis' 'Music its Origins and Influence' (1871), in which he asserts that music is a 'picture-image' of the interior life of the human being in that just as the emotions have '*elations* and *depressions*: Sound, as manipulated by the art of music, has its *elations* and *depressions*, since musical notes go up and down in the scale'.[177] In 'Music and Emotion' (1870) he claims that since music presents the listener with an accurate conceptual understanding of man's inner-life in its entirety and not the edited highlights, as he would be in a painting or a tragedy, music possesses an educative and ethical capacity.[178]

Here, however, Haweis' soundly Schopenhauerian conclusions run into the buffers of Victorian Puritanism, and the influences of John Ruskin's *Queen of the Air* (1869) and his Rede Lecture 'On the Relation of National Ethics to National Arts' (1867) become obvious.[179] For Haweis musical comprehensiveness becomes a practical means of putting the moral fibre back into the listless Victorian middle classes. In language echoing the mid-century preoccupation with masturbation he argues that the arousal of emotions, albeit falsely, through listening to music is morally beneficial because it allows them to be ordered and disciplined. Listening to Beethoven, therefore, is like visiting a moral gymnasium where the sloppy emotional life is honed into shape by vigorous exercise.[180] In the aptly titled series of essays 'Music and Morals' which appeared in the *Contemporary Review* whilst under the editorship of James Thomas Knowles, which lasted from 1870 to 1877, he argues that ordered emotions are those cultivated to their highest activity, so music is capable of expressing emotions seldom felt before. Thus, those living listless lives, into which category Haweis places women en masse, are able to find some form of escape: to such 'music comes with a power of relief and a gentle grace of ministration little short of supernatural'.[181] Furthermore, music's capacity to organise emotions allows all the spiritual thoughts and feelings that the congregation had been struggling to express during prayer to be taken up with the first blasts of the organ and moulded into the clearest form of spiritual exultation.[182]

We do not have to look far in Hardy's fiction to find examples of music organising chaotic emotions: it is central to our understanding of the casual musical facility of Donald Farfrae, and the way that the desire of Jude and Sue finds expression in music. It plays some part in the powerful scene from *Desperate Remedies* discussed in Chapter 1, in which the organ playing of Charles Manston draws Cytherea to him against the Gothic backdrop of the thunder storm: 'the power of the music did not show itself so much by attracting her attention to the subject of the piece, as by taking up and developing as its libretto the poem of her life and soul, shifting her deeds and intentions from the hands of judgement and holding them in its own'.[183] Music, as John Hughes' perceptive analysis of this scene notes, has the effect of numbing her judgement whilst reconstituting her feelings (classified in the Romantic conception of a poem) regarding the executant.[184] It signals the beginning of their romance, as the sinister Manston takes upon the role of a mesmerist playing upon his susceptible victim who finds herself 'involuntarily shrinking up beside him'.

In *Tess of the D'Urbervilles*, Hardy presents us with a scene in which music acts as an antidote to such passion when his heroine attempts to escape the misery of her pregnancy in the music of a church service:

> She liked to hear the chanting – such as it was – and the Old Psalms, and to join in the Morning Hymn. That innate love of melody, which she had inherited from her ballad-singing mother, gave the simplest music a power over her which could well-nigh drag her heart out of her bosom at times.

And as the hymns begin, she reflects upon this power:

> She thought, without exactly wording the thought, how strange and godlike was a composer's power, who from the grave could lead through sequences of emotion, which he alone had felt at first, a girl like her who had never heard of his name, and never would have a clue to his personality.[185]

Initially the scene appears to reflect Haweis' contention that for troubled women 'music comes with a power of relief and a gentle grace of ministration little short of supernatural', the hymn seemingly organising her emotions within the context of religious observance. However, for Tess there is no succour to be found in the sense of community brought about by the singing, as religious ceremony quickly dissolves into scandalous gossip. Nor is help to be found in the Christian sentiments of the words, the effects of which remain unrecorded. Instead, Hardy establishes his heroine's susceptibility as part of her hereditary disposition, the suggestion of an 'innate love of a melody' aligning her pleasure with a Darwinian quality as pervasive as 'Nature's Law'.

There is, however, a deeper metaphysical significance to Tess' experience revealed by Hardy's focus on the role of the composer. Perhaps there is little wonder that as she is led through a wide variety of previously unfelt emotions without the usual drawback of pain (a combination which has, of course, being recently highlighted for her) Tess should naïvely attribute to the composer a godlike power. It is entirely consistent with Schopenhauer's assertion that the power of the composer approaches the divine because he is able to reveal the inner nature of the world, and expresses the deepest wisdom without the concomitant pain. In attributing to the composer a paternal guiding hand, however, Tess attributes a moral superiority that is absent in Schopenhauer's formulation, who insists that he does so in a 'language which his reason does not understand'.

It is, as will be observed later, a naïve assumption also made by the young Jude, who takes the step of visiting the composer of a piece of music that moves him in the hope of finding a solution to his problems. It is Sue who is nearer the mark in drawing the analogy between the power of the composer and the operation of the wider process: both lead their human beings through a wide variety of emotions, and both are ambivalent to the feelings of their victims. It is, unfortunately a truth that Tess is never able to grasp.[186]

In this chapter we have seen how Hardy's Classically inspired project brought together metaphysics and music drama to construct a narrative form that challenged the Realist school of fiction. In place of the gritty realism of Zola we are transported to a 'sequestered spot[] outside the gates of the world' and presented with a reinvigorated Sophoclean tragedy.[187] Instead of the psychological complexities that attend the characterisation of George Eliot, we are faced with sometimes vaguely drawn puppets, whose inner turmoil is played out through a process of mythological parallels and Aeolian music. Thus, there is no need to nudge us towards certain sympathies by authorial moralising, rather, Hardy places us at such aesthetic distance in his imaginary auditorium that we are able to observe the unfolding of not simply the domestic struggles of his characters, but also hear the music of a wider process which motivates their behaviour. Generally his characters remain deaf to this music, this is their tragedy, but there are occasions when they catch a glimpse of the true order of the universe, but by then it is usually too late. A tragic disharmony is at the centre of all Hardy's novels, whether it be an oversensitivity to the harshness of environment, an obstinate desire to take on fate and impose oneself on the universe, or a catastrophic love affair. The last element, becomes in Hardy's hands an emotion to be endured rather than enjoyed, a tragic tension which finds expression in the performance of music. It is this element that will be explored in the following chapter.

4

The Plucked Harp String: Desire, Courtship Ritual and the Debate Concerning Speech Theory

In the last chapter I sought to demonstrate how Hardy employs a web of musically delineated natural sounds to connect the activities of his puppets to the wider universal process. In no other aspect of their lives is this process more apparent than in the desire felt between the sexes. In Hardy's work falling in love is described continually by means of metaphors drawn from biology, metaphysics and mesmerism that emphasise the element of compulsion: Jude experiences 'a momentary flash of intelligence, a dumb announcement of affinity' between himself and the 'complete and substantial female animal' Arabella Donn;[1] Felice Charmond describes how she was 'seized by a hand in velvet' and driven into the arms of the handsome Fitzpiers, while his explanation of desire focuses upon the suitably electro-biological analogy of a Leyden-jar filled with electric current searching for a conductor through which to discharge his 'emotive fluid'.[2] The metaphor is mesmeric: the body is transformed into a 'galvanic battery' ready to conduct its 'magnetic fluid' under the influence of the mesmerist. Such power was not to be considered artificially induced, but, as the mesmerist Spencer Hall concluded, nothing more than the exercise of 'natural law'.[3] This, however, does not make it any less painful, the milkmaids in *Tess of the D'Urbervilles* being particularly acute victims of the 'oppressiveness of an emotion thrust on them by cruel Nature's law'. They become merely a 'portion' of a vast semi-anthropomorphised 'organism called sex', which causes them to 'writhe feverishly' in their cots at night.[4]

This last image is significant because it invokes both the Darwinian struggle for sexual selection and the 'brain-like network of currents and ejections, twitching, interpenetrating, entangling, and thrusting hither and thither the human forms' that make up 'the controlling Immanent Will' of *The Dynasts*.[5] In the work of both Darwin and Schopenhauer the idea of romantic love is replaced by the needs of the 'species' or 'will' to perpetuate itself. The brutal vision expounded in the *Origin of the Species* emphasises that the choice of a potential mate is governed by the need of the species, acting through the unconscious individual, to reproduce itself at the expense of its competitors. Ever-watchful Nature is partially anthropomorphised into a being that scrutinises each species with an infallible eye, rejecting failures and favouring each successful competitor.[6]

In Chapter 2 it was observed that Darwin was received by many Victorian intellectuals as a naturalist whose inductive speculations corroborated the deductive theories of Schopenhauer. Nowhere is this tendency clearer than when considering their writing on sexual relations. The mixture of terms specific to the writings of both men to be found in Zimmern's biography of Schopenhauer, suggests just how closely their ideas had become aligned in the mid-Victorian mind:

> The phenomenal world being the realisation of the eternal Will to live, the sexual instinct is, as respects the intelligent portion of it, the machinery employed by the will to accomplish this end. The aim of Nature merely regards the perpetuation of the species; the individual is as nothing to her. While seeming to act for himself, in reality he is impelled by the force of which he is the manifestation in time, and which aims at perpetuating itself through his action....
>
> All love, however ethereally it comports itself, is rooted solely in desire; indeed, is really but a certain, specified, individual sexual inclination.[7]

A similar blurring of terminology is to be found in David Asher's 'Schopenhauer and Darwinism' (1871), in which he asserts that

> real love, then, in man and woman is what Schopenhauer has defined it to be; viz., the law of natural selection implanted within us for the purpose of preserving the type of the human race in its greatest perfection; it is the instinct of the race or genus that prompts us to covet that particular woman for ourselves, deluding us with the idea of thereby gratifying our own individual desires, but, in reality, benefiting the race to which we belong.[8]

This emphasis on the powerlessness of the individual with regard to sexual relations is also made clear in Sully's *Pessimism*, in which he describes Schopenhauerian love as the will of the unborn child manifesting itself through its parents.[9] Such sentiments are echoed in Hardy's late verse 'The Mother Mourns', in which a personified Nature mourns that desire is nothing more than the 'lure that my species / May gather and gain'.[10] Furthermore, Zimmern's carefully argued diatribe against the marriage contract, in which two otherwise unsuitable people are united through a species instinct beyond their control, appears to form the single most important idea explored by Hardy through the marriages of characters such as Jude and Arabella, and Grace and Fitzpiers.

Since desire between the sexes provides the clearest example of the unconscious activity of Hardy's universal process, it is perhaps unsurprising to find its agency central to his dramatic ambitions in the novels. Indeed, as Terry Eagleton has observed, 'With Schopenhauer, desire has become the protagonist of the human theatre, and human subjects themselves its mere obedient bearers or underlings.... In a traumatic collapse of teleology, desire comes to seem independent of any particular ends, or at least grotesquely disproportionate to them.'[11] It is the 'grotesquely disproportionate' power of desire that Hardy depicts in the novels through his use of musical analogy: in figurative terms the web becomes a harp, the tones of which draw his protagonists together.[12] Perhaps predictably, in Hardy's hands such music is transformed from an ode to joy into a lament announcing the pain and confusion of desire.

This becomes literal in *The Trumpet Major* as Bob Loveday installs an Aeolian harp to win the love of Anne Garland. When the wind blows, 'the wires began to emit a weird harmony which mingled curiously with the plashing of the wheel' awaking in Anne repressed feelings for Bob:

> Every night after this, during the mournful gales of autumn, the strange mixed music of water, wind, and strings met her ear, swelling and sinking with an almost supernatural cadence... she marvelled pleasantly at the new depths of poetry this contrivance revealed as existent in that young seaman's nature, and allowed her emotions to flow out yet a little further in the old direction, notwithstanding her severe resolve to bar them back.[13]

Just as George Eliot uses the musicalised noise of the water mill to explore the emotional sensitivity of Maggie Tulliver, Hardy's use of water music has the effect, as Hughes has noted, of converting Anne's 'emotions into hydraulic form, as they overflow the sea-wall of conscious restraint, and "flow out yet a little further in the old direction"'. Indeed, such is the power of her feelings that she asks that the harp be removed since 'it affects me almost painfully at night'. Invoking Deleuze, Hughes argues that this becomes a moment of 'individuation', when Anne is transformed into a 'collection of intensive sensations' made to vibrate in consonance with the harp of Bob's construction. As such she is opened up to a new set of relations concerning the maker.[14] Of course, for Hardy such a moment is not without its grim irony, for when she learns that the harp was in fact John's idea then, as Michael Irwin has observed, 'its cries and moans become almost unbearable, reminding her of the trumpet major's hurt and her complicity in it'.[15] Like all Hardy's tragic love affairs, pain emerges from the powerlessness of the individual to control his or her desire.

In *A Laodicean* a similar tension between apparent self-control and the over-mastering nature of desire is demonstrated as the Aeolian harp is transformed into the 'musical threads' of the telegraph wire which draw George Somerset to Paula Power.[16] As he pauses in the middle of a dark field during his search for the village of Sleeping-Green, Hardy notes how:

> the wire sang overhead with dying falls and melodious rises that invited him to follow; while above the wire rode the stars in their courses, the low nocturn of the former seeming to be the voices of those stars,
>
> > Still quiring to the young-eyed cherubim.
>
> Recalling himself from these reflections Somerset decided to follow the lead of the wire. It was not the first time during his present tour that he had found his way at night by the help of these musical threads.[17]

Hardy's modernisation of the Romantic metaphor of the harp is not unusual, but reflects what Steven Connor has identified as a late-century artistic interest in the tension between the 'uncanny sound made by the wires in the wind and the messages they were conveying'.[18] Typical of this tradition, according to Connor, is John Payne's 1908 poem 'The Telephone Harp', in which he juxtaposes the cables carrying the vocalising of human beings '[d]runk with conceit and drugged with the wine of the Will-to-be' with the sound they make when touched by the 'hand of the storm-wind' so that 'they are also susceptible to a kind of otherworldly interference'.[19] Hardy's meaning is similar: we are invited to imagine Paula, the princess in her medieval tower, sending messages in an attempt to fashion her destiny, whilst the Aeolian music of the wires (which Hardy deliberately links to the wider harmony of the spheres) leads Somerset to her with an attraction analogous to gravitational force.

In both *Two on a Tower* and *The Woodlanders* Hardy employs similar Aeolian modulations to remind us that the power of 'Nature's Law' is to be suffered by the individual rather than enjoyed. In the former, Swithin leaves Lady Constantine alone on the tower at night whilst below her 'shouts mingled with the wind, which retained some violence yet, playing over the trees beneath her as on the strings of a lyre'.[20] For a moment Hardy externalises their passions through musical vibrations, the phallic tower combined with the 'violence' of the wind indicating the uncontrollable nature of their passion. Similarly, in *The Woodlanders* the confession of Felice to Grace of her adultery takes place in the hostile woodlands whilst 'the funeral trees rocked and chanted dirges unceasingly'.[21] Significantly, both women take shelter beneath a clump of hollies, a bush used throughout Hardy's fiction to symbolise virile sexuality.[22] Here, it scratches rather than protects the women; the Aeolian music of the trees contextualising this isolated sexual symbol within the wider web of compulsion afflicting both of them. Thus, despite her protestations that she had merely dallied with Fitzpiers, the music of the trees reminds the reader of the irresistible force acting through Felice, transforming her into a figure to be pitied rather than scorned.

In all of the above examples Aeolian music reminds the reader of the various laws determining the lives of Hardy's characters; my intention in this chapter is to explore how this cosmic music is related to the representation of musical performance in the novels. Musical execution as a metaphor for sexual attraction is not, of course, peculiar to Hardy: the piano became a favoured site of nineteenth-century fictional seduction for authors as diverse as the Brontës, Gaskell, Thackeray and Eliot, with women either portrayed as victims of male charms through their emotional susceptibility, or predators artfully using their accomplishments like latter-day sirens. As was seen in Chapter 1, Hardy's early work *Desperate Remedies* falls into this tradition, offering the reader an isolated exploration of the laws of attraction that would evade the censure of Mrs Grundy. By the mid-seventies, however, the maturation of Hardy's three principles meant that musical performance was more than simply an apt metaphor – it was a fundamental part of his metaphysics. In Hardy's depiction of the effects of music, the tangle of nerve fibres observed in *The Dynasts* that controls the activities of his characters is internalised in the nervous system of the individual. In essence his heroines, since it is generally women who are susceptible to music in the novels, are all highly strung 'harps' who vibrate in consonance with the musical strings plucked by their potential mates: a feature made quite clear through the various physiological and scientific terms used by Hardy to describe their reactions.

Contemporary anthropological, physiological, psychological and mesmeric theories concerning the affective power of music allowed Hardy to reinvigorate a Romantic image of the susceptible listener as a plucked harp string, thereby allowing musical performance to join those other laws such as heredity, sexual selection and the will, in determining man's behaviour.[23] As was observed in the introduction, the writing of Hardy's tragic novels coincided with an enormous growth in the number of articles appearing in mainstream periodicals (particularly the more liberal and progressive publications such as *The Contemporary* and *Fortnightly Reviews*), concerning the mystery of music's origin, meaning and function. Broadly speaking, their approach was Positivist: seeking first to identify the scientific laws underpinning musical power before proposing a social role leading to man's communal perfection. More specifically, many of these articles reflected the scientific work of the continental psychologists Gustav Flechner and Hermann von Helmholtz (particularly the latter's *On Sensation of Tone* (1877)), in which they sought to relocate the musical experience from a purely mental activity to a function of various physiological relationships within the individual body. Thus, the activity of listening to music became a quantifiable sensory experience, reflecting the nature of the external stimulus and the distribution of the nervous system. The sense of 'self' was at once strengthened and compromised: the individual was reduced to a simple cluster of sensations; and yet the subjective response reflected the composition of each individual nervous system.[24]

Typical of this new tradition were thinkers such as Haweis, who contributed a number of highly influential articles to the progressive *Contemporary Review* between 1866 and 1898.[25] In 'Music and Morals: Part III' (1871) he reinvigorates the image of the harp, arguing that women are susceptible to music because their constitutions 'are like those fine violins which vibrate to the lightest touch. Women are great listeners, not only to eloquence, but also to music. The wind has swept many an Aeolian lyre, but never such a sensitive harp as a woman's soul.'[26] Haweis' harp, however, is more than simply a convenient symbol; it is made up of the individual fibres of the nervous system which are made to vibrate in consonance with external musical chords. Thus, for those women with susceptible natures, listening to music can 'cultivate emotion into its highest activity' and even recreate exhausted emotions through the direct vibration of nerve tissues.[27]

The harp is an image depicted frequently in the musicological research of James Sully, most notably in a series of articles published in the *Westminster* whilst under the editorship of John Chapman in the mid-seventies. The place of publication is significant: the constantly precarious financial situation of the journal lead to a reliance on financial aid from Harriet Martineau in 1854 (which therefore ensured a more Positivist agenda). Meanwhile, the inability to pay contributors in the 1860s gave, as Sully himself observed, new writers a platform to explore their ideas.[28] His own contributions reflect these twin features: their inclusion of experimental physiology to unravel the mystery of music's emotional power is both indicative of the Comtean emphasis on scientific method as a means of explaining the behaviour of man, and too modern for the *Westminster*'s more traditional quarterly competitors.

Sully, as was observed in Chapter 2, was responsible for introducing Hartmann's philosophy of the unconscious to the periodical-reading public in a detailed essay which appeared in the *Fortnightly Review* in 1876. Significantly, as Hughes has noted, in the *Philosophy of the Unconscious*, the material and spiritual are brought together through musical analogy. According to Hartmann's vision, the nervous system is like an Aeolian harp vibrating in consonance with the stimulus it receives, 'producing "ideation" as a function (in the last analysis) of "cerebral vibrations", physical resonances'.[29] The vibrating string becomes analogous to the unconscious as it guides the conscious 'self' according to quasi-musical laws: 'we see indeed daily [. . .] the *unconscious*, how the soul without consciousness guides the fingers according to the laws of harmony, whilst it incites consciousness to new relations and actions'.[30]

In 'The Physics and Physiology of Harmony' (1875), Sully roots his discussion in Hartmann's analogy, and pushes it to its logical materialist conclusions. He argues that any pleasure derived from music is due purely to the stimulation of the nervous system which connects the ear to the brain and is independent of any mysterious 'sub-conscious' activities of the intellect.[31] Indeed, under this view the human nervous system is so constructed that

> the scala media of the cochlea resembles a keyboard, in function as well as appearance, the fibres of the corti being the keys, and the ends of the nerves representing the strings which the keys strike. . . . All our feelings and emotions, from the lowest sensations to the highest aesthetic consciousness, are ultimately referable to a purely mechanical cause.[32]

In this model, the mysterious power of music is reduced to a series of physical laws governing the relationship between tonal vibration and the impulse of electrical charges which are dispatched along nerve fibres to stimulate neurones. Since this fibrous web responds mechanically to specific tones, music becomes a physiologically determining agent and a direct representation of the emotions experienced by the listener.[33]

Both the inventor and physiologist Alexander Bain and George Eliot's polymath partner G. H. Lewes published works which sought to demystify music's affective power through the application of the physical sciences. Once again the image that recurs in their work is that of the harp, which, they argue, is animated not simply by musical chords, but also the human voice. Bain notes in *The Senses and the Intellect* (1855) that man continually expresses his feelings through his voice because 'the high tension of the medulla oblongata', caused by a build-up of emotions, needs to be relieved through the production of sound, whether screaming, singing or speaking.[34] The consequent vibrations are transferred to the tympanum of the ear, thereby allowing emotions to be transferred through purely physical means without the intervention of the intellect. Hardy's interest in Lewes' materialist philosophy is evident from a note taken from the latter's 'The Course of Modern Thought' in March 1877, which reads 'Physiology began to disclose that all the mental processes were (mathematically speaking) functions of physical processes, i.e. varying with the variations of bodily states; and this was declared enough to banish for ever the conception of the Soul, except as a term simply expressing certain functions.'[35] Lewes applies these materialist ideas to the voice in *Problems of Life and Mind* (1874), where he argues that the reason we respond uncontrollably to the tone of certain voices is because 'when a note is sounded by one chord it will set vibrating any other chords which are in sympathy with it and only those. It is thus also external voices awaken sympathetic tones in us.'[36]

The idea of the vibrating chord, whether musical or spoken, awakening 'sympathy' in the listener is also central to the musical theory of one of the most important influences on Hardy's thought, Herbert Spencer. He sets out his ideas in a provocative essay 'On the Origin and Function of Music' (1855), published in *Fraser's Magazine* while under the editorship of John William Parker.[37] It should be remembered that it was under his editorship that George Eliot published her similarly provocative 'Liszt, Wagner, and Weimar', the first article published in this country to offer a positive account of Wagner's aesthetics. Furthermore, the scientific nature of Spencer's article is typical of the type that Parker was commissioning at the time in an effort to play down the dashing, witty Regency style that had characterised the journal under its first editor, William Maginn (1800–1836), whilst appealing to the voracious appetite of the new middle-class readership for articles that attempted to explain the rapidly changing world around them. Thus, Spencer's work joined that of others at the forefront of scientific and philosophical thought, most notably G. H. Lewes, Anthony Froude and Arthur Helps.

Spencer's essay, like the work of Lewes, indicates quite clearly the Romantic/scientific dialectic that characterised mid-century treatment of music, for whilst continuing to consider music an 'idealised language of the emotion', he invokes the recent studies of Bain in order to assert that the emotional impact of music is reducible to the mechanical vibrations produced in a certain arrangement of nerve fibres by the consonant vibrations of piano chords.[38] This physiologically determinist position is part of Spencer's materialist vision of evolution, which posits the origins of music in the impassioned speech tones of man's distant ancestors, which, he argues, have since evolved into a dry 'language of the intellect'. This primitive emotional language, he argues, has evolved into modern complex music and still lingers in the musical element of modern speech voice tone. It is an emotional language which only those who have evolved a certain degree of sensibility can experience. To them the vibrating chord, whether musical or spoken, becomes a 'sympathetic medium of communication' which undermines attempts to express feelings through the clumsy means of the word.[39]

Spencer did not invent the 'speech theory' view of musical origin, it had been popularised by both Rousseau, whose position typified the mindset of the Enlightenment (the mystical force of music becoming a tangential offshoot of a rational and ordered means of verbal communication), and Hegel, whose Romantic credentials forced him to reassert the importance of pure emotional expression. Speech theory even formed the basis of an exchange of letters in the *Blackwoods Magazine* as early as 1819.[40] Spencer simply reinvented the theory for the age of science. Therefore, despite the earliness of the publication of his essay it is significant to note that his ideas remained highly influential throughout the seventies due largely to their incorporation into the work of advocates such as Joseph Godard and James Sully. Furthermore, his work also maintained public interest due to the notoriety it achieved through the opposition of Darwin. Darwin was generally critical of Spencer's synthetic philosophy because it rested on what he considered to be a priori conclusions. This is particularly so of Spencer's musical theory which he dismissed in *The Descent of Man* (1871) with the assertion that 'articulate speech is one of the latest as it is certainly the highest of the arts acquired by man', and not a stepping stone on the way to musical development, a conclusion he articulates clearly in a footnote:

> Mr Spencer comes to an exactly opposite conclusion to that at which I have arrived. He concludes, as did Diderot formerly, that the cadences used in emotional speech afford the foundation from which music has been developed; whilst I conclude that musical notes and rhythm were first acquired by the male or female progenitors of mankind for the sake of charming the opposite sex.[41]

The implication for the listener, therefore, is that he is moved by a piece of modern complex music not because he hears the impassioned speech tones of man's distant ancestors but because its combinations of tones awaken in him the same intense emotions felt by his distant progenitors during courtship ritual.

These two interpretations offered the poles between which theories concerning the origins, emotional power and function of music fluctuated throughout the middle of the sixties and seventies.[42] The musicologist Joseph Goddard, for example, who shared Spencer's belief in the Lamarckian principle of slow incremental change, and the Comtean principle of progress, argued in his *The Philosophy of Music* (1862) that music is not simply a necessary extension of the properties of tone and phrase observed in ordinary speech, it is their 'highest exemplification', turning it into a *'direct, original, and unalloyed language of human emotions.'*[43] Like Spencer, he argues that speech has since become a limited means of communication because it relies on the constituent element of 'the mechanical symbols of words'.[44] This primitive emotional language, however, remains in voice tone, through which a speaker is able to *'kindle within the listener* an effort *of imagination and glow of spirit*, of a kindred nature to that within the imparter', forming a special sympathy between speakers.[45]

James Sully tempered the determinist conclusions reached in his 'The Physics and Physiology of Harmony' (1875) with an essay published in the non-secular *Contemporary Review*, which, appropriately enough, sought to restore some of the quasi-mystical qualities attributable to music. In 'On the Nature and Limits of Musical Expression' (1874), Sully invokes Spencer's essay, which, he claims, 'has been recognised more or less clearly by nearly all writers on the subject', to argue that this mystery is intensified by an intellectual 'impulse' in man to 'project a living, throbbing soul behind musical tones' so that they seem to be the utterances of 'some unknown nature'.[46] This idea finds resonance with J. S. Mill's theory that the auditor of a piece of modern complex music tends to conceive of himself as 'overhearing' the more reflective emotional expression of some unknown being.[47]

By contrast, Edmund Gurney took issue with Spencer in his 'On Some Disputed Points in Music' (1876), rejecting 'speech theory' for a variety of different reasons, and concluding that 'I feel that my apprehension of music must differ so totally from Mr. Spencer's, that I perhaps fail fairly to catch his point of view.'[48] He does, however, acknowledge that the pleasure derived from listening to music is different to that experienced whilst observing, say, the symmetry of a building, and accordingly he reasons that the listener must therefore be moved by more than the melodic structure of music; a point which he proposes in an article published in *Nineteenth Century*, entitled 'On Music and Musical Criticism' (1878):

> Neither the complexity of proportional relations, nor the interest of following and balancing, nor the elementary sense of varieties of motion, seem to carry with them the requisite explanation of the tremendous emotional power of melody. For this we can only turn to the mighty aid of inherited association.... Mr Darwin's theory seems to me the only one yet suggested which at once accounts for the facts of music, and rests on a broad ground of evidence.[49]

In embracing Darwin, Gurney is not arguing that the listener responds to a modern melody because it has a dynamic resemblance with a form of pre-verbal mating ritual, rather he is filling in a gap left by Darwinian theory to suggest that what must have enabled man's distant progenitors to have found pleasure in the tones of pre-verbal courtship ritual was the presence of a 'rudimentary faculty'. When listening to a piece of modern complex music, therefore, an evolved, more elaborate, special faculty participates in an emotional experience which links the listener directly to the first emotional experiences enjoyed by his ancestors during courtship.[50]

Hardy was certainly aware of this debate: a brief annotation to a quotation copied into his *Literary Notebooks* from Gurney's essay indicates that he favoured Spencer's interpretation.[51] This, however, is hardly surprising, since Hardy was defending the system of synthetic philosophy against attacks even as late as 1915, asserting in a letter to Caleb Saleeby that 'I am utterly bewildered to understand how the doctrine that, beyond the knowable, there must always be an unknown, can be displaced.'[52] Hardy's apparent partisanship, however, is secondary to the fact that he took an interest in the debate at all; an engagement that, I believe, influenced the way he depicted the emotional power of musical performance and musically delineated voice tone in the novels.

Hardy was not alone in this, Delia da Sousa Correa has presented a convincing account of how the ideas of thinkers such as Spencer and Lewes influenced George Eliot's depiction of musical performance and voice tone in the novels.[53] She argues that when we consider the depiction of Maggie Tulliver in *The Mill on the Floss*, for example, it is apparent that Eliot's musical usage strays beyond the more traditional model offered by the Brontës and Gaskell and incorporates some of the physiological theories discussed above. Maggie is not simply moved by the singing of Stephen Guest, but in Eliot's careful depiction, her heroine's nervous system is transformed into a harp which vibrates in consonance with both his singing and bass voice tone. When he speaks, his tones are described as 'like [the] sudden accidental vibration of a harp close by her' sending an uncontrollable thrill through her body. Throughout the narrative the metaphor of the harp is reanimated as Eliot explores the repercussions of contemporary theories of physiological determinism, asking the reader to pity her heroine as she depicts her as an unwilling innocent 'being played on...by the inexorable power of sound'.[54] Essentially, musical vibrations are transformed into a modern physiological version of the Greek Fates against which Maggie, armed with a Feuerbachian will, must struggle in order to secure moral redemption in the exercise of her perceived duty.[55] It is a technique that Eliot employs again in *Romola*, in which Eliot's heroine does not make a conscious decision to follow the religious leader Savonarola, but rather has 'the sense of being possessed by [the] actual vibrating harmonies' of his 'musical' speech, against which she has no power.[56]

When we consider Hardy's heroines, they are all, like Maggie Tulliver, highly strung: indeed, as Tess observes, 'there are very few women's lives that are not – tremulous'.[57] This susceptibility is not simply used by Hardy to explore the patriarchal construction of femininity, but it also demonstrates the shortcomings inherent in Spencerian ideas concerning materialist progress. If, as Spencer asserts in 'Progress: Its Law and Cause' (1857), species continue to evolve in a Lamarckian fashion from the 'homogeneous to the heterogeneous', then Hardy's musical presentation provides an illustration of the possible consequences of over-specialisation and refinement.[58] It is a theme to which he alludes in *The Life* in a comment that reminds us of the intolerable antilogy central to his fiction: 'the human race is too extremely developed for its corporeal conditions, the nerves being evolved to an activity abnormal in such an environment'.[59] Since his characters are little more than nerve endings of a universal process they vibrate in consonance when these fibres are plucked – a condition which is demonstrated most clearly in the sexual impulse.

This imagery is apparent in Hardy's depiction of the sexually charged chess game between Knight and Elfride in *A Pair of Blue Eyes*. In Chapter 11 of *First Principles* Spencer illustrates his contention that nothing is static in the world of flux by asserting that if only we could 'look through a telescope of high power' we would be able to see how 'each pulsation of the heart gives a jar to the whole room'.[60] It is these pulsations that are made visible in this scene as 'some flowers upon the table [are] set throbbing by [Elfride's heart's] pulsations'. Indeed, so great is the strain that by the end of the scene her pulse is 'twanging like a harp string'.[61] Similarly, Sue Bridehead is described as a woman of 'nervous temperament', for whom 'the fibres of her nature seemed strained like harp-strings'.[62] Jude often remarks upon her 'quivering' nature, and observes that she is 'a harp which the least wind of emotion from another's heart could make to vibrate'.[63]

Throughout Hardy's narratives, then, the harp becomes the most common metaphor to indicate the nervous susceptibility of his characters. Musical performance and voice tone, therefore, become the invisible means by which harp strings are plucked, thus creating a sympathetic vibration, or unconscious desire, which draws his lovers together. This purely physiological metaphor, however, is augmented by Hardy's employment of terminology common to the popular field of mesmerism, which, as was observed in the last chapter, offered most Victorians the clearest picture of the power of the unknown mind.[64] Mesmerism raised a number of questions concerning the relationship between mind and body, reducing the individual to an electric machine galvanised by magnetic fluid. It was under the hands of the experienced mesmerist that this fluid was quite literally stroked (through a series of non-contact passes) into activity. Indeed, as Winter has shown, one of the most popular mid-century advocates of mesmerism, the young professor of practical medicine at University College, London, John Elliotson was caricatured in a cartoon in Punch (1843) as a concert pianist playing upon the skull of his patient.[65] Thus, for the mesmerist, the analogy between the nervous system and the strings of a piano or harp is reinvigorated, but with sinister undertones. The fact that most practising mesmerists were foreign and most subjects susceptible females, and the whole process involved unseemly stroking, played havoc upon the prurient middle classes, for whom the art struggled to lose its sexual undertones.

This became particularly evident, according to Winter, in the debate that emerged from the mid-century interest in an offshoot of mesmerism, 'Electro-Biology', which centered on whether the conscious person could be made to act unconsciously or not. Such was its importance that it involved the leading physiologists and psychologists of the day, James Braid (who later coined the term 'hypnotism'), Thomas Laycock and William Benjamin Carpenter. Mesmerism, according to Carpenter, heightened the sensitivity of the subject, transforming them into 'thinking automaton', who were still conscious, but behaved in an unconscious way according to 'mental reflexes'.[66] Laycock went further, and talked of 'sensitive females' being nervously arrested by the attention of their suitors. Significantly, as da Sousa Correa has noted, Laycock was simultaneously condemning the exciting effects of listening to music as a major cause of female hysteria and potentially damaging to the nervous and reproductive system.[67] During the same period E. J. Tilt warned of the powerful emotional effects of music on susceptible females – drawing particular attention to the harmful effect of vibrations on the sensitive nervous system.[68]

The sinister connection between mesmerism and music is perhaps most clearly explored in Hardy's work in the short story 'The Fiddler of the Reels' – a story that seems to dramatise the warnings of Laycock and Tilt.[69] Mop Ollamoor, is a creation designed to play havoc with late Victorian susceptibilities. The narrator grudgingly describes him as 'not ill-favoured', but 'a woman's man they said' (the reportage relieving the narrator from expressing opinions that might be construed as praise), possessing a catalogue of those attributes that might make women swoon whilst their men snort: he is 'un-English', his 'olive-skin' and unkempt, long, scented hair being indicative of his morally dubious character.[70] Even his musical ability merely provides an opportunity for the narrator to chide him for his lack of practice, summoning the testament of the wholly upstanding 'Mellstock quire-band' who 'in their honest love of thoroughness...despised the new man's style'.[71] Both they and the narrator, however, are unable to deny the power of his fiddling over women, particularly the young Car'line Aspent. In order to explain it with minimum appreciation, she is transformed into a victim through a gendered diagnosis which focuses on her 'fragile and responsive organization' and 'nervous passion'. Such is her susceptibility that even the sound of his footfalls could make her 'start from her seat...as if she had received a galvanic shock' – an effect it would require a 'neurologist' to explain.[72]

By reducing Mop's power to a simple physiological relationship, Car'line's honour is preserved: she is a victim of her nervous disposition rather than lax morality. To reinforce this notion, Mop's musicality is also presented as menacing rather than magical. His physical description reflects foreign soloists such as Liszt and Paganini (to whom he is compared), who, as Eliot explored through Julius Klesmer, were still regarded with suspicion by middle-class society. He also calls to mind the rather more morally dubious character of the mesmerist, a parallel which Hardy's narrator evokes through his description of the 'acoustic magnetism' which causes Car'line to dance 'slavishly and abjectly' as if she had lost 'her power of independent will.[73] Finally, both he and his music are demonised: the trusty Mellstock Quire warning that 'all were devil's tunes in his repertory'. He is at once seducer and sorcerer, observing the power of his 'weird and wizardly' music with a 'gimlet-like gaze'. Even his fiddle is transformed into a demoniac Familiar, which lets out an 'elfin shriek' when he has finished playing.[74]

A less sinister example can be found in *The Hand of Ethelberta* when, during a visit to a cathedral, Hardy's heroine finds herself drawn like a sleepwalker to the organ-loft where Christopher is playing:

> She knew the fingers that were pressing out those rolling sounds, and knowing them, became absorbed in tracing their progress. To go towards the organ-loft was an act of unconsciousness, and she did not pause till she stood almost beneath it.[75]

Once again Hardy invokes a power that is both physiological and mesmeric, the direct relation between fingers and sounds evoking Sully's reduction of the 'scala media' to a keyboard, or the Punch caricature of the mesmerist Elliotson as a keyboard player. Ethelberta, is reduced to a mesmeric state, her nerves to harp strings played upon by the unseen Christopher. Hence, as Hughes has noted of this scene, the music momentarily undermines Ethelberta's strong sense of duty, producing new arrangements of feeling *within* her concerning the player.[76]

This is also the case during the garden scene at Talbothays dairy, where the terminology of physiology and mesmerism is supplemented by a biological vocabulary rooted in Darwinian courtship ritual. The scene has a corollary in the sword display of sergeant Troy before Bathsheba Everdene, his swinging, thrusting arm making a scarlet haze 'like a twanged harp-string' before his petrified, yet appreciative audience.[77] In this more reserved scene, however, it is Angel's badly played harp that plucks the heartstrings of Tess:

> Tess, like a fascinated bird, could not leave the spot. Far from leaving she drew up towards the performer, keeping behind the hedge that he might not guess her presence.

The outskirt of the garden in which Tess found herself had been left uncultivated for some years, and was now damp and rank with juicy grass which sent up mists of pollen at a touch; and with tall blooming weeds emitting offensive smells – weeds whose red and yellow and purple hues formed a polychrome as dazzling as that of cultivated flowers. She went stealthily as a cat through this pro-fusion of growth, gathering cuckoo-spittle on her skirts, cracking snails that were underfoot, staining her hands with thistle-milk and slug-slime, and rubbing off upon her naked arms sticky blights which, though snow-white on the apple-tree trunks, made madder stains on her skin; thus she drew quite near to Clare, still unobserved of him.

Tess was conscious of neither time nor space. The exaltation which she had described as being producible at will by gazing at a star, came now without any determination of hers; she undulated upon the thin notes of the second-hand harp, and their harmonies passed like breezes through her, bringing tears into her eyes. The floating pollen seemed to be his notes made visible, and the dampness of the garden the weep-ing of the garden's sensibility. Though near nightfall, the rank-smelling weed-flowers glowed as if they would not close for intentness, and the waves of colour mixed with waves of sound.[78]

Perhaps only Hardy could get away with calling his hero 'Angel' before furnishing him with a harp! In this scene, however, he is more an Adam playing opposite to Tess' Eve, a relationship that Hardy invokes repeatedly to characterise their courtship.[79] If, however, they are the first two people on the earth, then Tess has already been expelled from the sanitised Eden of the creationist myth to an uncultivated portion of the garden where a Darwinian nature oozes with sexuality, and 'rank...juicy grass' sends up mists of pollen.[80] In Chapter 19 of *The Descent of Man*, Darwin argues that the listener is moved by music because certain combinations of tones awaken the same intense emotions felt by his distant progenitors during courtship. At this time 'the male pours forth his full volume of song, in rivalry with other males' in order to attract a mate and perpetuate the species.[81] Hardy's reading of Gurney's outline of the theory in his 'On Some Disputed Points in Music' (1876) is significant when considering how Tess and Angel are transformed into a version of Adam and Eve who comply with these rules of courtship.[82] A synaesthetic quality attends Hardy's description of the way in which Angel's notes, which have 'a stark quality like that of nudity', mingle with these clouds, so that 'the floating pollen seemed to be his notes made visible', focusing the reader's attention on the sexually magnetic qualities of the music.[83]

Under their influence Tess is transformed into a 'fascinated bird, [which] could not leave the spot', and then a cat who moves stealthily through the garden towards the source. As she progresses the garden adorns her with its juices and stains, affirming her as part of that nature which 'writhes feverishly' under the governance of the laws of sexual selection.

In his reading of the scene, Ebbatson is alive to the mesmeric sensations felt by both Tess and the reader as the 'hypnotic approach and dance-like movements [of Tess] are mimed by the reading mind's stumbling through the dense syntax. The pleasurable insidiousness of hypnosis is hinted at in this undulating movement.'[84] Similarly, for Hughes, Hardy's writing here means that 'the distinction between bodies seems to be suspended by the process of music', which includes 'the reader's response [which] becomes indeterminate, passing into Tess' sense of things, and outside again'.[85] Thus, not only does the synaesthetic quality of the music reveal a new relationship between Tess and Angel, it also collapses the distance between the narrator and the reader, allowing us to experience the new sense of relations which envelop Tess with a sense of immediacy. Joan Grundy, chooses to focus on the moral aspects of the scene, arguing that whilst the harp is attracting Tess' sexual nature her purity is maintained because her spirit has been removed in a way similar to the affects of 'gazing at a star'.[86] But this is not how the passage reads. For Hardy, the fallen Tess is simply an extension of the natural laws surrounding her; accordingly, Angel's harmonies are not simply heard, but 'passed like breezes through her', evoking the same intensely sexual reaction that marks Hardy's description of the garden.[87]

Clearly, Angel's harp ensnares Tess in the web of determinism making up what Hardy refers to in the novel as 'Nature's Law'. And just as this power, whether it be of the will or species, objectifies itself through the vibrating strings of Angel's harp, it also manifests itself in the vibrations of his voice tone. As has already been noted, physiological speculations concerning the relationship between music and voice tone reached a climax in 1876 when a number of articles were published focussing on the arguments of Spencer and the speech theorists. The year 1876, however, is also the date when epistemological debates concerning aurality in general and the voice in particular were ignited when Alexander Graham Bell filed a patent for the telephone, which not only allowed the voice to be disengaged from the speaker for the first time since Echo, but, as a review in *The Times* made clear, allowed the 'little incidents of human utterance... a whisper, a cough, a sigh, a breath...to pass along miles of wires'.[88] Then, in 1877, Charles Edison patented the phonograph, which not only allowed the individual to hear his own voice, but recorded it for perpetuity. Thus, as both Kahn and Connor have observed, the voice was no longer to be apprehended in a fleeting moment, occupying its own space and time: it now no longer disappeared. Furthermore, because the phonograph recorded all sounds, including previously barely perceptible sounds which it could play back greatly amplified, the human voice lost its pre-eminence and became one of many competing sounds.[89] Connor notes that Edison himself was fully aware of the philosophical implications of his invention and developed the idea of a 'spirit catcher', an instrument of such delicacy that it could record the configuration of vibrating atoms of sounds made long ago: thus, just as the telescope could make visible the ancient light from distant stars this machine offered 'the startling possibility of the voices of the dead being reheard.'[90]

It is an idea which looks back not only to the Classical myths of Rumour and Echo, but also, as Kahn has argued, to Charles Babbage's attempts to shore up religion against the advance of science in his *Ninth Bridgewater Treatise* (1837). In it he argued that that 'the pulsations of the air, once set in motion by the human voice, cease not to exist . . . the waves of the air thus raised, perambulate the earth and the ocean's surface, and in less than twenty hours every atom of its atmosphere takes up the altered movement'.

> Thus considered, what a strange chaos is this wide atmosphere we breathe! Every atom, impressed with good and with ill, retains at once the motions which philosophers and sages have imparted to it, mixed and combined in ten thousand ways with all that is worthless and base. The air itself is one vast library, on whose pages are for ever written all that man has ever said or woman whispered. There, in their mutable but unerring characters, mixed with the earliest, as well as the latest sighs of mortality, stand for ever recorded, vows unredeemed, promises unfulfilled, perpetuating in the united movements of each particle, the testimony of man's changeful will.[91]

It is the world of Clifford's 'mindstuff' or the Paterian world of 'flux' made audible, with all sounds reduced to their subatomic units never to be destroyed but simply re-configured. Kahn notes how Dickens certainly held an interest in Babbage's ideas, noting in a speech given at the Birmingham and Midland Institute in 1869 that 'it was suggested by Mr. Babbage, in his *Ninth Bridgewater Treatise*, that a mere spoken word – a mere syllable thrown into the air – may go on reverberating through illimitable space for ever and ever . . .'.[92] Significantly, as Kahn makes clear, it is an idea that continues to maintain weight in the scientific world, modern attempts to eavesdrop on the dead being typified by Raudive voices: the sounds of apparently fragmented voices recorded and decoded in what appear to be 'silent' areas.[93] William Burroughs concludes from this that 'maybe we are walking around under a magnetic dome of pre-recorded word and image, and Raudive and other experimenters are simply plugging into the prerecording'.[94]

It is quite clear, then, that Hardy's writing of *The Return of the Native* coincided with a period when sound, and particularly the human voice, for the first time possessed the qualities of amplification, repetition and disengagement from its source: features that characterise the soundscape permeating many of Hardy's novels and stories. This influence can be seen in the world of *The Dynasts*, which, in the tradition of Bertolt Brecht, is a play for voices. In the drama, sound becomes a means by which Hardy telescopes time and challenges the pre-eminence of his central characters in relation to their environment. Crucial events in the drama, such as the battle of Ulm or the procession of Princess Maria Louisa to her wedding, are obscured by 'the gauze' of 'heavy rains', emphasising that in a world governed by the Immanent Will the individual remains unimportant.[95] Even Napoleon and Wellington are reduced to indistinguishable 'talking shapes': during the battle of Salamanca the reader becomes an auditor of Wellington and his officers, who are merely 'vague figures on horseback [who] are audible in the gloom'.[96] The scene then switches immediately to the field of Borodino – where our viewing position places us outside Napoleon's tent, so we can hear his disembodied voice addressing his generals.[97] The implication is simple: not only is the semi-chorus of the years correct in dismissing 'Space and Time' as an irrelevant 'fancy', but also Hardy is underlining the fact that his central protagonists are largely interchangeable. They are merely masks through which the universal process objectifies itself, or, in accordance with the mesmeric paradigm, puppets through which the mesmerist projects himself through a form of mental ventriloquism.[98]

The novels, I would argue, resonate to a similar soundscape, Hardy's characters being transformed into masks through which the wider process objectifies itself in a form of ventriloquism. Hardy even gives his heroines musically delineated voices, Eustacia the 'viola voice', Tess a 'flute-like voice', and Paula Power the tones of 'a flute at the grave end of its gamut', emphasising that they are merely 'organ-stops' on a vast cosmic instrument.[99] Their powerlessness is demonstrated clearly in the way that Hardy subverts the cliché of 'love at first sight' by bringing them together with their lovers through the power of the 'arresting voice'. Connor argues that 'because a voice is an event in time, something that happens to us, even happens on us, in a way that an object presented for sight is not, the experience of hearing something with one's own ears is much more importunate and encroaching than seeing it with one's own eyes', and the most powerful of all voices is that which is 'a voice without an origin,... a voice immune to the powers of the eye and the categorical cognitive functions associated with it'.[100] It is just such a voice that interrupts the reverie of Angel one morning during breakfast at Talbothays, drawing him to the unseen Tess.[101]

The scene is crafted around musical allusion, with an interesting precedent in George Eliot's *Daniel Deronda* (1876). For Eliot it is the singing voice of Deronda which is first heard by Mirah Cohen as she stands on the river bank. The narrator notes that 'apparently his voice had entered her inner world without her having taken any note of whence it came', turning her away from her contemplated suicide (in accordance with Schopenhauerian theory concerning will-annihilation) and creating a bond of sympathy with the unknown singer.[102] For Hardy, the self-absorbed Angel is depicted rehearsing in his imagination a recently conned musical score to which all those present quiver in harmony, except for the 'flute-like voice', which is out of harmony with his orchestration. Through voice tone she is marked out and selected by Angel, Hardy noting that he 'seemed to discern in her something that was familiar, something which carried him back into a joyous and unforeseen past, before the necessity of taking thought had made the heavens grey'.[103] Although ostensibly referring to the chance meeting at the dance, this observation seems to allude to a deeper Darwinian familiarity that precedes the birth of consciousness, which announces the same 'affinity *in posse*' that passes between Jude and Arabella.[104]

From this moment onwards such tone acts as a privileged means of communication between them: Angel 'persistently wooed her in undertones like that of the purling milk' so that 'every sound of his voice beginning on the old subject [of marriage] stirred her with a terrifying bliss'.[105] Ultimately his voice becomes part of the web of compulsion against which the fallen Tess must struggle in order to maintain her conception of her own purity, a conflict that Hardy presents in physiological terms: 'every see-saw of her breath, every wave of her blood, every pulse singing in her ears, was a voice that joined with nature in revolt against her scrupulousness'.[106]

Repeatedly in Hardy's fiction it is the disembodied voice, often at night and in isolation, that brings Hardy's lovers together. Felicia Miller Frank links the power of such a voice to Edmund Burke's aesthetics of the sublime – 'a source of intense stimulation that is uncapturable in representation'.[107] There is certainly a sense of the sublime in the single disembodied 'goodnight!' that draws Eustacia to Clym in the darkness of Egdon Heath, and the similarly isolated meeting of Ethelberta and Christopher Julian on a lonely heath.[108] Both offer no mere attraction: in the latter Hardy describes how 'at hearing him speak all the delicate activities in the young lady's person stood still: she stopped like a clock. When she could again fence with the perception which had caused all this she breathed.'[109] As with the late poem 'The Destined Pair' or 'The Convergence of the Twain', there is a sense in which Ethelberta has found her predestined 'mate'.[110] The Titanic, a ship and therefore feminine, is depicted on its maiden voyage as bent upon a coincident path with its 'sinister mate', the 'Shape of Ice' fashioned by 'the Immanent Will that stirs and urges everything'.[111] Just as the ship and iceberg form 'twin halves of one august event', Ethelberta's poetry and Julian's music are presented as two 'parts of an organic whole'. When they are performed together, Hardy is at pains to emphasise the physiological impact upon Ethelberta – the consummation brought about as two hemispheres jar – and she finds herself 'walk[ing] in circles about the carpet' of her bedroom attempting to dissipate the excess of nervous energy.[112]

We have already remarked upon the quasi-scientific manner in which Hardy presents desire in *The Woodlanders*, but this becomes most obvious in his use of voice tone to indicate the mutual attraction of Fitzpiers and Felice Charmond. It is noticeable that no such tone attends his relationship with Grace; the impetus here is always visual, often reflected. Fitzpiers idealises Grace in order to fall in love with her, and then immediately falls out of love when she has been captured. It is a succession of events that he labels 'Nature's Law', a principle Hardy distils into a frosty entry in *The Life*: 'Love lives on propinquity, but dies of contact.'[113] This process does not influence Fitzpiers' wooing of Felice, however, since her unobtainability keeps his ardour from cooling. If, as he candidly acknowledges, he is 'charged with emotive fluid like a Leyden jar with electric, for want of some conductor', then the physiological metaphor finds its corollary in the 'vibratory tones' which attend their brief romance.[114] It is Felice's voice that spans time and links the present encounter with the interrupted love affair carried on in Heidelberg, thus convincing Fitzpiers of the powerlessness of the 'human will against predestination'.[115] It is also her voice tone that undermines the language of the intellect, and therefore her conscious attempt to control their passion. When, for example, she attempts to assert her sense of morally appropriate behaviour and begs Fitzpiers not to visit her again, it is contradicted by 'tones whose modulation incited him to disobey'.[116]

Perhaps the clearest example of Hardy's use of voice tone as an agent of compulsion is to be found in *The Well-Beloved*, in which a casual conversation about laundry between Jocelyn Pierston and the second incarnation of Avice Caro is transformed into an illustration of the laws of attraction. Indeed, Hardy's reference to a capitalised 'Nature... working her plans for the next generation under the cloak of a dialogue on linen', invokes directly the sacrifice of the individual to the species discussed by both Asher and Zimmern.[117] Hardy expands upon this theme when Pierston hears Avice's voice in another room:

> she attracted him by the cadences of her voice; she would suddenly drop it to a rich whisper of roguishness, when the slight rural monotony of its narrative speech disappeared, and soul and heart – or what seemed soul and heart – resounded. The charm lay in the intervals, using that word in its musical sense. She would say a few syllables in one note, and end her sentence in a soft modulation upwards, then downwards, then into her own note again...
>
> The subject of her discourse he cared nothing about – it was no more his interest than his concern. He took special pains that in catching her voice he might not comprehend her words. To tones he had a right, none to the articulations. By degrees he could not exist long without this sound.[118]

Significantly, it is not the content of Avice's discourse that is important, but the musicality of her tone, which in common with Hardy's other musical threads indicates the activity of wider process undermining the language of the intellect.

The privileging of voice tone as a means of communication between sensitive individuals begs the question, what happens to Spencer's 'dry language of the intellect' in Hardy's novels? It was concluded in Chapter 2 that the free will of Hardy's puppets is comparatively small, their lives for the most part being directed by forces beyond their control. Consequently, both plans and actions that attempt to impose the will of the individual on the universe are at best meaningless and at worst catastrophic. The only path to true harmony lies in the use of free will to adapt to the harsh effects of necessity.[119] In the novels, therefore, the language of the intellect is relatively unimportant: a fact illustrated by a cameo in *The Dynasts* that shows several characters in the crowd that gathers to celebrate the victory of Nelson at Trafalgar admonishing one onlooker for 'opening and shutting his mouth like the rest' but emitting no sound.[120] In his defence he states that since his voice makes no difference in the general hubbub he may as well conserve his breath on grounds of economy. In effect, since speech is a function of the intellect which is subordinate to the wider universal process, words cannot alter the destiny of man, rather they are, as Metternich observes, mere 'bubbles…aimless in their shape'.[121]

Much of the dialogue in Hardy's novels consists of Metternich's 'bubbles'. Pities criticises parliament for believing that any 'power lay in their oraclings', an admonishment that could be extended to Alec d'Urberville as he delivers his sermon in the Evershead village barn. Here, the 'good new words' are delivered in Alec's 'bad old notes', the 'lineaments' of his face 'seem[ing] to complain' because they were being 'diverted from their hereditary connotations to signify impressions for which Nature did not intend them'.[122] Thus, despite Alec's devotion to the words of his text, these are merely a function of the intellect, or bubbles. He is still a puppet through which the 'bad old notes' of his brutal ancestors objectify themselves, and therefore he is powerless to divert himself from the destiny laid out by his heredity endowment.

In the novels, then, all speech, all plans and indeed all acts based upon the intellect are a gamble upon the destiny of the individual: a belief Hardy emphasises by the inclusion of a playing card motif to describe some exchanges between characters. In *A Laodicean*, for example, William Dare continually gambles on his destiny by manipulating his father in a series of reminiscences sprinkled with references to card play.[123] In *The Mayor of Casterbridge* Lucetta Templeman plays with a pack of cards whilst reinventing her past history, therefore gambling with both time and destiny before a circumspect Elizabeth-Jane.[124] In *The Return of the Native*, Hardy demonstrates the awkwardness of words as a means of emotional communication by peppering certain exchanges with references to gambling. Diggory Venn's highly charged meeting with Eustacia is brought to a head by his decision to play 'the card of truth'; and Mrs Yeobright is described as not playing '*every* card' at her disposal in her negotiations with Wildeve.[125]

Perhaps not surprisingly, words are at their most futile in the dialogues between Hardy's lovers; a fact illustrated by the first exchange between Eustacia and Clym (which will be analysed in Chapter 5) and the following conversation between Tess and Angel immediately following the garden scene:

'What makes you draw off in that way, Tess?' said he. 'Are you afraid?'
'Oh no, sir…not of outdoor things; especially just now when the apple-blooth is falling, and everything so green.'

'But you have your indoor fears – eh?'
'Well, yes, sir.'
'What of?'
'I couldn't quite say.'
'The milk turning sour?'
'No.'
'Life in general?'
'Yes, Sir.'
'Ah – so have I, very often. This hobble of being alive is rather serious, don't you think so?'
'It is – now you put it that way.'[126]

The contrast with the perfectly weighted garden scene could not be greater: the mixture of bucolic detail and homespun philosophy appears awkward, indeed, Hardy at his worst, whilst Angel's curiosity and Tess' passivity transforms the whole exchange into an interrogation rather than a love scene. But Hardy's apparent clumsiness simply underlines the inadequacy of words as a means of expressing their feelings. They exist in two separate linguistic worlds, which never seem to touch: the social inferiority of Tess is immediately highlighted by her deferential 'sir', whilst her inability to find words to express the way she feels is marked by her 'I couldn't quite say.' Similarly, Angel is unable to speak to Tess, but rather carries on a conversation with his idealised 'virginal daughter of Nature' about what he believes are suitably countrified worries. Ironically, as he stumbles into the clichéd 'Life in general' he identifies a common source of concern, squeezing into the constraining lexicon of words those feelings that Tess has actually suffered. It is music that breaks through the constrictions of the 'dry language of the intellect', releasing those dimly felt emotions which become, for Tess, something against which she must struggle.

In a similar way, the attempts of Jude and Sue to find the appropriate words to express their feelings often means that their dialogues are reduced to the exchange of aphorisms accumulated from contemporary and ancient authors. As J. I. M. Stewart has observed, 'Sue talks of the house of Atreus and Jude immediately comes back at her with the house of Jeroboam.'[127] In one characteristic example, Sue clothes herself in the aphorisms of Mill to explain why she is parting from her husband, leaving a bemused Phillotson to exclaim, 'what do I care about J. S. Mill!'[128] The only time they appear to connect with one another is, as will be seen later, under the influence of music and voice tone. Jude, like Hardy's other tragic lovers, is initially drawn to 'certain qualities of his own voice; softened and sweetened', which he can detect in the accents of

Sue.[129] This is their true medium of communication, Jude picking up 'every vibration in Sue's voice', enabling him to 'read every symptom of her mental condition'.[130]

In a fictional world in which the individual is ensnared in a web of merciless determinism, falling in love is transformed into a brutal and often violent experience. Hardy's characters become puppets through which the universal process, which incorporates both the will of Schopenhauer and the species instinct of Darwin, objectifies itself. Hardy evokes the powerlessness of the individual by reinvigorating the Romantic symbol of the harp, the strings of which not only invoke his wider web, but also, in accordance with contemporary scientific research, the fibres of human nervous system. The shock of instantaneous desire felt by a number of Hardy's tremulous heroines, therefore, is an ungovernable reaction brought about when this harp is made to vibrate in consonance with Hardy's male protagonists by means of either musical performance or simply the qualities of voice tone. In its most physical manifestation, Car'line Aspent's susceptible nervous disposition means that she is physiologically determined to react to the vibrating strings of Mop Ollamoor's violin. In a more complex example such as that of the garden scene at Talbothays dairy, Tess is deliberately aligned with an uncultivated, fecund nature, and Angel's harp playing with the mating call by which man's distant progenitors sought to attract their partners during a form of Darwinian courtship ritual.

The harp string plucked by musical performance also vibrates in consonance with the vocal chords, lending to speech tone a power of sexual attraction otherwise unaccountable for in Hardy's fiction. Voice tone, according to the principles of speech theory, is the musical element of language which hearkens back to the primitive language of the emotions by which man's distant progenitors communicated. Hardy's musically delineated voice tones objectify the wider process, penetrating individual spheres of consciousness, and bringing together all his lovers under an irresistible force of compulsion. From their first meeting, the voice is central to the relationships of all Hardy's central protagonists, undermining the emptiness of the language of the intellect, objectifying the wider process and performing the function of the chief medium of communication between characters of a similar sensibility.

In the chapters that follow it is my aim to analyse how our knowledge of Hardy's employment of musical allusion enriches our reading of *The Return of the Native*, *The Mayor of Casterbridge* and *Jude the Obscure*. All share the broad characteristics that have been explored both in this and in the previous chapter, but each presents very different variations, which precludes a more thematic type of study. One particular advantage of this chronological method of analysis is that the evolution of Hardy's art towards a more experimental novelistic genre can be seen clearly. Another advantage of this method is that it demonstrates quite clearly how music acts in the novels as that medium that draws together the events unfolding in the narrative into an organic unity. With these considerations in mind, I turn to *The Return of the Native*, in which it is possible to see the 'sad music of humanity' underpinning Hardy's own version of the 'Artwork of the Future'.

5

A Tale of 'Tragical Possibilities': Music and the Birth of Consciousness in *The Return of the Native*

In a note made in *The Life* on 22 April 1878 Hardy acknowledges his debt to the Dutch landscape artist Meindert Hobbema for the idea of using man-made features to infuse human emotion into the baldest external scenes of nature.[1] In the painterly description of the road dissecting Egdon Heath, which employs such techniques as chiaroscuro and alterations in perspective and viewpoint, Hardy appears to be attempting just such an infusion, not of a single emotion, but of human consciousness. The thread-like sinuousness, yet inviolate brightness of the road appears like 'the parting-line on a head of black hair'; whilst the surrounding dark shades of the heath compose 'The face upon which Time makes little impression' (p. 34). It is the face of a partially anthropomorphised universal process which, like Spencer's Absolute, is subject to the same laws that it propagates. Yet despite the harshness of these laws, the heath endures, its undulating contours making it impervious to the harsh 'unweeting wind' of necessity.

Such a face also appears in the 'everlasting heath' covered with barrows 'like warts on a swarthy skin' in *The Hand of Ethelberta*,[2] and also in Hardy's presentation of the dunes surrounding Scheveningen in *A Laodicean*, of which De Stancy notes 'it always seems to me that this place reflects the average mood of human life'.[3] While Paula screens herself by means of an umbrella, and the small village snuggles behind its sea wall, the dunes endure through their very mediocrity. Like Scheveningen, Egdon in the twilight was:

> Perfectly accordant with man's nature – neither ghastly, hateful, nor ugly: neither commonplace, unmeaning, nor tame; but, like man, slighted and enduring. . . . It had a lonely face, suggesting tragical possibilities. (p. 33)

It is a face which not only reflects the qualities necessary for survival in Hardy's harsh universe, but also hints at the 'tragical possibilities' brought about through the birth of consciousness. Indeed, if Egdon is Hardy's Eden 'before the birth of consciousness', then the sinuous road is his malicious snake, bringing with it the 'disease of feeling'.[4] For with consciousness comes not only the capacity for the individual to understand the hopelessness of his situation, but also the belief that he can use his free will to change it. Through this last course of action the individual attempts to impose his will upon the universe, which leads to a Promethean conflict with tragic consequences. For in Hardy's world survivors are not those who attempt to change their circumstances with energy, but rather those who accept their lot and use their modicum of free will to make life endurable.

Egdon's tale is recorded not simply in its enduring features, but also in the faces of those who live upon it. Hardy's privileging of this feature coincided with a new attitude to the face brought about by the publication of Darwin's *The Expression of Emotions in Man and Animals* (1872). Prior to this date, as Jonathan Crary's work has made clear, the face was a feature to be interpreted according to the terms of rhetoric set out in Charles Le Brun's 1698 treatise on emotional expression. Darwin was the first to make the face both a 'symptom of an organism's anatomical and physiological functioning and its relative impenetrability . . .'.[5] For Hardy the face is both, like the inky depths of Egdon, impenetrable, and also symptomatic of the struggle between consciousness and the wider process. In the spring of 1876 he was reading Jowett's *Dialogues of Plato*, from which he noted the Hellenic ideal of the 'beautiful youth'.[6] But in the face of Clym Yeobright he acknowledges that the 'ideal physical beauty is incompatible with emotional development and a full recognition of the coil of things' (p. 162). This is the face of the future: a face that bears testimony to the 'destructive interdependence of spirit and flesh'. It is revisited in the face of George Somerset, which 'had more of the beauty – if beauty it ought to be called – of the future type than of the past', and also the 'half-apathetic expression' of Susan Henchard, a woman who 'deems anything possible at the hands of Time and Chance except, perhaps, fair play'.[7]

It is also a tale told through Hardy's soundscape, underpinned by the music of the heath which collapses both space and time in accordance with the Classical unities of the novel. To take a stroll on Egdon, therefore, as we are invited to do by Hardy's narrator (who constantly varies the narrative distance and implicates us in the text through the allusion to vagaries such as 'an emotional listener') is to enter Babbage's 'great library'. Hardy achieves the same effect at the beginning of the short story 'The Melancholy Hussar of the German Legion', in which the narrator opens by taking a walk on the downs at night and catches the sounds of the soldiers who camped there ninety years ago:

> At night, when I walk across the lonely place, it is impossible to avoid hearing, amid the scourings of the wind over the grass-bents and thistles the old trumpet and bugle calls, the rattle of the halters; . . . guttural syllables of foreign tongues, and broken songs of the fatherland.[8]

Here, the narrator is transformed from a nostalgic storyteller to a being sensitive to the sounds of a romance which still resonate in the air. The tale, therefore, does not exist in memory, but is recorded on the very air and in the earth of the downs upon which the romance took place – a narrative structure which has great bearing for the conception of Egdon's tale. Whereas the downs echo to the 'broken songs of the fatherland', which evoke an atmosphere of melancholy nostalgia, Egdon's music possesses a 'great resemblance to the ruins of human song' – a description that invokes both Spencer's ideas concerning the origins of music and speech, and Schopenhauerian metaphysics.

As was established in Chapter 4, in the mid-century the art of song was held as an important staging post in terms of evolutionary theory, with Darwin, Gurney and Spencer offering very different interpretations of its role in the emotional and linguistic development of man. Spencer's unusual Lamarckian interpretation presents 'song' as the perfect fusion of intellect and emotion, in which impassioned speech is exaggerated and systematised according to musical laws. In evolutionary terms, Spencer argues, this fusion has been corrupted through the irresistible principle governing all phenomena, which asserts that 'organic progress consists in a change from the homogeneous to the heterogeneous'. As a consequence, song has evolved in two divergent directions, the language of the passions eventually evolving into music, the language of ideas continuing to evolve into the dry 'language of the intellect'.[9] Hardy's support for Spencer's 'speech theory' in the *Literary Notebooks* is helpful in interpreting his analogy between the music of the heath and the 'ruins of human song' here, for it evokes the passing of a time when man was able to express his feelings before the evolution of the intellect led to a reliance upon language.[10] In a novel that focuses clearly on the difficulty of communication, the music of Egdon offers an alternative means of emotional expression to the limited power of words, those 'rusty implements of a by-gone barbarous epoch' incapable of encompassing real feeling or shaping destiny (p. 190).

Like Babbage's great library, then, the heath echoes to the songs of men who were in harmony with each other and the world around them, and it is these songs that are reincarnated in the performances of the present 'crop of the heath', the Egdon rustics – most notably those of Grandfer Cantle. This sense of reincarnation is important, for invoking distant ancestors Hardy is asking interesting questions concerning the relationship between music and memory. For Hughes 'the evocation of the sounds of the past' that opens the tale of the Melancholy Hussar offers 'the narrator a way of banishing the present, and moving into the earlier time of the romance between the hussar and Phyllis': in effect music becomes a 'veritable time machine'.[11]

But Hardy is not simply evoking a lost historical moment through the music of Egdon, rather he is reawakening it in the mind of the listener. In this context, as Tim Armstrong has noted, the work of Spencer and Haweis is significant, for they argue that music does not simply echo previously experienced emotions, but it reanimates them in the listener through its capacity to re-create the same physiological state. This position accords entirely with Schopenhauer, who argued that musical experience does not offer an actual moment, but rather the abstract suffering of the will.[12] To say that its music is transferable to the present chorus of rustics, therefore, is not simply to recognise a nostalgic connection with the past, but to identify in their singing the indestructible qualities of the wider process.

The music of Egdon, therefore, telescopes history, adding to the sense that the tale about to unfold has been told many times before. Unfortunately, his central protagonists remain deaf to such music, Hardy noting of Eustacia's vigil on top of Rainbarrow that she 'took no notice of the windy tune still played on the dead heath-bells' (p. 73), and it is within this deafness that Hardy locates the 'tragical possibilities' of the novel. Around it he is able to construct his vision of 'the art of the future', a Classically inspired work in which the Aeolian modulations of Egdon and the songs of the rustics perform the function of a Wagnerian chorus continually reminding the reader of the wider process that underpins the behaviour of his characters.[13] Hardy makes this quite clear in the 'prelude' of Eustacia's twilight vigil on top of Rainbarrow, in which her apparent dominance of her surroundings is undermined by Hardy's careful orchestration of the heath music. Through its music Hardy collapses the linear nature of time into a transcendent moment to remind us that she is simply an extension of her environment – a truth to which she remains tragically deaf.

Hardy also illustrates these Wagnerian aspects of the novel in the opening description of the 'sky-backed pantomime' of the heathmen on top of Rainbarrow: a scene that acts as a dumb show to the rest of the novel as the main themes are worked out under the influence of music. As with the prelude, there is in Hardy's orchestration of this scene a hypnotic quality that embraces the author, narrator and reader into a transcendent moment. The scene is infused with uncertainty: initially the observing consciousness is that of Diggory Venn, but as this telescopes out through the 'traveller's eye' and the 'imaginative stranger' to the 'looker on', it is clear that this latter figure is to perform the function of a 'surrogate reader', thereby giving the dramatic display a sense of immediacy (pp. 37–38). Ostensibly the heathmen gather to celebrate November Fifth, but Hardy's allusion to the myth of Prometheus transforms their bonfire into a symbol of the gift of consciousness. Like Eustacia, the heathmen do not arrive on the barrow but emerge from the inky depths of the heath, the first appearing like 'a bush on legs' (p. 39). This blurring of the distinction between the organic and the inorganic continues as the flames momentarily elevate them from the 'dark stretches' of the heath to 'some radiant upper storey of the world' where 'all was unstable; quivering as leaves, evanescent as lightning' (p. 41). In this Paterian flux the heathmen are transformed from men into phantoms bearing the attributes of men, with cavernous 'lantern jaws', nostrils like 'dark wells', and 'shadowy eye-sockets' in which 'eyeballs glowed like little lanterns' (p. 41). Their conversation revolves around the subject of dancing, and as Timothy Fairway enumerates the times when he has enjoyed its pleasures – Christmas, christening and marriage, all except a funeral – it is clear that Hardy is looking beyond these specific examples to the wider 'dance of life', which marks the evolution of man through the various stages of his life (p. 45).

To illustrate this point, Hardy has Grandfer Cantle, who is nearing the end of this cycle, participate in two dances (one of joyous rebellion and one of resignation), and also sing a song. Both are important in establishing Hardy's Wagnerian chorus. Warmed by the flames he begins 'to jig a private minuet', but the presence of his walking stick and his lack of breath reminds the reader of the vulnerability of both human consciousness and individual action in the determined world (p. 42). Because of his infirmity he is forced to cease until, as the fire begins to burn out (signifying the individual relinquishing consciousness), he becomes a 'three-legged object' in a dance which takes place in its embers (p. 52). Rainbarrow is transformed into a 'whirling of dark shapes amid a boiling confusion of sparks' animated by 'the strumming of the wind upon the furze-bushes, which formed a kind of tune to the demoniac measure they trod' (p. 52). It becomes one of Hardy's dances, demonstrating that even the rebellious individual can achieve a degree of equanimity by submerging his portion of the will in the wider process. Thus, as Hardy's perspective is enlarged, the pagan pantomime is transformed into a dumb show underpinned by a Wagnerian chorus which informs both participants and readers of the message central to the tale about to unfold: that it is wiser for the individual to accept his fate and dance in tune with the universal process, than rebel and find oneself out of step. The warning given, the participants sink back into the heath to form the thorn bushes shaped like 'jumping madmen, sprawling giants, and hideous cripples' observed by Johnny Nunsuch during his journey after his duties as Eustacia's fire tender (p. 87).

Cantle's song is also significant in establishing the part played by the rustics in Hardy's Wagnerian chorus. On one level his breathless rendition signifies the irrepressibility of human endurance and a determination to spread good cheer, a theme to which Hardy returns in the short poem 'Christmastide'. In it a despondent narrator trudging along a dark road with only the 'sighing' bushes for company, is cheered by a chance meeting with a 'sodden tramp', who, despite the poverty of his condition, breaks into a 'thin song' whilst wishing 'A merry Christmas, friend!'[14] It offers a striking image of Hardy's conception of the human condition: the life of man is reduced to that of an isolated individual navigating his way through the gloom surrounded by the discordant tones of a suffering universe. Enlightenment comes through suffering: the tramp offers a model of endurance combined with a determination to make the best of limited opportunities for happiness and to spread good will. Thus, Cantle's song echoes the ruined songs of his distant ancestors, men who understood this message and lived in harmony with the music of the heath.

Cantle's song also, as C. M. Jackson-Houlston has observed, has a very real choric function in this scene, in that Hardy uses its text to comment on the main love triangle between Wildeve, Eustacia and Clym.[15] 'Queen Eleanor's Confession' tells the tale of Eleanor's seduction by the Earl Marshall prior to her marriage to King Henry, and her subsequent confession when the two men visit her disguised as friars.[16] The unhappy king is only prevented from executing his rival through a promise he had cleverly extorted earlier. Through Cantle's ludicrously inappropriate rendition here Hardy is able to introduce the theme of infidelity into the general talk of marriage, and hint, in a way that would bypass the censorious pen of Mrs Grundy, that Eustacia has been Wildeve's mistress before her marriage. Furthermore, the focus on confession also anticipates the prevarication of Wildeve before the inquisition of Mrs Yeobright, and the arrogance of Eustacia before Venn's patient questioning. Ironically, as Jackson-Houlston notes, confession remains something that Eustacia is bad at, leading to tragic consequences.

Hardy's text is permeated with the songs of the Egdon rustics, mainly those of Grandfer Cantle. His ribald repertoire focuses almost exclusively on sexual matters, thus reminding the reader of the Darwinian instinct that underlies so many of the awkward protestations of love. This is particularly apparent in his proposed rendition of 'Down in Cupid's Gardens' and 'The Foggy Dew' to serenade the newly married Thomasin and Diggory Venn, songs that cut through Diggory's stultifying sense of chivalry and inability to articulate himself to ensure through double-entendre that 'Cheerfulness Again Asserts Itself at Blooms-End'.[17]

Through the set pieces of the 'prelude' and 'dumb show' that take place on Rainbarrow Hardy is seeking to establish for the reader an understanding of the appropriate relationship between his characters and the forces motivating their behaviour – a connection explored further through the mumming of St George. As was seen in Chapter 3, Hardy's insistence on the powerlessness of his puppets in *The Dynasts* led to his depiction of them carrying out their activities in a dream-like state, whilst their lines were delivered in the 'curiously hypnotising...automatic style' of the Christmas mummers, who resemble 'persons who spoke by no will of their own'.[18] Hardy seeks to achieve a similar effect in *The Return of the Native*, actually introducing the Christmas mummers into the second part of the novel to perform the function of a 'play within a play' demonstrating the correct relationship between his characters and the controlling influence of the heath. Indeed, Eustacia objects to the whole performance, as well she might, because 'the agents seem moved by an inner-compulsion to say and do their allotted parts whether they will or no' (p. 128). In effect, within the novel as a whole Hardy's central protagonists are little more than mummers taking on roles that have been handed down for generations in the 'Timeworn Drama' of love and betrayal: Eustacia is the passionate heroine; Clym the self-absorbed thinker; Wildeve the pantomime lady-killer; and Mrs Yeobright the aggrieved mother.[19]

Hardy draws out this parallel further through his emphasis on how the speech of his characters contributes to the soundscape of the novel, in particular the attribution of various 'murmurings'. The verb of speech is significant, since it is applicable to the sound made by natural phenomenon such as the wind in the trees or the movement of water (both of which might be considered objectifications of the universal process) and it also evokes the art of mumming.[20] Thus, the murmur joins the chorus of other pre-verbal expressions such as groans and sighs that signal the presence of the universal process, indicating that Hardy's puppets are speaking 'by no will of their own' and are simply fulfilling the role to which they have been assigned in the 'Timeworn Drama'. Mrs Yeobright's resignation to the inevitability of her son's attraction to Eustacia, for example, is signified by her murmured 'there is no help for it' (p. 178); Eustacia, tempted by Wildeve's contemplation of a trip to Paris, utters a murmur 'that was nearly a sigh' which expresses the re-emergence of her true desires (p. 277); a self-absorbed Clym murmurs 'mother' in his sleepy response to her rap at the door (p. 263); and Wildeve's envy of Clym is captured in his murmured 'if he were only to die' (p. 288).

Hardy repeats this technique in *The Well-Beloved*, in which the love affair of Jocelyn Pierston and Marcia Bencomb is undermined by their own murmured comments. These provide a sub-plot which suggests that, despite their love and devotion, they are simply puppets through which their ancestors are playing out their animosity. These ancestral tones are first heard in the 'sardonic voices, and laughter in the wind' which Pierston hears during the 'development of his little romance'.[21] But it is quickly transformed into murmured exchanges, such as Marcia's murmured 'your father is my father's enemy', and Pierston's murmured acquiescence to the prophetic observation that 'I don't think we shall get over it at all.'[22] Ironically, both not only acknowledge the role of heredity in the failure of their romance, but also its intrinsic theatricality: a point made apparent in Pierston's reference to their doomed forbears: 'hereditarily we are mortal enemies, dear Juliet'.[23]

In Hardy's world, all other speech is a function of the intellect and therefore meaningless; a state of affairs emphasised through the playing card motif used in the exchanges between several characters to indicate that words are simply a gamble on destiny. Diggory Venn's highly charged meeting with Eustacia, for example, is brought to a head by his decision to play 'the card of truth'; and Mrs Yeobright is described as not playing '*every* card' at her disposal in her negotiations with Wildeve. The limitations of language are also emphasised by the poverty of some of the dialogue in the novel, something illustrated by the following exchange which passes between Eustacia and Clym when they are actually face to face for the first time:

'Are you a woman – or am I wrong?'
'I am a woman.'
His eyes lingered on her with great interest. 'Do girls often play as mummers now? They never used to.'

'They don't now.'
'Why did you?'
'To get excitement and shake off depression,' she said in low tones.
'What depressed you?'
'Life.'
'That's a cause of depression a good many have put up with.'
'Yes.'
A long silence. (p. 147)

Such an exchange anticipates that which passes between Angel and Tess following the garden scene, and seems to vindicate Rutland's dismissal of the dialogue as an 'unconvincing blemish' on the novel.[24] He has rather missed the point: the dialogue is stilted because Hardy wishes to emphasise its emptiness. Words are what Metternich describes in *The Dynasts* as mere 'bubbles... aimless in their shape', Eustacia and Clym are brought together by means other than the intellect, which is why 'no language could reach the level of their condition' (p. 190).

The poverty of language is also made abundantly clear during the first tryst between Eustacia and Wildeve. As the lovers attempt to untangle their emotions, gambling with words and seeing what effect they have on one another, the only sound of true purport can be heard in a lull in their conversation when the Wagnerian chorus of the heath reminds the reader of the wider process controlling their desire:

> the pause was filled up by the intonation of a pollard thorn a little way to windward, the breezes filtering through its unyielding twigs as through a strainer. It was as if the night sang dirges with clenched teeth. (p. 96)

And a little later,

> acoustic pictures were returned from the darkened scenery; they could hear where the tracts of heather began and ended;...in what direction the fir-clump lay, and how near was the pit in which the hollies grew; for these differing features had their voices no less than their shapes and colours. (p. 97)

The harshness of the image created by the 'thorn' and 'unyielding twigs' combines uneasily with the sexual connotations that lie behind the submerged fronds of the 'hollies' to remind the reader that in Hardy's universe desire is an emotion to be suffered rather than enjoyed. This is particularly so for Eustacia, whose passion is not focused upon the individual, but rather upon the general need 'to be loved to madness' (p. 84). Having ensnared Wildeve, she is dissatisfied and searching for something new, a psychological state that Hardy explores, not as George Eliot may have done, through his heroine's introspection, but through the Wagnerian chorus of the heath. For one of the voices brought to her is that of the fir clump, which was 'enclosed from the heath land in the year of [Clym's] birth', and therefore performs the function of a leitmotif bringing musical 'Tidings of the Comer' (pp. 115, 201).

From the first premonitory sounds of the trees, then, there is an inevitability that surrounds their relationship, a quality identified by one of the first reviews of the novel printed in the *Saturday Review* of 4 January 1879, which states that Hardy's protagonists seem to be drawn 'towards each other instinctively', and in such a way that 'harmony' between 'highly pitched' minds could only end in 'discord and tragedy'.[25] The choice of metaphor is significant, because it demonstrates an instinctive grasp of the musical tissue through which the wider process is made to operate in the novel. It is heard again almost immediately following Eustacia's exposure to the voice of the firs, as Hardy isolates her at Mistover Knap and allows the disembodied voices of the rustic chorus to pass down the chimney 'instinctively coupl[ing]' Clym and herself as 'a pair born for each other' and in perfect 'harmony' (p. 117).

Hardy further emphasises this sense of inevitability by focusing on the physiological power of Clym's voice tone over Eustacia. In the simple disembodied 'single goodnight' with which Clym first greets her, Hardy is careful here to emphasise that 'it was not to the words that Eustacia listened' but to Clym's 'accents'. In accordance with the physiological research of both Spencer and Bain, her reaction is recorded not in terms of thoughts, a response that engages the intellect, but in the physical alterations of her features as they 'went through a rhythmical succession' of changes enabling her to 'picture' the man 'for whom she had predetermined to nourish a passion' (p. 124). Tone, therefore, not sight or language, acts as the physiological agent of necessity drawing them together; Hardy's invocation of Dr Kitto, whose memoirs emphasised the human capacity for the blind to draw pictures from sound, lending to this a physiological credibility.[26] Hardy actually read about Kitto in his copy of Spencer's *The Principles of Biology* (1864), his work generally challenging the conception of a transcendent 'self' in favour of a series of 'psychical states' which conform to laws just as easily as simple reflex action.[27] For Spencer, then, this disembodied voice has a physiological effect that produces in Eustacia a new set of relationships concerning its owner.

This is manifested, as it is with Kitto, in what Connor has described as an instinctive attempt to create pictures out of sound 'to fix and spatialize... what is by its very nature transient'.[28] Ironically for Eustacia it is just such a picture that emerges from her subconscious in 'the Great Dream' – a medium which is both transient and unreliable.

In the latter half of the nineteenth century, as the research of Henri Ellenberger has demonstrated, dreams, like so many other aspects of psychological study, were being dissected in the laboratory, culminating in the dynamic psychology of Freud.[29] The Romantic conception of the dreaming soul escaping from the ties of the body was being replaced by a physiological model in which, according to Johannes Volkelt's *Dream Phantasy* (1875), dreams translate 'bodily impressions directly into symbols'.[30] This, of course, allowed dreams to become a more accurate guide to a sub-conscious explorable by scientific means, whether by experimenting with external stimulation (popular in the work of Maury, *Sleep and Dreams* (1861)) or interpreting symbols (Friedrich Theodor Vischer's studies on dreams are typical (1875)).[31]

Eustacia's girlish dream of dancing with a knight in shining armour is open to just such fashionable interpretation, highlighting as it does the paradox central to her character: for the knight's visor remains shut, indicating that Clym's 'awakening voice' does not provoke desire for him, but a 'long[ing] for the abstraction called passionate love more than for any particular lover' (pp. 84, 126). Although she interprets the dream as being 'meant for Mr. Yeobright', the crumbling of the knight 'into fragments like a pack of cards' upon removing his helmet reminds the reader that attempts to deduce one's destiny remain nothing more than a gamble (pp. 124, 125). The only correct conclusion to be drawn from the dream is that Eustacia is only in harmony with the 'wondrous music' of the ambivalent process when she is satisfying her objectless passion (p. 124).

Despite the vagaries of Eustacia's character Hardy makes it quite clear during their first meeting at Mistover Knap (during which Clym joins the other heathmen to retrieve the bucket from Captain Vye's well) that they are a pair destined for each other. Details such as his mother's murmured warning, the description of his walking 'with a will, ... as straight as a line', and the shadow advancing in front of him emphasise the inevitability surrounding this meeting that transforms it into 'The First Act in a Timeworn Drama' (p. 178). This sense is further increased by the seemingly innocuous addition to the original manuscript of the word 'kiss' to describe the sound of the bucket striking the water (p. 179). As with the term 'murmur', the malleability of this term makes it an ideal tool to express the immutable and indestructible universal process manifesting itself through the organ-stops of both man and Nature. It becomes part of Babbage's great library, a feature made more explicit in the late poem 'A Kiss', when it becomes a sound that circles the earth waiting for a mask, either organic or inorganic, through which to objectify itself: 'That kiss is gone where none can tell – / Not even those who felt its spell: / It cannot have died; that know we well'.[32] In this particular scene the kiss of the bucket acts as the dominant, unifying tone, to which, through another alteration to the manuscript, Eustacia adds her spirit-like disembodied tones from an elevated position.[33] It reminds the reader of the kiss denied to Eustacia in her dream; it anticipates the sound of her voice at the window as well as Clym's desire to kiss her rope-burned arm, and their eventual passionate kisses (pp. 179, 182).

As was suggested in Chapter 3, Mrs Yeobright has a 'singular insight into life' that periodically raises her above the role of the aggrieved mother and allows her to take in at a glance the wider process underpinning the domestic drama (p. 85). She understands the dangers of Eustacia's bewitching charms and she also realises that the next step in the 'Time-worn Drama' will be for this witch to turn Clym against his mother – 'it is always so' (p. 231). Significantly, she seems at times to hear the music that surrounds her and understand its meaning, a capacity that Hardy makes clear in her reaction to the wedding. Mrs Yeobright is not present at the service, rather Hardy isolates her at Blooms End and reinforces her powerlessness to determine the future of her son by announcing the wedding through the 'notes of distant bells'. Simultaneously, Hardy introduces a 'whispered chorus' of 'husky grasshoppers', similar to those that will accompany her during her death, to remind the reader that despite the intensity of the domestic drama the mechanical universe carries on 'busy in all the fulness of life' (pp. 207, 267). Briefly, through this chorus, the two plots are combined to demonstrate that the domestic is simply a product of the wider process, a truth that the intuitive Mrs Yeobright seems to grasp in a moment of bitter revelation:

'Then it is over,' she murmured. 'Well, well! and life too will be over soon. And why should I go on scalding my face like this? Cry about one thing in life, cry about all; one thread runs through the whole piece. And yet we say, "a time to laugh"!'. (p. 207)

Her fatalistic murmuring reminds the reader of her role as the aggrieved mother in the unfolding drama, and yet by her identification of the 'one thread' she appears to grasp the existence of the web weaving her fate together with the wider power of the universal process. In this moment of revelation she dismisses self-pity as a possible response to such ills and instead reveals a strain of stoicism born of experience – her resignation being combined with a malicious determination to make the best of it.

How one comes to terms with living in a world governed by such harsh laws is, to a large extent, the subject of the second half of the novel. As troubles beset Clym and Eustacia, their responses are not stoical, but variations on Schopenhauer's methods of extracting oneself from the misery of the will-governed world. The first of these, as was made clear in Chapter 2, is the submersion of the individual will in the wider process, a means Hardy indicates through the dance. The second is by means of the 'mortification' of the will in the performance of some ascetic discipline, a means Hardy indicates through furze-cutting.

Eustacia's determination to lose herself in the tones of the East Egdon band suggests her elevation to the preliminary stage of Schopenhauer's process. The dance is not simply a social occasion, and the beating hearts do not depict a community spirit, rather, as Hughes notes, Hardy's 'writing captures the independent and "perfect individuality" of the dance (in Deleuze's phrase) as an event woven out of the coming together by moonlight and the "whole village-full of sensuous emotion, scattered abroad all the year long, [which] surged here in a focus for an hour" '.[34] It is a set piece that looks back to the 'dumb show' of Rainbarrow and anticipates the Duchess of Richmond's Ball on the eve of Waterloo, in which the whirling figures abandon themselves to the music of the wider process.[35] Here, however, the tone is sensuous, Hardy emphasising that the combination of 'tone of light' and dancing 'drives the emotions to rankness, the reason becoming sleepy and unperceiving in inverse proportion' (p. 244). The emphasis on sleepiness reminds us that for an individual to give himself up to the wider process is to become an automaton guided by, in this case, the 'rank' instinct of Darwinian sexual selection. It is not surprising, therefore, that Eustacia began 'to envy those pirouetters, to hunger for the hope and happiness which the fascination of the dance seemed to engender within them' (p. 244).

When she eventually joins in, her proximity to Wildeve does not lead to the palpitations that characterise their passionate relationship, rather, as Hughes notes, we are invited to conjecture as to her feelings, which are presented using metaphors ranging from the physiological to the supernatural as the varying narrative perspective drifts from external inspection to sympathy with her internal debates concerning Wildeve.[36] Significantly, her story is told in her face, which is presented as 'rapt and statuesque;

empty and quiescent', a peculiar observation for so passionate a woman. Hardy returns to such a description in the short story 'On the Western Circuit', when Raye, Hardy's hero, is depicted first observing his bride-to-be revolving on a roundabout animated by a barrel-organ:

> she was absolutely unconscious of everything save the act of riding: her features were rapt in an ecstatic dreaminess; for the moment she did not know her age or her history or her lineaments, much less her troubles.[37]

It is an apt symbol of the clockwork nature of Hardy's universe: Hardy's heroine is transformed into a figure on a musical box, her expression capturing the Schopenhaurian reverie when the most complex operations of the nervous system give way to automatic functioning and she finds herself at one with the wider process. The contemporary physiologist William James noted of such an expression that 'the eyes are fixed on vacancy, the sounds of the world melt into confused unity...and the foreground of consciousness is filled, if by anything, by a sort of solemn sense of surrender of the empty passing of time'.[38] As Eustacia whirls in her hypnotic state, her internal debate focusing not on desire but on the expendability of Wildeve as a partner: for fulfilment comes not from his love but rather from giving into her desire 'for the abstraction called passionate love more than for any particular lover' (pp. 84, 245).

Initially, Clym's response to the breach between his mother and Eustacia appears to be superior, since it follows Schopenhauer's second, and more elevated, principle of extracting oneself from misery. Schopenhauer argues that the will must be annihilated through the contemplation of love for one's fellow man followed by a gradual withdrawal from the world and its alluring pleasures and the performance of some monotonous activity, which allows the individual, in Hueffer's phrase, to become 'a calm looker-on at its own deeds'.[39] It is, of course, a condition arrived at by the tramp in 'Christmastide', who finds solace in singing a song whilst spreading good cheer through his greeting. As Clym takes up the ascetic discipline of furze-cutting and 'Sings a Song' it appears that he too has succeeded in renouncing his ambition, a rejection which harmonises him with those distant ancestors whose songs are echoed in the music of the heath. However, despite the apparent moral superiority of this response, Hardy's addition of the detail of the French origin of the song suggests that at this stage of his evolution Clym's asceticism does not provide the foundation for his altruism, but rather gives free reign to the self-absorption and nostalgia which are central to his character (a theme Hardy makes explicit through the introduction of the blindness motif). Implicit in this choice of physical affliction is a metaphor that criticises Clym's particular brand of asceticism when compared with the stoicism of his mother or Diggory Venn. Whereas these characters accept their lot and move forward with a grim determination and a faith in the possibility that human ingenuity may bring some comfort, Clym simply capitulates and wallows in a selfish preoccupation with his own doom.

These two musical reactions are repeated in the activities of the insects passed by Mrs Yeobright on her fateful journey across the heath. In the spring of 1876 Hardy read and made notes on J. G. Wood's *Insects at Home* (1872), of which Walter Wright has noted that it will have presented Hardy with some 'philosophical implications for the life of man'.[40] This is undoubtedly true, insects being a favoured image of both Darwin and Schopenhauer to exemplify a world governed by the principle of instinct. It is these implications that we find worked out in *The Return of the Native* through the reduction of the heathmen to ants and 'the maggoty shapes of innumerable obscure creatures' crawling over the face of haggard Egdon (p. 256). Around the feet of the 'woman not disinclined to philosophize' the dancers at East Egdon are transformed into the 'independent worlds of ephemerons', the happiness of which kindles in her a hope that her visit might be a success (p. 256). Hardy's choice of the verbs 'carouse', 'heave' and 'wallow', however, betray her latent disgust of Eustacia's sensuality, therefore warning the reader of the imminent disaster. Furthermore, Clym becomes to her eyes both 'of no more account in life than an insect' and a being bearing the characteristic walk of her 'husband', details through which Hardy reminds the reader that his characters are simply temporary objectifications, both temporal and phenomenal, of an ambivalent process (p. 257).

As she sits down to rest above Clym's cottage, this objectification re-emerges through the 'perpetual moan' of the fir and beech plantation surrounding their marriage home:

> the wet young beeches were undergoing amputations, bruises, cripplings, and harsh lacerations, from which the wasting sap would bleed for many a day to come, and which would leave scars visible till the day of their burning. Each stem was wrenched at the root, where it moved like a bone in its socket, and at every onset of the gale convulsive sounds came from the branches, as if pain were felt. (p. 201)

Clym is now observed centre stage, and the trees planted in the year of his birth (and meant to have been more explicitly connected with him in the serial version), perform the function of a letimotif playing out his inner agony.[41] As they tower above the rolling contours of Egdon, the trees provide an apt symbol of those who have sought to defy the dictates of the wider process. Their 'perpetual moan which one could hardly believe to be caused by the air' echoes that of the pines planted by Marty South in *The Woodlanders*, or the dirge-like tones which tell 'Yell'ham Wood's story'.[42] Significantly, although such music also reflects the pain of Mrs Yeobright, whose determination to replace Eustacia in her son's affections defies the 'inevitable movement onward' in Egdon's tale, she is able to momentarily detach herself from the domestic drama and 'dismiss thoughts of her own storm-broken and exhausted state to contemplate theirs' (p. 201). It is another one of those moments when, through the music of the heath, Mrs Yeobright is able to contextualise her domestic troubles within the wider process, leading to a reinforcement of her stoical resistance.

Mrs Yeobright's re-entry into the domestic drama and her knock at the door, as Ian Gregor has observed, 'dramatically "freeze" the scene, and for an instant the emotional complex of the Yeobrights' and of Wildeve is laid bare'.[43] Hardy now re-creates the Christmas mummers play, but with his characters more explicitly performing the roles assigned to them by the wider process. Central to this careful unravelling is the way Hardy's characters add their tones to the musical moan of the Devil's Bellows, so that their participation in two plots is made apparent. For example, Eustacia's role in the domestic plot is signalled by Wildeve's dissatisfied observation that she has been 'playing the same tantalising part' of the lover (p. 262). When he observes that she has dropped into her 'old mournful key' he unwittingly connects her fickleness with the wider aspect of her character, which yearns for the dream of 'music, poetry, passion, war' and is dissatisfied by the reality of each (p. 262). Wildeve reciprocates in the role of the impetuous lover, whilst on a different level his 'murmurs' provide a brief history of failed ambition and personal calamity, which prefigures the fate of Clym. Furthermore, Hardy's peculiar mixture of tense in Wildeve's assertion that Clym 'probably doesn't know what it is to lose the woman he loved' makes explicit the participation in two plots, for whilst ostensibly referring to Eustacia, it also signifies Mrs Yeobright, who is at that moment standing on the doorstep trying to capture the conscious attention of her son (p. 262). As has already been stated, Clym's murmured 'mother' signifies – paradoxically – his self-absorbed character; and Mrs Yeobright's murmured 'he lets her shut the door against me!' indicates her continued role as the distressed mother (p. 264).

The death of Mrs Yeobright momentarily awakens Clym's slumbering reason, illuminating as it does the paradox central to his character. Not only does his intention of educating the Egdon Eremites sit uneasily with the malicious pleasure that he takes in the heath's re-integration of Wildeve's plot, but he is also incapable of understanding that his capitulation to the heath entails a surrender of his belief in the power of the word. Unlike his mother, he remains deaf to the Wagnerian chorus surrounding him, remaining instead committed to Spencer's 'language of the intellect'. This blinkered belief in the moral validity of words without any attempt to investigate the meanings lying behind them manifests itself in the dogged pursuit of his mother's deathbed utterance: words which Hardy carefully informs the reader were 'too bitterly uttered in an hour of misapprehension' (p. 284). With bitter irony, Hardy undermines Clym's self-indulgent recriminations over her death – characterised by such melodramatic exclamations as 'if any man wants to make himself immortal by painting a picture of wretchedness, let him come here!' – with Eustacia's 'shivering sigh', which proves to be the only real expression of emotion to pass between them (pp. 283–284). Importantly Clym misses this because, as we might expect, he 'was too deeply absorbed in the ramblings', which were not, as Hardy's authorial intrusion makes clear, an expression of his remorseful state, but 'incidental to' it (p. 284).

The dramatic climax of the domestic plot is complemented by the simultaneous crescendo in the Wagnerian chorus that has pervaded the narrative. Hardy's careful orchestration of the natural tones of the storm in the final chapters is not simply a piece of theatre, but is used to demonstrate the degree to which his characters have evolved in their understanding of their relationship with the process governing their lives. For, although Egdon remains the conditioning influence of all who live on it, its effects are amenable to individual interpretation. Crucially, both Eustacia and Clym remain to the end deaf to the music that surrounds them. Eustacia's flight in the wind and the rain presents her last attempt to shape her own destiny, but it fails because she has no money. As she rails Lear-like against the vindictive external agents that she remains convinced have blighted her life, she demonstrates that she has not evolved beyond the young woman who blamed all her troubles on some 'indistinct, colossal Prince of the World' (pp. 274, 321). But in Hardy's world there are no slighted gods, her fetishistic belief mocked by the music of the heath, which appears 'as if it whistled for joy' (p. 277).

It is typical of Clym that his final attempt to alter the destiny of both himself and Eustacia should take the form of a letter. It is equally characteristic of the workings of Hardy's universe that it should remain undelivered, providing an apt symbol of the limitations of the word as a means of expression. As the letter sits on the mantelpiece, the only reply to Captain Vye's attempts to locate his daughter is that of the Aeolian chorus 'which seemed to gnaw at the corners of the house' reminding us that in Hardy's universe the governing principle is that of 'chance and senseless circumstance' (p. 419). It is, of course, a truth to which his self-absorbed hero has remained deaf throughout the narrative, Hardy symbolising it here by isolating Clym at Blooms End whilst he paces from room to room attempting to stop and muffle the 'strange noises in windows and doors' (p. 324).

For Thomasin, however, Egdon 'was no monster whatever, but impersonal open ground' upon which 'a person might experience much discomfort . . . and possibly catch cold' (p. 329). Whereas Clym and Eustacia have employed their energies in altering their perceived destiny, with the consequence that they are left like the young Jude to complain that 'events did not rhyme quite as [they] had thought',[44] the patient Thomasin, who eschews extremes of action and accepts the vagaries of events around her, has learned to accept her fate, seeing it as simply life unfolding. Like Susan Henchard, she is in tune with the music of the mechanised universe, a quality Hardy illustrates through his description of her sleeping figure at the beginning of the novel: 'she seemed to belong rightly to a madrigal – to require viewing through rhyme and harmony' (p. 58).

Eustacia, however, only finds fulfilment through death, her death mask capturing the 'momentary transition between fervour and resignation', the latter being the 'more recently learnt emotion' to which Egdon appeals (pp. 32, 339). And what of Clym? Hardy certainly seems at pains to suggest that he remains arrogantly self-absorbed to the end: he visits his mother's grave regularly and venerates a lock of Eustacia's hair; he dismisses Venn as too common for his cousin's hand; and when toasts are drunk at the wedding, he continually asks Charley why they are drinking to his health. And yet there seems to be, in Clym's moral lecturing that takes place on a sunlit Rainbarrow, a more positive note which indicates the conquest of enlightenment over the darkness of the heath. D. H. Lawrence dismisses Clym's preaching as the last resort of a man who was empty, an opinion seemingly reflected in Hardy's own presentation of his hero constantly wallowing in words, and his rather dismissive comment that 'some believed him, and some believed not' (p. 365).[45] However, what is important here is not the contents of Clym's sermons, which the reader may suspect contain little more than collections of moral platitudes, but the 'tones of his voice, which were rich, musical, and stirring', with which they are delivered (p. 364).

Hardy's meaning here is illuminated by consideration of the late poem 'The Pedestrian', which makes an interesting companion-piece to 'Christmastide'. Once again the narrator is depicted travelling on a lonely road on a dark heath, but this time he meets a young philosopher (a student of Schopenhauer), who takes his ritual constitutional knowing that he has only six months to live. What impresses upon the narrator is:

> His voice was that of a man refined,
> A man, one well could feel, of mind,
> Quite winning in its musical ease;
> But in mould maligned
> By some disease;[46]

There is no weak song of good cheer here, instead the ravages of thought are, like Clym, etched upon his face. Hughes' analysis of the poem focuses on how Hardy's careful use of rhythm allows for an act of poetic ventriloquism in which the narrator finds expression through the musical voice of the student, and the student is able to speak through the narrator who remembers him.[47] Hardy's meaning is similar here, the music of the wider process objectifying itself through the shattered organ-stop of Clym, whilst Clym attempts to articulate his story of the heath. Despite his reliance upon the word, he remains an object-lesson to his auditors, his musical voice adding to the Wagnerian chorus that has permeated the novel warning of the dangers of attempting to impose oneself on the universe.

6

'A Tragedy Appropriate for Its Time': Music and the Story of a 'Man of Character'

The sign of the Three Mariners Inn which stands in the centre of Casterbridge depicts three sailors 'represented by the artist as persons of two dimensions only...so that they were but a half-invisible film upon the reality of the grain, and knots, and nails, which composed the signboard' (p. 57). It is to this inn that the three travellers – Farfrae, Susan and Elizabeth-Jane – gravitate when they first enter the town, leading the reader to connect their function in the narrative with the monolithic representations on the signboard. R. H. Hutton, reviewing the novel in the *Spectator* in 1886, found some 'failure of art' in the anaemic representation of these characters; but this is to misread Hardy's aesthetic purpose, which appears to have been to use their particular human attributes to explore specific elements of Henchard's temperament.[1] For, in this novel Henchard dominates the narrative in the same way that his forcefulness enables him to eclipse those around him. Thus, when we consider the full title, *The Life and Death of the Mayor of Casterbridge: A Story of a Man of Character*, it is quite clear that Hardy's narrative is not to focus on a human relationship, since none of the characters surrounding him is strong enough to sustain an equal part in any kind of alliance. His story is, rather, the connection between a man's character and his destiny.

Hardy's insistence upon the importance of this latter element means that for critics it has remained central when considering the tragic stature of the novel: put simply, Hardy presents the reader with a Greek tragedy in which Henchard, having violated an external moral order, is left to struggle against the retribution meted out by offended gods.[2] But there are no gods in Hardy's universe, just, as Jude Fawley observes, 'man and senseless circumstance'.[3] Thus, if, as Frederick Karl has observed, Hardy's incorporation of some elements of the Classical theatre suggests that what he 'evidently intended was a Greek tragedy', it was to be one 'appropriate for his own time'.[4] To this end his tragic mechanism has less to do with the avenging Fates than the Promethean tension which arises from the attempts of the individual to impose his portion of the will upon an indifferent universe.[5] When we consider the opening wife-sale, therefore, it is important to recognise that it does not act as a trigger for divine retribution, but rather it displays a force of character that is ill-adapted for a world which rewards flexibility.

So what can we say of the character of Michael Henchard? Quite simply, he is a more energetic version of farmer Boldwood in *Far from the Madding Crowd*, of whom Hardy noted that 'if an emotion possessed him at all, it ruled him; a feeling not mastering him was entirely latent' (p. 147). Such a description is of interest in the context of various mid-century debates concerning the nature of character and the self. In his 'The Aesthetic Aspects of Character' (1871), James Sully offered a model in which he attempted to order different character types according to their harmonious adaptation to environment. He identifies a 'simple character [as] one which presents one or two dominant phases instead of numerous qualities subtly interwoven . . . readers of George Eliot's works may find examples of this effect in such types of character as Savonarola and Dinah Morris'.[6] We could add to this list, Michael Henchard, whose unswerving energy is contrasted with the flexible Farfrae, in whom, as Lucetta observes, the 'commercial and the romantic' are woven like different-coloured threads in a cord, 'intertwisted, yet not mingling' (p. 150). Henchard is a man with no middle ground, his massive emotions emerging in a series of impulsive acts of increasing moral repugnance.

The trajectory of his decline is of interest when we consider Schopenhauer's ideas concerning character. In *The World as Will and Idea* he argues that the character of the individual is another name for the immutable will which bypasses the intellect and manifests itself through the 'blind incessant impulse' which is the 'inner content, the essence of the world'.[7] The term 'impulse' is one of many Schopenhauer uses interchangeably with that of 'will', and to contemporary English critics operating within an intellectual community dominated by the biological vocabulary of Darwin, 'impulse' proved a more accessible term. 'Impulse' is also a term favoured by Hardy: Tess' seduction by Alec follows from her 'abandon[ing] herself to her impulse', Fitzpiers 'impulsively' pursues Suke Damson through the woods following the Midsummer Eve ritual, and Jude 'impulsively' seizes the hand of Sue on one of their outings from the Melchester Training College.[8] Significantly, for Schopenhauer, 'what is bad in the character will always come out more strongly over time', the first impulsive, morally abhorrent act being the precursor of many similar ones.[9] In such circumstances repentance is futile, since it does not demonstrate an altered will, simply recognition of the pain caused.[10] It is an understanding of character that accords entirely with Henchard's personal history: his first immoral act of selling his wife is carried out on impulse and is followed by a highly theatrical and ultimately futile oath of abstinence (pp. 38–39).[11]

Henchard is portrayed as much as of a victim of his own impulsive acts as those around him, transforming him at times into the horrified spectator of his own misdeeds. Henchard's lie to Newson concerning the paternity of Elizabeth-Jane is given on impulse and is immediately followed by Hardy's observation that 'Henchard, scarcely believing the evidence of his senses, rose from his seat amazed at what he had done' (p. 253). His impulsive decision to meet the royal personage finds him 'stagger[ing]' into public view in a state of reverie rather than mischief, 'blandly' holding out his hand in greeting (p. 232). Henchard even excuses the wife-sale with the observation 'I was not in my senses, and a man's senses are himself' (p. 252). It is when Henchard is not in his senses, whether through the effects of alcohol or by his lapsing into a state of reverie, that his destructive impulses emerge. When he becomes conscious of his deeds, he is at once horrified and remorseful, and finds himself attempting to understand the motives for his behaviour, and make up for it through futile gestures.

If Hardy intended *The Mayor of Casterbridge* to be 'a Greek tragedy appropriate for his own time', then Henchard's conscious struggle to control his character is his tragic mechanism. As with *The Return of the Native*, however, Hardy does not present Henchard's story as a psychological drama: his characters do not, like George Eliot's, find themselves engaged in inner-dialogues between various competing moral choices. Rather, in accordance with the Classical project, the human psyche is reduced to a series of exemplary parallels and metaphors. Henchard, for example, is continually associated with a variety of 'mythical' figures synonymous with particular character traits. We learn little of his loneliness, other than through his association with outcasts such as Coleridge's ancient mariner and the Biblical Cain. His melancholia is explained by parallels with Saul, and his friendship for Farfrae by means of Saul's love of David. What Hardy achieves by this broad spread of associations is a mythologising of Henchard's specific troubles, which lends to his decline a universal quality.

Central to this process is Hardy's use of music, a fact that many critics tacitly acknowledge in their division of the novel into musical parts. Both Millgate and Goode refer to the various stages of Henchard's demise as 'movements', and Gregor goes so far as to suggest that the function of the opening two chapters is to 'serve as an overture to the novel as a whole'.[12] Their seemingly intuitive grasp of the essential musicality of the novel derives from Hardy's use of musical allusion to constantly undermine Henchard's grandiose vision of his place in the universe. For, whereas Henchard blames his downfall on vindictive gods outraged at the initial crime of selling his wife, Hardy once again employs a Wagnerian chorus of musically delineated natural sounds to continually remind the reader that there are no gods, rather an ambivalent universal process indifferent to personal suffering. Raging against unseen gods, therefore, is a particularly egocentric and futile activity: it is better to acknowledge the central message of the novel, that life is nothing more than a 'brief transit through a sorry world', in which happiness derives from making 'limited opportunities endurable' (pp. 285–286). It is a lesson grasped by Hardy's stoical survivors – Susan and Elizabeth-Jane – but which remains unheeded by Henchard.

This music is first heard in the carefully stage-mannered opening scene which acts as Wagnerian prelude, raising the story to a mythical status above the limitations of particular times, places and characters, helping to create the sense of foreboding, which is, as Millgate has observed, implicit in the *'Life and Death'* of the title.[13] The scene is characterised by a theatricality similar to that observed at the beginning of both *The Return of the Native* and *The Woodlanders*: Hardy explicitly positioning his characters before 'some grand feat of stagery [observed] from a darkened auditorium' (p. 35). Once again the road transforms itself into a spatial representation of time: the details of the cloud of 'stale familiarity' hanging over the couple; the 'thick hoar of dust' covering their shabby garments; and the 'doomed leaves' of the hedgerows, fill the reader with a sense of foreboding appropriate for the tale that is about to unfold (pp. 27, 28). It is a sense increased by Hardy's careful inclusion of music in the form of the

> voice of a weak bird singing a trite old evening song that might doubtless have been heard on the hill at the same hour, and with the self-same trills, quavers, and breves, at any sunset of that season for centuries untold. (p. 28)

The bird is idealised, a representative of the many that have sung the same song for centuries, and therefore it lends universality to the narrative. This quality is immediately strengthened by Hardy's vagueness with regard to both the time and place in which the story is set, and his description of the anonymous central group in terms of assemblages of clothes. The bird is also 'weak', a detail that looks back to the vulnerability of Grandfer Cantle and anticipates poems such as 'The Darkling Thrush' and 'The Blinded Bird', both of which deal with themes germane to Hardy's presentation here. In the former the despair of the narrator is reflected in the desolation of his surroundings, characterised, as with the road upon which the Henchards travel, by Hardy's description of the 'Winter's dregs'. The only prevailing sound is the music emerging from the 'tangled bine-stems' which resound 'like strings of broken lyres', their state of disrepair adding to the sense of despair that governs the poem.[14] Emerging as a contrast to this music, however, is the song of the 'Darkling Thrush':

> At once a voice arose among
> The bleak twigs overhead
> In a full-hearted evensong
> Of joy illimited;
> An aged thrush, frail, gaunt, and small,
> In blast-beruffled plume,
> Had chosen thus to fling his soul
> Upon the growing gloom.
>
> So little cause for carolings
> Of such ecstatic sound
> Was written on terrestrial things
> Afar or nigh around,
> That I could think there trembled through
> His happy good-night air
> Some blessed Hope whereof he knew
> And I was unaware.

The similarity with the song of the 'weak bird' is striking, as it chooses, through the medium of music, to 'fling his soul' into an inhospitable universe. The real focus of Hardy's poem, rather like 'Christmastide', is the bemusement of his narrator that any creature could find cause to sing in such inauspicious circumstances. This question becomes much more direct in the 'Blinded Bird', with Hardy's narrator noting of the pitiful creature:

> So zestfully canst thou sing?
> And all this indignity,
> With God's consent, on thee![15]

It is this power of endurance that the observer of the blinded bird finds 'Divine', deliberately and ironically contrasting it with the callous indifference of God. The auditor of the darkling thrush remains perplexed to the end, attributing to the bird some 'blessed Hope' – a process of anthropomorphism which highlights a human need to project oneself into the future rather than endure the present. It is this human frailty that will be worked out fully in *Jude the Obscure*, in which Jude's naïve striving towards illusory goals highlights the tension between his hope and the grim reality that thwarts him. Music provides the perfect analogue for such experience; both Schopenhauer and Haweis arguing that musical movement through expectation, tension and thwarted resolution offers an image of the workings of the unconscious. Significantly, in such a model 'hope' merely allows the individual to suffer unending misery, tied, to use Schopenhauer's image, to a perpetually turning 'wheel of Ixion'. In the auditor's attribution of some 'blessed Hope' to the song of the thrush he has rather missed the point: Hardy's combination of upper-case and 'blessed' pointing to the ironic intention of the statement. For, if the music of the 'broken lyres' invokes the Aeolian music of poems such as Coleridge's 'The Eolian Harp' and Wordsworth's *Prelude*, their broken state reminds us that in Hardy's universe 'Nature's Holy Plan' is non-existent.

Thus, the song of the weak bird suggests not transcendence above, but accommodation with, the immediate environment. Essentially, his song outlines the principle that is central to *The Mayor of Casterbridge*, that life is harsh and happiness derives not from illusory hopes (that time will thwart), but from enduring, adapting and making 'limited opportunities endurable' (p. 285).

The song of Hardy's idealised bird in the first scene of the novel provides the same function; crucially it is a song to which Henchard remains deaf. Even our first glimpse of him is full of foreboding, since it is apparent that he is unhappy with the staleness of his present life and eager to transform his destiny. Significantly, Hardy does not present this dilemma in terms of an inner-dialogue, or even a dialogue between the characters, rather he dramatises it amidst the highly theatrical surroundings of the fair (with its 'peep-shows', 'wax-works', 'inspired monsters' and 'readers of fate') through a series of competing strains of musically delineated sounds. Initially, his self-absorption and determination to impose his own will upon the universe is signalled by his preferring to read, or, indeed, *pretending* to read, his own music from 'a ballad sheet' rather than listen to the music of the bird. As the voice of the bird is transformed into the 'bird-like chirpings' of his family cautioning moderation, Henchard continues to turn a 'deaf ear' to it, preferring instead to take up the 'strain' of the auctioneer's cry 'who'll take the last lot for a song?' (p. 31). In the furmity booth Henchard makes his Faustian pact to rid himself of his past and trades two songs for his freedom: that of his family calling for moderation, and the song of the weak bird counselling acceptance (p. 29).

Even the respite offered by the interruption of the swallow is ignored, a detail that demonstrates very clearly the perilousness of Henchard's self-absorption. For Hardy appears to be making an ironic allusion to Psalm 84, in which a swallow is taken as a symbol of good omen for a pilgrim who sings of his dissatisfaction with his present life and envy of the swallow who has made 'a nest for herself, where she may lay her young'.[16] Nothing could be further from Henchard's thoughts than such a nesting instinct!

Hardy also appears to be drawing a parallel with Bede's sparrow, whose flight through the great hall of the Saxon king is used by an attendant councillor to demonstrate that man's life on earth is a journey through pain and sorrow: 'for the few moments it is inside, the storm and wintry tempest cannot touch it, but after the briefest moment of calm, it flits from your sight, out of the wintry storm and into it again. So this life of man appears but for a moment; what follows or indeed what went before, we know not at all.'[17] Once again, it is a bird that reiterates the lesson that life on earth is a 'brief transit through a sorry world', a lesson already grasped by Susan who wears a 'half-apathetic expression of one who deems anything possible at the hands of Time and Chance except, perhaps, fair play', and learned by Elizabeth-Jane through harsh experience (pp. 28, 286). Thus, there is no forward movement in the narrative, merely a cycle in which Hardy's characters come to terms with their position. Unfortunately, it is an accommodation that Henchard never achieves, as he ignores the diversion offered by the bird and doggedly returns to his impulsive decision to sell his wife. Once again, it is a determination that Hardy presents through musical metaphor, Henchard returning to the 'old strain' of the auctioneer 'as in a musical fantasy the instrument fetches up the original theme' (p. 32).

Anticipating our horrified response to these events, Hardy takes this opportunity to mock both the reader's and Henchard's belief that an external order has been violated. He lifts the tent flap to remind us of the tranquil stage scenery outside, coaxing us to 'abjure man as the blot on an otherwise kindly universe', before gently reminding us that sometimes Nature may rage while man sleeps innocently (p. 35). He also ridicules Henchard's oath, depicting him searching for a 'fit place and imagery', kissing 'the big book' and then journeying without pause 'till he reached the town of Casterbridge, in a far distant part of Wessex' (pp. 38, 39, 40). All that is missing from Henchard's progress is the seven league boots!

The prelude establishes the cyclical pattern of impulsive act, consequence and futile gesture of remorse that will mark the decline of Henchard. Henceforward Hardy's narrative sets out to explore the destructive capabilities of such a psychology. As stated previously, he is to some extent an uncomprehending spectator of his own impulse; his increasingly morally repugnant acts combining with magnificent gestures of self-abasement designed in his own mind to appease offended gods. But Henchard is not the glorious victim of the vindictive agents he perceives himself to be – a lack of comprehension that lays at the heart of Hardy's tragic ambitions in this novel. Throughout the narrative Henchard's tendency to perceive himself as the solitary victim of malign forces is constantly undermined by Hardy's carefully orchestrated Wagnerian chorus, which reminds the reader that if the term 'tragedy' is applicable at all, it derives from the dangers of any individual action that is out of harmony with the wider music. It can be heard, for example, in the 'single big blue fly buzz[ing] musically round and round' the awaking figure of Henchard following the wife-sale (p. 37). If it evokes the vindictive plague sent to punish Pharaoh or the swarms that torment Io in Aeschylus' *Prometheus Bound*, its bumbling oversized appearance and lonely drone mocks them.[18] Henchard has not violated an external moral order; he has not even committed a crime! He has simply failed to exercise control over his impulsive character. It simply suits Henchard's own egotism to reinvent himself as Cain – the first ever victim. He is not Cain, but is closer to Hamlet, a victim of his inability to see himself properly; a shortcoming that Hardy dramatises later in the novel by bringing Henchard face to face with the effigy of himself floating in the weir stream of the ten hatches.

There is then in Hardy's narrative a deliberate mockery of Henchard's grandiose vision of himself, a policy made clear by the presentation of his denouement, not through the presence of the avenging Fates, but by the arrest of the furmity woman for urinating against the church wall. Through the comical sordidness of her behaviour, she is transformed from an agent of the gods, which is how Henchard sees her, into a part of his past that he would simply like to forget. For, if there is any tragic mechanism in the novel, it is simply that given time the individual will be brought face to face with the consequences of his actions, which is exactly what Hardy achieves through the reintroduction of Susan and Elizabeth-Jane into the narrative following a lacuna of nineteen years. Their function is made abundantly clear by Hardy's careful stage management: not only does the road function as a spatial representation of time, but the description of the musical clocks, chiming 'like a row of actors delivering their final speeches before the fall of the curtain', which greet their entry into Casterbridge, reminds us that both characters are little more than puppets in Hardy's clockwork universe. This sense is reinforced through Hardy's description of the way in which the clocks' stammering rendition of Psalm 19 undermines the town band's energetic performance of 'The Roast Beef of Old England'. If the latter announces Henchard's extravagant success, then Hardy's reduction of a hymn in praise of God as the creator of both Nature and the Laws to badly wrought clockwork simply reminds us that in Hardy's mechanical universe time will catch up with his errant hero.[19]

The dissonant tones of the clocks are taken up by the Casterbridge locals observing the pantomimic spectacle of the dinner at the King's Arms, which shows Henchard at the height of his powers. As one voice at the lower end of his dining table ('not quite in harmony with those at the head; just as the west end of a church is sometimes persistently found to sing out of time and tune with the leading spirits in the chancel') raises complaints as to the quality of the bread, the question is taken up by the chorus of 'loungers outside' and transformed into the broader appeal, 'what are you going to do to repay us for the past?' (p. 53). It is a question that embraces the situation of the anonymously observing Susan and her daughter.

Henchard's answer is ostentatiously theatrical. It is quite within character that he should choose the ruined Roman amphitheatre as a suitably magnificent venue for the grand reconciliation with his wife. Yet despite the apparent nobility of his action, Hardy's careful stage-management of the scene, particularly his orchestration of the prevailing Wagnerian chorus, leads to Henchard's motives being undermined. It is clear that he is motivated not by 'amatory fire or pulse of romance' but rather a sense that he must put right past wrongs, thus the obstinacy that surrounds the pursuit of the utterance of the single word of forgiveness (p. 89). As with the oath of abstinence he puts great faith in the moral validity of the word, seeing in it some protection against an external moral order which he is afraid that he has violated. But, as Hardy reminds the reader through the 'Aeolian modulations' that animate the scene, there are no affronted gods, simply an ambivalent process (p. 81). There therefore can be no grand gesture, Henchard's pursuit of forgiveness paling into insignificance in comparison with the barbaric acts for which the arena has been employed previously. Indeed, the whole arena is transformed in Hardy's description into a mere 'spittoon of the Jötuns' (p. 80). It is therefore entirely in accordance with Hardy's deflation of Henchard's magnanimity that Susan's reply should remain muffled and unheard.

Hardy employs a similar chorus during Henchard's disastrous attempt to eclipse Farfrae in his spectacular entertainment. The juxtaposition of the two fetes is designed to demonstrate the essential difference in the character of the two men: the cautious Farfrae organises his entertainment in an 'ingeniously constructed' tent sheltered from the vicissitudes of the weather, in which, much to the delight of the Casterbridge locals, he dances and cavorts (p. 107). Such is his success that the authorial observation that nobody 'so thoroughly understood the poetry of motion as he' reaches beyond his present performance, to an acknowledgement that he is in tune with a universe that rewards moderation (p. 108). Henchard's entertainment, by contrast, is planned on an extravagant scale and positioned upon the most elevated spot in the surrounding region as if, in his own mind, to challenge the gods. When the storms duly arrive they are described by an observing consciousness drifting between Hardy and Henchard as 'a monotonous smiting of earth by heaven' (p. 107). This is Henchard's reinvention of his situation: he is selected for special punishment and must suffer. And yet, as 'the wind play[s] on the tent-cords' of his rain-sodden marquee, the 'Aeolian improvisations' once again remind the reader that he is not Cain, but rather an extravagant character in a world that rewards qualities of quiet endurance (p. 107).

We hear it again in the Aeolian modulations of Yalbury Wood following Henchard's attempts to convince the suspicious Farfrae that he must return home to tend the sick Lucetta. Henchard's failure leads to the type of recriminations that have become typical of his egocentricity in that they focus on the anguish caused by the loss of his name rather than the consequences for the dying Lucetta. Hardy transforms him into a despairing 'repentant sinner' and a 'less scrupulous Job' who curses the day he was born (p. 248).[20] But once again, what Hardy is offering in this description is Henchard's own somewhat heroic assessment of his own ability to withstand affliction; a judgement echoed in his later defiant addition of a negative into his inversion of Cain's pleading with God: 'I – Cain – go alone as I deserve – an outcast and a vagabond. But my punishment is *not* greater than I can bear!' (p. 269).[21] But as the 'moan' of the wind blowing 'among the masses of spruce and larch of Yalbury Wood' reminds the reader, Henchard's self-abasement is futile since he has not been selected for special punishment, but simply suffers in common with the rest of mankind (p. 247).

Another character attempting to avoid the past is Lucetta Templeman. She remains, like the architecture of her house, a facade of moderation behind which sits the leering face of intrigue. Like Henchard, she fashions phantoms with which to punish herself for past indiscretions, but whereas he accepts his past and reinvents for himself the role of heroic victim, Lucetta's fear of public ridicule and censure lead her to avow that 'I won't be a slave to the past' (p. 164). As with Henchard's inability to understand himself, the medium through which Hardy explores Lucetta's paranoia is not a form of internal dialogue (as might have been favoured by George Eliot), but by externalising her fears by means of his Wagnerian chorus: first through Farfrae's songs, and secondly through the 'rude music' of the skimmington (p. 243).

As will be observed in the next section, Hardy generally uses Farfrae's singing as a means of measuring the emotional and moral evolution of his characters. It is his songs that draw all those he meets into his sphere of emotional influence, a feature which extends to his liaison with Lucetta. However, here Hardy uses the texts of his songs to maintain an ironic commentary on their developing relationship. When, as Jackson-Houlston has observed, she requests him to sing her a song to shake him out of the unhappiness caused by Henchard's antagonism towards him, it is Burns' song 'Tibbie Fowler', which is about a woman with a multiplicity of lovers. Not only does her choice highlight some crassness on her behalf, but also the subtext, which condemns the value of money in attracting lovers, highlights the moral dubiousness of one of her prime assets. For, as Jackson-Houlston quite rightly points out, neither Henchard nor Farfrae are indifferent to her wealth.[22]

It is through his music that the unwary Lucetta is first drawn to him, as he lies unobserved beneath his seed drill singing 'the lass of Gowerie' (pp. 156–157). It is a romantic song of exile, alluding, as Ian Gregor has observed, to the young '"Kitty wi" a braw new gown'.[23] Once again, Hardy's choice of song is ironic, for Lucetta is wearing a new gown as red as the machine, 'to be the cherry-coloured person at all hazards' (p. 155).

The pun on 'hazards' alerts us to the *gamble* that she is taking in wearing such a provocative dress, for although she becomes alluring she also *risks* disapproval. This censure is made public in the 'satirical mummery' of the skimmington, when her effigy will be adorned with the same red dress, thus transforming her into that which she most fears – a scarlet woman.

The skimmington is, as Millgate notes, a surreal scene, with more in common with Hawthorne's romances than contemporary realist fiction, in which the reader is invited to observe Lucetta watching the exhibition of her own worst fears.[24] Central to its aesthetic success in exploring her psychology is the way in which Hardy's Wagnerian music re-emerges in the cacophonous sound of phallic 'serpents' and 'rams'-horns' and 'other historical kinds of music' (p. 243). It is a music that evokes the Darwinian courtship ritual of man's distant progenitors, in so doing highlighting the promiscuous sexuality that Lucetta has been unable to control. Significantly, when the town magistrates, Stubbord and Grower, attempt to investigate the cause of the cacophony, nothing can be found aside from the ubiquitous Jopp, who claims to have heard nothing except 'the wind in the Walk trees [which] makes a peculiar poetical-like murmur tonight' (p. 244). It is an observation reinforced by Hardy's authorial intervention, linking his 'rude music' with that of the Aeolian modulations that have continually undermined Henchard's grand gestures of repentance. It reminds the reader that in Hardy's mechanical universe there are no vindictive gods, simply the inevitability that given time the individual will be confronted with their past. It is a truth to which both Henchard and Lucetta remain ignorant, the Mixen lane gossip Nance Mockridge grasping it in her observation that the scandal that surrounds them "twill out in time' (p. 91).

I want now to turn to the way in which Hardy uses the musically adept Farfrae to measure the development of his characters. This commentary begins with Farfrae himself, who, as has already been observed, embodies all the qualities absent from Henchard. Once again, Sully's observations concerning character are of interest, for in seeking to identify that character type that exhibits 'Correspondence with its immediate Environment', he argues that

> the character may be regarded either as a Product of external causes, or as an Instrument fitted for a recognised destiny. In the first instance the character seems natural; in the second, suitable.... A character which appears thus suited to the demands of its environing world assumes the pleasing aspect of a beautiful well-ordered structure.

The quality of fitness may attach itself to prudence, considered as a condition of individual happiness.[25]

In Hardy's novel of 'Character and Environment' Farfrae is prudent in a universe that rewards moderation, exhibiting the Darwinian characteristic of 'adaptation' to the 'demands of his environing world'. These are characteristics depicted in the voice: whereas Henchard's laughter expresses strength of purpose, Farfrae's 'voice musically undulated between two semitones' suggesting flexibility (p. 98). He is able to adapt and compartmentalise his feelings, a feature that Hardy indicates by aligning Farfrae with his innovative seed drill, a realisation of Sully's 'beautiful well-ordered structure'.

> The machine was painted in bright hues of green, yellow, and red, and it resembled as a whole a compound of hornet, grasshopper, and shrimp, magnified enormously. Or it might have been likened to an upright musical instrument with the front gone. That was how it struck Lucetta. 'Why, it is a sort of agricultural piano,' she said. (p. 155)

The intimate connection between music and machine gives some indication as to why his singing captivates many, for, as he informs the women, with the drill there is no wastage, each grain hits 'its intended place, and nowhere else' (p. 157). So whereas Henchard's emotions are massive but, like broadcast seed, directionless, Farfrae's much shallower feelings are guided right to the spot.[26]

It is Farfrae's ability to compartmentalise his feelings that allows his singing to take possession of all present at the Three Mariners on the first evening. They

> began to view him through a golden haze which the tone of his mind seemed to raise around him. Casterbridge had sentiment – Casterbridge had romance; but this stranger's sentiment was of differing quality. Or rather, perhaps, the difference was mainly superficial; he was to them like the poet of a new school who takes his contemporaries by storm; who is not really new, but is the first to articulate what all his listeners have felt, though but dumbly till then. (p. 67)

With the efficiency of his seed drill, Farfrae's singing expresses in an ordered fashion those dimly felt emotions which are difficult to articulate.

We are reminded of Haweis' physiological approach to psychology in his 'Music: Its Origin and Influence', which states that music has the capacity to organise the thoughts of both singer and auditor so that it not only 'arouses and cultivates emotion to its highest activity', but also 're-creates exhausted emotion by nerve currents generated through direct vibration of the nervous tissues', enabling the listener to experience emotions seldom felt before.[27] This faculty suggests for Haweis the function of music, which is to allow those living listless enclosed lives some form of escape. This certainly appears to have been the experience of Coney, Buzzford and Longways, who begin to view Farfrae as an idealised 'Scotchman' from a 'land o' perpetual snow... where wolves and wild boars and other dangerous animalcules be as common as blackbirds' (p. 67). Clarity of emotion, however, does not signal depth: a warning encoded in Hardy's speculation that Farfrae's superiority of sentiment is 'superficial' rather than real. It is a warning to which all his listeners remain deaf, since they continually attribute to Farfrae a degree of emotional sensibility which actually resides in his songs.

A more complex response is articulated by Elizabeth-Jane, who concludes from his 'fascinating melodies' and a brief chat with the Casterbridge locals that Farfrae

> seemed to feel exactly as she felt about life and its surroundings – that they were a tragical rather than a comical thing; that though one could be gay on occasion, moments of gaiety were interludes, and no part of the actual drama. It was extraordinary how similar their views were. (p. 68)

Such deductions are surprising since they are drawn from evidence which is at best thin and at worst mawkish, immediately challenging Hardy's earlier remark that 'she sought further into things than other girls in her position' (p. 45). Indeed they only seem explicable if we consider Schopenhauer's contention that music reproduces 'all the emotions of our innermost nature, but entirely without reality and far removed from their pain'.[28] It is this image that the 'subtle-souled girl' who saw deeper into things than most girls of her age apprehends in Farfrae's music, allowing her to draw the conclusions she does (p. 117). Hardy's ironic tone in this appraisal, however, suggests that there is a vast difference between intuition and knowledge gained from experience. Thus, despite Elizabeth-Jane's suspicions, Hardy allows the girl who arrives at Casterbridge to be as yet 'incomplete', possessing all the 'raw materials' of a human being, but requiring settlement in 'their final mould' (p. 45). She is not at this stage the 'seer' who colludes with Hardy in telling the story, but a snob who chides her mother for talking to the furmity woman and argues that 'we must be respectable' as an excuse for putting up in a hotel they cannot afford (pp. 58, 159). It is this youthful Elizabeth-Jane who attributes the emotional depth which actually resides in the music to Farfrae, allowing him to exploit his casual musical facility in her seduction.

Music is never far from their lovemaking: in her capacity of temporary maid, Elizabeth-Jane first overhears him as he saunters up and down 'humming a tune', and is then summoned into his presence by the service bell (p. 64). The mechanism anticipates their romance, Farfrae's nonchalant musicality plucking the harp string that will draw Elizabeth-Jane towards him. And yet in the intimate rendition of a romantic ballad with which Farfrae serenades her, Hardy encodes a warning, for once he is within his room 'the scene and the sentiment ended for the present' (pp. 68, 69). His sentiments are not insincere, but since he possesses the characteristics of the 'well-braced musical instrument' his shallow feelings have an effect out of proportion to his actual character (p. 148). As he admits to her during their misconceived tryst in the hayloft, 'it's well you feel a song for a few minutes, and your eyes they get quite tearful; but you finish it, and for all you felt you don't mind it or think of it again for a long while' (p. 98).

The truth of Farfrae's admission becomes apparent through the ease with which he controls his feelings: he makes a conscious decision not to play the 'Romeo' with Elizabeth-Jane following Henchard's disapproval, instead transferring his affections to Lucetta with a business ease (p. 115). When, however, Farfrae and Elizabeth-Jane eventually marry it is quite clear that the latter is perfectly aware of her husband's shortcomings. Hardy makes this apparent at the wedding feast, played before the observing consciousness of Henchard who stands to one side 'like a dark ruin' (p. 279). Primarily, he is perplexed by the fact that Farfrae, a widower, and his daughter-in-law, who 'long ago appraised life at a moderate value', should find such comfort in dancing (p. 279). Marriage for him was no dancing matter, but an act of duty. However, it is noticeable that 'the pair were not dancing together' and 'their emotions breathed a much subtler essence than at other times' (p. 279). In effect, both have grown through experience, and though they are both in harmony with the wider music of the ambivalent process, they participate on their own terms. Elizabeth-Jane, like Grace Melbury, enters her union with no illusions, determined to make use of the limited opportunities for happiness it affords. Significantly, it is a lesson that Henchard never learns.

Henchard's reaction to Farfrae's first performance at the Three Mariners is predictable only in that it is massive:

> When the Scotsman sang his voice had reached Henchard's ears through the heart-shaped holes in the window-shutters, and had led him to pause outside them a long while.
>
> 'To be sure, to be sure, how that fellow does draw me!' he had said to himself, 'I suppose 'tis because I'm so lonely.' (p. 69)

Quite what it is in Farfrae's music that moves him to this emotional extreme requires careful consideration. Towards the latter third of the novel Hardy notes of Henchard that 'he was the kind of man to whom some human object for pouring out his heat upon – were it emotive or were it choleric – was almost a necessity' (p. 122). Thus, having at Weydon-Priors traded love for power, the Henchard we meet at the King's Arms has fulfilled his economic ambitions, but is, by his own admission, lonely and in need of affection. As a confessed 'woman-hater' such a role is not to be fulfilled by his wife, to whom he can extend a sense of duty only, but rather by Farfrae. In him he recognises the two separate threads of business and sentiment woven but not mixed. In economic terms Henchard perceives him as his total opposite: whereas he regards himself as a 'rule o' the thumb sort of man', he claims Farfrae is a man of 'judgement and knowledge' (p. 63). Yet in Farfrae's singing, heard through apertures shaped like idealised hearts, Henchard believes that he recognises a man of deep emotions. Thus, the outsider is idealised into a combination of a hard-nosed business partner, and a brotherly figure who will fulfil Henchard's need for an emotional focus.

There are, however, a number of ironies in this sudden affection for Farfrae, which Hardy explores through his use of musical allusion. It is ironic, for instance, that Henchard's attachment to Farfrae as a man of moderation should be characterised by the emotional energy typical of 'a man who knew no moderation in his requests and impulses' (p. 84). It is also ironic that Henchard should, like Elizabeth-Jane, mistake Farfrae's well-guided sentiment for the expression of emotions as large as his own; a mistake that will allow the young Scotsman to play upon him 'as on an instrument' (p. 239).

This element of emotional control leads, as Julian Moynahan has observed, Hardy to draw parallels with the relationship between King Saul and David in the Old Testament.[29] Saul was a ruler who, like Henchard, was destined to lead a lonely and melancholy life until he met the younger David, whose singing charms him. It is a relationship which founders upon Saul's enviousness of his protégé's power, leading to a downward spiral of resentment, jealousy and eventually persecution. This pattern is reflected in the alliance of Henchard and Farfrae: the former's initial affection is poisoned by his impulsive and ill-advised decision to confide in Farfrae 'the secrets of his life' (p. 104). His 'dim dread' that this information will be used against him causes Henchard to misinterpret any questioning of his authority as an abuse of trust; a fear dramatised by Farfrae's support for the trouserless Abel Whittle against the idiosyncratic disciplinary methods of his master (pp. 103, 104).

This resentment is fanned further in a musical incident immediately following this scene, when Henchard accompanies Farfrae, who has been asked for by name, to the cottage of a deceased farmer to price a stock of hay. As the two men approach the door Farfrae is depicted practising 'a piece of music *sotto voce*', only stopping as they get closer because, as he notes, 'As their father is dead I won't go on with such as that' (p. 104). Henchard's sneered response, 'Do you care so very much about hurting folks' feelings?' appears initially to be an insight into the essential shallowness which lies behind his friend's musical ability: Farfrae desists, as Martin Seymour-Smith notes, as a gesture to the dead rather than from compassion for the living (p. 104).[30] Henchard's petulant addition of 'Especially mine!', however, dispels this delusion, revealing as it does a brooding self-absorption that will prove fertile ground for resentment to blossom into jealousy (p. 104).

Such a blossoming takes place at Farfrae's entertainment, when Henchard is forced to acknowledge 'the immense admiration for the Scotchman that revealed itself in the women's faces' and listen to the tributes paid by his fellow councillors (p. 108). His rash decision to dismiss his lieutenant is, of course, disastrous, for he not only loses his business manager, but also the focus of his love. Since there is no middle ground for Henchard, having fulfilled the role of the Mayor's idealised brother, the young Scot now re-emerges for Henchard as the equally unrealistic extreme of devil incarnate (p. 122). Music is central to Henchard's reinvention of their relationship, transforming itself in his mind from an expression of sincerely held emotion to the insidious means by which Farfrae 'got over me, and heaved me out' (p. 208). Thus, Henchard conceives of himself as the benevolent victim of a scheming outsider who had used his songs to manipulate his downfall. In this light the cacophonous rendition of Psalm 109 – by which Henchard publicly curses his enemy – can be read as an attempt to steal the power of music and turn it against its malevolent owner.

This performance is full of ironies which will be explored presently, but for now I want to make one further observation concerning Henchard's process of idealisation. This activity is only effective when Henchard is distanced from Farfrae, as he is when he hears his singing through heart-shaped holes. In his presence the process becomes more problematic, a difficulty Hardy demonstrates in the wrestling match in the hayloft – a scene where music plays a central, if unexpected, role. The Henchard who awaits his unsuspecting adversary sees himself, as Robert Kiely has observed, as a force of righteousness just about to engage in an epic encounter with evil.[31] He has even tied one arm to his side to ensure that his victory over his weaker opponent will be honourable. Unfortunately for his plan, when Farfrae enters he is humming the tune of 'the song he had sung when he arrived years before at the Three Mariners', causing Hardy to make the following observation of his hero: 'Nothing moved Henchard like an old melody. He sank back. ' "No; I can't do it!" he gasped. "Why does the infernal fool begin that now!" ' (pp. 236–237). Once again it is an allusion to music which both baffles and strains the reader's credulity. But through it Hardy demonstrates quite clearly Henchard's idealising tendency. Under its influence the pendulum of Henchard's emotions swings back to the idealised Farfrae who he had first heard in the Three Mariners. When the music stops, however, he can continue his crusade against malevolence. It is only when, as Kiely notes, he looks into his defeated adversary's eyes and sees not the devil or his brother but another human being that Henchard's game disintegrates, leaving him ashamed and confused, crouching in the corner in a womanly attitude (p. 239).[32]

The same sense of his own heroic stature attends Henchard's conducting of Psalm 109. More than ever, as Moynahan makes clear, he becomes identified with Saul, but in his own eyes he is a wronged ruler whose compassion prevents him doubling up his adversary 'as if [he] were a twig' (p. 208). Instead, he chooses to curse his enemy, ironically through a hymn written by David which presents an accurate record of Henchard's decline and future demise: the last line of the fourth verse, for example, echoes Henchard's desire to be remembered by nobody.[33] Significantly, when the choir has finished its rendition, Henchard is depicted with his eyes downcast, his disposition introspective and his speech broken. 'Don't you blame David' he muses:

> he knew what he was about when he wrote that!...If I could afford it, be hanged if I wouldn't keep a church choir at my own expense to play and sing to me at these low, dark times of my life. But the bitter

thing is, that when I was rich I didn't need what I could have, and now I be poor I can't have what I need!'. (p. 207)

There is intimation here of one of those false dawns which accompany Henchard's decline, for in this contemplative mood he appears to perceive the moral centre of the novel: that life is made to suffer. It is a message that we have heard encoded in the Aeolian modulations, the song of a weak-voiced bird and the music of the River Blackwater. This is a message, however, that Henchard has constantly ignored. In wishing for a choir to remind him of it he simply justifies our conviction that, unlike David, he never knows 'what he is about'; a supposition immediately vindicated when he raises his eyes and spies Farfrae passing: 'there's the man we've been singing about' (p. 207). Henchard is a fetishist who is much happier dealing with external agents arranged against him than the vagaries of self-analysis. Thus, despite his boorishness, the Henchard who stands with his back to the door, poker in hand, is a rather pathetic figure, whose tragedy lies in his continued obliviousness to the music surrounding him.

In the latter part of the novel Hardy dramatises Henchard's inability to understand himself through a series of visits to the banks of the 'Schwarzwasser': The introduction of the German pseudonym immediately elevating the river from a topographical feature identifiable on a map to an idealised stretch of water conducive to introspection (p. 124). Hardy's choice of location seems apt, immediately evoking the concept of the 'stream of consciousness', a term in psychology, as da Sousa Correa has noted, used by James Sully in 1881, long before it was appropriated by the Modernists.[34] In Hardy's analogy, however, the river fuses with music to provide a clear expression of the unconscious forces that motivate Henchard's behaviour.

> The wanderer in this direction who should stand still for a few moments on a quiet night, might hear singular symphonies from these waters, as from a lampless orchestra, all playing in their sundry tones from near and far parts of the moor. At a hole in a rotten weir they executed a recitative; where a tributary brook fell over a stone breastwork they trilled cheerily; under an arch they performed a metallic cymballing; and at Durnover Hole they hissed. The spot at which their instrumentation rose loudest was a place called Ten Hatches, whence during high springs there proceeded a very fugue of sounds. (p. 256)

The harmonising of the polyphonic strains into a fugue indicates the unified nature of the ambivalent process underlying the phenomenal world, and the fact that the orchestra is lampless – that is, unable to read its music – emphasises its essential blindness. Significantly, Henchard remains deaf to this music; rather, it is a Wordsworthian wanderer who acts as auditor, reminding us of the River Derwent in *The Prelude*, which becomes something of an earth mother to the poet, blending 'his murmurs with my nurse's song' and 'mak[ing] ceaseless music that composed my thoughts'.[35]

Henchard is never able to compose his thoughts, he never comes close to understanding his character, largely because he eschews the vagaries of self-analysis in favour of a fetishistic belief in external agencies. This is made clear through his visit to the river immediately following the revelation of the true paternity of Elizabeth-Jane. In his chosen spot he is greeted with the 'ruins of a Franciscan priory, and a mill attached to the same, the water of which roared down a back-hatch like the voice of desolation' (p. 124). The voice echoes the 'eternal note of sadness' heard by Matthew Arnold on 'Dover Beach' as he listened to the Sea of Faith recede.[36] The message too is similar: now that belief in a benevolent God lies in ruins, where can man find comfort in the harsh universe? Strangely, Henchard's comfort derives neither from religious belief nor from the stoicism displayed by his dead wife, but rather from the conviction that his suffering is unique. Thus, ignoring the music of the water his eyes are drawn to a 'square mass' protruding from the prison on the opposite bank which is 'like a pedestal lacking its statue' (p. 124). The missing feature is the corpse of a man, a vacancy that Henchard perceives himself as filling.

Hardy also recalls Henchard's egotism in his visit to the river following his impulsive lie to Newson, when, 'amazed at what he had done', he resolves to commit suicide (p. 253). As a despairing Henchard stares into the waters of the Ten Hatches, Hardy informs the reader that

> if he could have summoned music to his aid his existence might even now have been borne; for with Henchard music was of a regal power. The merest trumpet or organ tone was enough to move him, and high harmonies transubstantiated him. But hard fate had ordained that he should be unable to call up this Divine spirit in his need. (pp. 255–256)

Craig Raine notes some bemusement at this previously unrecorded love of music and argues that the passage can only be understood if we replace the term 'music' with 'love'.[37] However, it is not music and love that are analogous in Hardy's presentation, rather music and the impulse towards suicide, an admittedly bemusing combination that is only explicable in the light of Schopenhauer's reflections on the subject. In *Pessimism*, Sully states that 'Schopenhauer seeks to make clear what he means by denial of will to live by contrasting it with the impulse of suicide.... The self-murderer really wills to live; he wills "the unimpeded existence and affirmation of the body." '[38] Thus, suicide is futile since the indestructible will lives beyond its temporary objectification in a particular individual, the only sure means of escape derives from will-annihilation through the apprehension of art – and the highest form of art is music. Henchard's invocation, therefore, is pregnant with irony, for not only does his egotism in wishing to 'summon[] music' make him deaf to the 'singular symphonies' immediately before him, but in alienating Farfrae, much in the same way that Saul drove away David, he has succeeded in driving away the only person capable of creating music that will elevate the Mayor above his despair (p. 256).[39]

The irony is increased further through the way in which Henchard is prevented from carrying out his intention: it is not by a sudden apprehension of the music around him, but rather by the appearance in the water of an effigy which was not simply 'a man somewhat resembling him, but one in all respects his counterpart, his actual double' (p. 257). In effect, Hardy brings Henchard face to face with himself. He is not, however, moved to greater self-awareness – he remains impervious to psychological analysis – preferring instead to maintain the myth of external agencies and conceive of himself 'in the actual presence of an appalling miracle' (p. 257). If previously he was the figure missing from the gallows, then now he feels himself freed from punishment and 'in Somebody's hand!' – somebody who, for whatever reason, wishes to keep him alive (p. 258).

Throughout the novel, then, Henchard's desperate attempts to understand his character are undermined through Hardy's bringing together of music and water as an exploration of the unconscious forces controlling his behaviour. This choric role is made particularly clear when Henchard does indeed appear to change. When, for example, following his economic ruin he acknowledges to Farfrae that 'I – sometimes think I've wronged 'ee!', and stoically decides to enter his employment as a hay trusser, he does indeed appear to be a repentant sinner ripe for salvation (pp. 202, 203). This optimism, however, is undermined by Hardy's reintroduction of the musical theme through his description of the two bridges over the Schwarzwasser to which 'all the failures of the town' gravitate to contemplate their fate (p. 199). Already, there is a change in Henchard's position here, for he is now not alone but rather one of many. Furthermore, although both bridges have 'speaking countenances' each has a unique disposition reflecting the personality of those who stare over its parapets (p. 198). The first attracts those of 'lowest character' who spit at their adversities and reject the idea that 'the iron had entered their souls', claiming instead that 'they [are] down on their luck' (p. 199). In effect, they perceive their unhappiness as a temporary state that must be endured, rather than either a permanent psychological state, or a punishment meted out by vindictive gods. This is the bridge frequented by such characters as Jopp, Mother Cuxsom and Abel Whittle, who, for all their faults, are survivors.

The bridge further from the town is for those 'of the politer stamp' who are embarrassed by their failure (p. 199). They do not consider themselves 'down on their luck', but afflicted with 'lucklessness', a distinction which suggests that they believe themselves permanently tainted rather than momentarily indisposed. As a result, whereas the former bridge generates camaraderie in defiance of adversity, their condition is one of communal self-absorption. The loungers here spend their days not stoically making the best of it, but rather dreaming of improbable solutions to their problems, or contemplating suicide. None can hear the purling of the music below, for to do so would be to deny the exclusivity of their own suffering. This is the bridge favoured by Henchard, his belief that he is persecuted by a malign intelligence being entirely consistent with the egotistical outlook of the other loungers. Thus, despite all the signs that Henchard is coming to terms with his fate, these remain merely cosmetic. In fact, as Hardy intimates, if he has undergone any moral change at all it is for the worse, his recent setbacks not affecting a stoical resistance, but rather a quickening of the sinister qualities within him.

In reality, Henchard's character does not change throughout the novel, it remains an expression of the wider process, and therefore mysterious and inviolate. Even when his reunion with his daughter seems to offer the possibility of a happy ending, it is significant that his decision to 'school himself to accept her will' and 'not be the Henchard of former days' is motivated by a desire not to lose her rather than by a greater understanding of himself (p. 262). As in his earlier wife-sale, he has gambled the twin cards of love and ambition, and is eager to see them pay off. Thus, when his serenity is destroyed upon Newson's return, it should come as no surprise that Henchard immediately returns to his old fetishistic ways and jumps to the conclusion that he has been selected for further punishment. Accordingly, he reinvents himself as Cain and makes the theatrical gesture of a pilgrimage to Weydon-Priors to abase himself at the scene of what he describes as his 'crime' (p. 273). But Henchard's transgression has nothing to do with wife-selling. If any crime has been committed at all, it is simply that of trying to impose oneself on the ambivalent universe, a fact to which his egocentricity makes him deaf and blind.

It is apt, therefore, that his wedding gift to Elizabeth-Jane should be a 'caged goldfinch' wrapped in paper, a blind 'little singer' that invokes the 'trite evening song' of the 'weak bird', which Henchard had ignored in favour of his own 'ballet sheet' (pp. 276, 282). We are reminded of the late poem 'The Caged Goldfinch', in which the narrator is depicted musing on the 'jailed' bird apparently abandoned 'on a recent grave'. As it 'hops from stage to stage' the observer notes how it 'tried to sing', but gave up, to be replaced by a look of 'inquiry in its wistful eye'.[40] In this nihilistic vision, the determination to endure life's misery made apparent in the songs of both the 'Darkling Thrush' and the 'Blinded Bird' has given way to a despairing puzzlement shared by the bird, narrator, poet and reader as to 'him or her who placed it there, and why'. It is an appropriate symbol of Henchard's position at the close of the novel, the man of character turning into the more wistful Henchard who spends his time staring into the depths of the Blackwater attempting to understand the workings of the universe. It is, of course, a mystery that he never solves to his satisfaction, and it remains entirely fitting that his present should be forgotten and left to die a lonely death.

Similar conditions surround Henchard's own lonely death on Egdon Heath, where Cain is tended by his Abel. It is a scene entirely in keeping with Henchard's penchant for the theatrical, his litany of despair evoking parallels with Job and David in addition to Cain. But once again Hardy diffuses Henchard's claims as to the exclusivity of his suffering, this time by the presence of 'a blasted clump of firs on the summit of a hill' (p. 283). Like the fir trees growing above Clym Yeobright's cottage, they remind the reader of the tragical potentiality inherent in the attempts of the individual to impose his will on the universe. Their blasted state drives home the need for calm acceptance, a message evidently understood by Elizabeth-Jane, who excuses her bitter parting from her step-father with a fatalistic 'But there's no altering – so it must be', and carries out his will only 'as far as practicable' (p. 285). In effect, Henchard's sense of the tragic is entirely undermined by Elizabeth-Jane's common sense. So, in the same way that at the end of *The Return of the Native* Hardy places hope in the audience of Clym Yeobright, who remains to the end absorbed in his own tragedy, hope emerges in *The Mayor of Casterbridge* from the quiet determination of those characters, such as Elizabeth-Jane, who find harmony with the music of the wider process and respond with flexibility to its harsh rhythms.

7

'All Creation Groaning': A Deaf Ear to Music in *Jude the Obscure*

Having read the 'terribly sensible advice' contained in the letter of T. Tetuphenay, the disheartened Jude entered a local Christminster tavern:

> He stood at a bar and tossed off two or three glasses, then unconsciously sauntered along till he came to a spot called The Fourways in the middle of the city, gazing abstractedly at the groups of people like one in a trance, till, coming to himself, he began talking to the policeman fixed there.
> That officer yawned, [and] stretched...
> Here the two sexes had met for loving, hating, coupling, parting; had waited, had suffered, for each other; had triumphed over each other; cursed each other in jealousy, blessed each other in forgiveness.
> [Jude] began to see that the town life was a book of humanity infinitely more palpitating, varied, and compendious than the gown life. These struggling men and women before him were the reality of Christminster....
> He had tapped the real Christminster life. A band was playing, and the crowd walked about and jostled each other, and every now and then a man got upon a platform and sang a comic song. (pp. 138–139)

It is one of those revelatory moments in Hardy's writing, such as Mrs Yeobright's vision of the maggoty world of ephemerons on Edgdon Heath, when a character glimpses the correct relationship between man and the universe. As the Spirits of *The Dynasts* continually remind the reader, mankind is simply a 'writhing, crawling, heaving and vibrating' mass controlled by the Immanent Will, which Hardy illustrates by means of his inharmonious cosmic music.[1] In her youth, Sue Bridehead imagined the First Cause operated like a 'melody composed in a dream...

147

wonderfully excellent to the half-aroused intelligence, but hopelessly absurd at the full waking' (p. 351). As Jude dulls his intellect through alcohol, he enters the semi-conscious state (signified by the yawning policeman) in which he is able to perceive mankind as it participates in the somnambulistic 'dance of life' animated by this cosmic music. This is 'the real Christminster life', which consists not in illusory dreams of academic degrees, but in accepting one's place inside the jostling 'book of humanity', and finding happiness when available.

The tragedy of *Jude the Obscure* emerges from the fact that the insights of both his central characters remain momentary, their complex characters generally making them deaf to the music surrounding them. From his youth, Jude is both unwanted and out of harmony with his environment, characteristics Hardy dramatises through the very opening scene of the book:

> The schoolmaster was leaving the village, and everybody seemed sorry.... [T]he only cumbersome article possessed by the master, in addition to the packing-case of books, was a cottage piano that he had bought at an auction during the year in which he thought of learning instrumental music. But the enthusiasm having waned he had never acquired any skill in playing, and the purchased article had been a perpetual trouble to him ever since in moving house.
>
> The blacksmith, the farm bailiff, and the schoolmaster himself were standing in perplexed attitudes in the parlour before the instrument. The master had remarked that even if he got it into the cart he should not know what to do with it on his arrival at Christminster, the city he was bound for, since he was only going into temporary lodgings just at first.
>
> A little boy of eleven, who had been thoughtfully assisting in the packing, joined the group of men, and as they rubbed their chins he spoke up, blushing at the sound of his own voice: 'Aunt have got a great fuel-house, and it could be put there, perhaps, till you've found a place to settle in, sir.' (p. 33)

In a novel which focuses so closely on the themes of failed ambition, obscurity and the inadequacies of conventional means of emotional communication, this scene is revealing. It is the piano that Phillotson never learned to play, becoming a symbol of failed ambition, to be replaced, as it will with Jude, by his equally futile Christminster dream. The emotional sterility which will undermine his relationship with Sue is made clear in the reduction of a potential source of pleasure into a 'cumbersome article' that he did not know what to do with. Indeed, even his intention to play is transformed into the scholarly pursuit of learning 'instrumental music', which Hardy links with the 'packing case of books'. We are reminded of how Hardy employs the piano in his poem 'An East End Curate' to symbolise the stifling of emotional potential by a combination of monotonous routine and abeyance to Christian principle. The piano remains unplayed, 'its keys much yellowed', and the potential for pleasure offered by the presence of 'Novello's Anthems' and 'a few glees' is silenced by the oppressiveness of the 'Laws of Heaven for Earth' in a frame upon the wall.[2]

There is a sense of alienation that pervades the scene: we are placed on the outside, looking in as the narrator speculates as to the 'seeming' feelings of the central participants. Their identity, as Hughes has noted in his excellent analysis of this scene, remains anonymous beyond their social context, even Jude is perceived from the outside as an obscure 'little boy of eleven . . . blushing at the sound of his own voice' as he attempts to capture the attention of those around him.[3] The voice, that 'feature of my self', as Connor argues, 'whose nature it is thus to move from me to the world, and to move me into the world' is depicted as a source of embarrassment for the young Jude, who is too sensitive to articulate himself.[4] It is a muteness that will undermine both his intellectual and emotional ambitions throughout the novel. Just as Farfrae's emotional flexibility was aligned with the 'agricultural piano' that was his innovative seed drill, Jude's plight is mirrored in that of the piano: he is too highly strung for his environment, a 'cumbersome article' finding temporary accommodation with Aunt Drussila.

Hardy further emphasises Jude's dislocation from his environment in the very next scene, where he is placed in the 'wide and lonely depression' of Mr Troutham's cornfield and surrounded by the echoes of the 'songs from ancient harvest-days' (p. 38). The proximity of these ancient harvesters to the formulation of the laws by Sue's great composer suggests that they were in harmony with this environment in a way that Jude, whose sensitivity is signalled by his unwillingness to tread upon earthworms, is not (p. 41). In Schopenhauerian terms, they had learned to find happiness by submerging their portion of the individual will in the wider process. Their songs, like those of the Egdon rustics or the 'Darkling Thrush', remind us that in Hardy's universe happiness derives from the ability to endure and make the best of limited opportunities for happiness. Furthermore, as with the music of Egdon, these songs evoke a Spencerian evolutionary period when man's distant ancestors were able to communicate through the 'language of the emotions' before feeling became dissected from thought and man evolved a reliance on the word.[5]

In a novel in which the expression of feeling will prove so difficult, it is significant that Jude remains out of harmony with these songs. Instead of scaring the unwanted rooks, he establishes a bond of common sympathy with them, leading him to the hope that all might be happy. This dream, however, is rudely interrupted by the impassioned admonishment of farmer Troutham, following which Jude resigns himself to a moment of contemplation whilst lying upon his back 'on a heap of litter near the pig-sty':

> Events did not rhyme quite as he had thought. Nature's logic was too horrid for him to care for. That mercy towards one set of creatures was cruelty to another sickened his sense of harmony. As you got older, and felt yourself to be at the centre of your time, and not at a point in its circumference, as you had felt when you were little, you were seized with a sort of shuddering, he perceived. All around there seemed to be something glaring, garish, rattling, and the noises and glares hit upon the little cell called your life, and shook it, and warped it.
>
> If he could only prevent himself growing up! He did not want to be a man.
>
> Then, like the natural boy, he forgot his despondency, and sprang up. (p. 42)

This scene establishes the pattern that will mark Jude's life as one of dreaming, striving, disillusion, perplexed contemplation and fresh hope. Unfortunately for him, his wish is granted: he never matures sufficiently to arrive at an accommodation with the harsh universe, but continues to spring up with new hopes, which are met by ever more ferocious disappointments. In Schopenhauerian terms, music provides the perfect analogue for such experience, since it moves the listener to experience expectation, tension, thwarted resolution and renewed expectation. Hardy emphasises the musical patterning of Jude's decline through his presentation of the main events of his life through a chorus of 'musicalised noise' – the external sounds that continue to assail the 'little cell' of his young life.

Hardy's presentation of Jude's mental processes is of interest in the light of recent developments in auditory psychology. Connor has argued that since it is impossible to turn the ears off, sound is crucial to our development of a sense of homogeneity. He argues that the baby develops in a 'sonorous envelope' which defines, limits and shapes the baby's sense of 'self' whilst blocking out the disintegrating and confusing effects of dissonant noise. As the infant develops, music takes the place of this earlier envelope:

> the perceived regularities of rhythm, tone, melody, and harmony have the effect of articulating (breaking up and co-ordinating) and thus specializing what would otherwise be an undifferentiated torrent of noise. Music, and musicalized noise, is sound that holds us (arrests us, supports us) in the shapeliness that we have ourselves afforded it, in the patterning response of our musical attention. Music is sound which appears to have become autonomous, achieving solidity and form separate from its occasion or medium.[6]

Throughout *Jude the Obscure*, Hardy's young hero is continually depicted in a state of bewilderment, assailed by competing choices which are presented in the form of 'musicalised noise'. We never really see Jude, rather he is transformed into a 'packet of sensations', in Deleuzean phrase, which is continually in the process of responding to external stimuli. Thus, the momentary perplexity that follows the crumbling of his dream of food for all is quickly replaced by the Christminster dream, which, characteristically, asserts itself through the medium of music.

Hardy's careful depiction of the vanes, slates and freestone work in minute particularity is not the product of the image seen by Jude as he stands on the ladder of the Brown House, but, as Geoffrey Thurley as noted, an imaginative representation of reality.[7] Essentially Christminster is the distillation of a city in the real world perceived through Jude's idealism. The medium binding these images together is music, which for Connor allows the 'surrender of the visual individual to a structured community of sensation'.[8] Hardy's insistence on the transcendent and idealistic qualities of sound over sight has a good pedigree, Jonathan Reé noting that for both Hegel and Berkeley it was not eyesight but hearing that was the true sense of the ideal, liberating us from our dependence on the material world.[9] It is no accident, therefore, that Jude first hears 'the voice of the city, faint and musical' in the form of the church bells announcing 'we are happy here!' (p. 47). This musical appeal is emphasised further by a passing carter who claims that 'there's beautiful music everywhere in Christminster. You med be religious, or you med be not, but you can't help striking in your homely note with the rest' (p. 49). This observation gives to the alienated Jude a hope that he may find harmony within its precincts as well as 'something to anchor on, [and] to cling to' (p. 49).

The Christminster dream established, Hardy allows Jude to go some way to fulfilling it before reasserting those elements of his character through which the wider process will thwart his progress. In a letter to Edmund Gosse, Hardy claimed that 'the "grimy" features of the story go to show the contrast between the ideal life a man wished to lead, and the squalid real life he was fated to lead'.[10] There is perhaps no grimier way of puncturing the 'little cell' of Jude's dreams than the slap of a pig's pizzle on the back of the neck, which heralds the appearance of the 'complete and substantial female animal', Arabella Donn, whose primitive sexuality holds Jude on 'the spot against his intention' through the unvoiced Darwinian 'call of woman to man' (pp. 62, 64). As his own sexual nature emerges, however, Jude manages to sanitise it through a process of apotheosis that transforms Arabella into a figure of pastoral innocence just as unrealistic as his dreams of Christminster. In this way Jude allows the music of the Christminster bells to be replaced by the 'chime of church bells', which reduce themselves to 'one note, which quickened, and stopped' (p. 78). It is the death knell of the university dream and the reassertion, through the bells of a church wedding, of the life Jude is fated to lead.

When any hope of a happy marriage proves as false as Arabella's dimples and hair, and even Jude's belief that 'his idea of her was the thing of most consequence, not Arabella herself' is compromised by his discovery of the deception played upon him, he falls, once again, in to a slough of despair: 'events did not rhyme quite as he had thought' (pp. 81, 42). His youthful wish to be out of the world finds expression in a half-hearted suicide attempt, but this magnificent gesture eventually gives way to the less painful alternative of drunkenness. It is left to the eminently practical Arabella to find a solution, and sail for Australia on the grounds that 'she had grown tired of him' (p. 95).

Once again, Hardy allows his striving individual to throw off his despondency and spring up 'like the natural boy' (p. 42). Arabella has, however, awakened Jude's sexual instinct, so that the Christminster dream that reasserts itself is complicated by his attraction to his cousin, Sue. In Jude's own mind, however, Sue is merely to bless his new theo-logical project, by offering him a focus for his nobler thoughts, a process that begins with his reverent kissing of the photograph of the 'ideal character, about whose form he began to weave curious and fantastic day-dreams' (p. 112). It is, however, a deluded hope, something that Hardy makes apparent through his use of music.

During a Christminster church service Hardy places Jude behind 'the girl for whom he was beginning to nourish an extraordinary tenderness', and then animates the scene with a rendition of Psalm 119 (p. 115). For Jude, who has been abasing himself as a 'wicked worthless fellow' who has given in to his animal passions, the Psalm is pertinent for it asks, 'wherewithal shall a young man cleanse his way?' As 'the great waves of pedal music' connect him with the woman who appears 'steeped body and soul in church sentiment', she seems to offer the possibility of an 'anchorage for his thoughts, which promises to supply both social and spiritual possibilities' (pp. 114, 115). Hardy's choice of Psalm here, however, is instructive for a full interpretation of the scene:

> By taking heed thereto according to thy word...
> O let me not wander from thy commandments.
> Thy word have I hid in mine heart,
> that I might not sin against thee.
> Blessed art thou, O Lord:
> teach me thy statutes.
> With my lips have I declared
> all the judgements of thy mouth.
> I have rejoiced in the way of thy testimonies,...
> I will delight myself in thy statutes:
> I will not forget thy word.[11]

The Psalm's emphasis on 'words' as a means of maintaining the purity of the soul offers an apt objectification of Jude's religious belief, which comprises words expressed with suitable reverence. Jude creates his faith like his dream, finding something morally beneficial and virtuous in the mere utterance of the articles of his belief. Reé reminds us that for Freud, the attribution of special powers to words is the defining mark of all kinds of pre-scientific superstitions.[12] Hardy illustrates this characteristic through Jude's recitation, with 'reverent loudness', of the 'strange syllables... [and] words that had for Jude an indescribable enchantment' of his Griesbach text (p. 119).[13] It is these articles of faith that he intones drunkenly in a Christminster inn, berating his congregation afterwards for not being able to distinguish between them and 'the Rat Catcher's Daughter in double Dutch' (p. 143). This is precisely the point: his words could be nonsense for all concerned, particularly Jude. This failure to go beyond the word means that his theology will never be strong enough to counter his sexual impulse. Protected by the sounds of his faith accentuated and given power by music, he really feels that Sue can appeal to his better nature. But as the music ceases he is brought face to face with 'the real nature of the magnetism', and the feelings that 'seemed to have an ecclesiastical basis during the service' reveal themselves in all their animalism (p. 115).

The dream of theological advancement blessed by Sue's spiritual comradeship is also compromised by the fact that their convergence is predetermined. As with Clym and Eustacia, Hardy's medium for demonstrating this desire is musical vibration: a channel which breaks through the 'little cell' of their individual lives, undermining the awkwardness of words. Significantly, both Sue and Jude are presented as being too sensitive for their environment: Sue is depicted as less of an individual than a 'mere cluster of nerves' for whom 'the fibres of her nature seemed strained like harp-strings' (pp. 241, 367). Hardy often remarks upon her 'quivering' and tremulous nature, and observes that she is 'a harp which the least wind of emotion from another's heart could make to vibrate' (p. 292).[14] Hardy's employment of the Romantic symbol of the harp, however, has less to do with the patriarchal construction of femininity, than an illustration of the possible consequences of over-specialisation and refinement for species evolving according to the Spencerian principle of materialist progress from the 'homogeneous to the heterogeneous'.[15] It is a fear to which he alludes in *The Life*: 'the human race is too extremely developed for its corporeal conditions, the nerves being evolved to an activity abnormal in such an environment'.[16]

In physiological terms, Jude and Sue are too highly strung for their environment, enabling musical vibration to become an exceptionally refined means of communication – a condition which is demonstrated most clearly through the sexual impulse. Thus, it comes as no surprise that Jude should be drawn to Sue in the ecclesiastical warehouse, even before he has seen her, by the 'qualities of his own voice; softened and sweetened' in hers (p. 111). From this point onwards, in accordance with Spencerian theory, voice tone becomes a privileged means of communication between them, Hardy noting that even when 'they talked on an indifferent subject...there was ever a silent conversation passing between their emotions, so perfect was the reciprocity between them' (p. 221). This 'extraordinary affinity, or sympathy' between the pair, as Phillotson describes it, is illustrated clearly when all three meet at the model of Jerusalem. Here, Sue's apparent happiness is undermined by the 'momentary revelation of feeling' accorded by her tremulous voice. Briefly, Jude is able to glimpse her emotional confusion and her inability to put her meaning into words, which leads to her impulsive seizure of his hand (pp. 245, 129).

A similar loss of physical control follows their musically inspired meeting in the schoolroom at Shaston. Thinking himself alone, Jude begins to play upon an old piano modulating into a 'hymn which had so affected him in the previous week'. Both the instrument and the music are of significance: it is the piano that Phillotson never learned to play, and the hymn that had seemed to connect Jude to Sue during the church service. Thus, the emotional histories of the three central characters converge on the piano: as Phillotson's emotional sterility is present in the choice of instrument, so the emotional fulfilment enjoyed by Jude and Sue is in the quavering chords. As Jude plays, the vibrating chords of the piano momentarily allow both he and Sue to explore their feelings for one another without the encumbrance of words. For both Schopenhauer and particularly Haweis, music offered a means by which otherwise chaotic emotions could be ordered and expressed succinctly, a quality otherwise absent in their relationship:

> A figure moved behind him, and thinking it was still the girl with the broom Jude took no notice, till the person came close and laid her fingers lightly upon his bass hand. The imposed hand was a little one he seemed to know, and he turned.
>
> 'Don't stop,' said Sue. 'I like it'. . . .
>
> Sue sat down, and her rendering of the piece, though not remarkable, seemed divine as compared with his own. She, like him, was evidently touched – to her own surprise – by the recalled air; and when she had finished, and he moved his hand towards hers, it met his own half-way. . . .
>
> She played on, and suddenly turned round; and by an unpremeditated instinct each clasped the other's hand again. (pp. 219–220)

Ian Gregor notes of this scene that 'the darkening room and the rich melancholy music conspire to weave the spell which enables their relationship to take on an added intensity, an intensity made possible by the fact that the music succeeds in awakening Sue's emotions, but at the same time provides a suitably "spiritual" mode of expression'.[17] I think that this is mistaken: the point of the music in this scene is that it releases both from the artificiality governing their lives and shows them acting according to instincts that contravene the 'spiritual' nature of their relationship. It is not the spiritual qualities of the music that are important, but the fact that it expresses the feelings of suffering and yearning felt by Jude and Sue. Furthermore, the intensity of feelings has never been the issue, certainly as far as Sue is concerned, rather it has been the articulation of emotions. To this end, Jude is depicted as absorbed by the music, an isolated idealistic cell outside which Sue, his loved one, is a mere 'figure', a person with a small hand which extends into, and imposes upon, his world. The focus switches to Sue, who is so moved by the piece that she reaches out to touch Jude's outstretched hand, and is then surprised at her own reaction. Tentative physical touching quickly follows the emotional touching of chords as gesture follows music and non-verbal communication replaces the awkward phrases that usually characterise their conversations. The only dissonant tone in this moment of perfect reciprocity is that of the kettle, Jude's wedding gift, which 'sang with some satire in its note' (p. 220).

And well it might, for although such moments indicate that they are indeed a destined pair, their path is strewn with the obstacles typical of a Hardy narrative: a previous marriage, an unfavourable hereditary disposition and a joint tendency to dislocate the intellectual from the emotional. It is quite clear, however, that, unlike *The Woodlanders*, the question of marriage is not to be the rock upon which this particular relationship founders, since not only are both able to divorce with comparative ease, but their own marriage could quite easily have avoided the social opprobrium which pursues them from town to town.[18] It is rather a hereditary fear of the constrictions of the marriage contract, a 'sommat in [their] blood that won't take kindly to the notion of being bound', as Aunt Drusilla explains, which prevents their consummation (p. 94).[19] This fear of commitment paralyses not only their actions, but also their transference of personal experience into public discourse. They are, like Clym and Eustacia, emotionally mute, which is why so many of their conversations deteriorate into an exchange of intellectual phrases in an attempt to find the one appropriate for their situation. As Al Alvarez notes, 'despite all the troubles they have seen together, Jude and Sue speak to each other as though they had just been introduced at a vicarage tea-party'.[20]

Sue's inability to express her feelings is allied to her tendency to use words to externalise her impulses towards self-protection and self-indulgence, inclinations which have dire consequences for Jude. Not only does she deliver a continuous stream of jibes in 'the delicate voice of an epicure in emotions' whilst administering the punishment of the rehearsal of the marriage ceremony, but her 'curiosity to hunt up new sensation' leads her to lambaste Jude's theological beliefs whilst 'putting on flippancy to hide real feeling' (pp. 191, 171). As Ian Gregor has observed, she, like Jude, has allowed words to become detached from their consequences, allowing them to act as both a sword and a shield.[21]

Occasionally, however, this protective barrier is penetrated, an event illustrated quite clearly in an exchange that takes place shortly after Sue's marriage:

> There was something in her face which belied her late assuring words, so strictly proper and so lifelessly spoken that they might have been taken from a list of model speeches in 'The Wife's Guide to Conduct'. Jude knew the quality of every vibration in Sue's voice, could read every symptom of her mental condition; and he was convinced that she was unhappy. (p. 206)

Momentarily the vibrations of voice tone link together these two sensitive souls, undermining the tension between internal experience and the language in which it is expressed. The harp string is plucked and the two halves of the whole are drawn together along invisible threads. It is these vibrations that provide the invisible medium in which their love exists, which is why they are closest when the obscuring qualities of language are absent. This is illustrated clearly when, following one of the more acrimonious exchanges between them, Hardy reduces his heroine to nothing more than a voice that 'seemed trying to nestle in [Jude's] breast' (p. 172). The 'two-in-oneness' is complete, their consonant vibrations replacing the 'mechanical murmur of words' making up the marriage service (pp. 347, 298).[22]

For Jude, already locked into a pattern of hope, striving, disillusion and despair, the advent of Sue brings him into collision with the type of unpredictable personality that is most likely to destroy him. Her marriage to Phillotson, combined with the eventual shattering of his university dream, marks one of the lowest points of his life, when he is overcome by the 'hell of conscious failure', in both ambition and love (p. 145). Lying on his boyhood bed at Marygreen, the shattered Jude is left once more to muse that 'events did not rhyme quite as he had thought'. During one of Jude's earlier fits of despondency, a paternal Hardy had reflected that: 'somebody might have come along that way who would have asked him his trouble, and might have cheered him .... But nobody did come, because nobody does' (p. 55). At the lowest points of his life, however, people do come, offering solutions to Jude's problems. Significantly, these characters remain ill-drawn in their presentation, Hardy choosing to concentrate on the way that their message is brought to Jude through 'musicalised noise' breaking in upon his 'sonorous envelope', shaping his future progress in accordance with the three stages of Comtean evolution.[23] We hardly meet the young curate who modifies Jude's ecclesiastical ambitions with the 'altruistic life' of a church licentiate (p. 149). Rather, this new project 'hit upon the little cell' of Jude's life in the form of the 'mournful wind [which] blew through the trees, and sounded in the chimney like the pedal notes of an organ':

> each ivy leaf overgrowing the wall of the churchless churchyard hard by, now abandoned, pecked its neighbour smartly, and the vane on the new Victorian-Gothic church in the new spot had already begun to creak. Yet apparently it was not always the outdoor wind that made the deep murmurs; it was a voice. He guessed its origin in a moment or two; the curate was praying with his aunt in the adjoining room. (p. 145)

As with Hardy's poem 'Voices of things Growing in a Country Churchyard', we are reminded that the natural world is transformed into a series of masks through which the universal process objectifies itself. The dirge-like tone of decay mingles with the sounds of the aggressively 'pecking' ivy, suggesting that the principle of the 'survival of the fittest' extends to the church and man's beliefs as well as to the natural environment. Man, is simply another organ-stop through which the 'unweeting wind' of necessity blows, the 'murmurs' of the curate mingling with the organ music of the trees to remind us that in Hardy's world he is little more than a Christmas mummer delivering lines already scripted for him. Nevertheless, his disembodied tones allow the new dream of the church licentiate to supplant that of the high church and the university degree in Jude's boyish mind. However, even though Hardy seems to be offering the new church as a solution to Jude's problems, he notes that its weather vane has 'already begun to creak', suggesting that this new-found faith is already showing signs of weakness. Indeed, soon after its inception, Jude himself seems to be aware that his new project has less to do with faith than his feelings for Sue, 'an ethical contradictoriness to which he was not blind' (p. 150).

Jude's dreams of entering the church as a licentiate founder on his licentiousness. Not only does 'his passion for Sue trouble...his soul', but an evening of 'lawful abandonment to the society of Arabella' following her return from Sydney leads him to reflect that 'taken all round, he was a man of too many passions to make a good clergyman; the utmost he could hope for was that in a life of constant internal warfare between flesh and spirit the former might not always be victorious' (p. 210). Once again a despondent Jude is left to reflect on the disharmony of the universe, when a hymn that he has been rehearsing as part of a church choir awakens the new idea that its composer may be able to understand his position. Accordingly, the impulsive Jude, 'like the child that he was', sprang up with the half-formed intention of visiting him (p. 211).

In the same way that Hardy's introduction of Henchard's previously unacknowledged love of music seems a curious observation to be made while a man contemplates suicide, the episode of the composer must puzzle the reader. Ostensibly, Jude is drawn to him because the harmonies of the hymn suggest that he has found the perfect balance between his passions and the spiritual, thus allowing music to lever him above the misery of the world. However, when considered in relation to Hardy's metaphysical music it functions not only as an illustration of Jude's essential deafness, but also an indictment of Sue's great composer. Like Elizabeth-Jane before him, Jude has made the mistake of attributing to the composer qualities which actually reside in his composition. We are reminded of the composer momentarily heard by Tess in the church at Marlott, who, in Schopenhauerian terms 'reveals the inner nature of the world, and expresses the deepest wisdom in a language which his reason does not understand'.[24] Like the cinema projectionist, Jude's composer cares little for the nature of the revelation, or for its effects on sensitive souls; it is a means of earning a living interchangeable with any other. His ambivalence to his creation transforms him into an embodiment of the First Cause glimpsed by Sue in her youth: both compose in a state of somnambulism, their works being impenetrable to reason. Effectively, Jude's visit anticipates late poems such as 'New Year's Eve' and 'A Philosophical Fantasy', in which a representative of mankind is able to ask the First Cause why he is out of harmony with the universe. Jude's composer proves every bit as ambivalent as Sue's, and rejects music as a 'staff to lean on' in favour of the alternative means of solace offered by his new profession of wine merchant – a solution which Jude knows only too well (p. 212).

Yet despite these setbacks, Hardy allows him to evolve his own heady mixture of 'Greek joyousness' with Sue. Together they reject 'what twenty-five centuries have taught the race' in favour of a determination to 'make a virtue of joy' on the grounds that it is 'Nature's law and *raison d'être* that we should be joyful in what instincts she afforded us' (pp. 309, 348). Hardy signals this evolution in their relationship by his changing use of music: for when both visit the Great Wessex Agricultural Show they become absorbed in the music of a public concert, which presents them with an image of 'their own lives, as translated into emotion' by music (p. 307). The source of the music is crucial here, for it reflects their rejection of both theology and metaphysics as 'a staff to lean on' in favour of the humanist alternative offered by community spirit. In terms of Schopenhauer's metaphysics (in which music presents a picture of the inner nature of the world without the concomitant pain), the music of the band offers an opportunity for release from the world of striving.[25] It is through such music that Jude and Sue find harmony with their surroundings at last, an accommodation only achieved previously during Jude's drunken observation of the Christminster bands, when ambition momentarily gives way to an engagement with the jostling 'book of humanity'.

Their happiness, however, is fleeting. Arabella condemns them as 'like two children' in their 'fools' Paradise', a precarious situation which Hardy brings to life in the 'Pavilion of flowers' (pp. 307, 317). Here Sue, the epicure of the emotions, places her nose within an inch of the blooms in the intoxication of sensual gratification, while Jude, unmindful of the rules, pushes her further in amongst them (p. 308). It is a simple sequence of events providing an allegorical exploration of precisely why their relationship founders. Primarily, their self-absorbed willingness to break the rules emphasises their capacity to ignore the social conventions which insist on their marriage. However, Hardy's symbolic annihilation of the Fawley curse with the death of Aunt Drusilla, combined with the ease with which Sue and Jude are able to divorce their respective partners, suggests that, in Hardy's mind at least, marriage was not to be the central impediment to their happiness. Their demise does not follow from social censure, but rather from personalities which demand different things from marriage. Sue seeks pleasure in placing herself within an inch of sensual gratification, and withholding herself as an object of such desire – an Epicurean personality trait which the marriage contract will compromise by imprisoning her.[26]

For Jude, conversely, marriage means total commitment, which includes satisfaction of his strong sexual desire through legal consent. He is not content with simply smelling the flowers, he wants to roll around in them. Significantly, Hardy once again presents the re-emergence of this 'animalism' through the 'sonorous envelope'. Late one evening during their sojourn at Albrickham, the disembodied tones of Arabella are heard calling out to Jude in the darkness. Evocative of Hawthorne's romances, the scene militates against a more realist reading of the text. Arabella re-enters the narrative to herald the arrival of Little Father Time, who figuratively reminds the reader of the impossibility of escaping the consequences of individual action. However, Sue's perception of the 'low-passioned woman' in Arabella's voice, and the 'inconvenient sympathy' that it arouses in Jude, indicates that it is the desire as well as the consequence that is catching up with them (p. 278). The harp is plucked, and Jude's latent sexual impulse emerges with the vehement expostulation, 'perhaps I am coarse too, worse luck!' (p. 280).

Having allowed his characters to find happiness in their mixture of 'Greek joyousness' and the modern spirit, Hardy dashes it on the rock of primitive instinct. The effect on Jude of Sue's pattern of intimacy and denial (which has already killed the undergraduate and inflicted pain on Phillotson) is that he turns in upon himself. Inside he finds 'a chaos of principles' in which the 'present rule of life [is] following inclinations' (pp. 336–337).[27] He finds himself 'groping in the dark', the only thing providing an anchorage being the dream of Christminster, which, despite his previous humiliations, reasserts itself through Hardy's reintroduction of the motif of the pealing bells (p. 336). The immediate consequence of this re-emergence is the reassertion of Jude's old egotism, which, upon his entry into the city, keeps him standing in the rain listening to the university Latin service when his duty to his family suggests that he should be looking for lodgings. Even when he eventually embarks upon this task, the dream interrupts duty, as a peal of bells distracts his attention from an inquiry in hand, eliciting a tart response from the landlady:

Two or three of the houses had notices of rooms to let, and the newcomers knocked at the door of one, which a woman opened.
'Ah – listen!' said Jude suddenly, instead of addressing her.
'What?'
'Why the bells – what church can that be? The tones are familiar.'
Another peal of bells had begun to sound out at some distance off.
'I don't know!' said the landlady tartly. 'Did you knock to ask that?'
'No; for lodgings,' said Jude, coming to himself. (p. 339)

At this stage of the narrative, the temporary nature of the accommodation of Jude and Sue is geographical, social and moral. It is now that Hardy delivers his searing blow, questioning the strength of their confused mixture of humanism and reinvigorated Hellenism when faced with real disaster. His vehicle, Little Father Time, is a creeping indictment of Comtean beliefs in human progress, a representative of a generation that has progressed beyond the comforts of both theology and metaphysics to be left face to face with the appalling callousness of 'Nature's Law'.[28] Alienated and out of harmony with his environment, his 'saucer eyes' are permanently focussed beyond the particularities of life to the underlying process, so that he lacks the childish impulse which allows his father to continually dream of better things (pp. 289, 291). And without dreams, as Hardy asserts through the death of his 'dwarfed Divinity', little is left for the overly sensitive individual who understands the true nature of the universe, other than 'the beginning of the coming universal wish not to live' (pp. 290, 346).

Hardy's catastrophe offers his characters a glimpse of the future, and subsequently allows him to explore the palliative offered by their particular brand of humanism. One solution immediately breaks in upon the 'little cell' of the death chamber in the form of a 'large, low voice [which] spread into the air of the room from behind the heavy walls' (p. 346). It is the college organist practising Psalm 73, by means of which Hardy reintroduces religion as a once discarded means of dealing with suffering. Like the Book of Job, which will later provide Jude with his deathbed oration, the subject of this Psalm is the struggle to maintain faith in a world in which the good appear to suffer while the wicked prosper. The psalmist, who has been thoroughly tried by suffering, confesses that his attempts to maintain his faith have thrown him into a state of despair. Salvation, however, is at hand: for God reveals that the symbols of earthly success are illusory, and will vanish like a dream when he decides to make his power manifest. Thus, the only sure path to happiness lies in an absolute devotion to the one God who will lead the doubter by the hand through his suffering. From this new perspective the psalmist dismisses his earlier doubts, and embraces God with a new found zeal.

The Psalm strikes a chord with Sue, whose youthful perception of the First Cause as a composer whose creation resembled a 'melody composed in a dream', is shattered by the appearance of an angry 'God' who she believes has sacrificed the children 'to bring home to [her] the error of [her] views' (p. 369). Thus, she finds herself amongst the wicked, attempting to reconcile herself with God through a combination of self-abasement and the repudiation of what she perceives to be her crime. In returning to Phillotson she is 'compelling herself . . . against her instincts' to honour the sacramental bond between the two, an act of penance which, characteristically, protects her with words (p. 375). For Jude, however, there is to be no peaceful reconciliation with God, and his cynicism leads Sue to accuse him of being like 'a totally deaf man observing people listening to music. You say "What are they regarding? Nothing is there." But something is' (p. 359). There is indeed, but as Hardy indicates immediately after the death of the children through his introduction of the overheard cavilling between two clergymen over the direction the celebrant should face during the Eucharist, this 'something' is not to be found by dogmatic religious means (pp. 346–347). It is in fact Jude's expostulation 'Good God – the eastward position, and all creation groaning!' that comes nearer to Hardy's truth: for here Jude appears to apprehend, albeit momentarily, the groans making up the continual dirge that signals existence in a world in which there is just 'man and senseless circumstance' (pp. 347, 351).

Sue's asceticism is really a form of self-mortification which deafens her to this music, something which Hardy illustrates through her final interview with the dying Jude at the schoolhouse at Marygreen. The scene opens with Jude listening to 'the usual sing-song tones of the little voices that had not learnt Creation's groan', and ends with Sue kneeling on the floor covering 'her ears with her hands' to prevent the coughs and groans of his retreating figure from arousing within her an uncomfortable sympathy (pp. 393, 395). It is a brief cameo through which Hardy presents the reader with three different types of deafness: that of the children, whose naïveté gives them hope; that of Jude, who never matures sufficiently to accept life for what it is; and that of Sue, whose religiosity is a deliberate denial of the dismal music surrounding her. For Hardy, Sue's refusal to engage is as counterproductive as Jude's drunkenness, for it requires a perversion of, rather than an accommodation with, her instincts. It is an exercise in self-mutilation that Hardy dramatises through her entry into Phillotson's bedroom on the evening of her sacrifice. For here her clenched teeth mark the suppression of feelings which would otherwise find expression in the agonised moan that characterises the sad music surrounding her (p. 403).

Although critical of Sue's response, Hardy is hardly less so of that of Jude. His solutions – alcohol, submission to the will of Arabella and a half-hearted suicide attempt – lead the reader to question what there is other than the illusion offered by either dreams or religious faith. Hardy's answer arrives when Jude is on his deathbed, and once again takes the form of life's dismal music breaking in upon his little cell.

As Jude lies in an obscure room in Christminster, the notes of bells ringing for local festivities roll 'into the room through the open window' (p. 407). For the watching Arabella, the temptation of this music is too much, and leaving Jude she is led by 'the notes of [an] organ' to the rehearsal for a coming university function (p. 407). In this instance the music is not religious, but is rather a celebration of Christminster, something which Arabella rejects as 'rather dull' (p. 408). As the notes of the organ reach Jude they are as 'faint as a bee's hum', a detail that reminds us of the musical bee that circles Henchard on the morning after the wife-sale, and in so doing undermines the litany of despair with which Jude's life comes to an end (p. 408). For, although Jude clothes himself in the words of Job in order to vent his anger at his persecution, it is clear that his target is not God, but rather the illusory nature of his Christminster dream, stimulated by the music of The Remembrance Games. He remains, like Clym and Henchard before him, self-absorbed to the end, considering the 'Hurrahs!' of the students that punctuate his speech as a mockery of his own ambition (p. 408).

For Arabella, Jude's death brings a moment of guilt, which is quickly submerged in 'the faint notes of a military or other brass band from the river [which] reached her ears' (p. 410). Despite the domestic drama, 'the dance of life' continues unabated, enticing those attuned to its melody to take pleasure where it can be found. It is with this music that the vulgar Arabella – curling her hair, practising her dimples and cutting her mourning short to pursue Dr Vilbert – finds herself in tune, enabling her to arrive at a position of ascendancy towards the close of the novel. For Jude, such music remains a mockery to the end. As the 'joyous throb of waltz' being performed in the ballroom of Cardinal College enters the death chamber, it conjures up for the reader images of happy partners revolving in harmony with one another, their easy happiness ridiculing Jude's troubled relationship with Sue (p. 412).

The ascendancy of Arabella privileges her with the final words, which cast doubt on Sue's belief that she has found peace in her new found religiosity: ' "She may swear that on her knees to the holy cross upon her necklace till she's hoarse, but it won't be true!" said Arabella. "She's never found peace since she left his arms, and never will again till she's as he is now!" ' (p. 413). Fulfilment will come, not through an illusion built upon words, but, as with Jude, Eustacia, Henchard and Tess, only through death.

Conclusion

In 1877 Walter Pater claimed that *'all art constantly aspires towards the condition of music'*, a maxim aptly illustrated at the time by the paintings of Whistler and, later on in the century, by the novels of George Moore.[1] The critic William Blissett claims that Moore's later novels are exercises in the 'effect of Wagnerian music drama', in which it is possible to observe the continuous melody gradually transforming itself into the unbroken narrative of the stream of consciousness.[2] Blissett traces this tradition through the influences of the continental symbolist movement, notably Stéphane Mallarmé and Paul Verlaine, and its effect on Irish writers such as Edward Martyn and James Joyce. He makes no room for Hardy in this evolution: and yet I hope that this book has gone some way to illuminating an earlier form of literary music drama which may offer an alternative bridge between the musicality of such texts as *The Mill on the Floss* and *Ulysses*.

With this in mind, an article published in the arts magazine *Concordia* in February 1876, by the historian and man of letters Henry Sutherland Edwards, is of interest. In it he notes:

> we have heard a brilliant novelist, who is not so highly, or rather not so widely appreciated as he ought to be, described on his own authority as the 'Wagner of literature.' As far as we can divine, the signification of this dubious eulogism is, that the writer to whom it is applied contrives to give subtle expression to his thoughts by a use of words so happy that it can be compared to nothing less than the use which it is imagined Herr Wagner makes of musical sounds.[3]

Who is this 'Wagner of Literature'?[4] Both Tim Armstrong and Neil Roberts favour Meredith, whose novels, especially *One of Our Conquerors*, make direct allusion to Wagner. Roberts also notes of the passage that 'the suggestion that the novelist in question is caviare to the general, and the emphasis on the prose style, as if this were in some way orchestrated' suggests Meredith.[5] If correct, then it is clear that Meredith offers an exciting avenue of research in relation to the field of musical aesthetics. The research presented in this book, however, offers the intriguing possibility that it could be Hardy, whose conceptualisation of a literary drama constructed upon a chorus of musicalised sounds fully deserves the epithet 'Wagnerian'.

Edwards is less mysterious in his appellation of 'the Wagner of poetry', and gives as examples both Walt Whitman and Robert Browning. Could Hardy be added to this list? Certainly, it would be interesting to reassess the musicality of Hardy's verse in the light of both Wagnerian and contemporary scientific theory. Much recent criticism, most notably P. E. Mitchell's 'Music and Hardy's Poetry', Denis Taylor's work on Hardy's prosody, and John Hughes' '*Ecstatic Sound*', has sought to re-evaluate earlier critical opinion which dismissed Hardy as 'a master of fiction, but not a master of music'.[6] In disassociating Hardy's poetry and music, early commentators agued that it was a stylistic consequence of Hardy's pessimism: put simply, Hardy had nothing to sing about![7] The work of Denis Taylor, however, has sought to contextualise Hardy's metrical inventiveness with regard to the interweaving of metre and the spoken language within the poetical developments of mid-century poets such as de Selincourt and Patmore. As Hughes notes, 'it is one of the further implications of Taylor's book that Hardy's ear was haunted not simply by the metrical form but by rhythms that preserved a proximity to music'.[8] Such rhythms are of particular significance in the light of the theories of Spencer and Wagner, both of whom sought to trace the emotional power of music to its roots in language.

Another area of interest in relation to the present study is the connection between music and memory in Hardy's poetry. Hughes is concerned with how Hardy's inventive use of metre can open up the complex issues of time, a feature displayed by his careful use of the rhythms of dance music to evoke a different period in the poem 'Reminiscences of a dancing Man'. He is also interested in the capacity of music to retain an ideality that exists outside the logic of the calendar, allowing it to become, in Hardy's hands, a privileged tool of memory capable of recapturing the ecstasies of the past. Thus, in poems such as 'Singing Lovers' and 'Lost Love' music serves to reawaken values and pleasures associated with the past, a period of greater happiness from which the present speaker is alienated.[9]

Tim Armstrong is also concerned with the way Hardy uses music to evoke pleasures of the past: but he is more interested in locating where such musical experience occurs; the technological storage of such experience; and the relationship of the musical experience to the instrument that produced it. He also employs the theories of Spencer, Haweis and Schopenhauer discussed at length in this book, and modern research into auditory psychology to argue that the musical power so evident in poems such as 'Music in a Snowy Street' is based less on the evocation of a specific occasion, than the emotions attendant upon such a moment.[10]

My own work, I hope, has offered a new reading of Hardy's novels by contextualising them within the Victorian intellectual world, focusing particularly on the way in which his engagement with various musical debates enabled him to employ musical motifs to reflect shifting attitudes to human consciousness and the depiction and transmission of emotions. The Hardy who emerges is a far more innovative figure than has been previously acknowledged, whose revitalisation of the Classical tragedy through the medium of music echoes the mid-century interest in Schopenhauer (for whom music offers a model of the unconscious or Will) and Wagnerian music drama (whose work offered a reconceptualisation of the chorus in the drama). Reading the novels in the light of such theories becomes a much more complex and enriching process, in which we become conscious of a chorus of dissonant musicalised sounds through which Hardy creates his gloomy universe, brings his characters into being and allows them to engage with the outside world.

Hardy offers the reader tragedies appropriate for his time, reflecting his interest in evolutionary theory, heredity, mesmerism, physiology, and the origins and emotional affectiveness of both music and voice. In Hardy's godless universe, these are the agencies against which his characters must struggle, a conflict depicted through musical tropes. This struggle is clearest when dealing with love: Hardy's evocation of the Romantic symbol of the Aeolian harp being internalised in the fibrous human nervous system which is played upon by external forces. His tragic characters are simply out of tune with the world that surrounds them, a truth which they glimpse from time to time. In general, however, this remains the preserve of those who are too old, blind or mad to make use of their insight. Instead, it is left to the reader to pity the magnificent but misdirected energy of Henchard, the struggles of Jude and Tess to master their sexuality, and Clym's overwhelming struggle with his intellect. It is an experience that lends itself to the cinema: Hardy's constant telescoping of scenes (such as Eustacia's standing on Rainbarrow) anticipating the camera zoom, and his use of music suggesting a form of soundtrack. In this, Hardy's fiction suggests an alternative route of evolution to that of the realists, and Hardy is transformed into an experimental artist unrecognisable from the 'good little Thomas Hardy' dismissed so patronisingly by Henry James.[11]

Notes

Introduction

1. *The Return of the Native*, pp. 71–72. All references to Hardy's works are to the New Wessex Edition, General Editor P. N. Furbank, published in fourteen volumes by Macmillan, 1975–1976.
2. Walter Pater, 'The School of Giorgione', *Fortnightly Review*, 22 n.s. (October, 1877), 526–538 (p. 528).
3. *The Critique of Judgement*, Book II, 'The Analytic of the Sublime', translated by James Creed Meredith (Oxford: Clarendon Press, 1986), p. 195.
4. Berlinger claims 'O, then I close my eyes to all the strife of the world – and withdraw quietly into the land of music'. Wilhelm Wackenroder, *Phantasien über die Kunst für Freunde der Kunst* (1799), translated by M. H. Schubert, reprint in *Musical Aesthetics: A Historical Reader*, edited by Edward A. Lippman, 3 vols (New York: Pendragon Press, 1988), II, p. 11.
5. E. T. A. Hoffmann, 'Beethoven's Instrumental Music', reprint in *E. T. A. Hoffmann and Music*, edited and translated by R. Murray Schaefer (Toronto: University of Toronto Press, 1975), p. 83.
6. R. M. Longyear, *Nineteenth-Century Romanticism in Music*, 3rd edn (Englewood Cliffs, New Jersey: Prentice Hall, 1988), p. 18.
7. Hoffmann, *Die Automate*, quoted in Schaefer, p. 7.
8. M. H. Abrams, *The Mirror and the Lamp: Romantic Theory and the Critical Tradition* (Oxford: Oxford University Press, 1953). The actual instrument was invented by Athanasius Kircher in 1650 and designed to be hung from a window frame, so that it could respond to passing winds, p. 51.
9. John Ruskin, *The Queen of the Air* (1869). The Greek goddess, Athena Chalinitis, represents the passionate expression of music; Apollo signifies the ordering of air and is therefore symbolised by a lyre which measures and divides the air into musical tones. *The Complete Works of John Ruskin*, Library Edition, edited by E. T. Cook and Alexander Wedderburn, 39 vols (London: George Allen, 1903–1912), XIX, pp. 342–343.
10. Thomson, James, 'The Castle of Indolence', in *Liberty, The Castle of Indolence and Other Poems*, edited by James Sambrook (Oxford: Clarendon Press, 1986), canto I. 40, ll. 352, 353. Thomson's image obviously attracted Hardy, for he employs it to describe Clym's soothing effects on the passionate Eustacia. *The Return of the Native*, p. 118. See also Geoffrey Grigson, *The Harp of Aeolus and Other Essays on Art, Literature and Nature* (London: Routledge, 1947), pp. 24–46.
11. 'The Eolian Harp', in *The Complete Poetical Works of Samuel Taylor Coleridge*, edited by Ernest Hartley Coleridge, 2 vols (Oxford: Clarendon Press, 1912), I, ll. 44–48. Grigson carries out an excellent analysis of this poem, pp. 30–40.
12. See John Hollander, 'Wordsworth and the Music of Sound', in *New Perspectives on Coleridge and Wordsworth: Selected Papers from the English Institute*, edited by Geoffrey H. Hartman (New York: Columbia University Press, 1972),

pp. 41–84. He notes Pope's satirical observation of musical allusion in ll. 350–352 of *An Essay on Criticism*: 'Where-e'er you find "the cooling western breeze," / In the next line, it "whispers thro' the trees" ' (p. 44).

13. In *Tess of the D'Urbervilles* Hardy asks in an authorial intervention where the poet [Wordsworth] 'gets his authority for speaking of "Nature's Holy Plan" ' (p. 49). See Wordsworth's 'Lines Written in Early Spring'.

14. Norcombe Hill is given a fringe of trees 'like a mane', *Far from the Madding Crowd*, p. 46; according to Elfride Swancourt the 'Cliff without a Name' even has a 'horrid personality', *A Pair of Blue Eyes*, pp. 165, 167.

15. Alfred Tennyson, *In Memoriam*, in *The Poems of Tennyson*, edited by C. Ricks, 2nd edn, 3 vols (Harlow: Longman, 1987), II, 56, l. 15. All future references to Tennyson's poetry are to this edition.

16. *Poems*, II, 3, l. 5.

17. Ibid., II, 96, ll. 15–17.

18. Ibid., Epilogue, l. 128, and Prologue, l. 28.

19. J. S. Mill, *Autobiography*, edited by J. M. Robson, 2nd edn (Harmondsworth, Middlesex: Penguin, 1989), p. 132.

20. Mill, *The Spirit of the Age: Part I, Examiner* (January, 1831), 20–22. Reprint in *The Collected Works of John Stuart Mill*, edited by J. M. Robson, 33 vols (Toronto: University of Toronto Press, 1981–1991), XXII, *Newspaper Writings: December 1822–July 1831*, 227–234 (p. 233).

21. Thomas Carlyle, *Sartor Resartus: The Life and Opinions of Herr Teufelsdröckh in Three Books*, notes and introduction by Roger L. Tarr, text established by Roger L. Tarr (Berkeley, London: University of California Press, 2000), p. 87.

22. Ibid., p. 182.

23. Ibid., p. 180.

24. Arnold, 'Bishop Butler and the Zeitgeist', in *Last Essays on Church and Religion* (1877), Source, Walter F. Houghton, *The Victorian Frame of Mind, 1830–1870* (Oxford: Oxford University Press, 1957), p. 9.

25. Tennyson, *Poems*, II, 55, l. 5. Matthew Arnold, 'Empedocles on Etna' (1852), in *The Poems of Matthew Arnold*, edited by Miriam Allot, 2nd edn (London: Longman, 1979), ll. 233–234. All future references to Arnold's poetry are to this edition.

26. Quoted in John D. Rosenberg, *The Darkening Glass: A Portrait of the Genius of John Ruskin* (London: Routledge & Kegan Paul, 1963), p. 183.

27. *Poems*, ll. 10–18.

28. This was the title of a lecture given by Ruskin in London in February 1884 in which he commented on the literally darkening skies and used them as a metaphor for the contemporary malaise.

29. James Thomson, *The City of Dreadful Night and Other Poems* (London: Watts, 1932), Pt I, p. 1.

30. Florence Emily Hardy, *The Life of Thomas Hardy 1840–1928* (London: Macmillan, 1965), p. 100. Robert Gittings argues that this is less an expression of heartfelt sentiment than a 'gambit in his temporary manoeuvres with [Leslie] Stephen'. *Young Thomas Hardy* (London: Heinemann, 1975), p. 196.

31. Hardy notes in *The Life* that 'he had not the slightest intention of writing for ever about sheep-farming, as the reading public was apparently expecting him to do', p. 102. This dilemma is brought out clearly by Dale Kramer in *Thomas Hardy: The Forms of Tragedy* (London: Macmillan, 1975), p. 14.

32. Hardy to H. W. Massingham, *The Collected Letters of Thomas Hardy*, edited by R. L. Purdy and M. Millgate, 7 vols (Oxford: Clarendon Press, 1978–1988), I, p. 250 (31 December, 1891).

33. Hardy, 'A Profitable Reading of Fiction', *Forum*, New York (March, 1888), 57–70, reprint in *Thomas Hardy's Personal Writings: Prefaces, Literary Opinions, Reminiscences*, edited by Harold Orel (London: Macmillan, 1967), p. 116. My italics.

34. Robert Gittings, *The Older Hardy* (London: Heinemann, 1978), p. 4.

35. Ibid., pp. 6–7.

36. See Walter Houghton, 'Periodical Literature and the Articulate Classes', in *The Victorian Periodical Press: Samplings and Soundings*, edited by Joanne Shattock and Michael Wolff (Leicester, and Toronto and Buffalo: Leicester University Press, University of Toronto Press, 1982), 3–27 (p. 7). Periodical facts are all taken from the headnotes to the *Wellesley Index to Victorian Periodicals 1824–1900*, edited by Walter Houghton, 5 vols (Toronto and Buffalo: University of Toronto Press, 1966–1989). Laurel Brake notes that, 'Mudie's, the largest and most famous of the circulating libraries, opened and 1842'. 'Writing, cultural production, and the periodical press in the nineteenth century', in *Writing and Victorianism*, edited by J. B. Bullen (London and New York: Longman, 1997), 54–72 (p. 58).

37. See Walter Graham, *English Literary Periodicals* (New York: T. Nelson and Son, 1930), p. 305.

38. Lynn Ruth, Binstock, 'A Study of Music in Victorian Prose' (unpublished doctoral thesis, University of Oxford, 1985), pp. 46–51.

39. Henry James to Robert Louis Stevenson (19 March, 1892), in *The Letters of Henry James*, selected and edited by P. Lubbock, 2 vols (London: Macmillan, 1920), I, p. 194.

40. Grundy, *Hardy and the Sister Arts* (London: Macmillan, 1979), p. 172.

41. *Jude the Obscure*, p. 42.

42. Richard Leppert, *The Sight of Sound: Music, Representation and the Human Body* (California: University of California Press, 1993).

43. Jonathan Crary, *Suspensions of Perception: Attention, Spectacle; And Modern Culture* (Cambridge, Massachusetts; London: MIT, 2001).

44. Douglas Kahn, *Noise, Water, Meat: Sound, Voice and Aurality in the Arts* (Cambridge, Massachusetts; London: MIT, 1999).

45. Steven Connor, *Dumbstruck – A Cultural History of Ventriloquism* (Oxford: Oxford University Press, 2000).

46. Jonathan Reé, *I See a Voice: A Philosophical History of Language, Deafness and the Senses* (London: HarperCollins, 1999).

47. Delia da Sousa Correa, *George Eliot, Music and Victorian Culture* (Basingstoke: Palgrave Macmillan, 2003).

48. John Hughes, *'Ecstatic Sound': Music and Individuality in the Work of Thomas Hardy* (Aldershot: Ashgate, 2001).

1 The road to Norcombe Hill: Hardy's musical evolution

1. *The Life*, pp. 15, 16.

2. Ibid., p. 23.

3. Most criticism with regard to Hardy and music has focused upon his employment of traditional folk songs in both his poetry and prose. Typical

of this tradition is F. B. Pinion's survey of the songs referred to in Hardy's novels, *A Hardy Companion: A Guide to the Works of Thomas Hardy and their Background* (London: Macmillan, 1968), pp. 187–191, 205–206. C. M. Jackson-Houlston carries this process a stage further by showing how the singing of such songs and their effects on the listeners are used by Hardy as a 'very precise moral and social touchstone'. Angel Clare, for example, is censorious of Tess' lyrics, and Farfrae's kind of music is continuously set up in opposition to Henchard's. C. M. Jackson-Houlston, 'Thomas Hardy's Use of Traditional Song', *Nineteenth Century Fiction*, 44 (1989–1990), 301–334 (pp. 313, 318, 330). P. E. Mitchell concentrates upon what he describes as Hardy's revitalisation of the folk song form in his poetry, a technique that has the effect of evoking ideas of an enduring social continuity that transcends the plight of the individual in the modern industrial world. P. E. Mitchell, 'Music and Hardy's Poetry', *English Literature in Transition*, 33 (1987), 308–321. Eva Mary Grew argues that Hardy's musical susceptibility not only guided him towards musical subjects and metaphors, but also caused him to think of natural sounds and voice tone in musical terms. 'Thomas Hardy as Musician', *Music and Letters*, 21 (1940), 120–142 (pp. 137–138).

4. Michael Millgate, *Thomas Hardy: A Biography* (Oxford: Oxford University Press, 1982), p. 37. Martin Seymour-Smith, *Hardy* (London: Bloomsbury, 1995), p. 27. F. B. Pinion notes that 'such ecstasy was roused in him as he performed his father's music that he could hardly hide his tears', *Thomas Hardy: His Life and Friends* (London: Macmillan, 1992), p. 14.

5. Sherman bases her conclusion on an assessment of the Hardy family's collection of songbooks 'Thomas Hardy: Lyricist, Symphonist', *Music and Letters*, 21 (1940), 143–171 (p. 145).

6. Sherman, p. 155.

7. Carl J. Weber, 'Thomas Hardy Music: With a Bibliography', *Music and Letters*, 21 (1940), 172–178 (p. 173).

8. Gittings, *Young Thomas Hardy*, p. 60.

9. *The Life*, p. 201.

10. Millgate, *Biography*, p. 79. Grundy, p. 150.

11. Hardy to 'a friend', quoted in Weber, p. 173.

12. da Sousa Correa, *George Eliot, Music and Victorian Culture*. See in particular her chapter 'Music and the Woman Question'.

13. See in particular H. R. Haweis' series of essays 'Music and Morals' printed in the *Contemporary Review*, 1870–1871; John Hullah's *Music in the House* (London: Macmillan, 1878); and John Curwen's teaching of music to the working classes through the 'Tonic Sol-fa' movement.

14. *Cornhill Magazine*, 8 (July, 1863), 93–98 (p. 98).

15. Leppert, *Sight of Sound*, p. 178.

16. See da Sousa Correa's sections 'The "minister of domestic discord"' (pp. 66–77) and 'The "most sensuous of accomplishments"' (pp. 77–91).

17. Thackeray, *Vanity Fair*, Norton Critical Edition (New York: W. W. Norton), p. 161.

18. Anne Brontë, *The Tenant of Wildfell Hall*, edited by Herbert Rosengarten (Oxford: Clarendon Press, 1992), pp. 230–238. See da Sousa Correa's section 'Music and the Woman Writer', pp. 91–101 (pp. 96–97).

19. See *Wives and Daughters* (Oxford: Oxford University Press, 1987), pp. 231, 281–284, and the analysis of da Sousa Correa, *George Eliot, Music and Victorian Culture*, p. 94.

20. *Middlemarch*, edited by David Carroll (Oxford: Clarendon Press, 1986), p. 94.
21. *Phoebe Junior* (London: Virago, 1989), p. 306.
22. Leppert, *Sight of Sound*, pp. 181–183. Date of Composition unknown.
23. Ibid., Date of Composition unknown, pp. 185–186.
24. For full exposition, see Leppert's chapter 'Male Agony: Awakening Conscience', and also Kate Flint, 'Reading *The Awakening Conscience* Rightly', in *Pre-raphaelites Re-viewed*, edited by Marcia Pointon (Manchester: Manchester University Press, 1989), pp. 48–49.
25. Edmund Gosse, 'Thomas Hardy's Lost Novel', *The Sunday Times*, 22 January, 1928. Quoted from William Rutland, *Thomas Hardy: A Study of his Writings and their Background* (Oxford: Basil Blackwell, 1938), p. 119.
26. Rutland, *Thomas Hardy*, pp. 119, 127.
27. Hardy, *An Indiscretion in the Life of an Heiress*, edited by Carl J. Weber (New York: Russell and Russell, 1965), pp. 97–98.
28. Ibid., p. 99.
29. Lawrence Jones argues that *The Poor Man and the Lady* is the common source for the musical episodes in *An Indiscretion in the Life of an Heiress* and *Desperate Remedies*. 'The Music Scenes from *The Poor Man and the Lady*, *Desperate Remedies* and *An Indiscretion in the Life of an Heiress*', *Notes and Queries*, 222 (Winter, 1977), 32–34 (p. 33).
30. *Desperate Remedies*, p. 158.
31. Hughes, '*Ecstatic Sound*', p. 38.
32. George Eliot, *The Mill on the Floss*, edited by Gordon Haight (Oxford: Clarendon Press, 1980), p. 367.
33. *A Pair of Blue Eyes*, p. 14.
34. Ibid., p. 14.
35. The most likely source for this arrangement is that which appeared in Bishop's *The Overture, Songs, Duets, Glees, and Choruses in Shakespeare's Play of the 'Two Gentlemen of Verona'* (London: Goulding, D'Almaine, Potter, 1821). However, Hardy may have been thinking of William John Agate's arrangement of 1873, or that published by Henry Simms (London: Cocks, 1863).
36. *A Pair of Blue Eyes*, p. 13. The poem was set to music by John Barnett in 1860 and is no. 2 of a 'Series of Contralto Songs' (London: Cramer, Beale & Chappell, 1860). See Burton R. Pollin, *The Music for Shelley's Poetry: An Annotated Bibliography of Musical Settings of Shelley's Poetry* (New York: Da Capo, 1974), p. 11.
37. Unwin (unpublished doctoral thesis, University of London, 1994) focuses on the relationship between gender and music, and is underpinned by an analysis of nineteenth-century pamphlets and essays which consider the moral and educative effects of music.
38. *Under the Greenwood Tree*, pp. 70–71.
39. Ibid., p. 69. My italics.
40. Ibid., p. 32.
41. In this scene the trees which 'writhed like miserable men' reflect her disappointment at her father's refusal for permission to marry. *Under the Greenwood Tree*, p. 156.
42. *Far from the Madding Crowd*, pp. 46–47. My italics.
43. *Desperate Remedies*, p. 223.
44. *The Literary Notebooks of Thomas Hardy*, edited with introduction and notes by Lennart Björk, 2 vols (London: Macmillan, 1985), 167, 442 and 546. *The*

Life, p. 217. Hardy owned *The Dialogues of Plato* translated, with analysis and introduction, by Benjamin Jowett, 4 vols (Oxford, 1871). Source, annotations to *Literary Notebooks*, 442. For further evidence of Hardy's Platonism, see 305, 475.

45. Hardy to Edmund Gosse, *The Collected Letters of Thomas Hardy*, edited by Richard L. Purdy and Michael Millgate, 7 vols (Oxford: Clarendon Press, 1978–1988), II, pp. 156–157 (31 March, 1897).

46. William Shakespeare, *The Merchant of Venice*, *The Riverside Shakespeare* (Boston and New York: Houghton Mifflin, 1974), V, 1, ll. 60–61. See *Thomas Hardy's 'Studies, Specimens &c.' Notebook*, edited by Pamela Dalziel and Michael Millgate (Oxford: Clarendon Press, 1994), pp. 77–78.

47. 'A Song for St. Cecilia's Day', in *The Poems of John Dryden*, edited by James Kinsley, 4 vols (Oxford: Clarendon Press, 1958), II, 1, ll. 6, 11, 15.

48. See *Studies and Specimens*, p. 30.

49. 'On the Morning of Christ's Nativity', in *The Poetical Works of John Milton*, edited by Helen Darbishire, 2 vols (Oxford: Clarendon Press, 1952–1955), II, 12, ll. 120–123. For Milton the concept of the music of the spheres had suffered debasement at the hands of successive generations, which, beginning with Aristotle, interpreted it far too literally. In the second 'Prolusion' he argues that the ability of Pythagoras to hear the cosmic music to which the rest of mankind is deaf, is a metaphor demonstrating that he has been chosen by the gods 'to share the most secret mysteries of nature'. Pythagoras, therefore, becomes a Christ-like figure who teaches man to live in harmony with the necessity and destiny prescribed by the orbiting stars. Modern man, however, is unable to hear this harmony because Prometheus corrupted him by indulging his self-interest and 'brutish desires', therefore dulling his sensitivity to the 'heavenly element'. *Prolusion II: On The Harmony of the Spheres*, in *The Complete Prose Works of John Milton*, 8 vols (New Haven: Yale University Press, 1953–1982), I, pp. 238, 239. See also M. N. K. Mander, 'Milton and the Music of the Spheres', *Milton Quarterly*, 24 (May, 1990), 63–71.

50. *Poetical Works*, II, 9, l. 95.

51. Ibid., II, 13. 'Ring out ye crystall sphears, / Once bless our human ears, / (If ye have power to touch our senses so) / And let your silver chime / Move in melodious time; / And let the Base of Heav'ns deep Organ blow, / And with your ninefold harmony / Make up full consort to th'Angelike symphony'.

52. Ibid., II, 16, l. 149.

53. Ibid., II, 23, l. 210 and 26, l. 234.

54. In *Studies and Specimens* Hardy copies out several phrases from the poem, the bulk of which are taken from the latter half (p. 30). Hardy copied several phrases from Milton's lines 232–234 into his notebook, and underlined numerous words. In the quotation which follows I have put Hardy's copied phrases into italics and left his underlining: '*The flocking shadows pale,* / *Troop to the infernal jail,* / Each fettered Ghost *slips to his severall grave,* . . .'. Hardy also notes the word 'dismal' (l. 210), which is linked to the image of the dismal dance.

55. *Studies and Specimens*, p. 30.

56. Phyllis Bartlett notes in her analysis of Hardy's copy of *Queen Mab and Other Poems* that 'there is only one marking in *Queen Mab* and two in *Alastor*, but with *The Revolt of Islam* . . . his pencil got busy, and by the time he reached *Prometheus Unbound* it was unstinting'. 'Hardy's Shelley', *Keats-Shelley Journal*,

4 (Winter, 1955), 15–29 (p. 16). Gittings notes that there is no doubt that Hardy read Shelley fervently in the 1860s, 'his marking of *Prometheus Unbound* was especially extensive', *Young Thomas Hardy*, pp. 79–80.

57. *Prometheus Unbound*, in *Shelley: Poetical Works*, edited by Thomas Hutchinson, 2nd edn (Oxford: Oxford University Press, 1970), IV, ll. 371–417. See also 'But now, oh weave the mystic measure / Of music, and dance, and shapes of light, / Let the Hours, and the spirits of might and pleasure, / Like the clouds and sunbeams, unite', IV, ll. 77–79.

58. *Poetical Works*, I, Ione – 'Hark, sister! what a low yet dreadful groan / Quite unsuppressed is tearing up the heart / Of the good Titan, as storms tear the deep / And beasts hear the sea moan in inland caves', I, ll. 578–581.

59. John Keats, 'The Eve of St. Agnes', in *The Poetical Works of John Keats*, edited by H. W. Garrod, 2nd edn (Oxford: Clarendon Press, 1958), l. 56. For Hardy's entry, see *Literary Notebooks*, 416.

60. Hardy, 'The Sleep-Worker', in *The Complete Poems of Thomas Hardy*, edited by James Gibson (London: Macmillan, 1976), l. 7. *The Dynasts: An Epic-Drama of the War with Napoleon, In Three Parts, Nineteen Acts, and One Hundred and Thirty Scenes*, edited and introduction by Harold Orel (London: Macmillan, 1978), II, V, 3. Hardy's italics.

61. *Far from the Madding Crowd*, pp. 46–47.

62. *Studies and Specimens*, pp. 17–18. *Poetical Works*, VI. 30, l. 2604, and VI. 28, l. 2586, and VII. 32, ll. 3114–3115. The previously unidentified epigraph to Chapter 18 of *A Pair of Blue Eyes*, 'And heard her musical pants', is taken from *The Revolt of Islam*, VI. 20, l. 2512.

63. *The Poetical Works of William Wordsworth*, edited by Ernest De Selincourt and Helen Darbishire, 5 vols (Oxford: Clarendon Press, 1940–1949). All future references to Wordsworth's poetry are to this edition, III, ll. 85, 87.

64. *Works*, I, ll. 365, 368 (1849 version).

65. *Works*, II. This is the 1807 'To The Cuckoo' published in *Poems of the Imagination*, from which Hardy used the phrase 'a wandering voice' for an epigraph to Chapter 15 of *A Pair of Blue Eyes*. 'The Solitary Reaper', *Works*, III.

66. Ibid., II, ll. 169–170.

67. Ibid., II, l. 177.

68. Ibid., II, ll. 187, 192.

69. *The Prelude or Growth of a Poet's Mind* (1805–1806 and 1850 edn) edited with introduction by Ernest De Selincourt, 2nd edn revised by Helen Darbishire (Oxford: Clarendon Press, 1959). All references are to the 1850 edn, I, ll. 271, 276, 281. See also a walk made during 'Schooltime', the narrator describes a 'power in sound' which would make him stand 'Beneath some rock, listening to the notes that are / The ghostly language of the ancient earth' (II, ll. 304, 308–309).

70. 'Lines Composed a Few Miles above Tintern Abbey, On Revisiting the Banks of the Wye During a Tour. July 13, 1798', II, ll. 88–95.

71. See introduction to *Studies, Specimens* in which it is claimed that the 1864 copy of 'Tintern Abbey' is extensively marked (p. 91). Walter Wright argues that Hardy 'underlined or otherwise marked in "Tintern Abbey": "The still sad music of humanity"', going on to observe that he marked it again in the 1896 edition of Wordsworth's *Poems*. *The Shaping of the Dynasts: A Study of Thomas Hardy* (Lincoln: University of Nebraska, 1967), p. 18.

72. Actually copied from J. A. Symonds, 'Matthew Arnold's Selections from Wordsworth', quoted in *Literary Notebooks*, 1151.
73. 'The Science of Fiction', reprint in *Thomas Hardy's Personal Writings: Prefaces, Literary Opinions, Reminiscences*, edited by Harold Orel (London: Macmillan, 1967), p. 137. This selective quotation is entirely consistent with others taken from Wordsworth's works which emphasise nature's harshness at the expense of its benevolence. In *The Woodlanders*, for example, he characterises the emotional suffering of George Melbury by referring to Wordsworth's 'The Small Celandine' which describes the flowers 'buffeting at will by rain and storm' (p. 52).
74. *The Life*, p. 147. Rutland notes 'Wordsworth certainly influenced him profoundly at one period' (*Thomas Hardy*, p. 15). Millgate notes that Hardy's 1864 copy of Wordsworth's poetry is 'extensively marked', adding that amongst the most marked poems is 'Tintern Abbey', *Studies and Specimens*, p. 91. See also Peter Casagrande, 'Hardy's Wordsworth: A record and Commentary', *English Literature in Transition*, 20 (1977), 210–237 (pp. 211–212).
75. 'Sometimes a soaking hiss proclaimed that they were passing by a pasture, then a patter would show that the rain fell upon some large-leafed root crop, then a paddling plash announced the naked arable, the low sound of the wind in their ears rising and falling with each pace they took', *Desperate Remedies*, p. 316. Smith hears the sounds of a toad 'labouring along through the grass' and 'the scurr of a distant night-hawk', *A Pair of Blue Eyes*, pp. 188–189.
76. *Under the Greenwood Tree*, p. 32.
77. Through the notes of the bird, the bride is reminded of her previous acceptance of Parson Maybold's unexpected proposal of marriage, a 'secret she would never tell', *Under the Greenwood Tree*, p. 192. In the scene from *A Pair of Blue Eyes* already mentioned, the tones are unified under the keynote of the 'rising and falling of the sea' (pp. 188–189).
78. *Far from the Madding Crowd*, p. 46.
79. Ibid., pp. 46–47.
80. Ibid., p. 293. Norcombe Hill has a 'mane' (p. 46) and eyes that glitter like those of dead men (p. 71).

2   'Silent workings of the invisible hand': Hardy's metaphysical evolution

1. Hardy to unidentified recipient (23 December, 1920). Quoted in *The Life and Work of Thomas Hardy by Thomas Hardy*, edited by Michael Millgate (London, Macmillan, 1984), p. 441. Such views are echoed in the preface to *Jude the Obscure*, which describes the novel as 'an endeavour to give shape and coherence to a series of seemings, or personal impressions, the question of their consistency or their discordance, of their permanence or their transitoriness, being regarded as not of the first moment' (p. 27).
2. Hardy in two letters to John Galsworthy, *Letters*, V, pp. 153, 156 (31 March, 1916) and (16 April, 1916).
3. Michael Millgate, *Thomas Hardy: His Career as a Novelist* (London: Macmillan, 1994), p. 177.

4. Schweik focuses on a passage in *Tess of the D'Urbervilles*, in which Hardy contradicts his declaration that Tess' sense of guilt was 'out of harmony with the actual world', with an idealist assertion in the very next paragraph that 'the world is only a psychological phenomenon'. See 'Moral Perspectives in *Tess of the D'Urbervilles*', *College English*, 24 (October, 1962), 14–18 (pp. 16–17). Gatrell focuses on a number of contradictions in *The Mayor of Casterbridge*, concluding that 'since the narrative voice is fundamentally contradictory, not anyway a homogeneous thing, the reader is left free to choose one or all of these methods of accounting for the way things turn out'. *Thomas Hardy and the Proper Study of Mankind* (Basingstoke: Macmillan, 1993), p. 92. See also Millgate, *Career as a Novelist*, p. 271.

5. Pierre D'Exideuil, *The Human Pair in the Works of Thomas Hardy: An Essay On the Sexual Problems as Treated in the Wessex Novels, Tales and Poems*, translated by Felix W. Crosse, 2nd edn (New York: Kennikat Press, 1970), pp. 51–52. My italics.

6. Miller, *Thomas Hardy: Distance and Desire* (Cambridge, Massachusetts: Harvard University Press, 1970), p. 16.

7. Green, *Hardy's Lyrics: Pearls of Pity* (London: Macmillan, 1996), p. 3. He states that 'the universe as disclosed by Hardy's personal experience and response to Victorian science – not only biology, but also astronomy and geology – [is] a non-moral, non-human order in which energies of inconceivable main and magnitude stream, flare, and lash, an order in which chance, causation, mutability and evolution obtain, and in which necessity "governs" both external Nature (that is, every organic and inorganic element, object, creature, and physical phenomenon outside a human being) and internal Nature (that is, heredity, sexual instinct, and emotions) – all this makes up a concept of the material conditions of man's life for which, to facilitate discussion, let us adopt the compound term *cosmic process*' (p. 30), Green's italics.

8. Millgate, *Biography*, p. 220.

9. Collins, 'If the voices narrating Hardy's fiction and verse are discordant, they are no more so than the spirit of the age into which he was born', *Thomas Hardy and his God: A Liturgy of Unbelief*, p. 6. See pp. 11–15, 47, 57–58, for discussion of Bakhtin's concept of 'polyphony'.

10. Ibid., p. 11.

11. Pater, *The Renaissance: Studies in Art and Poetry*, 2nd edn (1877) edited with Textual and Explanatory Notes by Donald L. Hill (California: University of California Press, 1980), pp. 150, 151.

12. Hardy to Alfred Noyes, *Letters*, VI, p. 54 (20 December, 1920).

13. Tennyson, 'Despair', *Poems*, 3, ll. 33–34.

14. See Gittings, *Younger Hardy* for survey of Hardy's loss of faith, pp. 88–99.

15. J. A. Froude, *The Nemesis of Faith* (Farnborough: Gregg, 1969 [a facsimile reprint of the 2nd edn, 1849]), pp. 27–28. Hardy's Impercipient is the observer of a Cathedral service who regrets that he 'knows not the ease' enjoyed by the congregation, since 'He who breathes All's Well to these / Breathes no All's-Well to me', *Complete Poems*, ll. 13–16. In 'God's Funeral' Hardy acknowledges that though he is unable to share the present faith of those weeping over the passing of God, he nevertheless 'did not forget / That what was mourned for, I, too long had prized'. *Complete Poems*, ll. 53, 55–56.

16. *Tess of the D'Urbervilles*, p. 146.

17. *Complete Poems*, ll. 10, 16–17. Feuerbach argues that God is simply an objectification of all the best qualities of mankind, designed to satisfy his needs.

18. 'God's Funeral', l. 21. Regret is replaced by outrage in 'God-Forgotten', in which Hardy creates a negligent deity who claims that the earth 'lost my interest from the first', *Complete Poems*, 4, l. 17.

19. For J. S. Mill, the rigidity of natural laws leads us to believe that every event could be caused by 'a specific volition of the presiding Power, provided that this Power adheres in its particular volitions to general laws laid down by itself', *Nature, the Utility of Religion, and Theism*, 2nd edn (London: Longmans, Green, Reader and Dyer, 1874), p. 136. In *The Life* Hardy notes of *On Liberty* that 'we students of that date knew almost by heart' (p. 330).

20. Quoted from Green, p. 28. This refers to Darwin, *On The Origin of Species* (1859) in *The Works of Charles Darwin*, edited by Paul H. Barrett and R. B. Freeman, 29 vols (London: William Pickering, 1986–1989), XV, p. 333.

21. Herbert Spencer, *First Principles*, 5th edn (London: Williams & Norgate, 1887), p. 41. A book which Hardy claimed acted 'as a sort of patent expander when I had been particularly narrowed down by the events of life', Hardy to Lena Milman, *Letters*, II, pp. 24–25 (17 July, 1893).

22. *The Life*, pp. 314–315.

23. *The Evolutionary Self: Hardy, Foster, Lawrence* (Brighton: Harvester Press, 1982), pp. xiii–xiv.

24. Pater, *Plato and Platonism: A Series of Lectures*, 3rd edn (London: Macmillan, 1910), pp. 14, 18–19.

25. John Morley, 'Three Books on the Eighteenth Century', *Fortnightly Review*, 22 (August, 1877), 259–284 (p. 268). See *Literary Notebooks*, 1065. Hardy's underlining.

26. John Tulloch, 'Morality without Metaphysics', *Edinburgh Review*, 144 (October, 1876), 470–500 (p. 476). See *Literary Notebook*, 872.

27. John Tyndall, 'Apology' appended to 'The Belfast Address', in *Fragments of Science: A Series of Detached Essays, Addresses and Reviews*, 5th edn (London: Longman, Green, 1876), p. 560.

28. Spencer, Herbert, *The Principles of Psychology*, 3rd edn, 2 vols (London: Williams & Northgate, 1881), I, pp. 617–618.

29. *Literary Notebooks*, 1357, see *Fortnightly Review*, 28 (1 November, 1885).

30. *The Life*, p. 230.

31. David Asher made a comparison between the theories of sexual attraction in Schopenhauer and Darwin, 'Schopenhauer and Darwinism', *The Journal of Anthropology*, I (January, 1871), 312–332 (p. 330).

32. 'Schopenhauer's Philosophy', *Mind*, 1 (October, 1876), 491–509 (pp. 491, 492). John Oxenford, 'Iconoclasm in German Philosophy', *Westminster Review*, 59 o.s., 3 n.s. (April, 1853), 388–407. At the time, the journal was under the editorship of John Chapman and George Eliot, whose encouragement of liberal free thought was only matched by Eliot's enthusiasm for German metaphysics and Biblical scholarship. She had already by this time published her translation *The Life of Jesus, Critically Examined*, by David Friedrich Strauss (1846) and was, as Chapman advertised in the June 1853 edition of the journal, in the

process of preparing a translation of Ludwig Feuerbach's *Das Wesen des Christenthums* for his new 'Quarterly Series'. Oxenford's article, therefore, cleverly prepared the public for Eliot's intended work. See Gordon Haight, *George Eliot: A Biography* (Harmondsworth, Middlesex: Penguin, 1985), p. 137.

33. Zimmern, 'Review of *Schopenhauer's Leben*, by Wilhelm von Gwinner', *Academy*, 13 (June, 1878), 573–574 (p. 573).
34. Zimmern, *Arthur Schopenhauer: His Life and his Philosophy* (London: Longmans, Green, 1876). Simcox, *Academy*, 9 (March, 1876), 265–266 (p. 265).
35. Sully, 'The Pessimist's View of Life', *Cornhill Magazine*, 33 (April, 1876), 431–443. *Pessimism: A History and a Criticism* (London: Henry S. King, 1877).
36. Hueffer, 'Arthur Schopenhauer', *Fortnightly Review*, 20 (December, 1876), 773–792. Interestingly Hueffer described Oxenford's essay as 'the foundation of Schopenhauer's fame, both in his own and other countries' (p. 785).
37. Hueffer, 'Arthur Schopenhauer', p. 788.
38. Zimmern, *Arthur Schopenhauer*, 1876 edn, p. 113.
39. Significantly in the revised edition of her book she illustrates Schopenhauer's conception of the will by stating that 'for him, the universal Will is essentially blind and purposeless, and in this sense non-rational or irrational, like "An automatic sense / Unweeting why or whence" of Hardy's *Dynasts*'. Zimmern, *Arthur Schopenhauer*, 2nd edn (London: George Allen & Unwin Ltd, 1932), p. 143.
40. Hueffer, 'Arthur Schopenhauer', pp. 789–790.
41. James Sully, 'Hartmann's Philosophy of the Unconscious', *Fortnightly Review*, 260 o.s., 20 n.s. (August, 1876), 242–262.
42. Sully, 'Hartmann', p. 247.
43. Ibid., p. 250.
44. Ibid., p. 251.
45. Anonymous review in *Spectator* (5 February, 1879), 181–182, reprint in *Thomas Hardy: The Critical Heritage*, edited by R. G. Cox (London: Routledge & Kegan Paul, 1970), p. 58. Cox speculates that the author of the review may be R. H. Hutton. For evidence of Hardy's ownership of Sully's *Pessimism* see Wright *The Shaping of the Dynasts*, p. 40. Also see *Literary Notebooks*, 495.
46. Grundy, *Hardy and the Sister Arts*, p. 174.
47. Timothy Hands speaks for many when he notes that the influence of Schopenhauer on the novels is an assertion which nowadays commands little support since, among other things, 'Hardy knew little German, [and] an English translation of Schopenhauer's *World as Will and Idea* was not published until 1883 . . . by which time his career as a novelist was all but over'. ' "A Bewildered Child and his Conjurors": Hardy and the Ideas of his Time', in *New Perspectives on Thomas Hardy*, edited by Charles P. C. Pettit (Basingstoke: Macmillan, 1994), pp. 137–155 (p. 148).
48. Hughes, '*Ecstatic Sound*', p. 204.
49. 'Arthur Schopenhauer', *Contemporary Review*, 21 (February, 1873), 440–463 (p. 449). The article reflects the desire of James Thomas Knowles (ed. 1870–1877) and a prominent member of the 'Metaphysical Society', to assuage the growing curiosity amongst the middle classes for philosophically speculative pieces.
50. *The Return of the Native*, p. 38.
51. *The Dynasts*, I.vi.3.
52. Ebbatson, *Evolutionary Self*, p. 45.

53. Zimmern, *Schopenhauer*, 1876 edn, p. 218.
54. *A Pair of Blue Eyes*, pp. 102, 105.
55. *Desperate Remedies*, pp. 227–228.
56. Ibid., p. 256.
57. Ibid., p. 265.
58. *The Dynasts*, II.v.5, and II.vi.2.
59. Hardy to Edward Wright, *Letters*, III, pp. 255–256 (2 June, 1907).
60. Zimmern, 1876 edn, p. 102. She makes this point very succinctly in the 1932 edn, p. 147. Interestingly a brief review of Zimmern's book focuses on this aspect of Schopenhauer's theory: 'an unconscious "will" (or instinct) . . . rules the world, and, in men of the normal commonplace kind, makes intellect the slave'. *The Athenaeum*, 2543 (July, 1876), 107–109 (p. 108).
61. Ibid., pp. 110–111.
62. Adamson, 'Schopenhauer's Philosophy', p. 505.
63. Sully, *Pessimism*, p. 93.
64. Arthur Schopenhauer, *The World as Will and Idea*, translated by R. B. Haldane and J. Kemp, 3 vols (London: Routledge & Kegan Paul, 1883), I, p. 254.
65. *Tess of the D'Urbervilles*, pp. 402–403.
66. See J. O. Bailey, *Thomas Hardy and the Cosmic Mind* (Chapel Hill: University of North Carolina Press, 1956), pp. 90–93, and Wright, pp. 47–54.
67. See *Literary Notebooks*, 2099–2140. See also 'Real Conversations. Conversation I – With Mr Thomas Hardy', *The Critic*, 38 (April, 1901), p. 316. Quoted in Wright, *Making of the Dynasts*, p. 47.
68. Sully, 'Hartmann', p. 252.
69. Ibid., p. 252.
70. Ibid., p. 254.
71. Ibid., p. 256.
72. Tyndall stated that the 'production of consciousness by molecular motion is to me quite as unthinkable as the production of molecular motion by consciousness', but had singularly failed to produce an alternative theory (*Apology*, p. 561).
73. W. L. Clifford, *Lectures and Essays*, edited by Leslie Stephen and Frederick Pollock, 2 vols (London: Macmillan, 1879), II, p. 85.
74. Ibid., II, p. 85.
75. Ibid.
76. W. H. Mallock, 'The Late Professor Clifford's Essays', *Edinburgh Review*, 151 (April, 1880), 474–511. For Hardy's notes, see *Literary Notebooks*, 1215.
77. Hardy to Roden Noel, *Letters*, I, pp. 261–262 (3 April, 1892).
78. *Spectator*, LV, p. 655. Annotation and quotation with variations and reversed word order, *Literary Notebooks*, 1281.
79. *The Life*, p. 405.
80. *The Dynasts*, I.iv.5, and I.v.4.
81. *Complete Poems*, ll. 21, 24, 41–42.
82. Ibid., ll. 3–4, 13, 15–16.
83. Ibid., ll. 16–20.
84. *The Life*, p. 202.
85. Ibid., p. 163. These sentiments are echoed in his comment that 'the emotions have no place in a world of defect, and it is a cruel injustice that they should have developed in it', *The Life*, p. 149.

86. Sully, *Pessimism*, p. 97.
87. Sully, 'Hartmann', p. 252. D'Exideuil speculates: 'was not the idea of the consciousness gradually penetrating the universe, as if to regenerate and save it, probably borrowed by Hardy from von Hartmann' (p. 42).
88. *The Life*, P. 405.
89. Ibid., p. 256, *Jude the Obscure*, p. 346.
90. Hardy to Edward Wright, *Letters*, III, pp. 255–256 (2 June, 1907).
91. *The Dynasts*, II.ii.3.
92. 'Hardy, History, and Recorded Music', in *Thomas Hardy and Contemporary Literary Studies*, edited by Tim Dolin and Peter Widdowson (Basingstoke: Palgrave Macmillan, 2004), 153–166 (p. 161).
93. *Literary Notebooks*, 2291.
94. Miller, *Distance and Desire*, p. 22.
95. *Complete Poems*, ll. 2, 9, 4. It is a bemused statement echoed by Napoleon in *The Dynasts*, who excuses the bloodshed he has caused by claiming 'Some force within me, baffling my intent, / Harries me onward, whether I will or no', *The Dynasts*, II.i.8.
96. Ibid., ll. 11–12.
97. Orel, *Thomas Hardy's Personal Writings*, p. 53.

3   The spider's web: Metaphysics into music drama

1. Orel, *Thomas Hardy's Personal Writings*, p. 120. From his appraisal of *A Pair of Blue Eyes* it is clear that good form was Hardy's measure of critical success. He recalls that the *Saturday Review* praised it as 'the most artistically constructed of the novels of its time – a quality which, by the bye, would carry little recommendation in these days of loose construction and indifference to organic homogeneity', *The Life*, p. 95. Furthermore, he noted with evident pride of *The Mayor of Casterbridge* that the plot 'was quite coherent and organic, in spite of its complication', *The Life*, p. 179.
2. *The Life*, p. 291.
3. *New Review* (April, 1891), 315–319, Orel, *Thomas Hardy's Personal Writings*, p. 137.
4. Orel, *Thomas Hardy's Personal Writings*, p. 114. Quoted with slight variations from 'Matthew Arnold's Selections from Wordsworth', *Fortnightly Review*, 26 (November, 1879), 686–701 (p. 689). *Literary Notebooks*, 1147.
5. Arnold, 'The Modern Element in Literature', reprint in *The Complete Prose Works of Matthew Arnold*, edited by R. H. Super, 11 vols (Ann Arbor: University of Michigan, 1962–1977), I, p. 20. Bjork notes that Hardy readily accepted 'a great deal of Arnold's literary criticism, both in its aesthetic and ideological ramifications' (annotations, 101).
6. Pater, *The Renaissance*, p. 143.
7. Pater, *Greek Studies*, Library Edition (London: Macmillan, 1910), p. 151.
8. *Social Life in Greece from Homer to Menander*, 5th edn (London: Macmillan, 1883), p. 1. Bjork notes 'that [Hardy] enjoyed and respected Mahaffy's study of Greek life is evident from the great number of entries based on it' (annotations, 500).
9. *Studies of the Greek Poets*, 3rd edn, 2 vols (London: Adam and Charles Black, 1893). Bjork asserts that 'judging from a number of entries ... Hardy seems to have valued Symonds' critical insight' (annotations, 167).

10. Ibid., I, p. 159.

11. *Culture and Anarchy* (Cambridge: Cambridge University Press, 1978), p. 132. Arnold's italics.

12. *Saturday Review*, 41 (June, 1876), 770–771, See *Literary Notebooks*, 464. *Tess of the D'Urbervilles*, p. 218, and *Jude the Obscure*, p. 309.

13. An anonymous review in the *Saturday Review*, 19 (May, 1865), 540–542, noted that the poem 'is an attempt to reproduce a Greek tragedy in its ideas as well as its form' (pp. 540, 541).

14. Bjork notes that Swinburne was 'one of Hardy's earliest and strongest literary infatuations' (*Literary Notebooks*, annotations, 1288). Wright notes that 'of all the Victorians Swinburne appears to have appealed most to Hardy', before going on to list the several copies in the Hardy library (*Shaping of the Dynasts*, p. 22). Millgate claims that 'the impact of Swinburne . . . is strongly signalled by the length of the passages from his early poems which Hardy went to the trouble of writing out from a friend's copy' (*Studies and Specimens*, p. xvii).

15. *The Life*, pp. 106, 114.

16. 'General Preface to the Novels and Poems', Wessex edn, I, 1912, reprint in Orel, *Thomas Hardy's Personal Writings*, 44–50 (pp. 45–46). It should be noted that in elevating ordinary people to the level of universal process he appears to be following the advice of his editor Leslie Stephen who argued that 'the very greatest writers are those who can bring their ideal world into the closest possible contact with our sympathies, and show us heroic figures in modern frock coats'. See 'Hawthorne', *Hours in the Library*, 2 vols (New York: Scribner, Armstrong and Company, 1875), I, pp. 206, 207.

17. *Psychologie als Wissenschaft, neugegründet auf Erfahrung, Metaphysik und Mathematik* (1824). Quoted in Henri F. Ellenberger, *The Discovery of the Unconscious: The History and Evolution of Dynamic Psychiatry* (London: Fontana, 1994), p. 312.

18. *Elemente der Psychophysik*, 2 vols (Leipzig: Breitkorpf and Hartel, 1860). Quoted Ellenberger, p. 313.

19. *The Life*, p. 204.

20. Ibid., p. 177. See also p. 218.

21. The Spirit of the Years notes, 'Yet but one flimsy riband of Its web / Have we here watched in weaving – web Enorm', *The Dynasts*, 'After Scene'.

22. *The Woodlanders*, p. 53.

23. 'Der Ring Des Nibelungen', *The Athenaeum*, 2544 (July, 1876), 154–155 (p. 155). It should be noted, however, that Schopenhauer's theory is quoted in order to reject it.

24. Gurney, 'On Some Disputed Points in Music', *Fortnightly Review*, 26 o.s., 20 n.s. (July, 1876), 106–130, pp. 121–122.

25. Schopenhauer, *The World as Will and Idea*, I, pp. 334–335.

26. In *Vorlesungen über die Philosophie der Kunst* he writes, 'The necessary form of music is *succession* . . . From this we comprehend the close relation of the sense of hearing in general and of music and speech in particular with consciousness of self.' Lippman, II, pp. 69–70.

27. He argues that the Ego's existence in Time is analogous to the existence of a single tone in a piece of music. Lippman, II, p. 106. Despite Schelling's relative obscurity, Hegel's philosophy was relatively well known in Britain due to

Lewes' 'Hegel's Aesthetics', *British and Foreign Review*, 13 (1842), 1–45. See Rosemary Ashton's chapter 'G. H. Lewes' in *The German Idea: Four English Writers and the Reception of German Thought 1800–1860* (Cambridge: Cambridge University Press, 1980), pp. 105, 112–119.

28. *The World as Will and Idea*, I, p. 335.
29. Pater, 'The School of Giorgione', quoted in Leppert, *Sight of Sound*, p. 223.
30. Appearing in Carlyle's translation as early as 1827.
31. Translated from German by Gonnop Thirlwall in 1825 (London: Whittaker, 1825). See V. Stockley, *German Literature as Known in England, 1750–1830* (London: George Routledge and Sons, 1929), p. 237.
32. For details of the anthologies, see Stockley, pp. 239–241.
33. *The World as Will and Idea*, I, p. 341. He notes, 'supposing it were possible to give a perfectly accurate, complete explanation of music, extending even to particulars, that is to say, a detailed repetition in concepts of what it expresses, this would also be a sufficient repetition and explanation of the world in concepts, or at least entirely parallel to such an explanation, and thus it would be the true philosophy' (I, p. 342).
34. Davis, 'Native to the Night: Form, the Tragic Sense of Life, and the Metaphysics of Music in Hardy's Novels', University of Maryland, College Park, 1987, Abstract.
35. In *Tess of the D'Urbervilles* she argues that Hardy creates a tension between the lyricism of the heroine and the wider D'Urberville rhythms surrounding her which follow the sonata form (pp. 201, 233). The 'D'Urberville rhythm' finds its most pronounced expression in the form of the 'footsteps-coming-up behind-Tess motif' as a number of characters overtake her on the open road. Her use of terms such as 'themes' and 'rhythms' to describe such sounds does not, however, disguise the fact that these are simply repeated noises with no pretensions to musicality.
36. Davis, 'Native to the Night', p. 58.
37. Ibid., p. 74.
38. Sherman, 'Thomas Hardy: Lyricist Symphonist', p. 161.
39. Pietch, 'The Relationship Between Music and Literature in the Victorian Period: Studies in Browning, Hardy and Shaw', North Western University, 1961, pp. 179–217. The most pertinent section, 'Some aspects of English Wagnerism', is, as the title suggests, very general.
40. 'Der Ring Des Nibelungen', *The Athenaeum*, 2544 (July, 1876), p. 154, col. c.
41. *Opera and Drama*, reprint in *Richard Wagner Prose Works*, 8 vols, translated by William Ashton Ellis (London: Kegan Paul, Trench, Trubner 1892–1899), II, p. 231. In an extraordinary footnote, he refuses to commit himself to a causal chain linking primeval melodic vowel sounds to speech, claiming 'I take the rise (*Enstehung*) of Speech from out of Melody, not as in a chronologic, but as in an architectonic order', thus side-stepping an issue which was to embroil English aestheticians for the latter half of the century (p. 225).
42. 'The Music of the Future', *Prose Works*, III, p. 335.
43. Ibid., p. 337.
44. Ibid., p. 339. In *Opera and Drama* Wagner denotes the 'Speaking-faculty of the Orchestra as the faculty of uttering the *unspeakable*' (*Prose works*, II, p. 316). Wagner's italics.
45. Ibid., p. 338.
46. Ibid., p. 340. Wagner's italics.

47. Ibid., p. 346.

48. Ibid., p. 349.

49. Chorley was a typical Victorian polymath; he produced a number of plays, poems and five unsuccessful novels. He was a recognised authority on a number of musical issues and, furthermore, appears to have been the only London critic to have experienced either Wagner's music, or his dramas, prior to the spring of 1854. Despite being at the vanguard, his musical tastes remained conservative: he never accepted Verdi, and his articles on Wagner are unashamedly prejudiced and hostile. In a review of *Lohengrin* he notes, 'Herr Wagner's attempt has been, to produce a work of pure declamation, without the slightest reference to melody'. 'Music at Weimar: A Review of *Lohengrin*', *The Athenaeum*, 1194 (September, 1850), p. 980, col. c. Furthermore, he described *Tannhäuser* as 'a wearisome straining after literal, verbal expression in music', *Modern German Music: Recollections and Criticisms*, 2 vols (London: Smith, Elder and Son, 1854), I, p. 363.

50. H. Davison, *Music During the Victorian Era: From Mendelssohn to Wagner – Being the Memoirs of J. W. Davison, Forty Years Music Critic of 'The Times'* (London: W. M. Reeves, 1912), p. 65. Furthermore *The Musical World*, the pre-eminent nineteenth-century English music journal, was written almost exclusively by Davison using a variety of pseudonyms: most notably, 'Otto Beard', 'Drinkwater Hard' and 'Sir Caper O'Corby'.

51. Ibid., p. 184.

52. 'M. Jullien's Concerts', *The Times* (11 December, 1854), p. 8, col. d.

53. 'London Philharmonic Concerts', *The Times* (26 June, 1855), p. 12, col. f.

54. 'Der Ring Des Nibelungen', *The Athenaeum*, 2544 (July, 1876), p. 154, col. c. 'A Retrospect', *The Graphic*, reprint in *The Musical World*, 55 (January, 1877), p. 41.

55. Hueffer, 'Richard Wagner', *Fortnightly Review*, 17 o.s., 11 n.s. (March, 1872), 265–287. He patronisingly dismisses 'Lyric Feuds', complaining that Mosely 'evidently has very little knowledge of Wagner's music'. *Half a Century of Music in England, 1837–1887* (London: Chapman & Hall, 1889), p. 68.

56. Eliot, 'Liszt, Wagner, and Weimar', *Fraser's Magazine*, 52 (July, 1855), 48–62 (p. 50).

57. See *Wellesley*, III, p. 547. In the 1850s the *Westminster* stood third amongst the serious periodicals.

58. Mosely, 'Lyric Feuds', *Westminster Review*, 88 o.s., 32 n.s. (July, 1867), 119–160 (p. 150). My italics.

59. It welcomed contributions from the publicly censured Swinburne, praised the pre-Raphaelites, Morris and Rossetti, and in an article written by Morely himself, supported Browning at the expense of the poet laureate: ' "On The Ring and the Book" by Robert Browning', *Fortnightly Review*, 11 o.s., 5 n.s. (January, 1869), 125–126.

60. Hueffer actually makes this comparison in 'The Wagner Festival: Part Two', *The Examiner* (August, 1877), reprint in *Francis Hueffer Musical Studies: A Series of Contributions* (Edinburgh: Adam and Charles Black, 1880), p. 199.

61. Ibid., p. 68. A letter to Liszt describing Schopenhauer as 'the greatest philosopher since Kant' suggests that he was delighted to be linked with the foremost metaphysician of the day. See *Correspondence of Wagner and Liszt*, translated by Francis Hueffer, 2 vols (London: H. Grevel, 1888), no. 168, pp. 53–55.

62. There is no mention here, for example, of the extraction of music from poetry, a fundamental principle of Wagner's aesthetic project worked out in *Opera and Drama*.

63. Bennett quotes Hueffer's assertion that ' "Schopenhauer seems to have considered music as an art of entirely independent and self-sufficient means of expression, the free movement of which could only suffer from a too close alliance with worded poetry" ' before remarking on Hueffer's puzzled observation that Wagner's rejection of these sentiments by his 'favourite philosopher,... "cannot but surprise us" '. Bennett might have drawn attention to the tentative 'seems', or the less than rigorous 'considered', for it is clear that there should be no 'surprise' for Hueffer: the positions highlighted are mutually exclusive, and require selective usage of Schopenhauer's ideas to make them consistent – a policy that was practised all too freely by Wagner himself. 'The Poetic Basis of Music', *The Musical World*, 52 (April, 1874), 226–228 (pp. 226–227).

64. Hueffer, *Richard Wagner and the Music of the Future: History and Aesthetics* (London: Chapman & Hall, 1874), p. 89.

65. Ibid., p. 90.

66. Hueffer, 'Richard Wagner and his *Ring of the Niblung'*, *The New Quarterly Magazine*, 4 (April, 1875), 159–186. Reprint in *Musical Studies*, from where this quotation is taken (p. 178).

67. *The Musical Standard* was merciless in its condemnation of Hueffer's article. Having candidly admitted that 'we have not found patience to read it all' the author attacks Hueffer's alleged long-windedness with the plea 'we think we hear the reader cry "Hold! enough!" but Dr. Hueffer goes on boring us with this rubbish for several more pages, and evidently likes it'. 'Hueffer on Wagner', *The Musical Standard*, 8 n.s. (May, 1875), Pt I, 278–279, Pt II, 293–294 (p. 294).

68. Dannreuther, *Richard Wagner, The Music of the Future, A Letter to M. Frederic Villot* (London: Schott, 1873). This organisation sponsored the first public concerts consisting of Wagner's music in London on the 19 February and 9 May 1873. *The Athenaeum* attacked the idea of performing excerpts from Wagner's work, arguing that 'his operas absolutely require, that they may produce their due effect, dramatic action and a *mise en scène*', 'The Wagner Society', 2366 (March, 1873), 288–289 (p. 288, col. c).

69. Dannreuther, *Richard Wagner: His Tendencies and Theories* (London: Augener, 1873). Hueffer notes that the brochure received a 'distinctly hostile' reaction, but it succeeded in opening for debate Wagner's aesthetics, *Half a Century*, p. 66.

70. Dannreuther, 'The Opera: Its Growth and Decay', *Macmillan's*, 12 (May, 1875), 64–72. 'The Musical Drama', *Macmillan's*, 33 (November, 1875), 80–85.

71. Bennett, *Macmillan's*, 20 (July, 1869), 260–265.

72. Dannreuther, *Tendencies and Theories*, pp. 12–13.

73. Ibid., p. 6.

74. Ibid., p. 4.

75. Dannreuther, 'Musical Drama', *Macmillans*, 33 (November, 1875), 80–85 (p. 85).

76. Dannreuther, Ibid., p. 82. See also 'The Music of the Future', translated by Dannreuther, p. 38.

77. Ibid., p. 83.

78. Ibid., pp. 83–84.

79. Editor from 1855 to 1895. Obituary by W. E. H. Lecky, *Edinburgh Review*, 183 (January, 1896), 267–271 (p. 270). William Stigand, 'Robert Browning's Poems', *Edinburgh Review*, 120 (October, 1864), 537–565 (pp. 537–538, 565); and R. Monckton Milnes, book review ' "Atalanta in Calydon: A Tragedy", by Charles Swinburne', *Edinburgh Review*, 122 (July, 1865), 202–216 (p. 215). *Wellesley*, pp. 420–421.

80. Statham, 'Wagner and the Modern Theory of Music', *Edinburgh Review*, 143 (January, 1876), 141–176 (p. 153, 173).

81. Ibid., pp. 171, 172. Statham links Wagner's artistic iconoclasm with that of the pre-Raphaelites (p. 176). This comparison is explored further in Edward Rose's article 'Wagner as Dramatist', in which he states that Wagner's work bears 'a strong likeness to certain schools of painting and of poetry now fashionable in England – to the productions of Burne Jones and of Swinburne . . . – to a certain extent, perhaps, he holds the creed of "arts for arts sake" '. *Fraser's Magazine*, 99 o.s., 19 n.s. (April, 1879), 519–532 (pp. 519–520).

82. Gurney, 'On Some Disputed Points in Music', p. 119.

83. Ibid., p. 118. Gurney's italics.

84. Ibid., p. 125.

85. Gurney, 'On Wagner and Wagnerism', *Nineteenth Century*, 13 (March, 1883), 434–452 (p. 447).

86. Sully, 'The Opera', *Contemporary Review*, 26 (June, 1875), 103–122 (pp. 107, 117).

87. Ibid., p. 117.

88. Bennett's articles in The Telegraph were collected into *Letters from Bayreuth: Descriptive and Critical of Wagner's 'Der Ring Des Nibelungen'* (London: Novello, Ewer, 1877), *'Letters from Bayreuth'*, p. 41. Bennett's reflections are also important because his outrage at the 'scenes of murder, incest, theft, deceit, and vulgar trickery' reveals the prurient underbelly of Victorian aesthetic criticism, which was remarkable in its absence in the articles of the period (p. 98). The only other condemnation of the moral content of *The Ring* I have been able to find is Louis Engel's 'Wagner', *Temple Bar*, 65 (July, 1882), 329–344. In it he poses the question 'what are the public to say to the gratuitous tendency to immorality to which [Wagner's] *Nibelungs Ring* lays itself open? There is not even an extenuating circumstance'. He concludes, 'If there was at least any dramatic necessity for the depicting of this incest, but nothing, absolutely nothing, is gained by it, except the aggravation of adultery' (p. 333).

89. *Letters from Bayreuth*, p. 89.

90. Haweis, 'Wagner', *Contemporary Review*, 29 (May, 1877), 981–1003 (p. 987).

91. Ibid., p. 988.

92. Halford Hawkins, 'The Wagner Festival at Bayreuth', *Macmillan's Magazine*, 35 (November, 1876), 55–63 (p. 63).

93. Percy Scholes, *The Mirror of Music, 1844–1944: A Century of Musical Life in Britain as Reflected in the Pages of the Musical Times*, 2 vols (London: Novello and Company, 1947), I, p. 254.

94. Circulation in 1877, 62, 193. Oliver Woods and James Bishop, *The Story of 'The Times'* (London: Michael Joseph, 1983), p. 120.

95. H. Davison, *Music During the Victorian Era*, p. 317.

96. 'Albert Hall Concerts', *The Times* (9 May, 1877), p. 10, col. d.

97. Ibid. (22 May, 1877), p. 9, col. f. See also 'Albert Hall Concerts', *The Times* (14 May, 1877), p. 8, col. e.

98. Haweis, *My Musical Life*, 2nd edn (London: W. H. Allen and Co., 1886), p. 448. Haweis' italics. Similar sentiments are expressed by *The Athenaeum*, which recorded that the greeting 'accorded to Herr Wagner is as enthusiastic as ever', 'Herr Wagner', 2586 (May, 1877), 650–651 (p. 651, col. a). Similarly *The Globe* acknowledges that 'much of the enthusiasm [for the 1877 concerts] has been probably genuine'. 'We Shall See', reprint in *The Musical World*, 55 (June, 1877), p. 413.

99. Anonymous, 'Richard Wagner in London', *Daily News* (4 May, 1877), p. 3. See *Literary Notebooks*, 1023.

100. In *The Life* Hardy asserts 'I prefer late Wagner, as I prefer late Turner, to early (which I suppose is all wrong in taste), the idiosyncrasies of each master being more strongly shown in these strains' (p. 329). See also 'I don't want to see original realities – as optical effects, that is. I want to see the deeper reality underlying the scenic. . . . The much decried, mad, late-Turner rendering is now necessary to create my interest' (p. 185).

101. *The Life*, p. 181. Hardy's italics.

102. Kahn, *Noise, Water, Meat*, pp. 86–87.

103. *New Musical Resources* (1919) (New York: Something Else Press, 1969), p. 20. Quoted from Kahn, *Noise, Water, Meat*, p. 88.

104. *The Mayor of Casterbridge*, p. 81.

105. *The Hand of Ethelberta*, p. 335.

106. *Tess of the D'Urbervilles*, pp. 402–403.

107. *The Well-Beloved*, p. 40.

108. Schopenhauer, *The World as Will and Idea*, l, p. 336.

109. *Jude the Obscure*, p. 351. The insight attributed to Sue is echoed in that of the Pities who asks over the dying Nelson why man should be born into such an inharmonious world: 'Things mechanized / By coils and pivots set to foreframed codes / Would, in a thorough-sphered melodic rule, / And governance of sweet consistency, / Be cessed no pain, whose burnings would abide / With That Which holds responsibility, / Or inexist' (I.v.4).

110. Hardy to Edward Wright, *Letters*, III, pp. 255–256 (2 June, 1907).

111. Armstrong provides a fascinating discussion of Hardy's poem 'Haunting Fingers' in this context. 'Hardy, History', p. 161. Armstrong notes how in the poem 'it is as if the freedom which Hardy had seen figured in the play of the pianist's hand has been released into its own proper space – the space of "stowage", of a ghost in the machine'.

112. Ibid.

113. See Alison Winter, *Mesmerized: Powers of Mind in Victorian Britain* (Chicago: University of Chicago Press, 1998), p. 136, See also Ellenberger, particularly the section entitled 'The Royal Road to the Unknown Mind: Hypnotism', pp. 112–120.

114. Winter, *Mesmerized*, p. 117.

115. Ibid., p. 309.

116. Ibid., p. 314. See also the Charivari caricature of 1868, in which all we see of Wagner is his bow (he is using it to conduct rather than a baton) as he lulls his audience into a trance with a shower of notes.

117. Hueffer, *Richard Wagner*, pp. 294–295. Quoted in Winter, *Mesmerized*, pp. 312, 314.
118. Nietzsche, *The Case of Wagner* (1888), translated by Walter Kaufmann (New York: Random House, 1967), pp. 171, 183, Crary, *Suspensions of Perception*, p. 252. Crary also notes the opinions of two early French critics. Eugène Véron noted of his experience of the *Ring* in 1878 that the production was of a dreamlike clairvoyance, unlike normal waking states, *L'esthetique* (Paris: C. Reinwald, 1878). Paul Souriau, writing in 1893, questioned whether 'Perhaps a new Wagner will soon write an opera for the magic lantern – an opera of dreamlike music and fantastic and virtually imaginary tableaus', *La Suggestion dans L'art* (Paris: Félix Alcan, 1893), pp. 176–177.
119. *The Complete Poetical Works of Thomas Hardy*, edited by Samuel Hynes (Oxford: Clarendon Press, 1995), 5 vols, V, p. 328.
120. *The Dynasts*, III.vii.7.
121. Ibid., III.iii.5. This feature led the contemporary reviewer, Arthur Bingham Walkley, to make the facetious yet perceptive observation that they were simply puppets of what Mr. Hardy calls the 'Immanent Will'. *The Times Literary Supplement* (29 January, 1904), p. 30, col. c.
122. Ibid., II.iv.8. Hardy also uses the image of an organ to describe the sound of the opening cannonade of the battle of Leipzig: a 'loud droning, uninterrupted and breve-like, as from the pedal of an organ kept continuously down' (III.iii.2). Hardy returns to this image in the 'victim shriek and song' of the 'Sleep-Worker'. *Complete Poems*, l. 21.
123. Hardy to Thomas Woolner, *Letters*, I, p. 73 (21 April, 1880).
124. *The Return of the Native*, pp. 71–72. Karen Davis also draws out the similarity between Hardy's presentation here and Schopenhauer's objectification of the will (p. 74).
125. Both Rutland (p. 179) and Jean R. Brooks quote A. Stanton Whitfield, who claimed that the scene is like 'the entry of the gods in Wagner. Large orchestras are not out of place in making the power of cosmic forces felt on the pulse.' See Brooks, *Thomas Hardy: The Poetic Structure* (London: Elek, 1971), p. 177. Frances Pietch, Karen Davis (p. 74) and Joan Grundy, however, make the comparison with the prelude to *Rheingold*. Grundy notes: 'a comparison with the beginning of *Rheingold* and its evocation in music of the waters of the Rhine seems even more appropriate. The existence of Gustav Holst's powerful symphonic poem *Egdon Heath*, confirms the impression that Hardy's chapter is in itself a poetic symphony' (*Hardy and the Sister Arts*, p. 165).
126. Davison, 'Wagner Festival', *The Times* (24 August, 1876), p. 8, col. a.
127. Hueffer, 'The Wagner Festival', *The Examiner* (August, 1876), reprint in *Musical Studies*, from where this quotation is taken, pp. 182–183.
128. Simon Gatrell, *Hardy The Creator: A Textual Biography* (Oxford: Clarendon Press, 1988), pp. 31–32.
129. Hughes does not actually refer to this specific scene, but it is certainly amenable to a Deleuzean interpretation. See Hughes, 'Ecstatic Sound' (p. 30), for specific references to Gilles Deleuze and Claire Parnet, See Hughes 'Ecstatic Sound' (p. 30) for specific references to, and detailed discussion of, the works of Gilles Deleuze and Claire Parnet.
130. *The Return of the Native*, p. 38, Having read *Marius the Epicurean* Hardy copied into the *Literary Notebooks* the suggestion that: 'The philosophic

mind might apprehend, in what seemed to be mass of lifeless matter, the movement of the universal life in wh. Things, and men's impressions of them, were ever "coming to be" alternately consumed and renewed... "Perpetual flux" of minds and things'. *Literary Notebooks*, 1549. For Pater, the appreciation of art is less an attempt to perceive things as they 'really are' in a Wordsworthian or Arnoldian sense, but rather it is a process of becoming in which the continually weaving and unweaving self realises itself in the object of perception. Central to his aesthetic is music, his claim that 'all art aspires towards the condition of music' privileging that art which annihilated the distinction between object and art.

131. Penny Boumelha points out that the plot shares many of the characteristics of *Far from the Madding Crowd* and *The Return of the Native*, such as the 'apparent recrudescence of the pastoral mode' and also the device of the returning native with a choice between lovers. *Thomas Hardy and Women: Sexual Ideology and Narrative Form*, 2nd edn (Wisconsin: University of Wisconsin Press, 1985), p. 98. See also the attempts of E. G. William, H. Matchett to create an ur-text of the novel, '*The Woodlanders*, or Realism in Sheep's Clothing', *Nineteenth Century Fiction*, 9 (1955), 241–261.

132. *The Woodlanders*, pp. 39–40.

133. Ibid., p. 37.

134. Ibid., pp. 37, 362.

135. Ibid., p. 93.

136. See Miller J. Hillis for a good discussion of this element in Hardy's fiction, *Thomas Hardy: Distance and Desire* (Cambridge, Massachusetts: Harvard University Press, 1970). He argues that Tess' movements across the landscape demonstrate how she 'travels a determined course through life toward her fated end' (p. 202). In 'The Absolute Explains' time becomes 'a dark highway' upon which man, 'plodding by lantern light', is only able to perceive the 'Now' by means of its dim rays, the 'Past' and 'Future' remaining obscure. *Complete Poems*, ll. 11–13, 16, 17.

137. *The Woodlanders*, pp. 38, 39.

138. *The Dynasts*, I.iv.5.

139. *The Woodlanders*, p. 84.

140. Ibid, pp. 52, 102. Melbury falls into a reverie when he establishes why he sent Grace away to school (p. 61), when he begins to accuse Felice Charmond of adultery (p. 248), and during his first speech to Fitzpiers regarding Grace's cold (p. 177).

141. *The Woodlanders*, p. 119.

142. Ibid.

143. Ibid., p. 92.

144. Ibid., p. 93.

145. Ibid., p. 123.

146. Ibid., p. 167.

147. Ibid., p. 169.

148. Ibid., pp. 170, 171.

149. Ibid., p. 173. It is also significant that the 'scurr of the distant night-hawk' is one of the sounds heard by Stephen Smith as he sits in the porch of Endlestow church waiting for Elfride Swancourt. By this stage of the narrative she has begun her liaison with Knight (p. 188).

150. Simon Gatrell, 'Hardy's Dances', *Thomas Hardy and the Proper Study of Mankind*, p. 34.

151. *Jude the Obscure*, p. 139.

152. *The Dynasts*, III.vi.2.

153. Ibid., 'Fore Scene'.

154. Hardy's description of the masked ball at Cambacérès is also designed to act as a grotesque dumb show for Napoleon's disastrous Russian campaign: 'the maskers surge into the foreground of the scene, and their motions become more and more fantastic. A strange gloom begins and intensifies, until only the high lights of their grinning figures are visible. These also, with the whole ballroom, gradually darken, and the music softens to silence' (II.v.1).

155. *A Laodicean*, pp. 138, 256.

156. In *The Dynasts* the dumb show which shows the progress of Maria Louisa's cavalcade to Paris to marry Napoleon is described as 'a file of ants crawling along a strip of garden-matting' seen through the 'heavy rains [which] spread their gauzes over the scene' (II.v.5). Also the French assault on Ulm is observed through 'the gauze of descending waters' (I.iv.4).

157. *A Laodicean*, p. 338.

158. *Tess of the D'Urbervilles*, p. 90.

159. Ibid., pp. 90–91. Hardy's italics.

160. Ibid., p. 92.

161. Hardy notes that Tess 'did not abhor dancing, but she was not going to dance here' (p. 91).

162. Hardy informs the reader that the interior of the Durbeyfield home 'struck upon the girl's senses with an unspeakable dreariness' (p. 45). Furthermore, Tess is described as feeling 'quite a Malthusian towards her mother for thoughtlessly giving her so many little sisters and brothers' (p. 62).

163. Ibid., 'The church clock struck, when suddenly the student said that he must leave – he had been forgetting himself – he had to join his companions. As he fell out of the dance his eyes lighted on Tess . . . owing to her backwardness, he had not observed her' (p. 42).

164. Ibid., p. 39.

165. Hardy's poem 'Heredity' seems entirely applicable to Tess, and explains the role of her sister, 'Liza-Lu, at the close of the novel: 'I Am the family face; / Flesh perishes, I live on, / Projecting trait and trace / Through time to times anon'. *Complete Poems*, ll. 1–4.

166. *The Hand of Ethelberta*, Ibid., p. 341.

167. Ibid., p. 340.

168. Ibid., pp. 335, 338.

169. Ibid., p. 341.

170. Mrs Yeobright's identification of the 'one thread [that] runs through the whole piece' actually comes through her bitterness at the marriage of Eustacia and Clym (p. 207).

171. *The Return of the Native*, p. 258.

172. In *The Dynasts* the Pities refers to 'the intolerable antilogy / Of making figments feel' (I.iv.5).

173. *The Dynasts*, II.vi.5.

174. Ibid.

175. Ibid.

176. *The Mayor of Casterbridge*, p. 98, *The Return of the Native*, pp. 58, 59.

177. 'Music: Its Origins and Influence', *Quarterly Review*, 131 (July, 1871), 145–176 (p. 155). Haweis' italics. This metaphor is quite literal in his in diagrammatic depiction of the depression and elation of a man dying of thirst who discovers water, and the correlative morphology of depression and elation to be found in the musical piece 'The Blue Bells of Scotland', 'Music and Emotion', *Contemporary Review*, 15 (October, 1870), 363–382 (pp. 372, 375).

178. Haweis, 'Music and Emotion', p. 375.

179. In the former he argues music is that art 'most directly ethical in origin', that which most directly expresses the moral goodness of the mind which produced it, and 'is also the most direct in power of discipline', it becomes 'the simplest, the most effective of all instruments of moral instruction.... Music is thus, in her health, the teacher of perfect order'. Unhealthy music, conversely, is indulgent and characterised by an undisciplined outpouring of passion. *Works*, XIX, p. 344 and p. 175. This Platonic argument is explored in Book III of *The Republic*, in which Socrates lectures Glaucon on the benefits of musical training, arguing that it is the most potent instrument of moral improvement 'because rhythm and harmony find their way into the inward places of the soul, on which they mightily fasten, imparting grace, and making the soul of him who is rightly educated graceful', *The Republic of Plato*, translated by Benjamin Jowett, 3rd edn (Oxford: Clarendon Press, 1888), III, p. 88.

180. Haweis, 'Music: Its Origins and Influence', p. 156.

181. Haweis, 'Music and Morals: Part III', *Contemporary Review*, 17 (July, 1871), 491–508 (p. 502).

182. Ibid., p. 506.

183. *Desperate Remedies*, p. 158.

184. Hughes, 'Ecstatic Sound', pp. 36–38.

185. *Tess of the D'Urbervilles*, p. 113.

186. A theory which is of interest in this context is George J. Romane's theory of Eject, which Hardy was reading and making notes on in 1886. An 'Eject' is a term coined by Professor Clifford to describe something (a sensation or mental state) which is neither an actual nor a conceivable object of our consciousness, but which is inferred to be a real existence analogous in kind to our own sensations or mental states. So, for Romane, listening to a piece of Beethoven has less to do with the type of physiological concerns highlighted by Helmholtz and Haweis than 'the mind of Beethoven communicating to my mind through the complex intervention of three different brains with their neuromuscular systems, and an endless variety of aerial vibrations proceeding from the pianoforte'. 'The World as Eject', *Contemporary Review*, 50 (July, 1886), 44–59 (p. 57). *Literary Notebooks*, 1383.

187. *The Woodlanders*, pp. 39–40.

4   The plucked harp string: Desire, courtship ritual and the debate concerning speech theory

1. *Jude the Obscure*, pp. 62, 63.

2. *The Woodlanders*, pp. 142, 251. Hardy notes of Grace that after his visit 'she felt like a woman who did not know what she had been doing for the previous hour' (p. 186).

3. Winter, *Mesmerized*, p. 131.
4. *Tess of the D'Urbervilles*, p. 174.
5. *The Dynasts*, I.vi.3.
6. Darwin, *Origin of Species*, *Works*, XV, p. 333.
7. Zimmern, pp. 221–222. Sully's 1876 review of Hartmann's philosophy reveals the 'unconscious purpose, or blind instinctive impulse, which gives all its meaning to the delights of courtship'. See 'Hartmann's Philosophy of the Unconscious', p. 249.
8. Asher, 'Schopenhauer and Darwinism', p. 331.
9. Sully, *Pessimism*, p. 92.
10. *Complete Poems*, ll. 51–52.
11. Terry Eagleton, *The Ideology of the Aesthetic* (Oxford: Blackwell, 1990), p. 159. Quoted from Crary, *Suspensions of Perception*, p. 57.
12. Interestingly, Joan Grundy alludes to the transformation from harp to web, but considers it in terms of Hardy's creative control rather than his metaphysics (p. 172).
13. *The Trumpet Major*, p. 194.
14. Hughes, *'Ecstatic Sound'*, p. 67.
15. Irwin, *Reading Hardy's Landscapes* (Basingstoke: Macmillan, 2000), p. 52.
16. *A Laodicean*, p. 49.
17. Ibid., Hardy's reference to 'dying falls' is an allusion to Shakespeare's *Twelfth Night*, I.i: 'That strain again. It had a dying fall'. Somerset's reflections centre on Lorenzo's speech from Shakespeare's *The Merchant of Venice*, V.i, in which he describes a Christianised version of the music of the spheres: 'There's not the smallest orb that thou behold'st / But in his motion like an angel sings, / Still quiring to the young-eyed cherubims'.
18. See *Dumbstruck*, p. 389 for a fascinating discussion of this phenomenon, particularly his analysis of the work 'Peter Progress'.
19. Connor, *Dumbstruck*, p. 389. The verse actually runs:

> One hears in the storm of sound the plaint of unknown powers
> The concert of wail that comes from other worlds than ours,
> The inarticulate cry of things that ill now were mute
> And speak out their need through the strings of this monstrous
> man-made lute.

20. *Two on a Tower*, p. 82.
21. *The Woodlanders*, p. 258.
22. A flirtatious Bathsheba Everdene considers the marriage proposal of a perplexed Gabriel Oak whilst standing behind a 'low stunted holly bush, now laden with red berries' (*Far from the Madding Crowd*, p. 64). Diggory Venn hides behind a holly bush to observe the sexually charged tryst of Wildeve and Eustacia (*The Return of the Native*, p. 94).
23. For a typical Romantic view, see Wackenroder, 'The Characteristic Inner Nature of the Musical Art and the Psychology of Today's Instrumental Music', Lippman (1988), II, p. 24.
24. According to Crary it was during the late seventies (particularly after the creation of the world's first psychology laboratory at Leipzig in 1879) that man became the focus of experiment. *Suspensions of Perception*, p. 29.

25. Haweis, 'Music and Morals: Part I', *Contemporary Review*, 16 (December, 1870), 89–101; 'Music and Morals: Part II', *Contemporary Review*, 16 (January, 1871), 280–297; and 'Music and Morals: Part III', *Contemporary Review*, 17 (July, 1871), 491–508.

26. Haweis, 'Music and Morals: Part III', p. 501.

27. Haweis, 'Music: Its Origins and Influence', *Quarterly Review*, 131 (July, 1871), 145–176 (p. 156).

28. Sully, *My Life and Friends: A Psychologist's Memories* (London: T. Fisher Unwin, 1918), p. 136. See *Wellesley*, III, p. 550.

29. Hughes, 'Ecstatic Sound', p. 209.

30. Hartmann, *Philosophy of the Unconscious*, 3 vols, translated by W. C. Coupland (London: Kegan Paul, 1893), I, p. 27. Quoted in Hughes, 'Ecstatic Sound', p. 210.

31. *Westminster Review*, 104 o.s., 48 n.s. (October, 1875), 432–453 (p. 453).

32. Ibid., p. 450.

33. This entirely mechanistic conclusion was explored further in E. Carey's essay 'Body and Music'. In it a fictional professor of physiology challenges the very existence of music, arguing that since what is called music is reducible to nothing more than the 'vibrations of the violin-string and sounding board ... transmitted ... along the auditory nerve and sensory ganglia to the cerebral hemispheres', it does not exist as an objective phenomenon. Carey, 'Body and Music', *National Review*, 5 (May, 1888), 382–390 (p. 386).

34. Alexander Bain, *The Senses and the Intellect* (London: John W. Parker, 1855), p. 311.

35. *Fortnightly Review*, 21 (1 March, 1877), p. 325. *Literary Notebooks*, 899, quotation with slight variations.

36. G. H. Lewes, *Problems of Life and Mind*, First Series, 2 vols, I, 'The Foundation of a Creed' (London: Trubner, 1874), p. 254. Quoted by da Sousa Correa, who provides an excellent discussion of its implications for the work of George Eliot (*George Eliot, Music and Victorian Culture*, p. 162).

37. Spencer, 'On the Origin and Function of Music', *Fraser's Magazine*, 56 (October, 1857), 396–408.

38. Spencer acknowledges his debt to Bain's *Animal Instinct and Intelligence* in a footnote on page 397. It is, however, probably Bain's *The Senses and the Intellect* (1855) that Spencer found more useful, since in the chapter 'On Hearing' Bain dismisses nebulous concepts such as beauty when exploring the sensuous pleasure derived from certain tones, and reduces it instead to a consideration of the shape of the ear's tympanum (pp. 202–204). It is an argument persued later by Spencer in 'The Physiology of Laughter', in which he reduces laughter to the 'quasi-convulsive contractions of the muscles' around the mouth caused by the 'undirected discharge of nervous energy into the muscular system'. Reprint in *Essays: Scientific, Political, and Speculative*, English reprint of 3rd series of US edn, 3 vols (London: Williams & Northgate, 1868), I, 194–209 (p. 201).

39. Spencer, 'Origin and Function', pp. 406, 407.

40. In 'Essai sur L'Origine des Langues' (1753), Rousseau states that 'melody, in imitating vocal inflexions, expresses laments, cries of sorrow or joy. ... It imitates the accents of languages, and the affective turns in every idiom that are caused by certain movements of the soul' (reprint in Lippman, I, p. 328). In *The Asthetik* (1820), Hegel declares that 'the purely natural cry of feeling,

whatever it may be, of horror...or the sobbing of grief...are themselves highly expressive; and indeed...the starting-point of music' (reprint in Lippman, II, p. 139). 'Speech theory' also formed the basis of an exchange in *Blackwoods* between 1819 and 1824, beginning with the question of the poet and political radical, Thomas Doubleday, who asks 'how happens it that the same succession of tones produces, in various persons, the same sentiment'. His answer is to propose a connection between the inflections of the human voice under passion and music. 'Letter to the Editor', *Blackwoods Magazine*, 5 (July, 1819), 400. See also the reply by A. B., 'On Musical Expression, In Answer to Musical Queries in Last Number', *Blackwoods*, 5 (August, 1819), and Doubleday's riposte (actually printed D. P., but this author is undoubtedly the same), 'On Musical Expression, In Defence of the Queries', *Blackwoods*, 5 (September, 1819), 694–697 (p. 694). It is later echoed in the assertion of Francis Fetis that 'music in its origin, is composed only of cries of joy or expressions of pain'. *Music Explained to the World or How to understand Music and Enjoy its Performance*; Pt I (London: H. G. Clarke, 1844), p. 3.

41. Darwin, *The Descent of Man, Works*, XXII, p. 595.

42. It is interesting to note that even as late as 1890 Spencer was still defending his theory from Darwin's attack. See 'The Origin of Music', *Mind*, 15 (October, 1890), 449–468, in which he argues that from observations made in his back garden (a frightening insight into the inductive method) it is plain that birds sing for the same reasons that boys do: 'overflow of energy'! (p. 452).

43. *The Philosophy of Music: A Series of Essays*, entitled, respectively, 'The relationship of music to the other fine arts'; 'The moral theory of music'; and 'The laws of life in art' (London: Boosey and Sons, 1862), p. 103. Goddard's italics.

44. Ibid., pp. 41–42.

45. Ibid., pp. 80, 81. Goddard's italics.

46. Sully, 'On the Nature and Limits of Musical Expression', *Contemporary Review*, 23 (March, 1874), 572–589 (pp. 575, 585).

47. Mill's essay is reprinted as 'Thoughts on Poetry and its Varieties', in *Collected Works*, I, 343–365 (see p. 350). Sully does acknowledge this essay on p. 584, but with mixed feelings.

48. Gurney, 'On Some Disputed Points in Music', p. 117. To begin with, he rejects the five similarities which Spencer had identified between the dynamic structure of impassioned speech and music, arguing that 'on not one of these heads does he seem to me to succeed in making out his case'. He takes the example of loudness, which he suggests is the most plausible, and notes that it 'is by no means a universal or essential element, either of song or of emotional speech' (p. 107). He then proceeds to use the research of Helmholtz to provide another distinction, arguing that the emotional voice tends to glide from pitch to pitch, whereas music tends to move in fixed intervals (p. 113). He concludes by stating that although there are certain effects in emotional speech which do play a part in a large number of musical effects, the relationship is one of common ground, not causality.

49. Gurney, 'On Music and Musical Criticism', *Nineteenth Century*, 4 (July, 1878), 51–74 (pp. 55–56).

50. Ibid., p. 57. Gurney expands on this appeal to a 'special faculty' in his seminal *On the Power of Sound* (London: Smith, Elder, 1880), p. 492.

51. He certainly owned a copy of *Essays: Scientific, Political and Speculative*, in which Spencer's 'On the Origin and Function of Music' was published, but it was auctioned off as part of the Hardy estate, forming item twenty-eight in the Hodgson catalogue of sale – therefore making it impossible to verify whether he had marked the text in any way. *The Catalogue of Messrs Hodgson and Co.* for May 26, 1938 is kept at the Dorset County Museum. I am grateful for the help of Lilian Swindall, curator of the Hardy collection, for her help in locating this document. However, it is clear from a quotation copied into his *Literary Notebook* from Gurney's essay which attacked the main principles of speech theory that Hardy not only knew about speech theory but supported it. Hardy's handwritten comment rebutting Gurney's criticisms '[no: Mr S. is right]' indicates agreement with Spencer. See Bjork's annotation, 495.

52. Hardy to Caleb Saleeby (28 January, 1915). There are two versions of this letter. The copy printed in *Letters*, V, pp. 78–79, does not contain this observation. However, this copy was revised by Hardy himself and this sentence, which refers to a notice in the *Cambridge Review*, 30 (January, 1915) of Alfred W. Tillett's *Spencer's Synthetic Philosophy: What it is All About* (London, 1914), was added. The latter version is reprinted *The Life*, pp. 369–370.

53. See her excellent discussion of physiology in *The Mill on the Floss* in *George Eliot, Music and Victorian Culture*, pp. 102–129, particularly, p. 106.

54. *The Mill on the Floss*, edited by Gordon S. Haight (Oxford: Clarendon Press, 1980), pp. 366, 380.

55. Eliot's understanding of the term 'Will' is similar to Ludwig Feuerbach's, whose *Essence of Christianity* she translated in 1852. He argued that it is the instrument of salvation, for it gives man the strength to follow his duty, and when it sleeps man becomes the instrument of others. In this he is diametrically opposed to Schopenhauer, who argues that the sleeping will is the root of all salvation. For pertinent summary, see Eliot's translation of *The Essence of Christianity*, 2nd edn (London: John Chapman, 1854), p. 39.

56. Eliot notes that 'his preaching was a music', *Romola*, edited by Andrew Brown (Oxford: Clarendon Press, 1993), pp. 514, 251.

57. *Tess of the D'Urbervilles*, p. 212.

58. Spencer, 'Progress: Its Law and Cause', *Westminster Review*, 67 o.s., 11 n.s. (April, 1857), 445–485 (p. 446). Lamarck's theory is set out in *Historie Naturelle des animaux sans vertebras* (1816), which states that organisms have a God-given faculty that allows them to produce organs by means of slow incremental change in response to their environment, 'acquired characteristics' that are then passed on to offspring. Despite the advocacy of this theory in Robert Chambers' *The Vestiges of Creation* (1844), Lamarck's ideas failed to gain currency amongst the majority of biologists or the general public, since they seemed to rely on a fanciful principle by which a creature could simply grow, say, a longer neck in response to a desire to eat leaves on a taller tree, a sleight of hand that Darwin's theory of natural selection avoided.

59. *The Life*, p. 218.

60. Spencer, *First Principles*, p. 252.

61. *A Pair of Blue Eyes*, pp. 135, 136. See also Grundy's discussion of this passage in *Hardy and the Sister Arts*, p. 138.

62. *Jude the Obscure*, pp. 116, 241.
63. Ibid., p. 292.
64. Winter, *Mesmerized*, p. 136, Ellenberger, *Discovery of Unconscious*, p. 113.
65. Ibid., p. 63.
66. Ibid., p. 287.
67. *A Treatise on the Nervous Diseases of Women: Comprising an Inquiry into the Nature, Causes and Treatment of Spinal and Hysterical Disorders* (London, 1840), pp. 140–141. See da Sousa Correa's excellent discussion of this topic, *George Eliot, Music and Victorian Culture*, p. 86.
68. *On the Preservation of Health of Women during the Critical Periods of Life* (London, 1851), p. 38 (da Sousa Correa, *George Eliot, Music and Victorian Culture*, p. 87).
69. 'The Fiddler of the Reels', in *Life's Little Ironies*, reprint in The New Wessex edition of *The Stories of Thomas Hardy*, edited and introduction by F. B. Pinion, 3 vols (London: Macmillan, 1977), II.
70. 'Fiddler', p. 123.
71. Ibid., p. 124.
72. Ibid., p. 126.
73. Ibid., pp. 127, 134, 136.
74. Ibid., pp. 124, 136.
75. *The Hand of Ethelberta*, p. 230.
76. Hughes, *'Ecstatic Sound'*, p. 31.
77. *Far from the Madding Crowd*, p. 204.
78. *Tess of the D'Urbervilles*, pp. 150–151.
79. Hardy observes of their early morning courting that 'the spectral, half-compounded, aqueous light which pervaded the open mead, impressed them with a feeling of isolation, as if they were Adam and Eve' (p. 157).
80. Ibid., p. 150.
81. *The Descent of Man, Works*, XII, p. 594. Significantly, Darwin's theory also supports Hardy's fear that man is becoming too sensitive to the world around him. For, as Sully argued in 'Animal Music' (1879) if 'from generation to generation the females of a particular species continued to choose males with fine voices, there would be a gradual improvement of vocal powers generally, according to Mr. Darwin's well-known principle of sexual selection'. *Cornhill Magazine*, 40 (November, 1879), 605–621 (pp. 616–617).
82. Modern man, Edmund Gurney argues, has evolved a 'special faculty' which enables him to derive from a piece of modern complex music an emotional experience which links him directly to the first intense emotions experienced by his ancestors during courtship. See also 'On Music and Musical Criticism' (p. 57).
83. *Tess of the D'Urbervilles*, p. 151.
84. Ebbatson, *Evolutionary Self*, p. 34.
85. Hughes, *'Ecstatic Sound'*, p. 32.
86. Grundy, *Hardy and the Sister Arts*, p. 146. She is referring here to Tess' earlier assertion that 'our souls can be made to go outside our bodies when we are alive' (p. 147).
87. *Tess of the D'Urbervilles*, p. 151.
88. *The Times*, 19 November, 1877, p. 9. Quoted Connor, *Dumbstruck*, p. 380.
89. Kahn, *Noise, Water, Meat*, pp. 217, 219. Kahn has observed that the phonograph was an instrument talked about before it was invented. He cites Lautreamont's novel *Les Chants de Maldoror* (1868), and the obscure Poe-pastiche, 'The

Automoton Ear' (1876), by the little-known American writer, Florence McLandburgh, in which a professor sets out to construct a device to aid the ear in hearing atoms (Kahn, pp. 4–5, 212–213).

90. *The Diary of Sundry Observations of Thomas Alva Edison*, edited by Dagobert D. Runes (New York: Philosophical Library, 1948), pp. 240–241. Quoted from Connor, *Dumbstruck*, p. 359.

91. *Ninth Bridgewater Treatise* (1837) (London: Cass, 1967), pp. 108–110, 111–112. Quoted from Kahn, *Noise, Water, Meat*, p. 211.

92. Kahn, *Noise, Water, Meat*, p. 212.

93. *Breakthrough: An Amazing Experiment in Electronic Communication with the Dead*, translated by Nadia Fowler (New York: Taplinger, 1971), p. 23. Quoted from Kahn, *Noise, Water, Meat*, p. 220.

94. 'It belongs to the Cucumbers', in *The Adding Machine* (New York: Seaver Books, 1986), p. 60. Quoted from Kahn, *Noise, Water, Meat*, p. 220.

95. *The Dynasts*, II.v.5, pp. 379–380. A fact emphasised by the description of the latter as the progress of 'ants crawling along a strip of garden matting'.

96. Ibid., III.I.3, 458.

97. Ibid., III.i.4, 460. This technique is used for light-relief at the Carlton House Ball as the philandering Prince Regent finds himself pursued by the disembodied voices of his late wife and new lover, the marchioness of Hertford, *The Dynasts*, II.vi.7, 424.

98. Winter, *Mesmerized*, p. 119.

99. *The Return of the Native*, p. 82, *Tess of the D'Urbervilles*, p. 147, and *A Laodicean*, p. 90.

100. Connor, *Dumbstruck*, p. 23. Sam Halliday notes Georg Simmel's argument that when we behold a person by ear as opposed to sight 'what we hear is the person's momentary character, the flow of their nature.' 'Sociology of the Senses', in *Simmel on Culture*, edited by David Frisby and Mike Featherstone (London, 1997). Halliday, 'Deceit, Desire and Technology: A Media History of Secrets and Lies', *Forum for Modern Language Studies*, 37: 2 (2001), p. 145.

101. *Tess of the D'Urbervilles*, pp. 146–147.

102. *Daniel Deronda*, edited by Graham Handley (Oxford: Clarendon Press, 1984), p. 171.

103. *Tess of the D'Urbervilles*, p. 148.

104. *Jude the Obscure*, p. 63.

105. *Tess of the D'Urbervilles*, p. 210.

106. Ibid., p. 206.

107. *The Mechanical Song: Women, Voice and the Artificial in Nineteenth-Century French Narrative* (Stanford, California: Stanford University Press, 1995), pp. 186–187. Quoted from Connor, *Dumbstruck*, p. 39.

108. *The Return of the Native*, p. 122.

109. *The Hand of Ethelberta*, p. 39.

110. In 'The Destined Pair' Hardy notes: 'Two beings were drifting / Each one to the other: No moment's veil-lifting / Or hint from another / Led either to weet / That the tracks of their feet / Were arcs that would meet'. He also raises the problem of mismatch, questioning whether it would have been kinder if Fate had kept them apart (*Complete Poems*, ll. 1–7, 15–16).

111. 'The Convergence of the Twain', *Complete Poems*, ll. 18, 19, 21, 29. The plot line of *Tess of the D'Urbervilles* follows a similar pattern. On her maiden voyage Tess is destined to meet her 'sinister mate', Alec d'Urberville.
112. *The Hand of Ethelberta*, p. 94. I also quote here from 'The Convergence of the Twain', l. 30, and the last line heralded by the Spinner of the years: 'And the consummation comes, and jars two hemispheres' (l. 33).
113. *The Woodlanders*, p. 214. *The Life*, p. 220.
114. Ibid., pp. 142, 215. During their first meeting, Hardy describes how Felice speaks 'with vibrations of feeling in her words' (p. 210), whilst Fitzpiers' wooing is carried out 'in his most vibratory tones' (p. 215).
115. Ibid., p. 210.
116. Ibid., p. 232.
117. *The Well-Beloved*, p. 96.
118. Ibid., p. 101.
119. Hardy illustrates this philosophy through the reactions of Troy and Bathsheba to the spouting gargoyle that destroys the grave of Fanny Robin. Whereas Troy wails against a vindictive Providence, Bathsheba quietly has the spout turned to avoid the grave, *Far from the Madding Crowd*, p. 328.
120. *The Dynasts*, I.v.5.
121. Ibid., II.v.3.
122. *Tess of the D'Urbervilles*, pp. 330–331.
123. His function in the novel is to encourage his father to gamble upon his destiny, for, as he tells him over a game of cards in the church vestry, 'It is better than doing nothing' (p. 176). As such his own life is made up of gambles, his claims of poverty leading to Hardy's observation that 'Dare knew that he played a pretty sure card in that speech' (p. 215). Furthermore, his illegitimacy also furnishes Somerset with 'a card which could be played with disastrous effect' against De Stancy (p. 192).
124. *The Mayor of Casterbridge*, p. 142.
125. *The Return of the Native*, pp. 102, 107. Hardy's italics.
126. *Tess of the D'Urbervilles*, p. 151.
127. J. I. M. Stewart, *Thomas Hardy: A Critical Biography* (London: Longman, 1971), p. 190.
128. *Jude the Obscure*, p. 239.
129. Ibid., p. 111.
130. Ibid., p. 206.

5 A tale of 'tragical possibilities': Music and the birth of consciousness in *The Return of the Native*

1. *The Life*, p. 120.
2. *The Hand of Ethelberta*, p. 344.
3. *A Laodicean*, p. 336.
4. See 'Before Life and After' in which Hardy talks of the period 'Before the birth of consciousness, / When all went well'. *Complete Poems*, ll. 3–4, 13.
5. Crary, *Suspensions of Perception*, p. 99.

6. Benjamin Jowett, Introduction to his translation of *The Dialogues of Plato*, 4 vols (Oxford, 1871), I, 3. *Literary Notebooks*, 443. Bjork goes on to make the point that for Hardy facial beauty is a thing of the past, when in the fullness of youth men were not weighed down by pessimistic philosophies.

7. *A Laodicean*, p. 5. *The Mayor of Casterbridge*, p. 28.

8. *Short Stories*, I, p. 40.

9. Spencer, 'Progress: Its Law and Cause', p. 446, and 'Origin and Function', p. 407.

10. *Literary Notebooks*, 495.

11. Hughes, '*Ecstatic Sound*', pp. 96, 159.

12. Armstrong notes of this relationship 'music cannot store a *particular* occasion for Schopenhauer, only the experience of termporarility *per se*; its qualities are the very opposite of the indexicality of the photograph'. 'Hardy, History', p. 159.

13. Hardy to Thomas Woolner, *Letters*, I, p. 73 (21 April, 1880).

14. *Complete Poems*, ll. 10, 14. John Hughes has taken this a step further, arguing that the musicality of the tramp is immediately picked up by the narrator, whose mental reinvigoration is reflected by the greater rhythmical intensity that guides the poem following their meeting. '*Ecstatic Sound*', pp. 112–114.

15. 'Thomas Hardy's Use of Traditional Song', p. 320.

16. Ibid., pp. 319–320.

17. Jackson-Houlston notes that the exact significance of the 'foggy dew' itself has been much debated, 'but certainly coming in from it involves a loss of virginity' (p. 328).

18. *The Dynasts*, preface, p. 8.

19. The mumming play of St George functions on several allegorical levels: as a pagan ritual it symbolises Eustacia's winter giving way to summer; on a theological level it could symbolise Christianity overcoming paganism, or just as easily humanism replacing superstition; and finally, within the context of the love story, it suggests that Clym, basking in the glittering romance of Paris – or the glow of rational enlightenment – will overcome Eustacia's oppressive nightly aspect. A point which is suggested by Hardy's observation that at one stage Clym's 'influence was penetrating her like summer sun!' (p. 129).

20. According to the *OED*, there are two definitions of 'mumming': one which alludes to people disguising themselves for the representation of a play; the other which states that it is an 'inarticulate *murmuring*; indistinct speech'. *The Oxford English Dictionary*, 2nd edn, prepared by J. A. Simpson and E. S. C. Weiner, 20 vols (Oxford: Clarendon Press, 1989), 10.

21. *The Well-Beloved*, p. 60.

22. Ibid., pp. 49, 59.

23. Ibid., p. 48.

24. Rutland, *Thomas Hardy*, 'Some of the dialogue in *The Return* – to pass to another blemish – is unconvincing' (p. 187).

25. *Saturday Review*, 47 (January, 1879), 23–24 (p. 23).

26. Ibid., p. 145. *The Lost Senses* (London: Charles Knight, 1845). Kitto begins his chapter on 'Percussions' by claiming that 'the absence of the sense [of hearing], concentrates the attention more exclusively upon the sensation which is through this medium obtained', so deafness makes a person susceptible to sound through the vibrations caused in other parts of the body (p. 32).

27. Spencer, *The Principles of Biology* (London, 1864), 2 vols, I, p. 69. See a quotation taken by Hardy in *Literary Notebooks*, 882. See also *The Principles of Psychology*, 3rd edn, 2 vols (London: Williams & Northgate, 1881), I, pp. 617–618.
28. Connor, *Dumbstruck*, p. 17.
29. See Ellenberger, *Discovery of the Unconscious*, pp. 303–311.
30. Ibid., p. 309.
31. Maury was interested in how external stimuli e.g. perfume, may alter a dream. Quoted in Ellenberger, *Discovery of the Unconscious*, p. 305.
32. *Complete Poems*, ll. 9–16. Hardy uses the same technique in *Desperate Remedies* when the kiss of Edward Springrove and Cytherea Graye joins the chorus of sounds that surround them, becoming an expression of their happiness: 'he kissed her again with a longer kiss.... The gentle sounds around them from the hills, the plains, the distant town, the adjacent shore, the water heaving at their side, the kiss, and the long kiss, were all "many a voice of one delight," and in unison with each other' (p. 76).
33. Gatrell, *Hardy the Creator*. He interprets this alteration as being motivated by Hardy's desire to indicate Eustacia's social superiority. Her voice, appropriately, is heard above Clym (pp. 45–46).
34. Hughes, 'Ecstatic Sound', p. 74.
35. *The Dynasts*, III.vi.2.
36. Hughes, 'Ecstatic Sound', p. 74.
37. *Short Stories*, II, p. 32.
38. Interestingly James began his *The Principles of Psychology*, from which this quote is taken, in 1878. It was actually published in 1890. Quoted in Crary, *Suspensions of Perception*, p. 101.
39. Hueffer, 'Arthur Schopenhauer', p. 790. See also Sully, *Pessimism*, pp. 100–101.
40. *Literary Notebooks*, 312 onwards. Wright, *Making of the Dynasts*, p. 25.
41. The original version reads, ' "I'll tell you," said Yeobright with unexpected earnestness. "I am not sorry to have the opportunity." *He leant his back against a tree, and went on.* "I've come home because..." ' (p. 198). The phrase in my italics was later extracted. See John Patterson, *The Making of The Return of the Native* (Westport, Connecticut: Greenwood Press, 1978), p. 60.
42. The message encoded in the story of Yellham Woods is ' "Life offers – to deny!" ', *Complete Poems*, l. 14.
43. Gregor, *The Great Web*, p. 95.
44. *Jude the Obscure*, p. 57.
45. Lawrence, 'Study of Thomas Hardy', reprint in *Phoenix: The Posthumous Papers of D. H. Lawrence, 1936*, edited by Edward D. McDonald (New York: The Viking Press, 1964), 398–517 (p. 414).
46. *Complete Poems*, ll. 22–26.
47. Hughes, 'Ecstatic Sound', p. 123.

6 'A tragedy appropriate for its time': Music and the story of a 'man of character'

1. *Spectator* (5 June, 1886), 752–753. Reprinted in *Thomas Hardy: The Critical Heritage*, edited by R. G. Cox (London: Routledge & Kegan Paul, 1970), pp. 134–140 (p. 139).

2. See Patterson, John, '*The Mayor of Casterbridge* as Tragedy', *Victorian Studies*, 3 (December, 1959), 151–172. Virginia Woolf argues that 'Henchard is pitted, not against another man, but against something outside himself which is opposed to men of his ambition and power.' *The Common Reader: Second Series*, 9th edn (London: The Hogarth Press, 1974), p. 255.

3. *Jude the Obscure*, p. 351.

4. Frederick R. Karl, '*The Mayor of Casterbridge*: A New Fiction Defined', *Modern Fiction Studies*, 6 (Autumn, 1960), 195–213 (p. 207).

5. See Karl, p. 211.

6. Sully, 'The Aesthetic Aspects of Character', *Fortnightly Review* (April, 1871), 247– 283 (p. 267).

7. Schopenhauer, *The World as Will and Idea*, I, p. 354.

8. *Tess of the D'Urbervilles*, p. 95; *The Woodlanders*, p. 171; and *Jude the Obscure*, p. 153.

9. Schopenhauer, *The World as Will and Idea*, I, p. 381.

10. Schopenhauer agues that 'repentance never proceeds from a change of the will (which is impossible), but from a change of knowledge', *The World as Will and Idea*, I, p. 382.

11. Hardy's description of Henchard's laugh suggests that any change has been superficial, and, just as it has always been, Henchard's 'personal goodness, if he had any, would be of a very fitful cast – an occasional almost oppressive generosity rather than a mild and constant kindness' (p. 51).

12. Millgate, *Career as a Novelist*, p. 226; Goode, *The Offensive Truth*, p. 82; and Gregor, *The Great Web*, p. 117.

13. Millgate, *Career as a Novelist*, p. 226.

14. *Complete Poems*, ll. 17–32.

15. Ibid., ll. 1–3.

16. The authorised King James version of 1611 used by Hardy reads 'my soul longeth, yea, even fainteth for the courts of the Lord: my heart and my flesh crieth out for the living God. Yea, the sparrow hath found an house, and the swallow a nest for herself, where she may lay her young', Psalm 84: 2–3.

17. *Bede's Ecclesiastical History of the English People*, edited by Bertram Colgrave and R. A. B. Mynors (Oxford: Clarendon Press, 1969), ii. 13, p. 185. I am grateful to Professors Janet Bately and Jane Roberts for their help in locating this scene and its connection with Psalm 84.

18. The fourth plague to ravage the kingdom of Pharaoh is that of gadflies (Exodus 8: 21). In *Prometheus Bound* the priestess of Argos, Io, complains to Prometheus of her punishment at the hands of Zeus, claiming that 'I, gadfly-maddened, still am driven from land to land, / Lashed by this God-appointed scourge' (ll. 679–680). Translated by Philip Vellacott (Harmondsworth: Penguin, 1961).

19. 'The heavens declare the glory of God; and the firmament sheweth his handywork', Psalm 19: 1.

20. See, Job 3: 1–2.

21. Genesis 4: 13.

22. Jackson-Houlston, 'Hardy and Traditional Song', p. 317.

23. See Ian Gregor's introduction to the New Wessex edition of the novel, p. 9.

24. Millgate notes the similarity with Hawthorne's 'My Kinsman, Major Molineux', *Career as a Novelist*, p. 231.

25. Sully, 'Aesthetic Aspects', pp. 268–269.
26. Hardy draws attention to Farfrae's shallowness in his reaction to Henchard's revelation of his dilemma concerning Susan and Lucetta: 'Donald showed his deep concern at a complication so far beyond the degree of his simple experiences' (p. 87).
27. Haweis, 'Music: Its Origin and Influence', p. 156.
28. Schopenhauer, *The World as Will and Idea*, I, p. 341. Karen Davis also draws attention to this aspect of Schopenhauerian theory, but she does not link it to the relationship between Farfrae and Elizabeth-Jane ('Deaf Ear to Essence', p. 198).
29. Moynahan, '*The Mayor of Casterbridge* and the Old Testament's First Book of Samuel: A Study of some Literary Relationships', *PMLA*, 71 (1956), 118–130.
30. See his introduction to Penguin edition of the novel (Harmondsworth: Penguin, 1985), p. 38.
31. Robert Kiely, 'Vision and Viewpoint in *The Mayor of Casterbridge*', *Nineteenth Century Fiction*, 23 (September, 1968), 189–200 (p. 193).
32. Ibid.
33. Once again Moynahan's analysis of this scene is excellent, p. 125. Psalm 109: 13 reads: 'let his posterity be cut off; *and* in the generation following let their name be blotted out'. Henchard's will requests 'that no man remember me' (p. 409).
34. da Sousa Correa, *George Eliot, Music and Victorian Culture*, p. 186. James Sully uses it in print in his *Illusions: A Psychological Study* (London: Kegan Paul, 1881), p. 241.
35. Wordsworth, *The Prelude*, I, ll. 271, 276, 281.
36. Matthew Arnold, 'Dover Beach', *Poems*, l. 12.
37. Craig Raine, 'Conscious Artistry in *The Mayor of Casterbridge*', in *New Perspectives on Thomas Hardy*, edited by Charles P. C. Petit (London: Macmillan, 1994), pp. 156–171 (p. 167).
38. Sully, *Pessimism*, p. 102.
39. See Moynahan's excellent discussion of this decision, pp. 124–125.
40. *Complete Poems*, ll. 3, 6, 47.

7 'All creation groaning': A deaf ear to music in *Jude the Obscure*

1. *The Dynasts*, Fore Scene.
2. *Complete Poems*, ll. 9, 10, 11.
3. John Hughes *Lines of Flight: Reading Deleuze with Hardy, Gissing, Conrad, Woolf* (Sheffield: Sheffield Academic Press, 1997), pp. 93–95. He draws our attention to the use of definite articles in the scene.
4. Connor, *Dumbstruck*, p. 7.
5. *The Return of the Native*, p. 71.
6. Connor, *Dumbstruck*, p. 29.
7. *The Psychology of Hardy's Novels: The Nervous and the Statuesque* (St Lucia, Queensland: University of Queensland Press, 1975), p. 186.
8. Connor, *Dumbstruck*, p. 28.
9. Reé, *I See a Voice*, p. 39.
10. Hardy to Edmund Gosse, *Letters*, II, p. 93 (10 November, 1895).

11. Psalm 119: 9–16, the Authorised Version of 1611 used by Hardy.
12. Reé, *I See a Voice*, p. 3.
13. Critical edition of the Greek New Testament by Johan Jackob Griesbach (1745–1812), first published in Halle in 1774–1777.
14. Sue's voice is described as 'tremulous' during her first meeting with Jude (p. 122); during a later exchange Hardy notes how 'her ever-sensitive lip began to quiver' (p. 153); and as she surveys the dead children 'her figure quivered like a string' (p. 348).
15. Spencer, 'Progress: Its Law and Cause', *Westminster Review*, 67 o.s., 11 n.s. (April, 1857), 445–485 (p. 446).
16. *The Life*, p. 218.
17. Gregor, *The Great Web*, p. 217.
18. Hardy's private correspondence emphasises that the novel was not principally concerned with the 'marriage question'. In a letter to William Archer he notes that 'the very last charges I expected them to bring against a book concerned merely with the doom of hereditary temperament and unsuitable mating in marriage were that it was an attack on marriage in general', *Letters*, II, p. 104 (2 January, 1896). In the letter to Edmund Gosse already quoted, Hardy states: 'it is curious that some of the papers should look upon the novel as a manifesto on "the marriage question" (although, of course, it involves it) – seeing that it is concerned first with the labours of a poor student to get an University degree, and secondly with the tragic issues of two bad marriages, owing in the main to a doom of curse of hereditary temperament peculiar to the family of the parties', *Letters*, II, p. 93 (10 November, 1895).
19. This is the legend of the Fawley curse, which, as Aunt Drusilla explains, means that 'the Fawleys were not made for wedlock: it never seemed to sit well upon us' (p. 94).
20. Al Alvarez, 'Thomas Hardy's *Jude the Obscure*', in *Beyond all this Fiddle: Essays, 1955–1967* (London: Allen Lane, Penguin Publishing, 1968), pp. 178–201 (p. 185).
21. Ian Gregor notes that 'Sue is blind to the effect her words will have, and she makes no attempt to go behind the letter of what she is saying. For her, words alone seem certain good.' See, 'A Series of Seemings', in *Hardy: The Tragic Novels, A Casebook*, edited by R. P. Draper (London: Macmillan, 1975), pp. 227–247 (p. 244).
22. Hardy dramatises the horror Jude and Sue feel towards the marriage contract by their watching a bride going through the formalities of the service: they 'could hear her mechanical murmur of words whose meaning her brain seemed to gather not at all under the pressure of her self-consciousness' (p. 298).
23. I am referring here to the Comtean idea, set out in the 'Cours de Philosophie Positive' (1842) and the *Système à Politique* (1852), that man's understanding must pass through a theological stage, a metaphysical stage, and finally a Positivist, or humanist, stage.
24. Schopenhauer, *The World as Will and Idea*, l, p. 336.
25. Ibid.
26. In an effort to explain her own sexual behaviour, Sue says to Jude, 'some women's love of being loved is insatiable' (p. 222), and 'sometimes a woman's *love of being loved* gets the better of her conscience' (p. 256, Hardy's italics).

Peter Casagrande notes that for Sue 'sexual pleasure derives in part from observing the distress in men from whom she withholds herself while at the same time living with them in relative intimacy'. See *Unity in Hardy's Novels: 'Repetitive Symmetries'* (London: Macmillan, 1982), pp. 211–212. Hardy himself noted in a letter to Edmund Gosse that 'there is nothing perverted or depraved in Sue's nature. The abnormalism consists in disproportion, not in inversion, her sexual instinct being healthy as far as it goes, but unusually weak and fastidious, *Letters*, II, p. 99 (20 November, 1895).

27. The complaint of the undergraduate was that she 'was breaking his heart by holding out against him so long at such close quarters' (p. 168). In the letter to Gosse quoted above Hardy claims that 'one of her reasons for fearing the marriage ceremony is that she fears it wd be breaking faith with Jude to withhold herself at pleasure, or altogether, after it; though while uncontracted she feels at liberty to yield herself as seldom as she chooses. This has tended to keep his passion as hot at the end as at the beginning, and helps to break his heart.'

28. The Doctor expresses much the same opinion when he talks of a new generation of boys who 'seem to see all [life's] terrors before they are old enough to have staying power to resist them' (p. 346).

Conclusion

1. Pater, 'The School of Giorgione', *Fortnightly Review*, p. 528.
2. 'George Moore and Literary Wagnerism', reprint in *George Moore's Mind and Art: Essays Old and New*, edited by Graham Owens (Edinburgh: Oliver & Boyd, 1968), pp. 53–76 (p. 73).
3. Untitled, *Concordia*, 2 (February, 1876), pp. 136–137.
4. I have looked into the most obvious sources to identify the subject, Edwards' 'The Literary Maltreatment of Music', *Macmillan's*, 33 (April, 1876), 552–558; *The History of Opera from Monteverdi to Verdi*, 2 vols (London, 1862); and *The Lyric Drama: Essays on Subjects, Composers and Executants of Modern Opera*, 2 vols (London, 1881).
5. Private correspondence with the authors.
6. T. H. Warren, Review in the *Spectator* (1902). Quoted in Hughes, '*Ecstatic Sound*', p. 138.
7. Mitchell, 'Music and Hardy's Poetry', p. 309.
8. Hughes, '*Ecstatic Sound*', p. 140.
9. See Hughes, 'Till Time Seemed Fiction', in '*Ecstatic Sound*', pp. 155–201.
10. Armstrong, 'Hardy and History', p. 157.
11. *The Letters of Henry James*, I, p. 194.

Select Bibliography

Primary sources

Periodical titles will be abbreviated as follows

Bk	*Blackwood's Edinburgh Magazine*
CR	*Contemporary Review*
CM	*Cornhill Magazine*
ER	*Edinburgh Review*
FR	*Fortnightly Review*
FM	*Fraser's Town and Country Magazine*
Mac	*Macmillan's Magazine*
Md	*Mind*
MW	*Musical World*
MS	*Musical Standard*
MT	*Musical Times*
NatRev	*National Review*
NewRev	*New Review*
NC	*Nineteenth Century*
QR	*Quarterly Review*
SatRev	*Saturday Review*
TB	*Temple Bar*
WR	*Westminster Review*

Adamson, R., 'Schopenhauer's Philosophy', *Md*, 1 (October, 1876), 491–509.

Aeschylus, *Prometheus Bound*, translated and edited by Philip Vellacott (Harmondsworth: Penguin, 1987).

Aidé, Charles Hamilton, 'Are the English Musical People?', *FM*, 43 (June, 1851), 675–681.

——, 'Survey of Music', *CM*, 6 (September, 1862), 408–411.

Anonymous articles in musical periodicals and *Blackwood's Magazine*

'Church Music', *MS*, 10 (October, 1869), 196.

'Letter to the Editor', *MS*, 11 (August, 1869), 90–91 [signed Exacetale].

'Occasional Notes', *MW*, 52 (March, 1874), 166.

'On the Music of Nature', *MW*, 48 (July, 1870), 459 [signed Idealizer].

'On Musical Expression', *Bk*, 5 (August, 1819), 556–558 [signed A. B.].

'Musical Queries', *Bk*, 6 (October, 1819), 69–70 [signed Ignotus].

'Opera and Drama', *MW*, 33 (May, 1855), 322–333.

'A Retrospect', *The Graphic*, reprint in *MW*, 55 (January, 1877), 41.

'Review of *The Philosophy of Music*, by Joseph' Goddard, *MW*, 40 (October, 1862), 629–630.

'Richard Wagner Comes', *MT*, 18 (April, 1877), 162–164.
'Wagner', *MS*, 8 n.s. (May, 1875), 278–279.
'The Wagner Festival', *Daily Telegraph*, 9 May 1877, reprint in *MW* (September, 1877), 656–657.
'The Wagner Festival', *MS*, 12 (June, 1877), 372–373.
'The Wagner Festival', *MT*, 18 (June, 1877), 276–277.
'We Shall See', *The Globe*, reprint in *MW*, 55 (June, 1877), 413.
Arnold, Matthew, *The Complete Prose Works of Matthew Arnold*, edited by R. H. Super, 11 vols (Ann Arbor: University of Michigan, 1960–1977).
——, *Culture and Anarchy*, edited by J. Dover Wilson (Cambridge: Cambridge University Press, 1978).
——, *The Poems of Matthew Arnold*, edited by Miriam Allot, 2nd edn (London: Longman, 1979).
Asher, David, 'Schopenhauer and Darwinism', *Journal of Anthropology*, 1 (January, 1871), 312–332.

The Athenaeum

[Articles written by Henry Chorley, music correspondent of *The Athenaeum* 1830–1866, are identified in parentheses].

'The Bayreuth Festival', 2548 (26 August, 1876), 281–282 [Music Critic].
'The Bayreuth Rehearsals', 2495 (21 August, 1875), 253.
'The Central Model Opera-House for Germany', 2498 (11 September, 1875), 350–351.
'Der Ring Des Nibelungen', 2545 (5 August, 1876), 186–187.
'Der Ring Des Nibelungen', 2546 (12 August, 1876), 217–219.
'Der Ring Des Nibelungen', 2547 (19 August, 1876), 250–251.
'Der Ring Des Nibelungen', 2548 (26 August, 1876), 282 [German Correspondent].
'Der Ring der Nibelungen', 2544 (29 July, 1876), 154–155.
'The Developed Lyric Drama', 2595 (21 July, 1877), 90–91.
'English Appreciation and English Talent', 1436 (5 May, 1855), 528 [Henry Chorley].
'Herr Wagner', 2585 (12 May, 1877), 618.
'Herr Wagner', 2586 (19 May, 1877), 650–651.
'Herr Wagner', 2587 (26 May, 1877), 682–683.
'Herr Wagner's *Flying Dutchman*', 2554 (7 October, 1876), 471–472.
'Herr Wagner's *Rienzi*', 2675 (1 February, 1879), 159–160.
'Herr Wagner's *Tannhäuser*', 2533 (13 May, 1876), 674–675.
'Music at Weimar: A Review of *Lohengrin*', 1194 (14 September, 1850), 980 [Henry Chorley].
'Obituary of Richard Wagner', 2886 (17 February, 1883), 224–225.
'Philharmonic society', 1431 (31 March, 1855), 385 [Henry Chorley].
'Philharmonic society', 1434 (21 April, 1855), 466 [Henry Chorley].
'Philharmonic society', 1438 (19 May, 1855), 592–593 [Henry Chorley].
'Review of *Arthur Schopenhauer* by Helen Zimmern', 2543 (22 July, 1876), 107–109.
'Review of *Der Fliegende Holländer*', 2582 (21 April, 1877), 521.
'Review of *Pessimism* by James Sully', 2604 (22 September, 1877), 365–366.
'Review of *The Ring* performed at Her Majesty's Theatre', 2846 (13 May, 1882), 612–614.
'The Richter Concerts', 2742 (15 May, 1880), 642–643.

'The Richter Concerts', 2744 (29 May, 1880), 704.
'The Richter Concerts', 2794 (14 May, 1881), 664.
'The Richter Concerts', 2795 (21 May, 1881), 697–698.
'The Richter Concerts', 2797 (4 June, 1881), 760.
'The Richter Concerts', 2799 (18 June, 1881), 825.
'The Wagner Society', 2366 (1 March, 1873), 288–289.
'Wagner's *Ring der Nibelungen*', 2846 (13 May, 1882), 612–614.
Bain, Alexander, *The Senses and the Intellect* (London: John W. Parker & Son, 1855).
Barry, William, F., 'Wagner and the Bayreuth Idea', *QR*, 187 (January, 1898), 1–30.
Bede, Venerable, *Bede's Ecclesiastical History of the English People*, edited by Bertram Colgrave and R. A. B. Mynors (Oxford: Clarendon Press, 1969).
Benedict, Julius, 'The Proposed University of Music', *NC*, 12 (July, 1882), 29–34.
Bennett, Joseph, 'The Condition of Opera in England', *Mac*, 20 (July, 1869), 260–265.
——, 'The Poetic Basis of Music', *MW*, 52 (April, 1874), 226–228.
——, *Letters from Bayreuth: Descriptive and Critical of Wagner's 'Der Ring Des Nibelungen'* (London: Novello, Ewer, 1877).
——, *Forty Years of Music 1865–1905* (London: Methuen, 1908).
Blind, Karl, 'Wagner's *Nibelung* and Siegfried's Tale', *CM*, 45 (May, 1882), 594–609.
Brontë, Anne, *The Tenant of Wildfell Hall*, edited by Herbert Rosengarten (Oxford: Clarendon Press, 1992).
Brontë, Charlotte, *Jane Eyre*, edited by Jane Jack and Margaret Smith (Oxford: Clarendon Press, 1969).
Capes, J. M., 'Music the Expression of Character', *FNR*, 70 o.s., 1 n.s. (April, 1867), 410–419.
Carey, E., 'Body and Music', *NR*, 5 (May, 1885), 382–390.
Carlyle, Thomas, *A Carlyle Reader: Selections from the Writings of Thomas Carlyle*, edited by G. B. Tennyson (Cambridge: Cambridge University Press, 1984).
——, *Sartor Resartus: The Life and Opinions of Herr Teufelsdröckh in Three Books*, notes and introduction by Roger L. Tarr, text established by Roger L. Tarr (Berkeley, London: University of California Press, 2000).
Chorley, Henry Fothergill, *Modern German Music: Recollections and Criticisms*, 2 vols (London: Smith, Elder, 1854).
——, *Thirty Years' Musical Recollections*, 2 vols (London: Hurst and Blackett, 1862).
Clifford, William Kingdon, *Lectures and Essays*, edited by Leslie Stephen and Frederick Pollock, 2 vols (London: Macmillan, 1879).
Coleridge, Arthur, 'Contemporary Music and Musical Literature', *WR*, 87 o.s., 31 n.s. (April, 1867), 384–400.
Coleridge, Samuel Taylor, *The Complete Poetical Works of Samuel Taylor Coleridge*, edited, with textual bibliographical, by Ernest Hartley Coleridge, 2 vols (Oxford, Clarendon Press, 1912).
Curwen, John, ed., *Singing for Schools and Congregations: A Grammar of Vocal Music, with a Course of Lessons and Exercises Founded on the Tonic-Sol-Fa Method*, 2nd edn (London: T. Ward, 1848).
Dannreuther, Edward, *Richard Wagner: His Tendencies and Theories* (London: Augener, 1873).
——, trans., *The Music of the Future: A Letter to M. Frederic Villot* (London: Schott, 1873).
——, 'The Opera: Its Growth and Decay', *Mac*, 12 (May, 1875), 64–72.
——, 'The Musical Drama', *Mac*, 33 (November, 1875), 80–85.

Darwin, Charles, *On the Origin of Species* (1859), in *The Works of Charles Darwin*, edited by Paul H. Barrett and R. B. Freeman, 29 vols (London: William Pickering, 1986–1989), XV.

——, *The Descent of Man in Relation to Sex* (1871), *Works*, XXII .

Donovan, J., 'Origin of Music: Passage Between Brute and Man', *WR*, 153 (March, 1900), 292–303.

Doubleday, Thomas, 'On The Metaphysics of Music and their Accordance with Modern Practice', *Bk*, 11 (May, 1819), 529–538.

——, 'Letter to the Editor', *Bk*, 5 (July, 1819), 400.

——, 'On Musical Expression, In Defence of the Queries', *Bk*, 5 (September, 1819), 694–697.

Dryden, John, *The Poems of John Dryden*, edited by James Kinsley, 4 vols (Oxford: Clarendon Press, 1958).

Edwards, H. Sutherland, *The History of Opera from Monteverdi to Verdi*, 2 vols (London: 1862).

——, 'Schopenhauer and Wagner', *Concordia*, 2 (February, 1876), 136–137.

——, 'The Literary Maltreatment of Music', *Mac*, 33 (April, 1876), 552–558.

——, *The Lyric Drama: Essays on Subjects, Composers and Executants of Modern Opera*, 2 vols (London: W. H. Allen, 1881).

——, 'An Operatic Crisis', *FNR*, 43 o.s., 37 n.s. (June, 1885), 842–851.

Eliot, George, 'Mr. Gilfil's Love Story' in *Scenes of Clerical Life* (1858), edited by Thomas A. Noble (Oxford: Clarendon Press, 1985).

——, *Adam Bede* (1859) (London: Everyman, 1994).

——, *The Mill on the Floss* (1860), edited by Gordon Haight (Oxford: Clarendon Press, 1980).

——, *Romola* (1863), edited by Andrew Brown (Oxford: Clarendon Press, 1993).

——, *Middlemarch* (1871–1872), edited by David Carroll (Oxford: Clarendon Press, 1986).

——, *Daniel Deronda* (1876), edited by Graham Handley (Oxford: Clarendon Press, 1984).

Engel, Louis, 'Wagner', *TB*, 65 (July, 1882), 329–344.

Fetis, Francis James, *Music Explained to the World: or How to Understand Music and Enjoy its Performance*, Pt I (London: H. G. Clarke, 1844).

Feuerbach, Ludwig, *The Essence of Christianity*, 2nd edn, translated by George Eliot (London: John Chapman, 1854).

Folkstone, Helen Matilda, 'The Wagner Festival at Baireuth' [sic], *FNR*, 46 o.s., 40 n.s. (September, 1886), 365–371.

Froude, James, *The Nemesis of Faith* (Farnborough: Gregg, 1969 – facsimile reprint of 2nd edn, London: John Chapman, 1869).

Fuller, Maitland, J. A., 'The Influence of Bayreuth', *NC*, 40 (September, 1896), 360–366.

Gardiner, William, *The Music of Nature: Or an Attempt to Prove that what is Passionate and Pleasing in the Art of Singing, Speaking, and Performing upon Musical Instruments is Derived from the Sounds of the Animated World* (London: Rees, Orme, Brown, Green and Longman, 1832).

Gillies, R. P., *German Stories: Selected from the Works of Hoffmann, de La Motte-Fouqué, Pichler, Kruse, and Others*, 3 vols (Edinburgh and London, 1826).

Goddard, Joseph, *The Philosophy of Music: A Series of Essays*, entitled respectively, 'The relationship of music to the other fine arts'; 'The moral theory of music'; and 'The laws of life in art' (London: Boosey and Sons, 1862).

Gurney, Edmund, 'On Some Disputed Points in Music', *FNR*, 26 o.s., 20 n.s. (July, 1876), 106–130.

——, 'On Music and Musical Criticism', *NC*, 4 (July, 1878), 51–74.

——, 'On Song', *FM*, 19 (February, 1879), 211–224.

——, *On The Power of Sound* (London: Smith, Elder, 1880).

——, 'A Musical Crisis', *FNR*, 38 o.s., 32 n.s. (October, 1882), 432–452.

——, 'On Wagner and Wagnerism', *NC*, 13 (March, 1883), 434–452.

——, *Tertium Quid: Chapters on Various Disputed Questions*, 2 vols (London: Kegan Paul, Trench, 1887).

Hadden, J. Cuthbert, 'Literature and Music', *Mac*, 75 (February, 1897), 267–274.

——, 'The Wagner Mania', *NC*, 44 (July, 1898), 125–131.

Hamilton, Edith and Cairns, Huntingdon, eds, *The Collected Dialogues of Plato* (Princeton: Princeton University Press, 1989).

Note

Hardy, Thomas, Parenthetical page-references to Hardy's novels throughout the text, unless otherwise stated, are to the New Wessex Edition, General Editor P. N. Furbank, published in fourteen volumes by Macmillan 1975–1976. Details given below include original date of publication.

——, *Under the Greenwood Tree*, introduction by Geoffrey Grigson (1872).

——, *Far from the Madding Crowd*, introduction by John Bayley (1874).

——, *The Return of the Native*, introduction by Derwent May (1878).

——, *The Trumpet-Major*, introduction by Barbara Hardy (1880).

——, *The Mayor of Casterbridge*, introduction by Ian Gregor (1886).

——, *The Woodlanders*, introduction by David Lodge (1887).

——, *Tess of the D'Urbervilles*, introduction by P. N. Furbank (1891).

——, *Jude the Obscure*, introduction by Terry Eagleton (1895).

——, *Desperate Remedies*, introduction by C. J. P. Beatty (1871).

——, *A Pair of Blue Eyes*, introduction by Ronald Blythe (1873).

——, *The Hand of Ethelberta*, introduction by Robert Gittings (1876).

——, *A Laodicean*, introduction by Barbara Hardy (1881).

——, *Two on a Tower*, introduction by F. B. Pinion (1882).

——, *The Well-Beloved*, introduction by Miller J. Hillis (1897).

——, *The New Wessex Edition of the Stories of Thomas Hardy*, edited and introduction by F. B. Pinion, 3 vols:

—— I, *Wessex Tales* and *A Group of Noble Dames*, 1888, 1891 (London: Macmillan, 1977).

—— II, *Life's Little Ironies* and *A Changed Man* (1894, 1913).

—— III, *Old Mrs Chundle* and other Stories, with *The Famous Tragedy of the Queen of Cornwall* (miscellaneous).

——, *An Indiscretion in the Life of an Heiress* (1878), edited by Carl J. Weber (New York: Russell and Russell, 1965).

——, *The Dynasts: An Epic-Drama of the War with Napoleon*, In Three Parts, Nineteen Acts, And One Hundred and Thirty Scenes (1903–1908), edited and introduction by Harold Orel (London: Macmillan, 1978).

——, *The Life of Thomas Hardy: 1840–1928* (London: Macmillan, 1965).

——, *Thomas Hardy's Personal Writings: Prefaces, Literary Opinions, Reminiscences*, edited by Harold Orel (London: Macmillan, 1967).

——, *The Complete Poems of Thomas Hardy*, edited by James Gibson (London: Macmillan, 1976).

——, *The Personal Notebooks of Thomas Hardy: With an Appendix Including the Unpublished Passages in the Original Typescripts of 'The Life of Thomas Hardy'*, edited with introduction and notes by Richard H. Taylor (London: Macmillan, 1978).

——, *The Collected Letters of Thomas Hardy*, edited by Richard L. Purdy and Michael Millgate, 7 vols (Oxford: Clarendon Press, 1978–1988).

——, *The Literary Notebooks of Thomas Hardy*, edited with introduction and notes by Lennart Björk, 2 vols (London: Macmillan, 1985).

——, *The Excluded and Collaborative Stories*, edited by Pamela Dalziel (Oxford: Clarendon Press, 1992).

——, *Thomas Hardy's 'Studies and Specimens & c.'*, *Notebook*, edited by Pamela Dalziel and Michael Millgate (Oxford: Clarendon Press, 1994).

Haweis, Henry, R., 'Music in England', *CR*, 7 (January, 1868), 36–53.

——, 'Review of *Musical Development* by Joseph Goddard', *CR*, 9 (September–December, 1868), 300–301.

——, 'Handel: Part One', *CR*, 10 (April, 1869), 503–529.

——, 'Handel: Part Two', *CR*, 11 (May, 1869), 60–78.

——, 'Mendelssohn's Elijah', *CR*, 14 (June, 1870), 363–376.

——, 'Music and Emotion', *CR*, 15 (October, 1870), 363–382.

——, 'Music and Morals: Part One', *CR*, 16 (December, 1870), 89–101.

——, 'Music and Morals: Part Two', *CR*, 16 (January, 1871), 280–297.

——, 'Music and Morals: Part Three', *CR*, 17 (July, 1871), 491–508. All three parts are reprinted with minor alterations in *Music and Morals* (1871).

——, 'Music: Its Origin and Influence', *QR*, 131 (July, 1871), 145–176.

——, 'Wagner', *CR*, 29 (May, 1877), 981–1003.

——, *My Musical Life* (London: W. H. Allen, 1884).

Hawkins, Halford, 'The Wagner Festival at Bayreuth', *Mac*, 35 (November, 1876), 55–63.

Hill, Octavia, 'Colour, Space, and Music for the People', *NC*, 15 (May, 1884), 741–752.

Hoffmann, E. T. A., *E. T. A Hoffmann's Musical Writings: Kreisleriana, the Poet and the Composer, Music Criticism*, translated by Martyn Clarke, edited by David Charlton (Cambridge: Cambridge University Press, 1989).

Holcraft, Richard, *Tales from the German, etc.* (London: 1826).

——, *Tales of Humour and Romance*, selected from the popular German writers, and translated by Richard Holcraft (London: Longman, Rees, Orme, Brown and Green, 1829).

Holmes, Edward, 'Some Words about Music and the Modern Opera', *FM*, 36 (October, 1847), 432–446.

Hueffer, Francis, 'Richard Wagner', *FNR*, 17 o.s., 11 n.s. (March, 1872), 265–287.

——, *Richard Wagner and the Music of the Future: History and Aesthetics* (London: Chapman & Hall, 1874).

——, 'Richard Wagner and his *Ring of the Niblung*' [sic], *NQM*, 4 (April, 1875), 159–186.

——, 'Arthur Schopenhauer', *FR*, 20 (December, 1876), 773–792.

——, 'The Chances of an English Opera', *Mac*, 40 (May, 1879), 57–65.

——, *Francis Hueffer Musical Studies: A Series of Contributions* (Edinburgh: Adam and Charles Black, 1880).

——, 'The Wagner Festival', *The Examiner* (August, 1877), reprinted in *Francis Hueffer Musical Studies* (Edinburgh: Adam and Charles Black, 1880), 179–200.

——, 'English Music During the Queen's Reign', *FNR*, 47 o.s., 41 n.s. (June, 1887), 899–912.

——, trans. and ed., *Correspondence of Wagner and Liszt*, 2 vols (London: H. Grevel, 1888).

——, 'Wagner and Liszt', *QR*, 167 (July, 1888), 65–87.

——, *Half a Century of Music in England: 1837–1887* (London: Chapman & Hall, 1889).

Hullah, John, *Wilhelm's Methods of Teaching Singing* (Kilkenny: Boethius, 1983 – facsimile reprint prepared by Leslie Hewitt of 1842 edn).

Huxley, Thomas, 'On the Physical Basis of Life', *FR*, 11 o.s., 5 n.s. (February, 1869), 129–145.

Kant, Immanuel, *The Critique of Judgement*, Book II, 'The Analytic of the Sublime', translated by James Creed Meredith (Oxford: Clarendon Press, 1986).

Keats, John, *The Poetical Works of John Keats*, edited by H. W. Garrod, 2nd edn (Oxford: Clarendon Press, 1958).

King, Henry, 'Rot your Italianos', *Bk*, 46 (September, 1839), 410–416.

Kitto, John, *The Lost Senses* (London: Charles Knight, 1845).

Klein, Hermann, *Thirty Years of Musical Life in London: 1870–1900* (London: Heinemann, 1903).

Lawrence, D. H., 'Study of Thomas Hardy', in *Phoenix: The Posthumous Papers of D. H. Lawrence, 1936*, edited by Edward D. McDonald (New York: The Viking Press, 1964), 398–517.

Lawrenny, H., 'Arthur Schopenhauer', *CR*, 21 (February, 1873), 440–463.

Lee, Vernon, 'Cherubino: A Psychological Art Fancy', *CM*, 44 (August, 1881), 218–232.

——, 'Orpheus in Rome: Irrelevant Talks on the use of the Beautiful', *CR*, 55 (June, 1889), 828–849.

——, 'Beauty and Sanity', *FNR*, 64 o.s., 58 n.s. (August, 1895), 252–268.

Lewes, G. H., 'Hegel's Aesthetics', *British and Fortnightly Review*, 13 (1842), 1–49.

——, *Problems of Life and Mind*, First Series, 2 vols, I, 'The Foundation of a Creed' (London: Trubner, 1874).

Lyell, Charles, *The Principles of Geology: An Attempt to Explain the Former Changes of the Earth's Surface by Reference to Causes now in Operation*, 3 vols (London: John Murray, 1830).

MacDonnell, M. J. B., 'Classical Music and British Musical Taste', *Mac*, 1 (March, 1860), 383–389.

Macfarren, George A., 'The English are Not a Musical People', *CM*, 18 (September, 1868), 344–363.

——, 'The Royal Academy of Music', *NC*, 12 (August, 1882), 256–269.

Mackenzie, Morrell, 'Speech and Song: Part I', *CR*, 55 (June, 1889), 850–863.

——, 'Speech and Song: Part II', *CR*, 56 (August, 1889), 179–193.

——, 'Art Versus Science in Song', *CR*, 56 (November, 1889), 777–780.

Mahaffy, John Pentland, *Social Life in Greece from Homer to Meander*, 5th edn (London: Macmillan, 1883).

Mainzer, Joseph, *Music and Education* (London: Longman, Brown, Green and Longmans, 1848).

Mallock, W. H., 'The Late Professor Clifford's Essays', *ER*, 151 (April, 1880), 474–511.

Marshall, Beatrice, 'Fredrich Nietzsche and Richard Wagner', *FNR*, 69 o.s., 63 n.s. (June, 1898), 885–897.

Marshall, Florence, A., 'Music and the People', *NC*, 8 (December, 1880), 921–932.

Mill, John Stuart, *Nature, the Utility of Religion, and Theism*, 2nd edn (London: Longmans, Green, Reader and Dyer, 1874).

——, 'Thoughts on Poetry and its Varieties', reprint in *Works*, I, *Autobiography and Literary Essays* (Toronto: University of Toronto Press, 1981), edited by John M. Robson and Jack Stillinger, 343–365.

——, *The Spirit of the Age: Part I, Examiner* (January, 1831), 20–22. Reprint in *The Collected Works of John Stuart Mill*, edited by John M. Robson, 33 vols (Toronto: University of Toronto Press, 1981–1991), XXII, *Newspaper Writings: December 1822–July 1831* (Toronto: University of Toronto Press, 1986), edited by Ann P. Robson and J. M. Robson, 227–234.

——, *Autobiography*, edited by J. M. Robson, 2nd edn (Harmondsworth, Middlesex: Penguin, 1989).

Milton, John, *The Poetical Works of John Milton*, edited by Helen Darbishire, 2 vols (Oxford: Clarendon Press, 1952–1955).

——, *The Complete Prose Works of John Milton*, 8 vols (New Haven: Yale University Press, 1953–1982).

Monckton Milnes, R., Book Review of '*Atalanta in Calydon: A Tragedy*, by Charles Swinburne', *ER*, 122 (July, 1865), 202–216.

Morley, John, Book Review of '*The Ring and the Book*, by Robert Browning', *FNR*, 11 o.s., 5 n.s. (January, 1869), 125–126.

——, 'Mr Pater's Essays (*The Renaissance*)', *FNR*, 19 o.s., 13 n.s. (April, 1873), 469–477.

——, 'Three Books on the Eighteenth Century', *FR* (August, 1877), 259–284.

Moseley, M. S., 'Lyric Feuds', *WR*, 88 o.s., 32 n.s. (July, 1867), 119–160.

Neumann, Angelo, *Personal Recollections of Wagner*, translated by Edith Livermore (London: Archibald Constable, 1909).

Newman, Ernest, '*Wagner's Ring* and its Philosophy', *FNR*, 69 o.s., 63 n.s. (June, 1898), 867–884.

Newman, John Henry, 'Christ Upon the Waters', *Sermons Preached on Various Occasions* (London: Burns and Lambert, 1857), 139–189.

Oliphant, Margaret, *Phoebe Junior*, 2nd edn (London: Virago, 1989).

Oxenford, John, 'Iconoclasm in German Philosophy', *WR*, 59 o.s., 3 n.s. (April, 1853), 388–407.

Pater, Walter, 'The Myth of Demeter and Persephone: Part II', *FNR*, 19 (February, 1876), 260–276.

——, 'Romanticism', *Mac*, 35 (November, 1876), 64–70.

——, *Plato and Platonism: A Series of Lectures*, 3rd edn (1893) (London: Macmillan, 1910).

——, *Greek Studies: A Series of Essays* (1895) (London: Macmillan, 1928).

——, *The Renaissance: Studies in Art and Poetry*, 2nd edn 1877, edited with Textual and Explanatory Notes by Donald L. Hill (California: University of California Press, 1980).

——, *Walter Pater: Three Major Texts (The Renaissance, Appreciations, and Imaginary Portraits)*, edited by William E. Buckler (New York: New York University Press, 1986).

Plato, *The Republic of Plato*, translated by Benjamin Jowett, 3rd edn (Oxford: Clarendon Press, 1888).

Read, Carveth, 'Review of *Modern Philosophy from Descartes to Schopenhauer and Hartmann*, by Francis Bowen', *Md*, 3 (January, 1878), 118–124.

Ritter, Fanny, *Woman as Musician, An Art Historical Study* (London: William Reeves, 1877).

Rose, Edward, 'Wagner as Dramatist', *FM*, 99 o.s., 19 n.s. (April, 1879), 519–532.

Rousseau, Jean Jacques, *La Nouvelle Heloise: Julie, or the New Eloise*, translated and abridged by J. H. Mc Dowell (University Park, P.A., London: Pennsylvania State University Press, 1987).

Rowbotham, J. F., 'The Origin of Music', *CR*, 38 (October, 1880), 647–664.

——, 'The Wagner Bubble', *NC*, 24 (October, 1888), 501–512.

Ruskin, John, *The Complete Works of John Ruskin*, Library Edition, edited by E. T. Cook and Alexander Wedderburn, 39 vols (London: George Allen, 1903–1912).

——, *The Literary Criticism of John Ruskin*, edited by Harold Bloom (New York: Da Capo, 1965).

Schmitz, Leonora, 'On the Study of Music', *FNR*, 4 (March, 1866), 222–227.

Schopenhauer, Arthur, *The World as Will and Idea*, translated by R. B. Haldane and J. Kemp, 3 vols (London: Routledge & Kegan Paul, 1883).

Shakespeare, William, *The Riverside Shakespeare*, 2nd edn (Boston and New York: Houghton Mifflin, 1997).

Shelley, Percy Bysshe, *Shelley Poetical Works*, edited by Thomas Hutchinson, 2nd edn (Oxford: Oxford University Press, 1970).

Simcox, G. A., 'Review of *Arthur Schopenhauer*, by Helen Zimmern', *The Academy*, 9 (March, 1876), 265–266.

Spencer, Herbert, 'Progress: Its Law and Cause', *WR*, 67 o.s., 11 n.s. (April, 1857), 445–485.

——, 'On the Origin and Function of Music', *FM*, 56 (October, 1857), 396–408.

——, *The Principles of Biology*, 2 vols (Edinburgh: Williams & Northgate, 1864).

——, *Essays: Scientific, Political, and Speculative*, English reprint of 3rd series of US edn, 3 vols (London: Williams & Northgate, 1868).

——, *The Principles of Psychology*, 3rd edn, 2 vols (London: Williams & Northgate, 1881).

——, *First Principles*, 5th edn (London: Williams & Northgate, 1887).

——, 'The Origin of Music', *Md*, 60 (October, 1890), 449–468.

Stanford, C. Villiers, 'The Wagner Bubble: A Reply', *NC*, 24 (November, 1888), 727–733.

Statham, Heathcote, H., 'Wagner and the Modern Theory of Music', *ER*, 143 (January, 1876), 141–176.

——, 'The Musical Cultus of the Day', *FNR*, 25 (June, 1879), 894–903.

Stephen, Leslie, 'Hawthorne', reprint in *Hours in the Library*, 2 vols (New York: Scribner, Armstrong and Company, 1875), I, 204–237.

Stewart, J. A., Review of *Frauenstadt's Neue Briefe über die Schopenhauer' sche Philosophie*, edited by Julius Von Frauenstadt, *Md*, 1 (April, 1876), 252–260.

Stigand, William, 'Robert Browning's Poems', *ER*, 120 (October, 1864), 537–564.

Sully, James, 'The Aesthetic Aspects of Character', *FR* (April, 1871), 247–283.

——, 'The Perception of Musical Form', *FNR*, 20 o.s., 14 n.s. (September, 1873), 371–381, revised as 'Aspects of Beauty in Musical Form', in *Sensation and Intuition: Studies in Psychology and Aesthetics* (1874).

——, 'The Basis of Musical Sensation', *FNR*, 17 o.s., 11 n.s. (April, 1872), 428–443, reprinted with minor revisions in *Sensation and Intuition: Studies in Psychology and Aesthetics* (London: Henry S. King, 1874).

——, 'On the Nature and Limits of Musical Expression', *CR*, 23 (March, 1874), 572–589, reprinted with minor revisions in *Sensation and Intuition*.

——, 'The Opera', *CR*, 26 (June, 1875), 103–122.

——, 'The Physics and Physiology of Harmony', *WR*, 104 o.s., 48 n.s. (October, 1875), 432–453.

——, 'The Laws of Musical Expression', *WR*, 49 n.s. (January, 1876), 210–218.

——, 'The Pessimist's View of Life', *CM*, 33 (April, 1876), 431–443.

——, 'Hartmann's Philosophy of the Unconscious', *FR*, 260 o.s., 20 n.s. (August, 1876), 242–262.

——, *Pessimism: A History and A Criticism* (London: Henry S. King, 1877).

——, 'Animal Music', *CM*, 40 (November, 1879), 605–621.

——, 'Review of *The Power of Sound*, by Edmund Gurney', *Md*, 6 (1881), 270–278.

——, 'Scientific Optimism', *NC*, 10 (October, 1881), 573–587.

——, *My Life and Friends: A Psychologist's Memories* (London: T. Fisher Unwin, 1918).

Swinburne, Algernon Charles, *The Swinburne Letters*, edited by C. Y. Lang, 6 vols (New Haven, Connecticut: Yale University Press, 1959–1962).

Symonds, John Addington, 'Matthew Arnold's Selections from Wordsworth', *FR*, 26 (November, 1879), 686–701.

——, *Studies of the Greek Poets*, 3rd edn (London: Adam and Charles Black, 1893).

Taylor, A. W., 'Wagner's Music', *MW*, 41 (July, 1863), 429.

Tennyson, Alfred, *The Poems of Tennyson*, edited by C. Ricks, 2nd edn, 3 vols (Harlow: Longman, 1987).

Thackeray, William Makepeace, *Vanity Fair: A Novel Without a Hero*, Norton Critical Edition (New York: W. W. Norton, 1994).

Thomson, James, *The City of Dreadful Night* (London: Watts, 1932).

Thomson, James, 'The Castle of Indolence', in *Liberty, The Castle of Indolence and Other Poems*, edited by James Sambrook (Oxford: Clarendon Press, 1986), 161–224.

Note

The Times:

[Articles written by James Davison, music correspondent of *The Times* 1846–1879, are identified in parentheses].

'M. Jullien's Concerts' (11 December, 1854), p. 8, col. d [James Davison].

'London Philharmonic Concerts' (14 March, 1855), p. 11, col. a [all by James Davison].

'London Philharmonic Concerts' (1 May, 1855), p. 9, col. f.

'London Philharmonic Concerts' (16 May, 1855), p. 11, col. f.

'London Philharmonic Concerts' (29 May, 1855), p. 12, col. b.

'London Philharmonic Concerts' (12 June, 1855), p. 12, col. e–f.

'London Philharmonic Concerts' (26 June, 1855), p. 12, col. f.

'Music Works of Wagner' (2 October, 1871), p. 12, col. b [James Davison].

'The Wagner Festival' (10 June, 1876), p. 12, col. d [Munich Correspondent].

'The Wagner Festival' (9 August, 1876), p. 4, col. e–f [all by James Davison].

'The Wagner Festival' (11 August, 1876), p. 5, col. d.
'The Wagner Festival' (14 August, 1876), p. 5, col. e.
'The Wagner Festival' (15 August, 1876), p. 3, col. d.
'The Wagner Festival' (16 August, 1876), p. 5, col. c.
'The Wagner Festival' (17 August, 1876), p. 3, col. e.
'The Wagner Festival' (18 August, 1876), p. 5, col. b.
'The Wagner Festival' (19 August, 1876), p. 10, col. a–b.
'The Wagner Festival' (21 August, 1876), p. 6, col. b–c.
'The Wagner Festival' (22 August, 1876), p. 5, col. d.
'The Wagner Festival' (23 August, 1876), p. 6, col. a–b.
'The Wagner Festival' (24 August, 1876), p. 8, col. a–b.
'The Wagner Festival' (25 August, 1876), p. 3, col. d–e.
'The Wagner Festival' (26 August, 1876), p. 4, col. a–b.
'The Wagner Festival' (29 August, 1876), p. 6, col. d–e.
'Wagner at the Lyceum Theatre' (10 October, 1876), p. 6, col. c [James Davison].
'Intended Visit to England of Wagner' (3 March, 1877), p. 10, col. c [Munich
    Correspondent].
'Account of Richard Wagner' (24 March, 1877), p. 5, col. d.
'Letter from Wagner to August Wilhelm' (24 March, 1877), p. 5, col. d–e.
'Address to Wagner on his Arrival in London' (4 May, 1877), p. 8, col. a.
'Albert Hall Concerts' (9 May, 1877), p. 10, col. d [James Davison].
'Albert Hall Concerts' (14 May, 1877), p. 8, col. e [James Davison].
'Albert Hall Concerts' (22 May, 1877), p. 9, col. f [James Davison].
'Concerts of Wagner' (7 May, 1879), p. 6, col. a.
'Generous Offer to America' (12 August, 1880), p. 3, col. f.
'A Wagner Season in London' (3 November, 1881), p. 7, col. e.
'Letter from Cosima Wagner to Angelo Neumann' (29 April, 1882), p. 7, col. e.
'Wagner's *Ring of the Nibelung*' (11 May, 1882), p. 6, col. c.
'Obituary of Richard Wagner' (14 February, 1883), p. 9, col. b.
Tulloch, John, 'Morality without Metaphysics', *ER*, 144 (October, 1876),
    470–500.
——, 'Pessimism', *ER*, 149 (April, 1879), 500–533.
Tyndall, John, 'The Belfast Address' (including apology), *Fragments of Sciences:
    A Series of Detached Essays, Addresses and Reviews*, 5th edn (London: Longman,
    Green, 1876), 473–563.
Wagner, Richard, *The Music of the Future, A Letter to M. Frederic Villot*, translated
    by Edward Dannreuther (London: Schott, 1873).
——, *Prose Works*, translated by William Ashton Ellis, 8 vols (London: Kegan
    Paul, Trench Trubner, 1892–1899).
Wakley, Arthur Bingham, 'Review of *The Dynasts*, by Thomas Hardy', *The Times
    Literary Supplement* (January, 1904), 30.
Wallaschek, Richard, 'How We Think of Tones and Music', *CR*, 66 (August,
    1894), 259–268.
Wordsworth, William, *The Poetical Works of William Wordsworth*, edited by
    Ernest De Selincourt and Helen Darbishire, 5 vols (Oxford: Clarendon Press,
    1940–1949).
——, *The Prelude or Growth of a Poet's Mind* (1805–1806 and 1850 edn), edited
    with introduction by Ernest De Selincourt, 2nd edn revised by Helen Darbishire
    (Oxford: Clarendon Press, 1959).

Young, Edward, Letters Summarising 'The Language of Music', *MS*, 11 (November, 1869), 247–248, and (December, 1869), 294.

Zimmern, Helen, 'Review of *Schopenhauers Leben*, by Wilhelm von Gwinner', *Academy*, 13 (June, 1878), 573–574.

——, *Arthur Schopenhauer: His Life and His Philosophy* (London: Longman, Green, 1876), also 2nd edn (London: George Allen & Unwin Ltd., 1932).

Secondary sources

Periodicals will be given full titles, with the following exceptions

NCF   *Nineteenth Century Fiction*
PMLA   *Publications of the Modern Language Association of America*

Abrams, M. H., *The Mirror and the Lamp: Romantic Theory and the Critical Tradition* (Oxford: Oxford University Press, 1953).

Alvarez, A., *Beyond all this Fiddle: Essays, 1955–1967* (London: Allen Lane, Penguin Publishing, 1968).

Anderson, Carol Reed, 'Time, Space, and Perspective in Thomas Hardy', *NCF*, 19 (December, 1954), 192–208.

Armstrong, Tim, 'Supplementarity: Poetry as the Afterlife of Thomas Hardy', *Victorian Poetry*, 26 (1988), 381–393.

——, 'Hardy, History, and Recorded Music' in *Thomas Hardy and Contemporary Literary Studies*, edited by Tim Dolin and Peter Widdowson (Basingstoke: Palgrave Macmillan, 2004), 153–166.

Aschkenasy, Nehama, 'Biblical Substructures in the Tragic Form: Hardy', *The Mayor of Casterbridge. Agnon, and the Crooked shall be Made Straight, Modern Language Studies*, 13 (Winter, 1983), 101–111.

Ashton, Rosemary, *The German Idea: Four English Writers and the Reception of German Thought 1800–1860* (Cambridge: Cambridge University Press, 1980).

Auerbach, Nina, 'The Rise of the Fallen Woman', *NCF*, 35 (June, 1980), 29–52.

Bailey, James Osler, *Thomas Hardy and the Cosmic Mind* (Chapel Hill: University of North Carolina Press, 1956).

——, *The Poetry of Thomas Hardy: A Handbook and Commentary* (Chapel Hill: University of North Carolina Press, 1970).

Banfield, Stephen, 'Aesthetics and Criticism': The Romantic Age – 1800–1914, Vol. 5, *The Athlone History of Music in Britain*, edited by Nicholas Temperley (London: Athlone, 1981), 455–473.

Barker, James, R., 'Thematic Ambiguity in *The Mayor of Casterbridge*', *Twentieth Century Literature*, 1 (April, 1955), 13–16.

Bartlett, Brian, ' "Inscrutable Workmanship": Music and Metaphors of Music in *The Prelude* and *The Excursion*', *Wordsworth Circle*, 17 (Summer, 1986), 175–180.

Bartlett, Phyllis, 'Hardy's Shelley', *Keats-Shelley Journal*, 4 (Winter, 1955), 15–29.

Barzun, Jacques, *Darwin, Marx, Wagner: Critique of a Heritage* (London: Secker and Warburg, 1942).

Beer, Gillian, *Darwin's Plots: Evolutionary Narrative in Darwin, George Eliot and Nineteenth-Century Fiction* (London: Routledge, 1983).

Binstock, Lynn Ruth, 'A Study of Music in Victorian Prose' (unpublished doctoral thesis, University of Oxford, 1985).

Bjork, Lennart, ' "Visible Essences" as Thematic Structure in Hardy's *The Return of the Native*', *English Studies*, 53 (1972), 52–63.
——, 'Thomas Hardy's "Hellenism" ', *Papers on Language and Literature*, edited by Sven Backman and Goran Kjellmer (Goteborg, Sweden: Acta Universitatis Gothoburgenis, 1985), 46–58.
Bloom, Harold, ed., *Thomas Hardy: Modern Critical Views* (New York, Philadelphia: Chelsea House Publishers, 1987).
——, *Thomas Hardy's Return of the Native* (New York, Philadelphia: Chelsea House Publishers, 1987).
Blissett, William, 'Wagnerian Fiction in English', *Criticism*, 5 (Summer, 1963), 239–260.
——, 'George Moore and Literary Wagnerism', in *George Moore's Mind and Art: Essays Old and New*, edited by Graham Owens (Edinburgh: Oliver and Boyd, 1968).
Boumelha, Penny, *Thomas Hardy and Women: Sexual Ideology and Narrative Form*, 2nd edn (Wisconsin: University of Wisconsin Press, 1985).
Brake, Laurel, 'Walter Pater of the Renaissance' (unpublished M.Phil thesis, University of London, 1968).
——, *Walter Pater* (Plymouth, Devon: Northcote House Publishers, 1994).
——, 'Writing, Cultural Production, and the Periodical Press in the Nineteenth Century', in *Writing and Victorianism*, edited by J. B. Bullen (London and New York: Longman, 1997), 54–72.
Brennecke, Ernest, *Thomas Hardy's Universe: A Study of a Poet's Mind* (London: Fisher Unwin, 1924).
Brooks, Jean, R., *Thomas Hardy: The Poetic Structure* (London: Elek, 1971).
Brown, Joanna Cullen, 'Variations on Two Enigmas: Hardy, Elgar and the Muses', in *Reading Thomas Hardy*, edited by Charles Pettit (London: Macmillan, 1998), 188–208.
Buckle, G. E., Stanley Morison, Iverach McDonald, and others, *The History of the Times*, 4 vols (London: Printed at the office of 'The Times', 1935–1952).
Buckler, William, E., ed., *On the Poetry of Matthew Arnold: Essays in Critical Reconstruction* (New York, London: New York University Press, 1982).
Budd, Malcolm, *Music and the Emotions: The Philosophical Theories* (London, New York: Routledge, 1992).
Bujic, Borjan, ed., *Music in European Thought 1851–1912* (Cambridge, New York: Cambridge University Press, 1988).
Bullen, J. B., 'Thomas Hardy's *Far from the Madding Crowd*: Perception and Understanding', *Thomas Hardy Journal*, 3 (May, 1987), 38–61.
Burgan, Mary, 'Heroines at the Piano: Women and Music in Nineteenth-Century Fiction', *Victorian Studies*, 30 (Autumn, 1986), 51–76.
Byerly, Alison, ' "The Language of the Soul": George Eliot and Music', *Nineteenth-Century Literature*, 44 (January, 1989), 1–17.
Campbell, Elizabeth, '*Tess of the D'Urbervilles*: Misfortune is a Woman', *Victorian Newsletter*, 76 (Autumn, 1989), 1–5.
Casagrande, Peter, 'Hardy's Wordsworth: A Record and Commentary', *English Literature in Transition*, 20 (1977), 210–237.
——, *Unity in Hardy's Novels: Repetitive Symmetries* (London: Macmillan, 1982).
Cassidy, John, A., *Algernon C. Swinburne* (New York: Twayne, 1964).
Cirillo, Albert, R., 'Salvation in *Daniel Deronda*: The Fortunate Overthrow of Gwendolen Harleth', *Literary Monographs*, I (1967), 201–243.

Clarke, G. W., ed., with the assistance of J. C. Eale, *Rediscovering Hellenism: The Hellenic Inheritance and the English Imagination* (Cambridge: Cambridge University Press, 1988).

Clinksdale, Edward, *The Musical Times: 1844–1900*, part of the 'Repetoire international de la presse musicale' series, 9 vols (College Park: University of Maryland, 1994).

Collins, Deborah, L., *Thomas Hardy and his God: A Liturgy of Unbelief* (London: Macmillan, 1990).

Connor, Steven, *Dumbstruck – A Cultural History of Ventriloquism* (Oxford: Oxford University Press, 2000).

Cooke, Deryck, *The Language of Music* (Oxford: Oxford University Press, 1959).

Cox, R. G., ed., *Thomas Hardy: The Critical Heritage* (London: Routledge & Kegan Paul, 1970).

Crary, Jonathan, *Suspensions of Perception: Attention, Spectacle; And Modern Culture* (Cambridge, Massachusetts, London: MIT, 2001).

Crozier, Eric, 'O Bygone Whirls!', *English Music*, 8 (July, 1980), 291–297.

Daleski, Matthew Hillel, *Thomas Hardy and the Paradoxes of Love* (Columbia: University of Missouri Press, 1997).

D'Agnillo, Renzo, 'Music and Metaphor in *Under the Greenwood Tree*', *The Thomas Hardy Journal* (May, 1993), 39–50.

Dave, Jagdish Chandra, *The Human Predicament in Hardy's Novels* (London: Macmillan, 1985).

Davis, Karen, Elizabeth, 'Native to the Night: Form, the Tragic Sense of Life, and the Metaphysics of Music in Hardy's Novels' (unpublished doctoral thesis, University of Maryland, College Park, 1987).

——, 'A Deaf Ear to Essence: Music and Hardy's Mayor of Casterbridge', *Journal of English and Germanic Philology*, 89 (April, 1990), 181–201.

Davison, Henry, *Music During the Victorian Era: From Mendelssohn to Wagner – Being the Memoir of J. W. Davison, Forty Years Music Critic of 'The Times'* (London: W. M. Reeves, 1912).

Deen, W., 'Heroism and Pathos in Hardy's *Return of the Native*', *NCF*, 15 (December, 1960), 207–219.

Delaura, D. J., ed., *Matthew Arnold: A Collection of Critical Essays* (New Jersey: Prentice Hall, 1973).

De Palacio, Jean, 'Music and Musical Themes in Shelley's Poetry', *Modern Language Review*, 59 (1964), 345–359.

D'Exideuil, Pierre, *The Human Pair in the Works of Thomas Hardy: An Essay on the Sexual Problems as Treated in the Wessex Novels, Tales and Poems*, translated by Felix W. Crosse, 2nd edn (New York: Kennikat Press, 1970).

DiGatani, J. L., *Richard Wagner and the Modern British Novel* (Rutherford: Fairleigh Dickinson University Press, 1978).

Dike, D. A., 'A Modern Oedipus: *The Mayor of Casterbridge*', *Essays in Criticism*, 2 (January, 1952), 169–179.

Dodd, Valerie, A., *George Eliot: An Intellectual Life* (Basingstoke: Macmillan, 1990).

Dolin, Tim and Widdowson, Peter, *Thomas Hardy and Contemporary Literary Studies* (Basingstoke: Palgrave Macmillan, 2004).

Draper, Ronald, ed., *Hardy: The Tragic Novels – Return of the Native, Tess of the D'Urbervilles, Jude the Obscure; A Casebook* (London: Macmillan, 1975).

——, 'The Mayor of Casterbridge', *Critical Quarterly*, 25 (Spring, 1983), 57–70.

Ebbatson, Roger, *The Evolutionary Self: Hardy, Forster, Lawrence* (Brighton: Harvester Press, 1982).

Edwards, Duane, D., 'The Mayor of Casterbridge as Aeschylean Tragedy', *Studies in the Novel*, 4 (Winter, 1972), 609–618.

Eggenschwiler, David, 'Eustacia Vye, Queen of the Night and Courtly Pretender', *NCF*, 25 (March, 1971), 444–454.

Ehrlich, Cyril, *The Piano: A History* (London: Dent, 1976).

——, *The Music Profession in Britain Since the Eighteenth Century: A Social History* (Oxford: Clarendon Press, 1985).

Eisley, Irving, 'Some Origins of Music: Communications and Magic', *Music Review*, 32 (1971) 128–135.

Ellenberger, Henri, F., *The Discovery of the Unconscious: The History and Evolution of Dynamic Psychiatry* (London: Fontana, 1994).

Ellis, William Ashton, 'Wagner and Schopenhauer', *FR*, 65 (March, 1899), 413–432.

Fernando, Lloyd, 'Thomas Hardy's Rhetoric of Painting', *Review of English Literature*, 6 (October, 1965), 62–73.

Fubini, Enrico, *The History of Musical Aesthetics*, translated by Michael Hatwell (London: Macmillan, 1991).

Garten, H. F., *Wagner the Dramatist* (London: John Calder, 1977).

Gately, Patricia-Ann, ' "A Transmutation of Self": George Eliot and the Music of Narrative' (unpublished doctoral thesis, University of Notre Dame, 1985).

Gatens, William, J., 'John Ruskin and Music', *Victorian Studies*, 30 (Autumn, 1986), 77–98.

Gatrell, Simon, *Hardy the Creator: A Textual Biography* (Oxford: Clarendon Press, 1988).

——, *Thomas Hardy and the Proper Study of Mankind* (London: Macmillan, 1993).

Gittings, Robert, *Young Thomas Hardy* (London: Heinemann, 1975).

——, *The Older Hardy* (London: Heinemann, 1978).

Glasenapp, C. F., *The Life of Richard Wagner*, translated by William Ashton Ellis, 6 vols (London: Kegan Paul, Trench, Trubner, 1900–1908).

Goddard, Dick, ' "As a Boy He had a Most Unusual Ear...": Folk Music and the Wessex Hardys', *English Dance and Song*, 32 (Winter, 1970), 14–15.

Godwin, Joscelyn, ed., *The Harmony of the Spheres: A Sourcebook of the Pythagorean Tradition in Music* (Rochester, Vermont: Inner Traditions International, 1993).

Goldberg, M. A., 'Hardy's Double-Visioned Universe', *Essays in Criticism*, 7 (1957), 374–382.

Gooch, Bryon, N. S. and Thatcher, David, ed., *A Shakespeare Music Catalogue*, 5th edn (Oxford: Clarendon Press, 1991).

Goodale, Ralph, 'Schopenhauer and Pessimism in Nineteenth Century English Literature', *PMLA*, 47 (March, 1932), 241–261.

Goode, John, *Thomas Hardy: The Offensive Truth* (Oxford: Basil Blackwell, 1988).

Graham, Walter, *English Literary Periodicals* (New York: T. Nelson and Son, 1930).

Gray, Beryl, *George Eliot and Music* (Basingstoke: Macmillan, 1989).

Green, Brian, *Hardy's Lyrics: Pearls of Pity* (London: Macmillan, 1996).

Gregor, Ian, *The Great Web: The Form of Hardy's Major Fiction* (London: Faber & Faber, 1974).

Grew, Eva Mary, 'Thomas Hardy as Musician', *Music and Letters*, 21 (1940), 120–142.

Grigson, George, *The Harp of Aeolus and Other Essays on Art, Literature and Nature* (London: Routledge, 1947).

Grundy, Joan, *Hardy and the Sister Arts* (London: Macmillan, 1979).

Guerard, Albert, *Thomas Hardy* (Norfolk, Connecticut: New Directions Paperbook, 1964).

Hagan, John, 'A Note on the Significance of Diggory Venn', *NCF*, 16 (September, 1961), 147–155.

Haight, Gordon, S., ed., *George Eliot: A Biography* (New York, Oxford: Oxford University Press, 1968).

——, *A Century of George Eliot Criticism* (London: Methuen, 1996).

Hall, Robert, W., 'On Hanslick's Supposed Formalism in Music', *Journal of Aesthetics and Art Criticism*, 25 (1966–1967), 433–436.

Hamilton, Ian, *A Gift Imprisoned: The Poetic Life of Matthew Arnold* (London: Bloomsbury, 1998).

Hands, Timothy, *Thomas Hardy* (London: Macmillan, 1995).

Havens, Raymond, D., *The Mind of a Poet: A Study of Wordsworth's Thought with Particular Reference to 'The Prelude'* (Baltimore: Johns Hopkins Press, 1941).

Heilman, Robert, B., 'Hardy's "Mayor" and the Problem of Intention', *Criticism*, 5 (Summer, 1963), 199–213.

Henigan, Julie, 'Hardy's Emblem of Futility: The Role of Christminster *in Jude the Obscure*', *The Thomas Hardy Yearbook*, 14 (1987), 12–14.

Higgins, Lesley, ' "Strange webs of Melancholy": Shelleyan Echoes in *The Woodlanders*', *Thomas Hardy Annual*, 5 (1987), 38–46.

Hollander, John, 'Wordsworth and the Music of Sound', in *New Perspective on Coleridge and Wordsworth: Selected Papers from the English Institute*, edited by Geoffrey H. Hartman (New York, London: Columbia University Press, 1972).

Houghton, Walter, F., *The Victorian Frame of Mind, 1830–1870* (Oxford: Oxford University Press, 1957).

——, 'Periodical Literature and the Articulate Classes', in *The Victorian Periodical Press: Samplings and Soundings*, edited by Joanne Shattock and Michael Wolff (Leicester, Toronto and Buffalo: Leicester University Press, University of Toronto Press, 1982), 3–27.

Howe, Irving, *Thomas Hardy*, 2nd edn (Basingstoke: Macmillan, 1985).

Hughes, John, *Lines of Flight: Reading Deleuze with Hardy, Gissing, Conrad, Woolf* (Sheffield: Sheffield Academic Press, 1997).

——, *'Ecstatic Sound': Music and Individuality in the Work of Thomas Hardy* (Aldershot: Ashgate, 2001).

Hyde, Derek, *New Found Voices: Women in Nineteenth Century Music* (Ash, Kent: Tritone Music Publications, 1991).

Hyder, Clyde, K., ed., *Swinburne: The Critical Heritage* (London: Routledge & Kegan Paul, 1970).

Ingham, Patricia, *Thomas Hardy* (London: Harvester Wheatsheaf, 1989).

Irwin, Michael, *Reading Hardy's Landscapes* (Basingstoke: Macmillan, 2000).

Jackson-Houlston, C. M., 'Thomas Hardy's Use of Traditional Song', *NCF*, 44 (1989–1990), 301–334.

James, Jamie, *Music of the Spheres: Music, Science and the Natural Order of the Universe* (London: Little, Brown, 1993).

Jarrett, David, W., 'Hawthorne and Hardy as Modern Romancers', *NCF*, 28 (March, 1974), 458–471.

Jenkyns, Richard, *The Victorians and Ancient Greece* (Oxford: Blackwell, 1980).

Johnson, Trevor, *A Critical Introduction to the Poems of Thomas Hardy* (London: Macmillan, 1991).

Jones, Lawrence, 'The Music Scenes from *The Poor Man and the Lady, Desperate Remedies* and *An Indiscretion in the Life of an Heiress'*, *Notes and Queries*, 222 (Winter, 1977), 32–34.

Kahn, Douglas, *Noise, Water, Meat: Sound, Voice and Aurality in the Arts* (Cambridge, Massachusetts, London: MIT, 1999).

Karl, Frederick, R., '*The Mayor of Casterbridge*: A New Fiction Defined', *Modern Fiction Studies*, 6 (Autumn, 1960), 195–213.

Kelly, Mary Anne, 'Hardy's Reading in Schopenhauer: *Tess of the D'Urbervilles'*, *Colby Library Quarterly, Waterville*, 28 (September, 1982), 183–198.

Kiely, Robert, 'Vision and Viewpoint in *The Mayor of Casterbridge'*, *NCF*, 23 (September, 1968), 189–200.

King-Hele, Desmond, *Shelley: His Thought and Work*, 3rd edn (London: Macmillan, 1984).

Kivy, Peter, 'Herbert Spencer and a Musical Dispute', *Music Review*, 23 (1962), 317–329.

Kramer, Dale, 'Character and the Cycle of Change in *The Mayor of* Casterbridge', *Tennessee Studies in Literature*, 16 (1971), 111–120.

——, *Thomas Hardy: The Forms of Tragedy* (London: Macmillan, 1975).

——, ed., *Critical Approaches to the Fiction of Thomas Hardy* (London: Macmillan, 1979).

——, *Critical Essays on Thomas Hardy: The Novels* (Boston, Massachusetts: G. K. Hall, 1990).

——, *The Cambridge Companion to Thomas Hardy* (Cambridge: Cambridge University Press, 1999).

La Valley, A. J., ed., *Twentieth Century Interpretations of Tess of the D'Urbervilles* (Englewood Cliffs, New Jersey: Prentice Hall, 1969).

Laird, J. T., *The Shaping of Tess of the D'Urbervilles* (Oxford: Clarendon Press, 1975).

Le Huray, Peter and Day, James, eds, *Music and Aesthetics in the Eighteenth and Early-Nineteenth Centuries* (Cambridge: Cambridge University Press, 1981).

Leppert, Richard, *The Sight of Sound: Music, Representation and the Human Body* (California: University of California Press, 1993).

Lippman, Edward, ed., *Musical Aesthetics: A Historical Reader*, 3 vols (New York: Pendragon Press, 1986–1990).

——, *A History of Western Musical Aesthetics* (Lincoln and London: University of Nebraska Press, 1992).

Longyear, R. M., *Nineteenth-Century Romanticism in Music*, 3rd edn (Englewood Cliffs, New Jersey: Prentice Hall, 1988).

McCann, Eleanor, 'Blind Will or Blind Hero: Philosophy and Myth in Hardy's *Return of the Native'*, *Criticism*, 3 (Spring, 1961), 140–157.

McLaughlin, T. P., 'Music and Communication', *Music Review*, 23 (1962), 285–291.

Magee, Bryan, *Aspects of Wagner* (Oxford: Oxford University Press, 1988).

Mallett, V. and Draper, Ronald P., *A Spacious Vision: Essays on Hardy* (Newmill, Cornwall: Patten Press, 1994).

Mander, M. N. K., 'Milton and the Music of the Spheres', *Milton Quarterly*, 24 (May, 1990), 63–71.

Mann, Karen, B., 'George Eliot and Wordsworth: The Power of Sound and the Power of Mind', *Studies in English Literature*, 20 (Autumn, 1980), 675–694.

Matchett, William, E. G., '*The Woodlanders*, or Realism in Sheep's Clothing', *NCF*, 9 (1955), 241–261.

Miller, J. Hillis, *Thomas Hardy: Distance and Desire* (Cambridge, Massachusetts: Harvard University Press, 1970).

Millgate, Michael, *Thomas Hardy: A Biography* (Oxford: Oxford University Press, 1982).

——, ed., *The Life and Work of Thomas Hardy by Thomas Hardy* (London, Macmillan, 1984).

——, *Thomas Hardy: His Career as a Novelist* (London: Macmillan, 1994).

Mitchell, P. E., 'Music and Hardy's Poetry', *English Literature in Transition*, 30 (1987), 308–321.

Monsman, George, *Walter Pater* (London: George Prior, 1977).

Moore, Kevin, Z., *The Descent of the Imagination: Postromantic Culture in the Later Novels of Thomas Hardy* (New York: New York University Press, 1990).

Morell, Roy, *Thomas Hardy the Will and the Way* (Kuala Lumpur: University of Malaya Press, 1965).

Morgan, B. Q., *A Critical Bibliography of German Literature in English Translation, 1481–1927* (New York and London: Scarecrow Press, 1965).

Morton, P. R., '*Tess of the D'Urbervilles*: A Neo-Darwinian Reading', *Southern Review: An Australian Journal of Literary Studies*, 7 (1974), 38–50.

Moynahan, Julian, '*The Mayor of Casterbridge* and the Old Testament's First Book of Samuel: A Study of some Literary Relationships', *PMLA*, 71 (1956), 118–130.

Newman, Ernest, *Wagner Man and Artist* (London: John Lane, the Bodley Head, 1925).

Newton, William, 'Hardy and the Naturalists: Their use of Physiology', *Modern Philology*, 49 (August, 1951), 28–41.

Orel, Harold, ed., *Thomas Hardy's Personal Writings: Prefaces, Literary Opinions, Reminiscences* (London: Macmillan, 1967).

——, 'The Literary Friendships of Thomas Hardy', *English Literature in Transition*, 24 (1981), 131–145.

Ousby, Ian, 'The Convergence of the Twain: Hardy's Alteration of Plato's Parable', *Modern Language Review*, 77 (October, 1982), 780–796.

Page, Norman, 'Visual Techniques in Hardy's *Desperate Remedies*', *Ariel*, 4 (January, 1973), 65–71.

——, *Thomas Hardy* (London: Routledge & Kegan Paul, 1977).

——, ed., *Thomas Hardy: The Writer and his Background* (London: Bell and Hyman, 1980).

Patterson, John, '*The Return of the Native* as Antichristian Document', *NCF*, 14 (September, 1959), 111–127.

——, '*The Mayor of Casterbridge* as Tragedy', *Victorian Studies*, 3 (December, 1959), 151–172.

——, *The Making of the Return of the Native* (Westport, Connecticut: Greenwood Press, 1978).

Peck, John, 'Hardy's Woodlanders: The Too Transparent Web', *English Literature in Transition*, 24 (1981), 147–154.

Peskin, S. G., 'Music in *Middlemarch*', *English Studies in Africa*, 23 (1980), 75–81.

Pettit, Charles P. C., ed., *New Perspectives on Thomas Hardy* (New York: St. Martin's Press, 1994).

Pietch, Francis, 'The Relationship Between Music and Literature in the Victorian Period: Studies in Browning, Hardy and Shaw' (unpublished doctoral thesis, North Western University, 1961).

Pinion, F. B., *A Hardy Companion: A Guide to the Works of Thomas Hardy and their Background* (London: Macmillan, 1968).

——, *A Commentary on the Poems of Thomas Hardy* (London: Macmillan, 1976).

——, *Thomas Hardy: Art and Thought* (London: Macmillan, 1978).

——, *Hardy the Writer: Surveys and Assessments* (London: Macmillan, 1990).

——, *Thomas Hardy: His Life and Friends* (London: Macmillan, 1992).

Pointon, Marcia, *The Pre-Raphaelites Reviewed* (Manchester: Manchester University Press).

Pollin, Burton, R., *The Music for Shelley's Poetry: An Annotated Bibliography of Musical Settings of Shelley's Poetry* (New York: Da Capo, 1974).

Raine, Craig, 'Conscious Artistry in *The Mayor of Casterbridge*', in *New Perspectives on Thomas Hardy*, 156–171.

Reé, Jonnathan, *I See a Voice: A Philosophical History of Language, Deafness and the Senses* (London: HarperCollins, 1999).

Riede, David, G., *Swinburne: A Study of Romantic Mythmaking* (Charlottesville: University Press of Virginia, 1978).

Rosenberg, John, *The Darkening Glass: A Portrait of the Genius of John Ruskin* (London: Routledge & Kegan Paul, 1963).

Rosenthal, Harold and Warrack, John, eds, *The Concise Oxford Dictionary of Opera* (Oxford: Oxford University Press, 1987).

Rutland, William, *Swinburne: A Nineteenth Century Hellene* (Oxford: Basil Blackwell, 1931).

——, *Thomas Hardy: A Study of his Writings and their Background* (Oxford: Basil Blackwell, 1938).

Schaefer, R. Murray, ed., and trans., *E. T. A. Hoffmann and Music* (Toronto: University of Toronto Press, 1975).

Scholes, Percy Alfred, *The Mirror of Music, 1844–1944: A Century of Musical Life in Britain as Reflected in the Pages of the Musical Times*, 2 vols (London: Novello, 1947).

Schweik, Robert, C., 'Moral Perspectives in *Tess of the D'Urbervilles*', *College English*, 24 (October, 1962), 14–18.

Sessa, Anne Dzamba, *Richard Wagner and the English* (Rutherford: Fairleigh Dickinson University Press, 1979).

Seymour-Smith, Martin, *Hardy* (London: Bloomsbury, 1994).

Sherman, Elna, 'Thomas Hardy: Lyricist, Symphonist', *Music and Letters*, 21 (1940), 143–171.

Sherman, G. W., *The Pessimism of Thomas Hardy* (London: Associated University Press, 1976).

Sousa Correa, Delia da, *George Eliot, Music and Victorian Culture* (Basingstoke: Palgrave, 2002).

Sperry, Stuart, M., *Shelley's Major Verse: The Narrative and Dramatic Poetry* (Cambridge, Massachusetts: Harvard University Press, 1988).

Spivey, T., ed., 'Thomas Hardy's Tragic Hero', *NCF*, 9 (December, 1954), 179–191.

Springer, Marlene, *Hardy's Use of Allusion* (London: Macmillan, 1983).

Starzyk, Lawrence, 'The Coming Universal Wish Not to Live in Hardy's "Modern" Novels', *NCF*, 26 (March, 1972), 419–435.

——, 'Hardy's Mayor: The Antitraditional Basis of Tragedy', *Studies in the Novel*, 4 (Winter, 1972), 592–607.

Stewart, J. I. M., *Thomas Hardy: A Critical Biography* (London: Longman, 1971).

Stockley, V., *German Literature as Known in England 1750–1830* (London: George Routledge & Sons, 1929).

Stoddard, Martin, *Wagner to 'The Wasteland': A Study of the Relationship of Wagner to English Literature* (London: Macmillan, 1982).

Stokoe, F. W., *German Influence in the Romantic Period 1788–1818: With Special Reference to Scott, Coleridge, Shelley and Byron* (Cambridge: Cambridge University Press, 1926).

Strunk, Oliver, ed., *Source Readings in Music History*, 5 vols, V, 'The Romantic Era' (New York: Norton, 1965).

Sullivan, William Joseph, 'Music and Musical Allusion in *The Mill on the Floss*', *Criticism*, 16 (Summer, 1974), 230–246.

Sumner, Rosemary, *Thomas Hardy: Psychological Novelist* (London: Macmillan, 1981).

Taylor, Dennis, 'Hardy's Missing Poem and his Copy of Milton', *Thomas Hardy Journal*, 6 (February, 1990), 50–69.

Temperley, Nicholas, 'The Lost Chord', *Victorian Studies*, 30 (Autumn, 1986), 7–24.

——, ed., *The Lost Chord: Essays in Victorian Music* (Bloomington: Indiana University Press, 1989).

Thurley, Geoffrey, *The Psychology of Hardy's Novels: The Nervous and the Statuesque* (Queensland: University of Queensland Press, 1975).

Turner, Frank, *The Greek Heritage in Victorian Britain* (Newhaven and London: Yale University Press, 1981).

Turner, Paul, *The Life of Thomas Hardy* (Oxford: Blackwell, 1998).

Unwin, Diana, S., 'Narratives of Gender and Music in the English Novel, 1850–1900' (unpublished doctoral thesis, University of London, 1994).

Van Ghent, Dorothy, *The English Novel: Form and Function* (New York: Harper Torchbooks, 1961).

Vigar, Penelope, *The Novels of Thomas Hardy: Illusion and Reality* (London: Athlone Press, 1974).

Weber, Carl, J., 'Thomas Hardy Music: With a Bibliography', *Music and Letters*, 21 (1940), 172–178.

Wickens, Glen, 'Literature and Science: Hardy's response to Mill, Huxley and Darwin', *Mosaic*, 14 (1981), 63–79.

——, 'Victorian Theories of Language and *Tess of the D'Urvervilles*', *Mosaic*, 19 (1986), 99–115.

Widdowson, Peter, *On Thomas Hardy: Late Essays and Earlier* (London: Macmillan, 1998).

Willey, Basil, *Nineteenth Century Studies: Coleridge to Matthew Arnold* (London: Chatto and Windus, 1949).

Winter, Alison, *Mesmerized: Powers of Mind in Victorian Britain* (Chicago: University of Chicago Press, 1998).

Woods, Oliver, and Bishop, James, *The Story of 'The Times'* (London: Michael Joseph, 1983).

Woolf, Virginia, 'The Novels of Thomas Hardy', *The Common Reader: Second Series*, 9th edn (London: The Hogarth Press, 1974).

Woolford, John, 'Periodicals and the Practice of Literary Criticism', in *The Victorian Periodical Press: Samplings and Soundings*, edited by Joanne Shattock and Michael Wolff (Leicester, Toronto and Buffalo: Leicester University Press, University of Toronto Press, 1982), 109–142.

Wright, T. R., *The Shaping of the Dynasts: A Study of Thomas Hardy* (Lincoln: University of Nebraska, 1967).

——, *The Religion of Humanity: The Impact of Comtean Positivism on Victorian Britain* (Cambridge: Cambridge University Press, 1986).

Yuill, W. E., ' "Character is Fate": A Note on Thomas Hardy, George Eliot and Novalis', *Modern Language Review*, 57 (1962), 401–402.

Index

Printed in the United States
66847LVS00001B/70